D1241036

BOUNDARY
BROKEN

By Melissa F. Olson

Disrupted Magic series

Midnight Curse
Blood Gamble
Shadow Hunt

Boundary Magic series

Boundary Crossed
Boundary Lines
Boundary Born

Scarlett Bernard novels

Dead Spots
Trail of Dead
Hunter's Trail

Nightshades series

Nightshades
Switchback
Outbreak

Short Fiction

Bloodsick: An Old World Tale
Companion Pieces: Stories from the Old World and Beyond

Also by Melissa

The Big Keep: A Lena Dane Mystery

BOUNDARY BROKEN

BOUNDARY MAGIC, BOOK 4

MELISSA F. OLSON

Published by 47North, Seattle

www.apub.com

Amazon, the Amazon logo, and 47North are trademarks of Amazon.com, Inc., or its affiliates.

ISBN-13: 9781542003841 (paperback)
ISBN-10: 1542003849 (paperback)

Cover design by Kirk DouPonce, DogEared Design

Printed in the United States of America

Dedicated to Brieta V., the godmother of this series.

Chapter 1

"For the last time, Lily," I said, not bothering to hide my impatience, "we are *not* using code names. There's no need."

"Copy that, Griffin. We are all set up on this end. Flower Child over and out."

I rolled my eyes and pressed the "Talk" button again. "Simon? What about you?"

"I kind of like the code names," came my friend's amused voice.

"That's not what—" I cut myself off and took a breath, pulling my knit hat down a little farther. It was late on a Wednesday night in December, and I was sitting cross-legged in the middle of Baseline Road in my hometown of Boulder, Colorado. My best friend, Lily, and her brother, Simon, were stationed at either end of the block, supposedly to direct traffic. Well, not "direct" so much as "ward off." Simon and Lily were witches, and they could do a pretty nifty spell to keep humans away while I did my thing.

Of course, that was assuming I could get the two of them to stay on task. It was after midnight, they'd both had long days at their nonmagical jobs, and they were clearly getting a little punch-drunk.

Or maybe they were just creeped out. As trades witches who worked with regular magic, the Pellars couldn't actually see the two children who ran skipping into this street every night after dark: the kids were remnants, minor ghosts who acted out the moment of their deaths over and over again in a loop, sometimes for centuries. They weren't sentient, and they couldn't hurt anyone, but even if you were used to seeing them, they were still kind of spooky. Then again, sometimes I wondered if it was more unsettling to see the remnants or to *not* see them but know they were there.

I pushed the button and tried again. "What I meant was, are you ready on your side, Simon?"

Silence.

"Simon?" Then I got it, and fought the urge to spike the walkie-talkie into the street. My boss, Maven, had gotten special encrypted handsets for me, just for this project, and they were probably expensive as hell. I sighed and said, "Are you ready on your side . . . Phoenix?"

"Ready over here, Griffin," Simon chirped. I heard Lily cackling over the line.

I clenched my teeth. Unlike my friends, I had been in the army, where we had actual missions and, yes, call signs. Using Lily's pop-culture version of military speak felt to me like playing with emotional matches, but I kept reminding myself that the Pellars were just having fun. And that they were out here in the cold in the middle of the night, using their sad excuse for spare time to help me. "All right," I said, "I'm going radio silent now, guys."

I turned the knob on the handset before Lily could respond. Tossing the handset on top of my backpack, I made myself glance over my shoulder. I'd been trying to avoid getting distracted by the remnants, but considering what I was about to do, it seemed more respectful to face them.

The two girls were near the same age, maybe ten or twelve years old, and they wore halter tops and pants that curved out at the bottom. I saw them whenever I drove through this part of town after dark, but this was the first time I'd come close enough to see the freckles that covered one girl's face and arms, or to realize that what I'd taken for a ponytail on the other girl was actually a long braid. Shit, they were so *young*.

When I'd first started my little pet project—laying Boulder's ghosts to rest—I had tried to do research on each of them beforehand. I had plenty of free time, so I'd spent hours at the library combing through ancient newspapers to find out who they were and how each one had died.

After a few weeks, though, I had to admit to myself that it didn't really matter—and that reading through so much death and horror wasn't particularly good for me. I'd decided to just focus on laying the ghosts.

I may not have known these remnants' names, but their cause of death was pretty obvious just from watching their loop. Both of them had their heads down, focusing on chasing something into the street—a ball, or maybe a small dog. Whatever it was, it hadn't left a psychic imprint behind, so I couldn't see it. The figures ran laughing into the middle of the road, and then the moment I'd dreaded arrived: the freckled girl turned her head in my direction, a look of horror materializing on her face just before she blinked out. Her friend never looked up. She disappeared before she even noticed the vehicle bearing down on them.

I closed my eyes, reminding myself that the two girls were gone, and had been for a long time. In a few seconds the whole scene would start over.

My working theory was that every ghost was a small piece of someone's soul, trapped on this side after death. Remnants like these two were the least sentient of the ghosts I'd encountered, but their presence still bothered me, in more ways than one.

Luckily, I could do something about it. Other witches often referred to boundary magic, my personal specialty, as death magic, and they hated those of us who could use it. But I tried to think of what I could do in terms of bridges, messages, reunions. I could put these ghosts to rest by sending the fractured parts of their souls across the boundary between life and death, where I assumed their spirits would become whole again.

At least, that's what I thought happened. I was still fairly new to this, and was making it up as I went along.

I unfolded my legs and crouched down a foot from the street's centerline, digging my big Swiss Army knife out of the backpack. I tried to pull out a cutting blade, but I kept fumbling it. We had done this routine a hundred times in the last six months, but now it was early December, and my fingers were stiff with cold.

I mumbled a few choice curse words, which steamed in the freezing air and drifted away. I blew on my fingers and rubbed them together until they were warm enough to work. When I finally got the blade out, I checked my hand and found the most recent scar was on my right pinkie. Tensing, I pricked my ring finger. I'd gotten a lot of practice at poking just hard enough for the amount of blood I needed.

The moment my blood hit the cold night air, the two girls paused, finally breaking their loop. There was boundary magic in my blood, and ghosts could somehow sense that. They didn't move any closer, but their laughing faces went slack and they turned their heads toward me, regarding me like a particularly sweet and tempting treat. This part never failed to unnerve me, and my uninjured hand automatically reached up to touch my birth mother's bloodstone where it hung on a leather cord under my clothes.

Still in the crouch, I turned in a circle, smearing the blood in a dark line that looked almost blue in the yellowish streetlights. I wanted to move as quickly as possible, to get those lifeless, staring eyes off me, but I forced myself to take care. The circle had to be completely intact, or I'd have to do this all over again.

I spent a few seconds filling in spots where the blood had smeared. There weren't any bad cracks in the road—I'd chosen this spot because it was the smoothest. When I was confident the circle would hold, I carefully stepped outside it. The Band-Aid was already in the outer pocket of my coat, and I taped it onto my bleeding finger. Then I looked up at the watchful girls.

The first time I'd made a doorway to the other side, it was almost an accident. Well, Simon referred to it as "psychic self-defense," and maybe that was a better description. My biological father, Lysander, had been attacking me with ghosts, something I hadn't even known was *possible* until that moment. Desperate, and with no other ideas, I'd done this same procedure more or less on instinct. I think I was even more surprised than Lysander when it worked.

Now I squatted back down, still outside the circle, and pressed my palms into the asphalt so the tips of my tattoos just touched the line of blood. Lily had designed the elaborate griffin tattoos, which helped me channel magic with more control. The bloodstone grounded and steadied me; the tattoos focused my magic like a funnel.

"Door," I said out loud, concentrating as hard as I could on the image of a doorway.

Inside the circle, the pavement disappeared, replaced by a sort of swirling smoke that led . . . somewhere. I hadn't opened a gate to, say, heaven or hell—that much I was pretty sure about. This was more of a neutral bridge to . . . wherever. Limbo, the gates of Saint Peter, Santa's workshop. I didn't know, and I wasn't the least bit tempted to find out.

When I was certain the door was stable, I looked back up at the two girls. "Go on," I said gently. "Be at peace."

The girls held hands as they approached the swirling mist without hesitation. They crossed the line of my blood with their chins up, eyes bright. I felt my own eyes fill as they vanished through the gate.

Blinking hard, I took a moment to glance around. Twice, when I'd done this, additional remnants had appeared from nearby buildings or bodies of water. They had heard the call of my blood, and were eager to take the path I was offering. I counted slowly to thirty, but there were no other takers tonight. I scuffed at the line of blood with my boot, breaking the circle. The smoky door vanished, replaced by ordinary pavement.

A rush ran through my body, the aftereffect of using pure boundary magic, and I had to brace myself on the ground for a moment. Sometimes this happened while the gate was still open, sometimes not until afterward, but there was always this feeling of joyous contentment when I laid ghosts to rest. It could last for minutes or hours, depending on the night.

Lily had once asked me, in her unfiltered Lily way, if it felt like an orgasm, and I'd had to think through how to actually explain it with words. "No, it's not sexual, or even sexual-adjacent," I had answered. "It's more like this overwhelming sense of"—I struggled for a phrase— "glorious purpose, I guess. It feels like I'm doing exactly what I was made to do."

I didn't explain that it was about the only time I really felt useful these days, but Lily had probably figured that out. My best friend was a lot more perceptive than she got credit for.

I let myself sag down onto the road, but after only a moment, I reached for the walkie-talkie. *Oh, what the hell.* I turned it on and pushed the button with a little smile.

"Griffin here," I said into the handset. "The eagles have landed. Over and out."

Chapter 2

It was after one in the morning by the time I drove the Pellars back to my cabin, where they'd left Simon's car. I was used to staying up most of the night—dating a vampire will do that to you—but I figured the two of them had to be exhausted. They both had normal human day jobs, plus specific responsibilities for their witch clan. Simon "liaised" with my boss, Maven, which mainly involved dealing with security issues alongside Quinn and me, and Lily . . . well, a year ago, their mother, Hazel, had declared that Lily would become the clan's next leader when she retired.

We probably should have seen it coming. The eldest Pellar sister had betrayed the family and gotten herself banned from the state, and the second-oldest sister, Sybil, was universally disliked. Somehow, though, nobody was more surprised by the news than Lily. Now she had special lessons with her mother several times a week to learn advanced magic, leadership, and diplomacy.

At any rate, I was expecting one or both of them to fall asleep in the car, so I was a little surprised when Lily said in a chirpy voice, "I'm *starving*! Do you have snacks?"

"Uh, yeah, I guess . . . Do you guys want to—"

She was already half turning in her seat so she could see her brother. "Si? You in for snacks? We could play cards or something."

We were nearly there, and I noticed that someone had turned on my outside lights. I grinned and hit the garage door button. "It's getting really late—" Simon began. As the door rose, it exposed the bumper of Quinn's car. "But I could stay for a little while," he finished. "Despite the obvious presence of that undead scum."

I laughed, pulling into the driveway. "Or *because* of it."

"I don't know what you mean," Simon said airily, as I parked and turned off the car. Interspecies friendship was apparently a little unusual in the Old World, so my witch friend and my vampire boyfriend were constantly insisting they hated each other.

As if to prove the point, Simon added, "That bloodsucking son of a bitch owes me *twenty bucks.*"

He yelled the last two words as he climbed out of the car, which is unnecessary when addressing someone with vampire hearing. The inner door to the house opened, and Quinn was suddenly there, wearing jeans and a black button-down shirt, looking cool and collected in his blond, craggy way. He raised an eyebrow at Simon, crossing his arms over his chest. "I already gave you your money," he said mildly. "Don't you remember?"

Simon was already in the garage, stomping his boots to clear the snow, but he actually paused for a second. "Don't try your Jedi mind tricks on me, vampire. I'm immune."

Vampires could press only humans, and Simon was one of the rare males with active witchblood. But Quinn still liked to mess with him. "Or is that just what I've led you to believe?" he said, deadpan. Simon just snorted in response.

Quinn turned sideways and held the door open so Simon and Lily could get past him into the house. I waited for them to go through, then went up and kissed Quinn on the lips.

I'd meant for it to be a brief peck, but he put his arms around my waist and I automatically reached up to wind my arms around his neck. "Hi," he said, pressing his forehead against mine.

"Hi." I have this stupid thing where I can't stop smiling when he looks at me like that. It's like a horrible teenage-girl tic. "Did you get done early?" I said, referring to his security work with Maven. "Or do you have to go back?"

"Nope, all done. It's another quiet night."

I made sure my expression didn't change, but Quinn gave me a sympathetic smile anyway. It's not easy being in a relationship with someone who can hear your pulse and smell changes in your pheromones.

When I'd first begun working for Maven, the Colorado Old World had been in a state of serious upheaval. Maven had killed the previous cardinal vampire, and it took some time for everyone, especially other vampires, to accept her new regime. While things were still settling down, there had been a string of supernatural catastrophes that complicated the transition further—including a killer sandworm *and* my biological brother showing up with my . . . well, I didn't like to use the word "father" in relation to Lysander, but I wasn't quite sure what to call him. "My biological mother's rapist" was awfully wordy.

At any rate, it had been more than two years since Maven's takeover, and everything had finally calmed down . . . a lot. I was supposed to be Maven's daytime security person, but lately she'd had very little for me to do. It had gotten to the point where I was picking up the occasional shift at my old convenience-store job just to fill the time.

I knew I shouldn't complain—having no emergency situations was a *good* thing. At least, that's what I kept telling myself, usually with a thick layer of guilt.

Quinn bent to kiss my forehead; then Lily's face popped back into view in the hallway. "Yo, hostess. Are we supposed to just forage for our own snacks during your make-out session?"

Rolling my eyes, I started toward Lily and the kitchen. "I think we both know Simon's already going through my fridge."

"Do you have any more of those beef sticks?" Simon called.

"You mean the ones I keep for my *dogs*?"

Quinn took over hosting duties so I could feed the menagerie of rescue animals I'd acquired since coming back from overseas. The cats were hiding, and Quinn had herded the barking or cowering dogs into the laundry room when he'd arrived. Animals, as a rule, do not care for vampires. We'd been dating for a couple of years now, though, and while the animals were never going to warm up to him, they were at least used to this routine.

I let the five dogs into the fenced-in backyard to do their business, then put four of them back in the spare bedroom, which used to house a crabby three-legged iguana named Mushu. To everyone's surprise, Mushu had taken a special liking to my biological aunt, Katia, another boundary witch. When Katia had moved to New Mexico, she'd taken Mushu with her, although his old aquarium remained in its usual spot for when she drove up to visit.

The four dogs—Cody, Chip, Pongo, and my newest foster, Stitch—weren't happy about being shut up again, but I promised myself I'd take them for a run the next day. The fifth dog, a fatally stupid Yorkshire terrier named Dopey, got to stay out in the hall. Unlike the other canines, Dopey was just too dumb to understand why she should be freaked out by Quinn. If he called her, and if she remembered her name at the moment, she would even jump up to sit in his lap.

She didn't follow me down the hall right away, so I left her snuffling around the floorboards like they might contain dog treats. I've given up trying to understand Dopey's thought process.

When I finally joined my friends in the living room, everyone was settled in their favorite spots: Quinn in the armchair, Lily and Simon on either end of the couch. The Pellars each had a beer, and Simon was eating from a Tupperware container of pretzels covered in white chocolate and dipped in red and green sprinkles. My mother had brought it over the previous afternoon as part of her campaign to push the holiday-cheer agenda. She had also offered to send my dad to help me put up some Christmas lights, but I needed to draw the line somewhere.

I snagged a handful of pretzels for myself and dropped into the other armchair. "What are we talking about?"

"Code names," Simon told me, in his most serious voice.

"I'm just saying, I get why Lex is Griffin, and Lily being Flower Child is *painfully* obvious," Quinn said. Lily gave him the finger. "But why is Simon Phoenix?"

"Simon Phoenix!" said both Pellars at once. They met in the middle of the couch to high-five. I felt a familiar stab of grief for my own sibling: my twin sister, Sam. We'd had our own in-jokes and near-telepathy. Sam could talk to me in my head sometimes thanks to boundary magic, but it wasn't the same as getting to hang out together.

Since the Pellars hadn't actually answered his question, Quinn looked at me with his eyebrows raised. I just shrugged. "I assumed it was because he died and I brought him back to life."

"Yeah, that too," Lily said. She was munching on a carrot from a bag I kept in the fridge just for her.

"Does Quinn get a code name?" I asked Lily.

She made a show of scrutinizing my boyfriend, who shot me a *thanks a lot* look. "Varney? Edward? Dracula, Dead and Loving It?"

"That's not funny," Quinn told her gravely.

Simon's hand shot up in the air like an eager third-grader's. "I think it's funny."

Quinn started to retort, but I slowly raised my hand too, causing both Pellars to burst into laughter. Quinn couldn't help but smile.

"Anyway . . ." he said with emphasis, obviously hoping to change the subject.

"What did you do today, Lex?" Lily asked.

I knew she was trying to pull me into the conversation—Lily was good at that—but I felt my expression sour. "Well, I worked out, picked up Maven's dry cleaning, and ran three errands for my mother."

Everyone else exchanged pitying looks. "Maven didn't have anything for you?" Lily asked. Quinn leaned forward in his chair to rest a hand on my leg.

"Nope. She's been preoccupied lately, so she hasn't had time to give me busywork." As soon as the words were out of my mouth, I regretted them. I had taken an oath of loyalty to Maven. I shouldn't be talking about her activities *or* criticizing her orders. I glanced sideways at Quinn and mumbled, "Sorry."

He shrugged it off. Quinn knew that I'd barely seen Maven lately. During the last couple of months, whenever I stopped by Magic Beans at night, she was on the phone in her office with the door closed.

Simon broke in to smooth over the awkwardness. "Any word on how Katia's settling into Albuquerque?" he asked me.

I brightened. "She's doing okay. She found a job as a nighttime security guard at the art museum."

Simon wrinkled his nose. "Albuquerque has an art museum?"

"And people want to *rob* it?" Lily added.

I tossed a pretzel at her. *"Anyway,"* I went on, "we talk every week, and she's coming to visit in a couple of weeks for Christmas. Maven gave the okay."

"That's cool," Lily said brightly. She had crouched down on the floor to pet Dopey, who had finally found her way out of the hall. "What are you going to get her for Christmas?"

"A children's book about art history," I said with a little smile.

Simon grinned. "Is your other friend coming again too?"

For some people, "your other friend" would be much too vague, but outside of the people in this room and my cousins, I had about two other friends, and only one of them had ever visited for the holidays. "Sashi? I'm not sure. The last few times we've talked, she's been with a new guy. It sounds pretty serious." Which would make for a very awkward holiday visit, since Sashi had dated my brother-in-law, John, for a while. I shrugged. "Maybe Grace will go to Las Vegas for the holidays this year."

Simon and Lily exchanged a dark look at the mention of Grace Brighton, and I wished I hadn't brought her up. Grace was Sashi's daughter and a nineteen-year-old college student here in Boulder. She was also human . . . because Sashi had never told her about the Old World. Witches had a window of time, right around puberty, to activate their magic, or it was lost to them forever. Sashi had chosen to let that window pass.

I hadn't actually *told* the Pellars that part, but they knew how strong Sashi was, and they'd met Grace. It wasn't hard to put two and two together.

Denying a witch her magic went against Simon and Lily's whole way of life—but then, they were clan witches. They had always known about magic, and they'd always had a place in the Old World. Like Sashi—and, I supposed, Katia—I was an outclan witch, born, raised, and living outside of the old customs. I had gone most of my life with no knowledge of the Old World, and there were days when I wished I could go back to that.

Clearly trying to change the subject, Simon poked his sister with the toe of his shoe. "Yo, Princess. Are we playing cards or what?"

Lily raised her head to glare at him. She and Simon jokingly referred to their mother as the witch queen of Colorado, so now he was getting a lot of mileage out of goading the new heir apparent. "Simon Aleister Pellar," Lily snapped, "we have discussed your use of that word."

He grinned, unapologetic. "What are you gonna do, your majesty?" Simon asked her. "Smite me? Send me to my tower?"

"Smiting has potential," Lily said, putting a finger to her chin as if in deep thought. "Especially if—"

Before she could finish, Quinn's head jerked, and he stood up so fast I barely saw the movement. "Quiet," he said sharply.

The whole room went still—we'd all trained to respond quickly during an attack. I strained to hear whatever Quinn had heard, but my human ears couldn't pick it up. "Someone's here," he murmured, still listening intently.

Simon, Lily, and I all stood up, and I instantly reached for the shredder stake I kept attached to my forearm with a couple of fitness headbands. I touched my chest, reaching for Valerya's bloodstone, but I had taken off the heavy crystal necklace for cleaning. Shit. I glanced at the Pellars, who had automatically moved away from the furniture and stood with their hands spread out, ready to cast.

"Vampire?" I asked Quinn. The local vampires had never come to my home before, but it seemed possible.

Quinn shook his head, his nostrils flaring, his eyes distant. His head turned back and forth. "Werewolves," he muttered. "At the back door too." Right on cue, a chorus of frantic barks rose from the back bedroom where I'd locked the dogs.

Werewolves didn't really travel alone. My fingers clenched around the shredder, hard enough to make my knuckles ache. My twin sister had been murdered by a werewolf a few years earlier, and more to the point, werewolves were supposed to be banned from the state of Colorado. This could only be bad.

I looked down at the wooden stake in my hand, realizing it was next to useless. The shredders were spelled to create a tiny explosion when they were driven into flesh, but that wouldn't slow a werewolf for very long. I had a small box of silver bullets in the gun safe, but that was in the back bedroom. The wolves could break down the door long before I made it there. And unlike vampires, a werewolf could walk right into my home.

"What do we do?" Lily whispered, looking at me. Her eyes were bright with fear, but her fingers were curled into conductors, sparks dancing between them. She and Simon had been working hard on their offensive magic.

"Quinn and Lily to the back door, Simon and I will take the front," I began, moving toward the kitchen. I thought I had a silver-plated fish knife in the junk drawer. If I could get it quickly—

The doorbell rang.

In the thick tension, the familiar chiming sound seemed almost offensively normal. We all looked at each other, mystified. I mouthed a word to Quinn: *Trap?*

Before any of us could speak, I heard a vaguely familiar male voice call, "Lex? It's Ryan Dunn. Can we talk?"

Quinn looked at me questioningly. I nodded, relaxing a little. Dunn was the alpha werewolf of the Wyoming pack that had helped me kill the sandworm three years earlier. I didn't exactly trust him, especially since he wasn't supposed to be in Colorado, but I had no reason to think he wanted to hurt any of us.

I went toward the front door, entering the hallway but staying about ten feet away. "What are you doing here?" I yelled. "How many of you are there?"

"Just me and Mary," he called back. Then he added, with a little impatience, "I'm calling in my marker."

Chapter 3

Thirteen years before I even learned about the existence of magic, a war for power was waged in Colorado.

Back then, a psychotic werewolf named Trask decided to unite all the Colorado packs and take control of the Old World in the state. That in itself could have worked out okay—werewolf packs had leadership roles in other places. But Trask hadn't cared about the most fundamental rule of the supernatural world: keep everything away from the humans.

After a number of people were killed, the peace-loving witch clans had tried to intervene, but that led to even more people getting caught in the cross fire—including Simon and Lily's father.

Hazel Pellar, the clan leader then and now, could have retreated into her grief and let Trask go unchecked. Instead, she had come up with a radical plan to stop him for good: she reached out to a very powerful vampire, Maven, and negotiated a deal. Maven would stop Trask and keep the werewolves out of Colorado, and in return the witches would be in her service for twenty years.

It was an uneasy peace, which had been tested several times since, including when Simon and Lily's older sister, Morgan, had caused magic to go crazy in the Boulder area, raising an evil snake monster. The Cheyenne werewolves had fought the sandworm with us, which was how I'd ended up owing the alpha a favor.

By Old World rules, Morgan Pellar should probably have been killed or imprisoned for her actions, but Maven had agreed on banishment—in exchange for letting the Cheyenne pack back into the state on the occasional weekend trip, mostly to run around the national parks during a full moon.

But the next full moon was more than a week away, and they'd certainly never come to my *house*. The dogs were barking loudly now, so I had to yell to be heard. "For what?"

"Two of the pack members have gone missing." This time, the voice came from behind us. I whirled around, shredder in hand, to see a thin, haughty woman leaning against the entrance to the back hall. The dogs had been too loud for us to hear her come in.

Quinn hissed at the sudden intrusion, an unnatural, vampire sound, and both Pellars took a step forward. I held out my arm to stop all three of them. "Mary," I said with exasperation. "Are you *trying* to get zapped?"

The female werewolf shrugged, looking unconcerned. "You were taking too long to let us in."

I'd only ever seen Mary in tiny dresses and sky-high heels, but tonight she was wearing loose, cheap cutoff sweatpants and an oversized red T-shirt with bleach stains on it. The kind of clothes you didn't care about ruining. That actually scared me.

I went to the front door and jerked it open. "Why didn't you just call?" I demanded, glaring at Dunn, who stood there with his hands in his pockets. He was a barrel-shaped man who looked to be in his late forties or early fifties, though werewolves aged slower than humans. "I would have come up to Cheyenne."

"Our packmates vanished here in Colorado," he said. "I want your help."

I motioned for him to come inside—the cold air was already making goose bumps appear on my bare arms. He walked past me, looking around with alert, wary eyes. I closed the door, but didn't ask him to remove his thick-soled work boots despite the snow. The idea of the alpha werewolf in my house in his sock feet was just too weird. "Let's sit down," I said, tired of trying to think through the politics.

I asked Quinn to get some folding chairs, and a couple of minutes later, two werewolves, a vampire, and three witches were all sitting in a semicircle in the living room, like the world's most bizarre AA meeting.

I focused on Dunn. "What happened?" I asked.

A smile flickered on his face. "That's what I like about you. No pleasantries." He cleared his throat, glancing at each of us in turn. "You know we've been given occasional permission to visit Colorado, right?"

I nodded. "The weekend pass. I'm aware."

Out of the corner of my eye, I could see Lily squirm in her folding chair. The Pellar family were the only witches who knew about the weekend pass. I didn't think they'd even discussed the arrangement with the rest of their witch clan. It was an uncomfortable reminder of Morgan's betrayal. "But Maven never gives us details about your trips," I added. "She says it's safer for everyone."

Out of the corner of my eye, I saw Quinn make the tiniest flinch. Nobody else caught it, because nobody else had been dating him for nearly three years. I filed the thought away for later.

"And she's right," Dunn replied. "Anyway, Maven and I were discussing a possible trip again this month. The pack has been itching to explore the Dunes."

The Pellars and I nodded automatically, but Quinn, who was not a Colorado native, looked confused. "The Great Sand Dunes National Park," I told him. "Four hours south of here."

"Oh, right," he said with a little shrug. "Heard of it, but I've never been." Vampires were predators; they mainly stayed in populated areas to be close to their food source. A hundred thousand acres of wildlife wasn't exactly a huge draw.

"It's stunning," Dunn said. It seemed like an odd word choice for a rough-looking guy in jeans and a flannel shirt, but his eyes practically glowed with enthusiasm. "And this is the off-season. With Maven's permission, I sent down my beta, Matt Ventimiglia, and his wife this morning to get the lay of the land and make sure there was enough space for us to run around unnoticed."

"Beta" meant the second-in-command of the pack, I knew. "What happened?" I asked.

"I talked to Matt at three o'clock this afternoon and everything was fine," Dunn answered. "They had stopped at the visitor's center during regular hours, gotten maps and things, and checked into a hotel in Alamosa. They were going back out to the Dunes tonight after dark, with Matt as a wolf and Cammie as his handler. That was the last I heard from them."

Quinn and I exchanged a wary glance. It seemed risky to have a werewolf running around a public park, even at night, but then, I didn't know much about werewolves. And given how worried Dunn looked, this was probably not the moment to ask about werewolf control. "What time were they supposed to call you?" I asked instead.

"Matt said no later than ten," he replied. "It starts to get dark around four thirty, so Matt and Cammie were going out there at five. I expected a call by nine. We've been calling every half hour or so since ten. When we couldn't reach either of them on the phone at midnight, Mary and I drove down here."

I glanced at the other werewolf. Mary had been silent throughout Dunn's explanation, and now she just sat and regarded me with those cool eyes. I couldn't read her.

"Why me?" I asked, looking back at Dunn. "Why not go right to Maven?"

His gaze shifted to Quinn. "What would Maven say if I called her with this?" he said, his tone challenging.

Quinn met his eyes, not backing down, but not pushing him either. Werewolf or not, Dunn was obviously worried about his people. "She would tell you to stay in Cheyenne, and send Lex and me down to the Dunes."

"And *you* can't go out in the sunlight," Dunn added, as though accusing Quinn of a crime. "Sunrise is five hours away. You wouldn't make it out on the dunes until sunset tomorrow night at best—and that's assuming you have a way to travel during daylight hours."

He was probably right. Under some circumstances, Maven would send me out alone during the day, but not if the situation involved werewolves—or something that could take down werewolves.

Dunn shook his head. "I can't risk waiting that long, and I sure as hell am not going to sit on my ass in Cheyenne while you go after my people." His eyes flicked to me. "I want *you* to come with us, as our official escort through Maven's territory. And I want to leave right now."

Chapter 4

Quinn looked ready to protest, so I sent him a look to say I had it under control. Dunn may have sounded pushy and arrogant, but I understood where he was coming from. We had both been in the military—Dunn as a marine, me in the army—with other soldiers under our command. I knew what it felt like to *need* to find your people.

Besides, I had been in the Old World long enough to know that he was really just opening a negotiation.

"We need to run this by Maven," I said firmly. "It can be on the phone, but she needs to at least know you're here, in case there's trouble." I elected not to describe what that trouble might look like. When it came to werewolves in Colorado, there were too many possibilities.

"I don't like the idea of you going without backup," Quinn said to me in a low voice.

"Uh, hello?" Mary said, waving a hand. "I can look after her."

Quinn didn't answer, but his look clearly said, *You're a werewolf.* He hadn't been in Colorado during Trask's rampage, but he knew the stories. He probably trusted the werewolves even less than I did.

Lily and Simon had been quiet through all this, though they'd traded several furtive looks. But now Simon spoke up, his eyes on Dunn. "I'll go with you."

Dunn looked at Simon speculatively, as though just now realizing he was there. "You were at the hot springs with us," he said, remembering. "You did that cloaking spell. Can you do it again?"

"Absolutely," Simon replied.

"If Si's going, I am too," Lily said. "I can help keep humans away from you guys."

I winced. "Lily . . ."

She gave me a stubborn look. "What?"

Simon did a little fishing and hiking, but Lily wasn't really an outdoors person. "It's December. The temperature is going to be in the teens, and it'll be windy as hell on the dunes."

"How do you know?"

"Because that's how they were created," I said patiently. "Look, we're going to need some serious cold-weather gear, and stores aren't open in the middle of the night. I've got some ski stuff, and Simon can borrow John's." My brother-in-law was clued in on the Old World and would help with whatever we needed. "You should stay in Boulder."

Lily chewed on a fingernail, thinking for a moment, then gave a reluctant nod. "Fine. But I want phone calls. Lots of them."

Dunn stood up, looming over me. "How soon can we leave?" he demanded.

Everything began to move quickly. Quinn called Maven at her coffee shop, Magic Beans, and I texted my cousins to beg off babysitting the next night. Simon found someone to proctor his exam at CU the next morning. I went to the closet in the spare bedroom to dig out my old ski gear, which was still in boxes from when I'd moved into the cabin. I hadn't gone downhill skiing since I'd been discharged from the army. Like many veterans, I had returned with a bad case of claustrophobia, and I'd worried that donning all the ski gear would feel too confining. But I would have to suck it up for this.

While all this was going on, I was feeling a little guilty for lying. My late sister, Sam, had owned ski stuff too, and it was probably in a box somewhere at John's. I could have let Lily come with us. But she would slow us down out there, and more importantly, I couldn't risk involving her. Simon and Lily had been able to help me in the past because of their unique status: they were part of a very respected witch family, but they had also been the youngest and least significant members.

Now, though, Lily was the designated next heir of Clan Pellar, and anything she did to help me could be seen as a political move. I knew she didn't care about that, but I also didn't want her to screw up her future. And if anyone in her clan found out she was helping the werewolves, however indirectly . . . that was exactly what could happen.

While I was still packing my gear in a backpack, Quinn came in with his cell phone. "Maven wants to talk to you," he said, holding it out to me.

I took the phone. "This is Lex."

"I don't like this plan," Maven said. She was using her real voice, rather than the ditzy-hipster tone she put on for her human customers at the coffee shop. She sounded controlled and wary, like a battlefield general.

But she hadn't said no. "I don't either," I replied. I didn't need to tell Maven that the whole thing could be a trap, or a way to get her boundary witch away from her. She'd survived for hundreds and hundreds of years; she understood strategy. "But I owe Ryan Dunn a favor. Unless you forbid it, I want to pay my debt."

"That's the only reason I'm going to allow it. We're already playing with political fire having werewolves in the state."

"I understand."

There was a long pause, and then Maven added, "For what it's worth, I did some background research on Dunn and his pack, to make sure he wasn't another Trask."

"And?"

"Dunn gives every impression of being a solid man and a good leader. I'm inclined to believe he's being straight with you."

I glanced through my open doorway and down the hall, to where an amused Ryan Dunn was crouched down petting a completely blissed-out Dopey. "So am I."

"Then go give him a hand," she said, as though I were about to hold a ladder so Dunn could clean out gutters or something. "I'll take precautions here. Keep Quinn informed. Oh, and Lex?"

"Yeah?"

"Be careful with Simon Pellar."

My brow furrowed. What was she implying? "I trust Simon."

Maven let out a short laugh. "No, I mean don't let anything bad happen to him. I have enough tension with the witches as it is."

Okay, that made more sense. "Yes, ma'am."

We discussed carpooling—the Boulder desire for energy efficiency runs deep—but after some uneasy debate, everyone settled on the werewolves driving Dunn's Forester to the Dunes, while Simon and I rode down in Maven's tricked-out Jeep. Both vehicles were outfitted with bullet-resistant glass and a few other safety precautions, and if something violent had happened to the Ventimiglias . . . well, I'd rather have all the protection we could handle. Dunn and Mary also wanted the option to go straight back to Wyoming, hopefully with the other two werewolves in tow.

Quinn drove my car to Magic Beans to discuss things further with Maven while Simon and I took Simon's Chevy to John's to pick up his cold-weather gear, including ski goggles. I felt bad about dropping by in the middle of the night, but at least I called ahead—first to John, and then to Charlie's vampire bodyguard, Clara. My niece is a null, a valuable commodity in the Old World, and Clara kept an eye on her during the night hours as part of a complicated deal I'd made with Maven.

Clara was, unsurprisingly, the one who answered the door: a tall, broad-shouldered, Nordic-looking woman, who always seemed like she should be on a stage singing opera with a horned helmet. Except for her mouth, which was a rosy pink bow that currently frowned down at me. "It is late," she said disapprovingly. Lots of vampires used old-fashioned syntax, from a time before contractions were common, but Clara also had an Eastern European accent that reminded me of the few times I'd heard my birth mother, Valerya, speak to me in my head. She and Katia had been born in the Ukraine, although Katia had lost her accent.

"It couldn't be helped," I told her, keeping my voice stern. I'd found that talking to Clara was kind of like talking to my dogs: the more confident and commanding I sounded, the better it would go.

Clara made a "hmph" noise and stepped aside so Simon and I could come into the foyer. John was just stumbling down the front stairs, wearing boxer shorts and a white undershirt, his eyes crusty with sleep. "Hey, Lex. Simon." John was human, but given Charlie's age and the previous attempts to kidnap her, Maven had given me special permission to tell him about the Old World. He and Simon had met a few times, usually when John picked up Charlie from my house.

"Hi, John," Simon said, reaching out to shake hands. "Thanks for this."

"Yeah. Sure." John's black hair was sticking up at all angles, and he ran a hand through it, which somehow made it even messier. I smothered a grin, but I did feel bad. John was a single parent to a four-year-old; he needed all the sleep he could get. He turned around and led us through the house to the garage, yawning.

"You need me?" Clara called after him.

John waved a hand over his shoulder. "Nah, go back to studying." Belatedly, I saw a pile of textbooks and a laptop computer spread out around the armchair in the living room as I passed by.

To Simon and me, John added, "Storage tubs are in the garage. You guys go ahead. I'm going to stop in the spare bedroom to grab some books and stuff we brought back from the Dunes last summer." He pointed down the hall, toward the garage door.

We went through the interior door into the garage, circling John's hybrid SUV to reach a massive rack of plastic tubs. John was a little fanatical about organization, and the bins were labeled with dry-erase tape. It took about twenty seconds to find the one marked "Ski Stuff."

"He went to the Dunes?" Simon said as I pulled the tub down and began pawing through it.

"Yeah, I forgot that he took Charlie for a couple of days." I tugged out a pair of goggles and handed them to Simon. "Try these on."

The goggles made him look like an enormous man-bug. "Have you gone to the Dunes before?" the bug asked me.

I grinned at him. "Once, when I was a kid, my folks took us camping there. I remember swimming in a creek and getting covered in sand. Not much else." I glanced down and saw that he was wearing Chuck Taylor All Stars, the official shoe of the professional nerd. "What's your shoe size?"

"Uh, thirteen."

"Hmm. John has winter hiking boots, but he's an eleven." I didn't have to check sizes—I had grown up with John. I pulled out a hat and thermal BUFF scarf. "You're gonna have to get sand in your shoes, I guess."

"You really think we'll need all this?" Simon sounded dubious. "It's not that cold."

I closed my eyes for a second. The memory of a different desert flooded me, and I swallowed the urge to spit. I may not have been to the Dunes since I was a kid, but if there was one thing I knew about, it was sand. "Trust me on this. The desert has a way of twisting the weather. Everything feels worse than it should."

"Oh," Simon said, in a tone that suggested he'd just remembered who he was talking to.

Lucky for us, at that moment John stumbled through the garage door, looking no more awake than when we'd arrived. "Here," he said, thrusting a small pile at me. "Books and maps."

"Thanks."

"Sure." John started to shove his hands into his pockets, then remembered he was wearing boxer shorts and awkwardly crossed his arms over his chest, shifting from foot to foot. The garage floor would be cold. "Did you find what you need?"

"Yup." Keeping my voice low, I asked, "What's Clara studying?"

John smiled, looking awake for the first time. "She gets bored, and I got tired of her sharpening her shashka collection in the living room, so I suggested she take some online classes."

Clara? "Let me guess," I said. "Medieval History? Weapons through the Ages? The Seven Actual Ways to Skin a Cat?"

"There are eleven ways," Clara's voice called from inside the house.

John shot me a smug look and I winced. Served me right for talking too loudly around a vampire. "American literature," John whispered.

Huh. I didn't know what to say to that, so I just shrugged and handed Simon a hat and a pair of lightweight snow pants, closing the lid on the tub. The three of us started toward the interior door, and then John stopped so abruptly I almost smacked into him. "What?" I asked.

"Almost forgot." John turned and went around the rack of tubs, reaching behind for something I couldn't see. He came out with two large, flat pieces of wood with black padding on them. "Sand sleds," he explained, holding them out. "Like for snow, but they have a slick back to go down the dunes. I decided to just buy instead of rent, figuring we'll go back next summer."

Simon and I exchanged another look, this one more positive. If the werewolves were injured—or worse—these could be very helpful in transporting them through the dunes. "Thanks," I said, meaning it. "Go back to bed."

John nodded. "Good luck," he mumbled, starting to turn away. "Charlie will probably FaceTime you sometime tomorrow. She wants to see"—he yawned—"the new foster dog."

Charlie had figured out how to FaceTime a year earlier, and John had given up trying to stop her from calling to chat. She was a social kid, and she missed me. And I realized, with a pang, I missed her too. I hoped whatever this was could be resolved in time for me to make my usual Friday babysitting date with her. "Give her a kiss for me, okay?" I said to John.

"Will do."

After we loaded the sleds into Simon's back seat and climbed in, I saw him looking thoughtfully back at the house, watching the front lights go off. "What?" I asked.

He shrugged. "Nothing. You're just . . . you're different with him. With your family."

"Isn't everybody?"

Simon blinked, and I realized my error. Simon *wasn't* different with his family, because they knew all the aspects of his life. It made me a little jealous.

He started the car and pulled away from the curb. "I don't know, you just have this whole Luther family thing going on, and the Old World has to stay separate, and John can know about some of it but not all . . . It must get confusing."

I considered his words for a moment, then shrugged. "I couldn't tell them about my work when I was in the army either. It's not that weird—medical doctors can't tell their families about patients because of privacy laws. People who work in government or technology have to keep professional secrets." I gave him a wry smile. "Maybe you're just spoiled, clan witch. We don't all get to have everything out in the open."

Simon snorted. "Spoiled. Right."

There was no traffic in the middle of the night, so it took no time at all to get to Magic Beans, where Quinn was waiting outside with the keys to Maven's Jeep and a large coffee in each hand. I went over to him and relieved him of the cups. "I could have gone in and gotten my own," I said.

"No need. Maven's on the phone anyway." Quinn's voice was easy, but there was worry in his eyes. The two of us weren't affectionate in public—there actually weren't that many people in the Old World who knew we were together—but he stepped close, his head bent toward me. He looked worried. "Be careful," he said quietly.

"Me? I'm always careful."

That got me a tiny smile. "Don't think I don't see how excited you are to finally have something interesting to do."

I winced, then tried to look like I wasn't excited about missing werewolves in Colorado. "Organizing Maven's barista schedule isn't exactly what I pictured for the direction of my life," I pointed out. "I'm not hoping for trouble, just . . . excited to feel useful."

"I know."

I pecked his cheek quickly and turned toward the Jeep. Simon was leaning against it, his eyes averted. When he saw me heading his way, he went around and pulled open the driver's door for me, reaching a hand out to take a coffee. "This one's yours," I said, handing him the coffee from my right hand.

"How do you know?"

I didn't bother to hide my smile. "Because *someone* wrote 'Geeky Mama's Boy' on the cup."

"Hey!" he yelled over my shoulder, but of course, Quinn had vanished inside.

In only a few hours, the traffic going through Denver would be nuts, but for now the roads were clear, and I was able to sail the Jeep down 36 at three miles over the speed limit. Maven had an arrangement with the Colorado Highway Patrol and Boulder PD—it wasn't exactly carte blanche, but no one would blink at the Jeep going twenty over. The werewolves wouldn't have the same perk, however, and we were trying to keep our profile low.

Simon spent the first part of the trip reading through the materials John had sent about the Dunes. In true Simon style, he seemed fully absorbed by the research, even looking through the coloring pamphlet for kids.

"Anything useful in there?" I asked in a very serious voice.

"No, but I think you might want to get Charlie in some art lessons. This is not good work."

"Hey, that's my niece you're talking about," I said, smiling. I gestured toward the pile in his lap. "What about the rest of it?"

Simon leaned back, sighing. "It's mostly just a refresher course on how the dunes were created by wind blowing through the various mountains and the kind of wildlife that lives there."

"There's wildlife in the dunes?" I said with surprise.

"Sure, plants and a few lizards and stuff. Nothing that will bother us."

He moved the pile of information to the back seat, carefully, and then there was an awkward silence. Simon and I didn't spend much time alone, which was intentional, at least on my part. There was a certain . . . tension? No, that wasn't the right word. I felt a connection to Simon, which made me uneasy.

I told myself the strange intimacy between us was the result of my saving his life once with boundary magic . . . and maybe that was even true. It didn't really matter, though, because Quinn and I were together, and Simon and Quinn were friends. Nobody wanted to change any of that, so we were both mindful of keeping a certain distance.

I wondered if Simon was seeing anyone seriously. It would make me feel better if he was, but it would also be ridiculously awkward to bring it up. I made a mental note to ask Lily. "Why don't you get some rest?" I suggested instead. "It's a four-hour trip, and I'm used to staying up." Simon, on the other hand, had to keep a diurnal schedule to go with his teaching job.

"Good idea," he said, looking relieved.

Simon fell asleep quickly, and my thoughts turned to the Cheyenne werewolf pack. My overall impression of werewolves had come a long way since one had murdered my sister, but part of me still saw them as enemy combatants. I'd seen what a werewolf had done to Sam's body, and I still had nightmares about it.

You know that was an isolated incident. Sam's voice said inside my head. I used to think this was just my brain predicting what she would say if she were still alive, but after I found out I was a witch, I'd realized that my sister and I were still connected, thanks to boundary magic. Sometimes her voice came through that connection, popping into my head like a catchy song. Tonight she sounded a little weary, like she was sick of making this argument.

"But it's not just me," I said under my breath, with a quick glance at Simon. He was deeply asleep. "Sashi has some kind of terrible history with werewolves. And they were responsible for killing Lily and Simon's dad."

There was no response, but this time I *could* predict what Sam would say, because we'd had this argument before, in my dreams. She would say that people were complicated, and werewolves were just people who'd gotten tangled up in magic, like me or Quinn or anyone else in the Old World. You would think that if *Sam* didn't hold a grudge against werewolves, I wouldn't either. Unfortunately, it didn't seem to work like that. Not with the image of Sam's ravaged body still in my memory. I had seen carnage in Iraq, but never with such brutality or disdain, like my twin's body was a chunk of useless meat.

I tried to pull my thoughts back to the current situation—and the current werewolves. Sam's killer was dead, and I did respect Ryan Dunn, werewolf or not. I had met him only twice, and he was brusque and pushy and concerned only with his own pack, but . . . I understood him. He and I would probably never be friends, but all that mattered was that I could work with him. Besides, it was just for this one thing. I owed him a debt, and he was calling it in.

Simple as that.

Chapter 5

Traffic was light on I-25, thanks to the early hour, and soon I was winding my way along 160, which curled around the bottom corner of the park and led to the park turnoff: a pretty, straight-shot road that probably provided a nice view of the dunes when it was light enough to see them.

By the time we reached the park entrance, the stars had faded away and a ribbon of orange-pink was spreading along the horizon. The visitor center wasn't open yet, so I drove right past it, following the sign to the parking area. "Simon," I said, reaching over to nudge his shoulder. "We're almost there."

He sat up, yawning and rubbing his eyes with the heel of his hand. He looked around for a moment at the miles of empty darkness and the straight road ahead. "Why are we going so slow?"

"The speed limit is ten."

"Why?"

"Probably because of them." I pointed to the handful of deer grazing on either side of the Jeep. You definitely wouldn't want to hit one of them at fifty miles per hour, especially in the near darkness.

"Oh." Simon still sounded sleepy. "You're so smart, Lex." I had to smile.

We reached a small, rectangular lot, which contained only a navy pickup truck splashed with mud. "That might be the missing couple's," Simon muttered.

"You're so smart, Simon," I replied, mimicking his voice.

Simon made a show of straightening up in his seat, faking pompousness. "Thank you. I know."

Grinning, I parked the Jeep a few spots away, right in front of the wooden fence that formed the border of the parking area. Behind it, I could make out wetland willow growing in a sort of second, natural fence, forming a border to the park itself. The lightening sky made silhouettes out of the dunes. I told myself that they probably didn't look quite so black and terrifying after the sun came up.

"Lex . . . you gonna be okay out there?" Simon had glanced sideways at me to watch my reaction.

I paused, not sure how to answer. I had been afraid wearing ski gear would set off my claustrophobia, and I hadn't laid eyes on a desert since I'd stumbled out of one after being left for dead. Now I was going to combine those two things.

"I have to be," I said at last. "Dunn called in his marker." I opened the car door before Simon could reply.

The Jeep's thermostat had said it was twenty degrees outside, but I'd taken off my heavyweight coat while I was driving, and the wind bit through my long-sleeved T-shirt. My nose immediately began running. I took a quick glance at the pickup truck to make sure it was empty and decided to get my cold-weather gear on before anything else. Grabbing the coat, I hurried to the back of the Jeep and opened the hatchback.

As quickly as possible, Simon and I started putting on the gear: lightweight snow pants, hiking boots for me, then the coats. I showed Simon how to pull his BUFF scarf over his head and turn it into a balaclava.

Dunn's battered Forester pulled up as we were still getting dressed, and he and Mary gave us a quick nod and headed straight for the pickup. Dunn pulled the door handle, found it locked, and put his hands over his eyes to peer inside. "Anything?" I called.

He shook his head. "They're still out there, or they've been taken by someone. We'll change now," he added abruptly, and he and Mary went toward the willow clusters, Mary already peeling her loose sweatshirt over her head, exposing a lot of pale white skin.

Simon and I went back to putting on hats and gloves, the goggles hanging around our necks. I insisted that he put a bottle of water, an energy bar, and a compass into his messenger bag even though he complained about the weight. As he slung the bag over his shoulder and began to turn away, I caught his arm. Making sure the werewolves weren't looking, I reached into a compartment in the Jeep and handed him a knife that Quinn had bought for me the previous Christmas. It was in a leather sheath and had a small clip to hook on one's pants. "It's silver," I said. "Just in case."

Simon rolled his eyes good-naturedly. "I'm a witch, remember? I can handle a physical threat, Lex."

"Yeah, but there's two of them, and not all of your spells will work against werewolves," I reminded him. As witches, Simon and I were in no danger of being turned into werewolves ourselves, but we could still be mauled to death by big-ass teeth and claws. I was carrying my revolver, loaded with silver bullets, and I would have offered Simon one too, if I'd thought he would carry it. Simon wasn't great with guns.

I extended the knife toward him again. "Humor me, okay? We might need to split up and follow different trails, and I don't want to be worried about you the whole time."

Simon gave a little headshake, but he took the knife, tucking it into his jeans underneath his snow pants. Hopefully the wolves wouldn't be able to smell the silver under the layers.

Simon began walking the parking lot's perimeter, setting up his humans-go-away spell. There was just no way to cast the spell around every single entry point to the dunes—the park and preserve covered more than a hundred and sixty square miles—but he could put a wide net around the entire parking area and the road leading to it. It was also the off-season for the park and early morning on a weekday, both of which worked in our favor. Add in the illusion spell that made the werewolves look like dogs, and I figured we were probably safe.

While Simon worked on the ward, I went to the Jeep's back seat and began unwrapping the two fifteen-pound rump roasts we'd bought on our bathroom stop. The change from human to wolf used up a lot of energy, and Ryan Dunn had suggested that they eat before we started the search, so they'd be better able to concentrate on tracking. I was just as happy not to be heading onto the sand dunes with two hungry werewolves.

When the roasts were unwrapped and set out near the edge of the parking lot, I wandered over to the Ventimiglias' pickup truck and peered inside, just out of curiosity. I understood immediately why Dunn hadn't bothered to break into the truck. Matt and Cammie clearly used it a lot—there was dust and some mud in the seats and footwells—but the tiny back seat held only a couple of neat piles of folded clothes, a gallon of water, and what looked like a roadside emergency kit. Nothing that would help us find them.

There was a loud grunt of pain from the direction of the willows, and I automatically glanced over, seeing the naked black branches shaking. I had never seen one of the werewolves change, and I planned to keep it that way. I looked for Simon, and saw him tramping back toward me, almost unrecognizable in his heavy coat and John's ski gear. He hadn't put the goggles on yet, and his eyes smiled at me.

"Done," he said, stamping his feet a little to warm them up. He leaned against the Jeep. The willow branches went still, and I figured they had to be almost finished. "Um, when they come out," Simon began, "we should probably try to look nonthreatening."

"I do," I said, looking down at myself. "I mean . . . right?" It wasn't like I was holding a weapon.

"Standing at parade rest is maybe a little threatening."

Oh.

"We've worked with them before," Simon said mildly.

I pushed out a breath. "For one night, three years ago, on our territory. That's not the same as trust." *And they killed my sister,* said an irrational voice in the back of my mind. I *knew* it was irrational, but I couldn't help having the thought.

"I don't necessarily disagree," Simon replied. "But let's maybe not start a fight we don't know we want?"

"Yeah. Okay." I stepped toward him and copied his body language, leaning against the Jeep.

A moment later, the two wolves emerged from the brush on our right, moving toward the rump roasts. Once again, I had to marvel at the insane *size* of them. I had seen natural wolves at a preserve, and those had been much bigger than I'd expected—but werewolves followed the law of conservation of mass. Dunn was two hundred pounds of muscle as a human, and as a wolf he was still two hundred pounds of muscle, which made him even bigger than Scarlett's bargest. He had thick fur that was dark gray on top, fading into white on his legs and tail.

Mary was smaller and sleeker, but her dark coloring and intelligent green eyes somehow made her equally terrifying. I made myself look away. Simon was right. There was no sense in challenging them. I'd come here to *help.*

The rump roasts were on the ground right in front of the Jeep, but to my surprise the wolves barely glanced at them. Moving cautiously, they walked right past the meat—and toward *us.*

Simon made a little noise in the back of his throat. Dunn was leading, and he moved closer and closer, his shoulders lowered slightly, coiling to spring.

I found myself pulling my sidearm, but I had never practiced with it in thick gloves. I fumbled it to the ground just as the wolves leaped toward us.

Chapter 6

"Down!" Simon shoved me hard, causing both of us to crash to the pavement. The wolves soared right over us—and raced across the pavement toward the cluster of deer that had caught their attention.

I had completely forgotten about the deer.

I would have breathed a sigh of relief, except Simon had knocked the wind out of me. I lay sprawled on the pavement, trying to get my lungs to *work*, dammit. I knew my eyes weren't actually bugging out like I'd been deprived of oxygen, but that's how it felt.

"Lex!" Shifting his body off mine and supporting himself on his elbows, Simon flapped off a glove. He used his uncovered hand to push the makeshift balaclava off my forehead, pulling it down below my chin, doing the same with his own.

Simon smoothed the hair from my face with a cool hand, murmuring, "I'm sorry, it's okay, it's okay, you'll breathe in a second, I promise."

Agonizing seconds ticked by while I struggled to force my diaphragm to do its thing. This had happened to me many times over the years, but it never ceased to be scary.

At last, my lungs reinflated, and I gasped in a great breath of air. Simon grinned ruefully, and I couldn't help but smile back. "I didn't mean to push you so hard," he apologized. "I'm clumsy in this gear."

"*I'm* sorry," I told him. "I thought they were attacking us. I feel really stupid."

"Me too. Let's not tell Lily, okay?"

I chortled, which hurt my chest. "Simon," I gasped.

"Yeah?"

"Can you get off me?"

His olive skin flushed, and he sat up and backed away from me. I had to laugh again at the mortified look on his face. "You didn't hurt me," I assured him. "It's cool. *We're* cool. I'm just going to lie here for a minute and feel like an idiot."

The pain in my chest was already receding. Simon relaxed; then there was a loud, wet *crunch*, and I think we were both relieved to turn our heads toward the werewolves. They had gotten one of the deer down and were nose-deep in the carcass. "I guess they prefer their food hot," Simon remarked. He stood up and extended his bare hand to me. Grunting, I took it and let him help me to my feet.

We spent a minute regrouping—he retrieved his glove, I fixed my headscarf in place and put the revolver back in my pocket. I got an old backpack with emergency supplies out of the back of the Jeep and strapped it on. By the time I straightened up again, the wolves were trotting toward us, licking blood off their lips.

Dunn approached me cautiously, and I had the sudden impression that he could smell the silver bullets. I wasn't going to leave the gun behind, so I fixed my eyes on the ground and held out a closed fist for him to sniff, while Mary and Simon did more or less the same thing.

"You remember us?" I asked, risking a quick glance at Dunn's eyes. "We're . . . friends. Well, allies, I guess." The wolf's expression didn't change, and I felt stupid all over again. What exactly was I expecting here? I gestured to Simon. "He's going to put an illusion on you so you can run around during the day without scaring people."

The wolves seemed to understand that, or maybe they just remembered Simon casting the illusion charm on them before our fight with the sandworm. Either way, they held still for a moment while he did his thing, pausing in front of each wolf, touching its head, and mumbling something I couldn't hear.

When he stepped back again, the wolves looked exactly the same to me. The last time we'd done this, Simon had explained that because magic didn't work well against itself, knowing there was an illusion allowed me to see right through it.

When he was finished with the casting, Simon slung his messenger bag over his shoulder and glanced at me. "The shirts?"

"Oh, right." I went over to Dunn's Forester, opened the unlocked passenger door, and found the paper Whole Foods bag he had told me about. Dunn and Mary had stopped at the missing werewolves' house before coming to Boulder. I reached into the bag for the two sweaters, holding them out for the wolves. They sniffed the fabric with increasing interest, and Dunn let out a low growl in the back of his throat. I'd spent enough time around canines to recognize it as a worried sound. "We're here to help," I said to him, "so try not to leave us behind, okay?"

Dunn let out a short bark and took off at a fast, relaxed lope, Mary at his heels. They disappeared into the brush almost instantly.

I handed Simon one of the sand sleds, tucked the other under my arm, and started after the wolves.

We caught up with them easily, to my surprise. They had stopped to sniff around the little strip of willows next to the parking lot where they'd changed earlier. Simon and I climbed down a sandy ramp to join them.

Now that we were inside the willow patch, I could see a wide expanse of damp sand stretching from here to the foot of the dunes. "That's the creek," I told Simon, pointing. "In the summer this whole thing is water, but it must run dry in the colder months." A few little rivulets of water were still moving sluggishly across it, but most of the remaining water had frozen over.

Simon nodded, adjusting his goggles, and I scanned the creek bed. I had sort of been hoping for giant wolf footprints leading us in one direction or another, but I saw right away that this was silly. The wind was constantly shifting the landscape, even over the wet sand. Footprints would disappear in an hour or two.

We watched the wolves for a few more minutes, and then they finally left the willows and began making their way across the creek bed. Simon and I started after them, with Simon picking his way around the puddles in his nonwaterproof shoes.

As soon as we left the protection of the brush, I felt the wind buffeting against my coat, searching for gaps in my gear. I hadn't left many, but soon a few tendrils of my hair writhed free of the headscarf and danced around my face. I tried breathing through the layer of scarf, but it was wet and cold and my nose began to run again. The goggles and gear immediately began to feel oppressive.

I decided that a cold, runny nose was preferable to claustrophobia, and pulled the scarf down, giving myself room to breathe—at least, when the wind didn't snatch my breath away. Between the wind and the gear, it was difficult to hear much, so Simon and I just lumbered after the werewolves, avoiding the patches of ice.

Dunn and Mary didn't seem bothered by the cold wind or the sand, but judging by their frequent backtracking and widening circles, they were struggling to track their missing packmates. As I watched them move in circles, I decided that Matt and Cammie likely had run around the creek bed for a while, stretching their legs and enjoying themselves.

Still, I figured they would have made their way to the sand dunes eventually, so to conserve energy, I gestured at Simon that we should keep going, trudging across the packed sand in a straight line. With the wind whipping at us, it seemed to take us an eternity just to cross the creek bed, and by the time we reached the foot of the dunes I could see Simon panting. I looked around for Dunn and Mary just as they trotted past us, heading up the nearest dune.

Turning to Simon, I pointed to the base of it, and he nodded, understanding. We went over and crouched down in the concave side of the dune, giving ourselves a few seconds' relief from the wind. "You okay?" I yelled to him.

Simon nodded again, but I could see the material around his mouth moving in and out with his fast breath. "That was a lot of exercise right after a lot of magic," he explained.

I winced, though he probably couldn't see it through my goggles. I had forgotten that Simon and Lily had done several wards for me the night before, and now he'd done two more big spells without much time to rest. "You need a minute?" I asked, but there was a yip from the other side of the dune. I stood up, trotting sideways along the base until it sloped enough for me to climb up.

I had gone running along the beach before, but moving on top of the sand dune was harder because my feet sank in *deep*, filling my hiking boots with sand. When I finally reached the top, I could see the two werewolves crouching over a bit of grass that poked through the sand bed. Mary lifted her head to sneeze violently, and Dunn looked up and saw me. He loped a few feet in the direction of the deeper dunes, then turned back to look at us.

"I think they found a trail," I yelled down to Simon. He struggled to his feet, sled in hand, and stumbled after me.

For the next half an hour, the wolves led us deeper and deeper into the sand dunes.

Except for the occasional massive sneeze as they were following a scent, Dunn and Mary seemed unaffected by the sand or wind. They kept their heads low and stole up and down through the dunes in a quick, fluid walk that looked easy. For us, though, every step was like slogging through shin-high water in space suits. It took forever for Simon and me to trudge up the crest of each dune, and once we did reach the top, it wasn't a simple point, like a mountain peak, but a snaking line that we had to walk along until we reached the downward slope on the far side.

That part was kind of fun, though, as Simon and I used the sleds to descend, careening down the long slopes. The quick downward trips allowed us to more or less keep up with the wolves, but controlling the sled was harder than I'd expected. The curves of the dune would occasionally cause one of us to arc sideways onto the wrong face, or fall off the sled partway down. The falls weren't dangerous—we'd just roll harmlessly to a stop—but I was constantly spitting out sand, and soon there was sand in my pockets and even inside my bra.

After a full hour of this, my nose was freezing, and my entire body felt gritty from the sand that had gotten through my clothes and glued to my skin. The sparkling, always gently moving sand was beginning to play tricks on my eyes, so I kept my gaze on either my feet or the wolves as they snuffled along the dunes. I occasionally checked on Simon, too. He was obviously flagging, taking frequent breaks to bend over and brace himself on his knees. I wasn't sure how much longer he could stay with us.

Just as I was about to suggest a longer break, we passed the crest of one dune and I saw something that finally interrupted the monotonous landscape: brittle, twisting branch tips, rising straight out of the ground like gnarled finger bones.

"It's a ghost forest," Simon called. He'd lagged behind and I waited for him to catch up. The wolves, meanwhile, beelined straight for the branches.

"What's a ghost forest?" I asked, wary of the term. I had all the ghosts I could handle, thank you.

"A new dune forms around . . . a group of trees," Simon panted. "Sand piles around them . . . Evergreens die, but cottonwoods . . . have adapted by . . . turning their lower branches . . . into roots."

Huh. At least it wasn't supernatural. By the time Simon finished his winded explanation, the werewolves had threaded through some of the branches and stopped, their paws digging at the sand. Simon and I dropped our sand sleds and hurried over to them, nearing just as they both stopped digging. Mary fell back, while Dunn raised his head and howled, an earsplitting, mournful sound that sent chills up my spine as we drew closer. Dunn leveled his gaze on me and I flinched, stopping a few feet away. I could see his upper lip twitching, as though he was about to bare his teeth at me. "What is it?" I asked.

I thought he was going to snarl at me, but Dunn seemed to get ahold of himself. He took a few steps backward, just enough so we could see into the wide, loose hole they'd made in the sand.

For a second, I thought I was looking at more of the twisting branches, but as I stepped closer I realized what I was seeing, and chills spread through the cold sweat on my back.

They were gray, lifeless fingers.

Chapter 7

Dunn howled again, and this time Mary joined him: a fluting, woeful sound that somehow contained grief and rage and a promise of revenge.

When the sound finally died down, Dunn and Mary began digging, taking care not to rake their claws over the fingers.

Judging from their reaction, I was pretty sure this was Matt or Cammie, or maybe both of them. We would need to take the bodies with us—the dunes were always shifting, and we couldn't risk them being found by a tourist or park ranger, especially without knowing how they had died.

Simon and I knelt down next to them and began to help. Dunn made a low growl when I got too close to his claws, so Simon and I started using our sleds to push away the sand the two wolves had already moved aside, making room for more.

After a few minutes of this, I had to stand and turn away, pulling up my scarf so I could take long, deep breaths without inhaling sand.

In Iraq, I had been left in a shallow grave much like this, dumped facedown in a heap. My connection to boundary magic—and, I believe, a small pocket of air under my head—had kept me from dying, but the Ventimiglias wouldn't have had that. Werewolves had incredible healing abilities, but they needed to breathe as much as any human or wolf would.

Had Matt and Cammie been dead before they were buried?

Simon touched my shoulder and I forced myself to turn back to the others. The werewolves had stopped digging, and I took one little step forward and looked down into the hole. The frozen face of Matt Ventimiglia was exposed now, along with his upper body and part of one leg. He'd been tossed carelessly into the hole, landing with his arm extended over his head and at an angle. His eye sockets seemed to be filled with sand, until I realized he must have died with his eyes open. Whoever had buried him hadn't bothered to close them, and the sand had stuck to the moisture in his eyes.

Simon must have been thinking along the same lines. "They must have been in a hurry," he said, sounding weary.

"Or they just didn't give a shit. Or both," I said, my voice coming out harsher than I'd intended.

The two werewolves shifted their feet around, and Dunn let out a low whine. I thought I understood—they didn't want to tear up the body with their claws. I looked at Simon. "You think you can help me lift him out?"

He gave me a grim nod. We each crouched down and took hold of a wrist, pulling gently as the wolves paced around us. The body was in rigor mortis and Matt had been heavily muscled, so it felt like trying to yank a boulder out of quicksand.

When the dune finally relinquished its prize, Simon and I nearly fell over. Matt's body was naked, frozen in a more or less prone position, with a thick layer of sand matted on his chest. Simon crouched down, using his gloved hand to brush at the sand on Matt's chest. It came away reddish, and Simon peered closer.

"I think this is a bullet hole," he reported, looking up at me.

"A lead bullet?" I asked, without much hope. I just really wanted this to be a random crime. Anything else was going to be a political nightmare for Maven.

Simon shook his head, of course. "A regular gunshot would have healed before they died. This was silver."

Next to him, Dunn let out a low growl of anger. Mary, who had been nosing around the hole left by the body, gave a sort of yip. We turned, looking in the hole, and I could see a small patch of purple fabric that had been uncovered when we'd lifted the body. "Cammie?" Simon asked, following my gaze.

"I think so."

We repeated the excavating process. The sand was still fairly loose, and it didn't take long to pull out Cammie's body and lay it beside her husband's. Unlike Matt, she had been wearing clothes: a dark purple windbreaker and jeans. She had a bullet wound too, but she had been shot in the head.

When the two bodies were side by side, the werewolves moved in, sniffing and nosing at their packmates with an air of mourning. Simon and I fell back to give them space. Simon collapsed on the ground to rest, and I let myself drop down beside him. Everything I was wearing was already full of sand; more wouldn't make a difference.

We took a moment to drink some water and eat an energy bar. "Do you think we were meant to find them?" Simon asked me, still chewing.

It was a good question. "Impossible to know," I said, after thinking it over. "If they were in a hurry, they might have made the grave shallow by necessity. It's also possible this grave *wasn't* shallow last night, if the winds changed and were strong enough. There are too many variables."

Dunn and Mary finally backed away from the bodies, and Dunn's massive head swung to look first at me, then in the direction we'd come from. Swallowing a sigh, I nodded and stood up. It was a long walk back to the parking lot. "Let's get them on the sleds."

Simon and I tied the bodies onto the sleds with some parachute cord from my backpack. Dunn and Mary both paced around us as we fumbled with the ropes, letting out the occasional short snarl as we bumped or pushed at the bodies. They were fairly terrifying, but I had gotten used to being around them, and managed to sound calm when I told Dunn there was no other way to get Matt and Cammie back. This seemed to pacify him, at least enough to stop snarling.

When we were finished, Matt's legs hung over the side of his sled, but there just wasn't any way to fit all of him on without mutilating the body. I removed my coat and my sand-smeared long-sleeved shirt. Shivering in a tank top, I quickly put the coat back on and wrapped the long-sleeved shirt over Matt's lower body, tucking the sleeves under so it would cover his groin. It was a little silly, but it was the only respectful thing I could think to do for him. Without a word, Simon did the same thing, taking off his own button-down shirt and tying it around Matt's legs where they extended past the sled. The shirt would be ruined, but at least his legs wouldn't get cut up by the sand.

We made a sad processional back through the dunes: Dunn in the lead, followed by two humans pulling sleds with corpses on them, and Mary bringing up the rear. My entire body was exhausted, like after a particularly grueling workout—and I was in good physical condition. Simon got a lot less exercise than I did, and I couldn't imagine how he must be feeling. He walked in front of me, and whenever he started to stagger, I called for a short break and some water. Dunn gave me a pointed look each time, but I didn't care. If Simon dropped from exhaustion, there was no way I'd be able to bring him, Matt, and Cammie across the dunes by myself.

It seemed to take us hours to reach the dry creek bed, but at last we came over a crest and I saw the glint of sunshine on small ice patches. I sighed with relief. There wasn't another car or person in sight, so Simon's ward was holding up.

By the time we tramped across the expanse of wet sand, my legs had started to tremble with exhaustion, but at last we reached the willow trees. Simon and I left the sand sleds there for the moment and went to collapse against the Jeep while we waited for the werewolves to change.

I glanced around the parking lot, trying to spot any video cameras. I didn't know much about the security systems at the national parks, but it certainly seemed possible they kept surveillance on the lot. "Do you have enough juice to do that security camera thing?" I asked Simon. "Before we bring the bodies closer?"

He sighed. "Maybe?" Leaning against the car for support, he struggled to his feet. "If I can walk that far on my jelly legs."

"Thank you!" I called as he trudged toward the center of the lot. One of Simon's trades witch spells was a hex that would short out video cameras in about a one-block diameter. Because it was delicate—"fussy," according to Lily—it would last only about half an hour. But we would be gone by then anyway.

The sound of painful cries from nonhuman throats began in the willows, and a few minutes later Simon was back, dropping down beside me on the asphalt. "So," he said in a low voice, " "who do you think killed them?"

I shook my head, wanting to be careful. I doubted the werewolves could hear us at the moment, but I wouldn't take chances. "I don't know. But whoever it was knew the wolves would be here, and I'm guessing that's not a long list."

We fell silent, too tired to talk, though we both stripped off the goggles, hats, and scarves now that the Jeep blocked the wind.

Eventually Dunn and Mary emerged from the willows, wearing the same loose, disposable clothes as before. Dunn was composed, but

Mary's face was clouded over with anger. She stalked straight toward me, towering over me with her hands on her hips. I was still exhausted and didn't want to stand, so I just tilted my head back to look at her. "Who did this?" she demanded.

I blinked. "How would I know? I didn't even know wolves were in Colorado until you showed up at my house." I was tempted to say *broke into my house*, but it wasn't the time.

"Did you smell anyone else out there?" Simon asked mildly.

Dunn answered first. "Yes and no. Whoever buried them had on too many layers—all I could smell was rubber and the kinds of durable fabrics commonly found in outdoor clothing. I might be able to recognize that exact combination of fabrics again, but if he's smart, he'll dump the clothes right away."

Mary pursed her lips, not ready to drop the subject, but Dunn raised his hands. His eyes were weary and sad. He was the alpha; Matt and Cammie were his responsibility. From his perspective, he'd failed them. "We can argue about who killed them later," he said tiredly. He shot Mary a look and promised, "And we will." Turning back to me, he added, "But right now we need to get them back to Cheyenne for a proper burial."

Mary's shoulders slumped, and as she turned away, her eyes were wet. "This is bullshit," she muttered, to no one in particular. I didn't hold it against her. If I were in her position, I'd be looking for someone to yell at too.

Dunn carried each of the bodies carefully to his Forester. Mary climbed in the back, and the two of them gently maneuvered the bodies into place. Simon and I stayed on the ground, leaning against the Jeep. The werewolves didn't seem to need any help, and at the moment I wasn't sure we could have mustered the energy to lift a bottle of water.

When they were finished, Mary stayed in the Subaru, emptying Cammie's pockets, although I couldn't see what she'd found. Dunn came over to stand in front of us. "Are you sure about this?" I asked Dunn, eyeing the Forester. "If you get pulled over for something . . ."

He gave me a wan smile. "We'll wrap them in a tarp, but we need to get them home."

I nodded slowly. It seemed like a huge risk, transporting the bodies so far, but I didn't have a better idea. There was a hidden compartment in the Jeep that could hold a body, but not two, and not in rigor mortis.

Mary hopped down from the Forester, holding what looked like a hotel room key card and the keys to the truck, which she jingled, frowning. "Why leave the truck here?"

Dunn looked thoughtful. "It does suggest he wanted us to go out there and look for them."

"Or it could just be that he forgot to take the keys out of Cammie's pocket before he buried them," Simon pointed out. "Or there's only one killer, and he didn't want to take the time to move the truck and come back for his own vehicle."

The alpha werewolf nodded. "When we get back to Cheyenne, we'll take a closer look inside, see if we can find anything." He looked at Mary. "We should get going. You drive the truck; I'll take the Forester."

Mary tightened her fist around the key ring but didn't move. "I should drive the Forester. You're alpha; if you get pulled over with bodies in the back—"

"My pack, my call," Dunn broke in, in a voice that left no room for argument. He stepped closer to Mary and rested his hand on her cheek for a moment. "I'll see you back home," he promised. "Go on."

Mary started toward the truck, but I called after her. "Where were they staying?"

She turned and gave me a perplexed look, and I added, "The hotel key? Where were they planning to spend the night?"

"Oh." She reached for the key card, which she'd shoved in the pocket of her cutoff sweatpants, and examined it. "The Holiday Inn in Alamosa," she said.

"Why? What are you thinking?" Dunn asked me.

"I'm thinking there's no way in hell Simon and I can make the drive back without rest, and I would deeply love a shower. He and I can go to the Holiday Inn and get our own rooms. While we're there we can pick up Matt and Cammie's stuff."

"I can just call there and have them ship it back up to Cheyenne," he pointed out, but there was interest in his eyes.

I shrugged. "If you'd rather. But if we're stopping anyway, we might as well clean it out for you."

Dunn nodded again, meeting my eyes. I didn't know a ton about wolves, but I'd been careful not to stare at him in a challenging way. It was a lot easier to make eye contact when I was sitting on the ground and he was standing. "Appreciate it."

Mary spun to look at him. Her head was lowered slightly in deference, but her expression was furious. "You're going to let Maven's lackeys mess with Matt and Cammie's stuff?" she growled. "What's to stop them from destroying any information they find?"

Okay, that was enough. I stood up and stepped toward her—not quite in her face, but getting close. "Mary," I said tightly, "I appreciate that you've lost someone today. But I haven't slept, and I just spent half a day hiking through my least favorite terrain on the planet. I look and feel like a walking bag of dirt. And yet here I am, offering to help you." Fuck werewolf politics. I met her eyes and didn't look away. "I came here in good faith to repay a debt, not as anyone's *lackey*. Do you want to get your head out of your ass and accept my help, or do you really think I suddenly developed a taste for mind games?"

Mary put her hands on her hips, glaring at me. "I can go to the hotel room," she snapped.

"I need you to drive the truck, and help me talk to the rest of the pack," Dunn said. "And we can't linger in this state; you *know* that. We're already pushing it by going home during the day, when Maven's not able to vouch for us."

"But—"

Dunn looked like he was about to lay down the law as alpha, but to my surprise, Simon spoke first. "Mary," he said quietly. Her eyes flicked down to him. "You saved my life two years ago. I haven't forgotten."

It was true; Mary had cut Simon out of the sandworm's throat while I was incapacitated. I had almost forgotten.

Her eyes softened just a little. Simon continued, "I know Lex has to represent Maven, but she's being straight with you. And *I* don't work for Maven. I don't really have a horse in this race, so to speak, but I do feel I owe you, personally. Please let us help."

Mary made a frustrated sound in the back of her throat and practically stomped over to him, tossing the hotel room key in his lap. Then she went to sit in the pickup truck, slamming the door behind her.

Dunn watched her go, then turned to look at us. "She was very close to Cammie," he said quietly. "They were roommates before she married Matt."

I winced. Dunn added, to me, "Thank you for your offer. I trust you'll call after you check the hotel room?"

I nodded. "Even if we find nothing, we'll pack up their stuff and get it back to you."

"Appreciate it." His eyes hardened. "I want a face-to-face meeting with Maven. Tonight."

I raised my eyebrows. Dunn was still a werewolf, and Maven rarely left the coffee shop, let alone Boulder. Getting the two of them face-to-face was a pretty huge demand. "You know what you're asking?" I said, keeping my voice even.

He nodded, his jaw set.

"Call Quinn after sunset," I told him. "He'll talk to Maven about setting it up. I don't know what she'll say, but . . . just call Quinn. We might not be back yet."

Simon and I turned to go, but Dunn called me back. "Lex . . . I do appreciate what you did today," he said quietly. "You and I are square," he said.

"Okay." Reflexively, I stretched out my hand and he shook it.

The flinty look hadn't left his eyes, though, and just for a moment he gripped my hand hard. "But I swear to you, when I find out who killed my wolves, whoever it is . . . there will be hell to pay."

Chapter 8

After the werewolves left, Simon went to dismantle his humans-go-away spell. I brushed off my clothes as much as I could and got inside the Jeep, getting the heater going. I made a quick call to Quinn's voice mail, explaining that we had found the bodies and were headed to Alamosa to rest for a few hours. Then I looked up the Ventimiglias' hotel on my phone, groaning as the trip estimate popped up. It was nearly another hour away, in the opposite direction from Boulder. I checked my watch. To my surprise, it was only a little before noon. I felt like we'd been out on the dunes for days, but just under four hours had passed. It didn't seem possible that I was this tired.

On a hunch, I called the hotel, identified myself as Cammie Ventimiglia, and asked if I had a reservation for one night or two. I didn't want anyone thinking the Ventimiglias were late to check out and messing with their stuff. But the clerk assured me the reservation was for two nights. Matt and Cammie must have decided to spend a second day in the area.

Before I hung up, I asked him when the hotel had been built. I'd learned the hard way that the older the hotel, the more ghosts inhabited it, and I didn't want to have to deal with hauntings under the current circumstances. To my relief, it was fairly new construction. I thanked him and hung up, yawning.

I wasn't the only one. Simon fell asleep before we went back through the National Park entrance, leaning against the window with his head propped on his messenger bag. I glanced over at him and had to smile. There were streaks of dirt on his face where sand had gotten trapped between his goggles and his skin, giving him a sort of raccoon/bandit look. Then I glanced in the visor mirror and saw that I had the exact same streaks, and directed my attention back to the road.

By the time we reached Alamosa I was starving, so I stopped at a sandwich shop, poking Simon's arm until he woke up to give me his order. I ran in to use the bathroom and get the food, and we cruised through town munching on our subs.

Like many small towns in Colorado, Alamosa wasn't particularly memorable on its own, but it did a brisk tourism trade because of its proximity to natural wonders. The town's main drag was a winding collection of strip malls, fast-food restaurants, and a handful of chain hotels. The Holiday Inn was nearly at the end of them, and it was exactly what you'd expect—generic, anonymous, and nonthreatening, with an overabundance of Christmas lights and tinny Christmas music playing in the lobby. The desk clerk, a pimply, slightly timid young man who looked about sixteen but was probably in his early twenties, didn't so much as raise an eyebrow when Simon and I walked in. "The Dunes?" he said, glancing at our filthy clothes and the light dusting of sand trailing behind us. He was clearly trying to suppress a smile.

Simon still looked too exhausted to speak, so I answered. "Yes. Our friends are staying here, and we were hoping to get a room as well. With two beds," I added quickly.

Unfortunately, the clerk informed me, they did not have a room available for us at the moment, as check-in didn't start until three. I glanced over my shoulder at Simon, who was swaying a little on his feet. Crap. I really didn't want to use the Ventimiglias' room because of the ick factor, but I was also too tired to go find another hotel. Stepping away from the desk, I pulled the hotel room key out of my pocket. It was in one of those little cardboard folders, and the room number was written on the inside: 126. "We'll just go visit with our friends," I told the clerk, trying not to sound resigned.

I led the way down the hall, with Simon trudging after me, until we reached the right door. I opened it cautiously, expecting . . . I don't know. A booby trap? Gunshots? It seemed unlikely that whoever had killed the Ventimiglias would stick around to ambush their hotel maid, but I still made Simon stay in the hall while I checked the room, my hand on the revolver in my pocket.

There was nothing. It was a perfectly average hotel room: shoebox-sized bathroom, sink and minifridge, king-sized bed, desk with a single chair, and TV sitting on a generic bureau. There were some toiletries in the bathroom and an extra-large, unzipped duffel bag on the wooden desk, and that was it.

I went back out and got Simon, who gave me a weak smile. "Why don't you shower first?" I suggested, taking pity on him. "I'll take a quick look at their things."

Simon nodded and shuffled into the bathroom while I went back to the duffel bag. It was a little dusty and worn, as though it got a lot of use. I perched on the edge of the desk chair, trying not to sand any more of the room than I needed to, and opened the bag's main compartment. I pulled out all the contents: a few changes of clothing, a Kindle, a couple of outdoor lifestyle magazines, and a large jar of peanut butter. There was no bread or anything, but I guessed the peanut butter was for Matt, who would be hungry after changing back into a human. Peanut butter was a good way to get a lot of protein, fat, and calories very quickly, if you could deal with it being stuck to the roof of your mouth.

I checked carefully, but there were no secret compartments, nothing hidden in the seams. I did find Matt's cell phone in one of the duffel bag's side pockets, which made sense: Why bring a new-model iPhone to the dunes, especially when you were planning to be a wolf the whole time? The phone was locked with a password, so I zipped it back in the duffel bag and turned to search the rest of the room—which took about thirty seconds. The fridge held only a six-pack of Snake River Pale Ale, and the drawers and closet were empty. If the Ventimiglias' murderer had even come to the hotel room, he or she hadn't left anything behind. Then again, what had I expected? Bloody handprints, or signed hate mail?

A moment later Simon came out of the bathroom wearing athletic pants and a long-sleeved white T-shirt. Like everyone else I'd met in the Old World, he always kept extra clothes with him. He mumbled something like, "Your turn," and went to collapse on one side of the king bed.

I stayed under the hot water for a long time, scrubbing the sand off my skin and shampooing my hair several times. There wasn't even much sand in my hair, thanks to the hat and scarf, but it was a psychological thing. I *felt* like the desert had spread through all my clothes and permeated my skin.

When I finally came out of the bathroom, wearing old jeans and a lightweight Luther Shoes sweatshirt, Simon was lying on the very edge of the bed. I had to laugh. He had built a fence of pillows going all the way down the bed's center.

Simon's eyelids cracked open and he smiled. "It's a little weird, right?"

"That you're a grown man building a pillow fort?"

He rolled his eyes. "Sharing a bed."

"Maybe a little," I admitted, circling the bed to climb under the covers on the other side. By unspoken agreement, Simon and I avoided intimacy, and now we were going to sleep together. Literally speaking, of course.

"You setting your alarm?" he asked, clearly trying to change the subject.

"Yeah." I fiddled with my phone, trying to decide how many hours we could afford to sleep. Ideally, I would have liked to be home before dark so I could go see Maven right away, but that was impossible: it was not quite two, and it would take at least four and a half hours to get back to Boulder. The sun would be down around 4:30. I texted Quinn again, telling him we were going to crash for a few hours and I would call him from the road, hopefully by 6:30. I figured he could handle whatever came up between sunset and then. Simon's car was already at Magic Beans, so I could go straight there to talk to Maven.

I barely managed to set the phone on the nightstand before I sank gratefully into sleep.

My dreams were filled with sand.

I should have expected it, really. I had spent all morning wandering around a desert landscape trying to avoid thoughts of my time in Iraq; of *course* I would have the Iraq nightmare.

I had done two tours overseas and I had seen—and, occasionally, been responsible for—all kinds of terrible things, but my nightmares tended to be about those last two days, and this time was no different.

My team and I climbed into the Humvee and started along the road. About fifteen miles into our route, the first IED blew under the truck.

I had just gotten to the part where I dragged myself away from the crumpled Humvee and turned back to see a severed left arm when I heard my name being called.

"Lex! *Lex!*"

My eyes flew open, but the room around me was dark. Before I could register where I was, or who was speaking, my fists thrashed out—right at Simon's face.

Simon, to his credit, was ready for it. He had one palm up, and as my right fist was about to connect with his nose, I felt it glance off something. His shield.

Panting, I went still. My eyes were adjusting to the near darkness, and I could make out the ruins of sheets and blankets around me. Sweat had soaked through my T-shirt and glued it to my chest.

"Shit," I whispered. I sat up and pressed my back against the headboard, pulling my knees in.

The lamp on Simon's side of the bed clicked on, and my friend reached for his glasses, jamming them on his face. His clothes and hair were rumpled, and there was a reddish mark on one cheek.

Shit.

"Did I hurt you?" I asked.

Simon blinked. "What? No."

"Your cheek is red."

"That's just where I was sleeping on it," he said, probably a lie. "You were, um, having a bad dream."

I choked on a laugh. "I guess you could say that."

"I've read about soldiers with PTSD," he said uncomfortably, "but I guess I never realized . . . Lex . . ."

I shook my head tightly. Simon, who had three sisters, recognized this as *Let's talk about literally anything else.* "What time is it?" I asked. The drapes were tightly closed, so I couldn't even tell if it was still light out.

He turned around to check the alarm clock behind him. "About five thirty," he reported.

Well after sunset. "We might as well get moving. I'll call Quinn on the way and check in."

"Okay." Simon shifted to stand up, but I didn't move. I didn't trust my legs yet, not when my head was still swimming with memories. Simon glanced back at me and seemed to realize this. "I'll, um, go use the bathroom first," he suggested. I nodded, but I didn't relax until I heard the door close behind him. Then I let the air out of my lungs with a great whoosh and scrubbed my face with my hands. That had been a bad one.

You're okay, though. I heard Sam's voice in my thoughts. *You're safe.*

I felt a rush of relief when my cell phone rang on the bedside table. I reached for the phone expecting to see Quinn's name on the screen, but the number was unfamiliar.

I answered it. "This is Lex."

"It's Mary." Her voice shook with tension.

"What's going on?" I asked.

"I'm almost back to Cheyenne, but I've been calling Ryan to check in and he's not answering."

I blinked hard, trying to force myself into the present. "He probably just doesn't have cell phone service," I said. "It's really spotty in—"

"You don't understand. I've been calling every twenty minutes for the last three hours. I just got off the phone with the pack's tech guy, and he says Ryan's phone GPS is just . . . gone."

"Maybe he lost it," I reasoned, but I was already standing up, starting to collect my few possessions from the room. "Or he could have dropped it."

Mary let out an aggrieved sigh. "Ryan is way too careful for that," she said, clearly at the limits of her patience. "Especially considering his *cargo*?"

Right. I had somehow forgotten about the two dead bodies Dunn was hauling up north. "Maybe he was in a fender bender? The phone might have gotten trashed."

"That's what I'm worried about. We can survive most car crashes, but if the cops searched the car and arrested him . . . I don't know if he'd get to make a phone call to us. I have no idea how that works. Jail, I mean. No one in the pack has been arrested before and I don't know how I would find him—"

She was babbling, so I broke in. "Okay, hang on. Where are you now?"

"I pulled over at a gas station near the state line. I'm trying to figure out if I should turn around and come back down there."

I thought that over. Mary was *not* supposed to be in Maven's territory. Every minute she was in Colorado without an Old World escort was another minute when she might be noticed by a witch or vampire, who might spread the word and create a political catastrophe.

Then again . . . "Mary," I said carefully. "I want you to go back to Boulder. You can hang out at my place, if you don't mind dogs and cats, or go to a hotel, but I don't think you should return to Cheyenne yet."

"Why not?"

Simon came out of the bathroom, a question on his face. I mouthed "Mary" to him.

"Lex? Why shouldn't I go home?"

Tell her the truth, or soften it with a lie? I decided to rip off the Band-Aid. "Because there are a limited number of people who knew where Dunn was going to be today. And I'm guessing most of them are in your pack."

Next to me, Simon's eyes widened, and there was a long silence on the phone. Finally, I said, "Mary? Are you still there?"

Her voice was a low rumbling growl, like she was struggling to control herself enough to speak. "You think *one of us—*"

"I'm saying I don't know," I interrupted, "and neither do you, not for sure. But it shouldn't hurt anything if you camp out for a few more hours while we find your alpha."

There was a long silence. "You have no idea what you're saying," she spat.

"Maybe not." I sighed. "Look, I'm not going to argue with you over the phone. But if you trust me even a little bit, please don't go back to Cheyenne until we find Dunn."

Another silence, then: "Where are you now?"

"We're just leaving Alamosa; we can retrace his route." Pinning the phone to my ear with my shoulder, I shoved my dirty clothes into my backpack and zipped it shut. Simon took the hint and began cramming stuff into his bag.

"All right," Mary said at last. "I'll go to your place."

"Thank you," I said with relief. "Can you tell me exactly where Dunn's signal disappeared?"

Chapter 9

Ten minutes later, Simon and I were back on the road, heading north toward Rio Norte, Colorado, where Dunn's cell phone had last pinged. It was less than thirty miles north of Alamosa, which worried me. When I'd talked to Mary, I'd assumed Dunn had gone off-grid hours away from here, maybe even in Wyoming. Rio Norte was too close.

Maven didn't answer her phone, but that was typical for this early in the evening—she was probably feeding. I called Quinn and filled him in instead, keeping to a brief account of what we knew. He promised to find Maven in person and update her. If Dunn had actually been arrested, I was going to need her help. I'd never covered up anything as big as someone getting arrested with dead bodies in the car. It was way above my pay grade, and would require vampire intervention.

"How are we going to find him once we get to Rio Norte?" Simon asked when I'd hung up the phone.

It was a reasonable question. I glanced over at Simon. "I don't suppose you have any magic that will help us find him."

Simon shook his head. "I could, but I'd need something that belongs to him. The idea behind locating magic is—"

"Simon?" I interrupted, sensing him moving into teacher mode. "We're almost to Rio Norte. Can I get the short version?"

He cleared his throat. "Right. Umm . . . the best bet would be spare keys to his car."

I thought that over for a moment. Mary would probably be able to get those for us, but it would require her to go back to Cheyenne, which would be time-consuming and possibly dangerous.

Then I had another idea. "What about Cammie and Matt?" I asked, pointing my thumb toward the back of the Jeep, where I'd stashed the duffel bag. "Cammie has a hairbrush in there. If you can find their bodies, that's where Dunn should be."

"Huh." Simon tapped his chin for a second, thinking. He had his scientist face on, and for a second I forgot my worry and had to smile. "That could work. I've never tried to find a dead body, but the body is human now, so the principle is sound." When vampires or werewolves died, the magic that had clung to them left their bodies as it had found them . . . which was why Matt's body had been human and nude when we'd uncovered it.

"Can you try it right now?"

"Better not. As you know, the most stable way for most witches to use magic is inside a circle. A moving car isn't ideal."

I nodded. Ahead of us, I saw a sign informing me that the Rio Norte exit was two miles away. "Okay, well, I don't want to pull over right here, since someone might stop to see if we need help or a ride. Let's get to Rio Norte and find an alley or deserted road or something."

"Sounds good . . ." His voice drifted off as he leaned forward, squinting through the windshield. You could see a long way in this flat, unpopulated area. "Lex . . . Are those what I think they are?"

The bright red and blue lights of police cars were flashing just to the right of the Rio Norte exit. A *lot* of them. "Yeah," I said, though my voice came out grim. "It's probably not connected to us, though," I added, sounding unconvincing even to myself.

I checked the speedometer and slowed to just under the speed limit, taking the exit off the highway. Just after we exited, I spotted a short metal bridge spanning the town's namesake, the Rio Norte River. The bridge obviously led straight into the small downtown area, but it was currently blocked off by a cluster of four police vehicles. Just past them, on the bridge itself, there was a massive tow truck, its orange and white lights blinking somberly. I couldn't see what the tow truck was actually doing, but a small crowd of onlookers was being contained on the far side of the bridge.

We reached the last intersection before the police cars, which was blocked off with sawhorses. A uniformed officer was standing in the road in a puffy, police-issue winter coat, trying to wave us along the detour with his big flashlight. Instead, I pulled up to him and rolled down my window. He automatically came over and bent his head to look in at us.

"What happened?" I asked.

The guy frowned, glancing beyond me like he was hoping for another car so he'd have an excuse to push me along. "A Subaru got T-boned and went off the bridge," he said, then gave me a stern look. "For your own safety, ma'am, please follow the detour into town."

I tried to ask another question, but he turned away, not having it. I rolled up the window and made the turn, glancing at Simon. He looked as worried as I felt, but neither of us wanted to voice our fear. There were lots of Subarus in Colorado.

I followed the detour, which snaked around the accident site, across a smaller, older bridge, and into downtown Rio Norte. I'd never been there before, but I'd been in similar places: small, scraped-together mining communities that were struggling to survive now that the silver or coal had run out. Colorado was littered with them, like a schoolyard strewn with abandoned toys.

We wound through the downtown streets until we were two blocks from the entrance to the bridge. I parked on the street, and without needing to discuss it, Simon and I walked down the street to join the crowd of onlookers. From this side I could see the spot where the vehicle had torn through the corrugated metal guardrail like it was ripping paper.

There were about thirty or forty people milling around, which had to be a pretty big percentage of the Rio Norte population. Most of them were talking to each other in tight, closed circles or muttering into cell phones, their expressions concerned or excited—or both. The whole scene on the bridge looked like something out of a movie, with all the flashing lights and the tow truck rope hanging down the gap in the ripped guardrail.

I sidled up to two harried-looking women in their thirties, both dressed in office clothes and parkas. I'd kind of hoped Simon would step up and do the talking-to-strangers part, like Quinn usually did, but he stayed at my shoulder, waiting for me to take the lead. Crap.

"Excuse me," I began. "We're just passing through town. Can you tell me what's going on?"

The one closest to me, a bleached blonde, gave me a brief glance and said, "They're about to pull up the car. They had to wait for the wind to die down a little."

"How did the guy go through the guardrail?" I asked.

Her friend, a Latina woman in a scuffed gray coat, answered. "Truck T-boned the side of it."

The blonde pointed to a small access road, barely more than a path, that ran parallel to the river on the opposite bank.

"We was just saying, we think the truck musta come off the front-age road. There are plenty of lights on the bridge, so . . ." She shook her head, mystified. "Why wouldn't he have stopped?"

The frontage road had no streetlights, and I could barely make out the handful of people down there. They were wearing black, and after a moment I realized these had to be divers, probably out of Pueblo or Colorado Springs. Rio Norte was way too small to have a team like that.

"Did anyone come out of the water?" I asked. "Any survivors?" Both women shook their heads.

Simon touched my arm and pointed at the tow truck. "Look," he said softly.

The thick chains had started moving, agonizingly slow, and with a horrific metallic screech that had a few people in the crowd covering their ears. It seemed like an hour before a wet, black mass emerged from the water, and my heart sank as I recognized Ryan Dunn's Forester. It cleared the surface of the water, dangling gently from the chains, and began a slow spin as a torrent of river water cascaded out the cracks.

I was too horrified to take in any details, but Simon bent his head to speak in my ear. "Lex, look at the windows."

I squinted, trying to see past the reflected lights bouncing off the wet metal. Then I realized what Simon meant: the inside of the Forester's bullet-resistant windows was scored with dozens of deep, ragged lines, clustered in groups of four.

Claw marks.

Chapter 10

"Lex," Maven said a few hours later, "I understand you're upset, but please try to calm down."

I snorted, continuing my tight circuit of the room. I didn't trust myself to speak yet.

We were in the large, concrete-floored back room at Magic Beans. Usually Quinn and I met Maven in her tiny office, but it was too tiny with the addition of Simon—and Maven had probably realized that I needed a hell of a lot more room. I'd been pacing for the last ten minutes while Simon had told the others about Dunn's Subaru.

I barely listened. I'd already provided a brief, edited-for-cell-phone-security explanation from the road, so Maven could dispatch a couple of her Colorado Springs vampires to Rio Norte. They were supposed to press minds and gather as much information as possible, and since we had a much longer drive than they did, Quinn had called with the first update before Simon and I made it into Boulder.

As I'd suspected, someone had tampered with Dunn's Subaru, sabotaging the door mechanisms so they wouldn't open from the inside. He had been trapped in there, panicked and unable to break through his specially reinforced windows, while he slowly drowned.

The only time someone could have messed with the Subaru was while the four of us were out on the dunes finding the bodies—which meant that Matt and Cammie had been bait. It was even possible that they'd been killed for no other reason than to lure Dunn into Colorado. And all that had happened on my watch.

By the time Simon and I arrived at Magic Beans, my hands were shaking with fury. It must have been obvious when we got inside, because neither Maven nor Quinn objected to Simon doing all the talking while I paced behind them.

Now, though, I turned to face the group. "I *won't* calm down," I snapped, not so much at Maven as to the room in general. "It was a trap, and I walked him right into it."

"You know it wasn't your fault," Quinn said, sounding infuriatingly calm.

"Wasn't it? He was supposed to be under my protection. That was the whole point of cashing in his favor, of bringing Simon and me along. And I let him get killed *right under my nose.*" I turned to continue my circuit of the room, but not before I saw Quinn and Simon exchange a look that I couldn't help but interpret as "bitches be crazy."

"About that," Maven said, her voice still perfectly calm. She was in her usual hippie/bag lady getup: a shapeless sweaterdress in tomato red that clashed with her orange hair, and piles of tacky costume neck-laces. The disguise fooled most people, but for me Maven practically pulsed with intensity. She was old, and powerful as hell. "Why do you think the two werewolves were shot with silver bullets, but Dunn was drowned? Wouldn't it have been easier to shoot him too?"

That brought me up short, and I paused in the middle of the con-crete floor. She was right. "They wanted Dunn's death to get attention," I concluded. "To make sure you—we—couldn't cover it up."

"I agree," Maven said dryly. "And it certainly worked."

She wasn't kidding. The crash had been all over the radio news dur-ing our drive back, with reporters leaning hard on the fact that there were two dead bodies in the back of Dunn's Subaru. I hadn't looked at a TV or computer yet, but I assumed it was all over every news outlet in the state.

Maven's vampires would contain the situation, at least before the ME found those silver bullets, but it was too late to keep the story from the audience most meant to see it—the witches. Those who remembered the werewolf war would know that Ryan Dunn was the name of the current Cheyenne alpha, and anyone who'd ever met a werewolf would recognize the claw marks on the window, which had apparently also made the news. Word would soon spread to everyone else. As far as any of us could figure, that had to be the point—showing the witches that Maven was allowing werewolves into the state, breaking the treaty as they understood it.

I went and sat down in the empty chair next to Simon. "Have the witches been calling?" I asked, a little cautious. I wasn't sure how much Maven would tell us in front of him.

"Me? No, they wouldn't dare," Maven replied. "But I heard from Hazel Pellar half an hour ago. She is being besieged by calls from the leaders of the other witch clans, wanting to know why they weren't informed about werewolves in our state."

"So they really didn't know?" I said, just to be sure. Lily had always talked like the Colorado witch clans had one hell of a rumor mill.

But Maven shook her head. "A few of them suspected, or had heard rumors, but no, the knowledge had been contained to Clan Pellar." Her eyes darted to Simon, whose face was tight.

"We kept it very quiet," he said heavily. "My mother was . . ." His fingers flexed as he searched for a word. "Embarrassed, I suppose. About Morgan. She didn't want the other clans to know about the weekend pass."

"Did anyone else in Clan Pellar know about it, besides you, Lily, and Sybil?" I asked.

Simon winced, glancing at Maven, and I realized it had been a mistake to ask him to rat out his fellow witches right in front of her. Crap. "I don't know for certain," Simon answered, his voice very careful. "It's possible."

"Pardon me," Quinn began. For a moment, I thought he was just trying to draw Maven's attention from Simon, and I was grateful. Then he said, "Is this really even our problem? You made a legitimate deal with Hazel to allow the occasional weekend pass. The witches are angry, but isn't that on Hazel? No offense, Simon," he added.

Simon looked miserable, but gave a little nod, and Quinn pushed on, his eyes on Maven. "When you okayed the weekend passes, you made it clear to Dunn's pack that they didn't actually have your protection, just your permission." He gave a small shrug, his tone neutral. "So . . . is this even our fight?"

The anger that had started to dissipate surged inside me, and I glared at my boyfriend. "It's *my* fight," I snapped. "Dunn was here under *my* protection."

Quinn raised an eyebrow, but didn't respond. He just looked toward Maven, who was staring at the air above his head, thinking it over. After a moment, she looked at Simon. "I appreciate you stopping in to help explain matters, but I'm sure you need to get back to the witch clan," she said.

Simon, who knew a dismissal when he heard one, nodded and stood. He looked tired. "Thank you," I said to him, meaning it. "For coming with me."

Simon nodded and rested a hand on my shoulder, just for a second, as he passed to go to the door.

Maven waited in silence until he was well out of earshot, then turned so she could look at both of us. "In three years, my treaty with the witches is over," she said without preamble. "When that happens, I want to permanently allow werewolves back into the state."

Chapter 11

I sat there blinking with surprise, but Quinn recovered faster. "Why?" he asked.

"Because it's going to happen one way or another. You two have firsthand experience with how difficult it is to keep them out of Colorado. If I were to invite a pack in, one that I already know and have had dealings with . . ." She waved her hand.

"It's the evil you know versus the evil you don't," I translated.

"More or less. At any rate, I've been . . ." She hesitated, wincing a little. "Well, I hate to use the word 'grooming' . . ."

Oh. I felt like an idiot. "*That's* why you've been letting them in the state. They're getting to know their future territory."

Maven nodded. "Of course, the entire state is too big for a single pack, but my goal was to get Dunn and his people in quickly and establish them as my allies. That would at least give pause to any other packs planning to rush in."

For a moment, I felt a great swell of pity for Maven. Most leaders had to think about the big picture, but she was also a vampire, capable of living forever. She had to think about the big picture *and* the long game simultaneously.

"In other words, killing Dunn and two of his wolves doesn't just trash their pack *or* your reputation," Quinn said, thinking out loud. "It trashes your plan for the future."

"Exactly." She frowned. "I suppose it's still possible that this was a squabble within the pack, but it's more likely that someone is trying to cut my feet out from under me." Maven gave a little headshake, like she was trying to fling something off her. "What troubles me most, however, is that this doesn't feel like a werewolf move."

"What do you mean?" I asked, wary.

She looked at me blankly for a moment, then nodded. "I keep forgetting that you've had very few interactions with the wolves. Both of you," she added, glancing at Quinn. "Werewolves *always* feel the prickle of their magic, like an itch under the skin. As a result, they're usually irritable, angry—impulsive. I can see a werewolf shooting the Ventimiglias out of anger, or spontaneously running Dunn off the road . . . but this was a careful plan, with multiple steps and risks. It was cold."

"Like a vampire plan," Quinn said softly.

"That makes no sense," I told both of them. "We've had no other signs that another vampire is involved in this mess."

"True," Maven allowed. "I suppose the bottom line is that I need to know who killed Dunn."

"So do I," I told them. *Both* of them.

"Hold on a moment." Maven got up and went into her office. While she was gone, I didn't look at Quinn, though I could feel him looking at me. Anything we said would be overheard by Maven and any other vampires in the building.

Maven returned with a small stack of files. "I had them investigated," she said. "I wanted to know who I might be getting into bed with. As werewolf packs go, this one seems—seemed—fairly stable and self-reliant. They had nine members, now down to six."

"Who will be alpha now that Dunn is dead?" I asked abruptly.

"That is the question, isn't it? Werewolf packs are usually led by a mated pair, sort of like parents in a large family."

"Wait. Did Dunn have a . . ." I waved a hand, not sure of the terminology. "An alpha partner?"

"Not yet. He had a human wife, who died a few years ago." She shook her head. "Ordinarily the beta wolf would step into the alpha role, but Matt Ventimiglia was the beta, and he's gone."

"Leaving a power vacuum," Quinn put in.

"Exactly." She handed me the top two files on her stack. "My best guess is that one of these two will try to take over."

The top file was Mary's, which surprised me a little. She didn't really project leadership qualities. Then I felt a stab of guilt. Mary was holed up at my house, and I hadn't even called her to tell her about Dunn yet. I may have been fuming the whole way home, but I still recognized that Maven needed to know first.

I lifted the cover of the second file, which was for a man named Finn Barlow. The name meant nothing to me. "Not Jamie?" I asked, referring to the blond, surfer-looking werewolf who'd helped us fight the sandworm, along with Dunn and Mary.

Maven shook her head. "He moved back to Australia last year."

"So what do you want us to do?" Quinn asked Maven. "Head up to Cheyenne?"

I let the file close and looked up at her. Maven's eyes went distant for a moment, the only indication she was weighing a difficult problem. "Ordinarily, yes, but we need to move as quickly as possible, and Mary Hollis is still in Boulder." She glanced at me.

Trying not to squirm, I said, "If they set one werewolf trap, there could be more. I thought it was better to be unpredictable." And I was damned sure not going to lose Mary too.

Maven nodded. "At any rate, I want Quinn to go up to Cheyenne and assess the situation. Do *not* attack the werewolves," she told him, with a note of warning. "But I'd like to know how they're reacting, what they're doing. And take a close look at this Barlow."

She turned her attention to me. "Lex, speak to Mary Hollis. Try to find out if she was involved in Dunn's death." She handed me the stack of files. "Then look through the rest of these and see if anything jumps out at you." She paused just for an instant, and added, "You have silver ammunition for your weapons, right?"

"Yes, but . . . I just can't see Mary being involved. She was really upset about Matt and Cammie, and even more worried about Dunn. She thinks it was the witches. Or you," I added.

"Then we have to keep her safe," Maven concluded. "If this was Barlow, or any of the other wolves, Mary may be a target too."

Maven told me to get some sleep after I talked to Mary; then Quinn and I were summarily dismissed.

Outside, I wrapped my arms around the files and stalked toward my car like I had blinders on. By the time I unlocked the door and dropped the files on the back seat, Quinn was there, catching my arm. "Hey. What's wrong?"

I half turned, not meeting his eyes. I was still angry, and there was a chance that I might press him by mistake. Instead, I glared down at his arm until he let go of me. "Is this even *our* fight?" I said, mimicking his tone.

He gave a little shrug. "It wasn't personal. I'm in charge of Maven's security. I need to look at the big picture."

I blew out a breath. "You're just so . . . cold. People *died*. People we could have saved."

"Werewolves," he pointed out, still maddeningly calm. "Who live in another state and knew the risks."

I clenched my fists, conflicted. In a way he was right, and I had no great love of werewolves anyway. I knew, at least intellectually, that I wasn't responsible for these deaths.

But Ryan Dunn had been a leader looking for his people, and I'd given my word that I would help. Simple as that.

I had no idea how to express any of that to Quinn, though. Instead, I heard myself picking a fight. "You knew the Ventimiglias were going to be at the Dunes last night, didn't you?"

I couldn't help but look at him now, but I kept a grip on my magic. He blinked, taking the tiniest step back from me. "Does it matter? Everything would still have happened the same way if you'd known about it in advance."

"It matters to me."

"Then yes, I knew. Like I said, I'm in charge of Maven's security. I needed to be aware in case any of the witches found out."

"Who else knew?" Maven had always implied she was the only one who knew the details about the weekend passes, but obviously I couldn't trust that.

"No one. Just Maven and myself."

"Why didn't you tell *me*?"

A look of slight confusion crossed his face. "Because there was no reason for you to know."

I threw up my hands. "I'm supposed to be daytime security, aren't I?"

Now he frowned. This was a lot of facial expressions for Quinn. "Lex. It should have been a completely routine weekend pass. You weren't involved in the others."

"Because I thought Maven was handling them herself!"

Understanding flooded his face. "So you're upset because she told me and not you?"

"No! . . . Yes! I . . . argh!" I turned and slammed the back door, yanking open the driver's side and climbing in without another word. After I turned the ignition, I felt, rather than saw, Quinn drift away from the car.

I sat there for a minute while the car warmed up, flexing and closing my fingers. I was fuming—and trying to figure out what the hell was going on with me. Quinn and I had had plenty of arguments, but this time I wasn't even sure what we were fighting about.

I just felt so useless. Dunn had come to me for help, and I'd done exactly jack shit for him. If I'd known the werewolves were coming in advance . . .

No, Quinn was right. It probably wouldn't have changed anything. I just hated that he was keeping things from me.

But you knew they weren't telling you everything. It wasn't Sam's voice this time, just the taunting of my own subconscious. When I'd made my deal with Maven, pledging my service in exchange for Charlie's safety and childhood, I'd made it clear that I wouldn't kill anyone for her, and I wouldn't hurt any innocents. Since then, I *had* killed several vampires, either in self-defense or to save someone else, but I had no issues with that.

Quinn, however, had a very different deal with our cardinal vampire. He was bound to her by magic oath, so if she told him to kill someone, he would have to. And he might decide he needed to spare me from knowing about it.

Uncomfortable as it was, I made myself consider the possibility that Quinn might have had something to do with the murders. Maven wasn't above killing in cold blood, but no matter how I turned it around in my head, I couldn't see any reason for her to allow three werewolves into Colorado, then kill them—or ask Quinn and me to look into the murders. If Maven had wanted Dunn or the Ventimiglias dead for any reason, she would have done it quietly, and they would have just disappeared.

And I would never have known about it.

That's *what's bothering you, dummy,* came Sam's voice. *Both Quinn and Maven are keeping things from you. You're not all the way in* or *all the way out.*

"That's ridiculous," I said out loud. "Of course I'm all the way in. Look at the things I've done in service to Maven."

There was no answer from my dead sister. Of course. I sighed and turned the key in the ignition, a wave of exhaustion breaking over me. It was time to talk to Mary.

When I finally returned to the cabin, just after midnight, I found Mary fast asleep in the center of the couch with Dopey curled up on her stomach. The rest of the dogs were obviously locked up in the back bedroom again, either by her or my cousin Jake, whom I'd called that morning during the drive to the Dunes. Jake was a veterinarian, and he'd given me the animals to begin with; he didn't mind stopping by on occasion when I needed help caring for them.

I paused for a moment in the entrance to the living room, looking at the werewolf on my couch. Mary was sprawled out on the center cushion, with one long leg draped up over the back of the couch, and the other flopping over the armrest. She was wearing only a cropped T-shirt and bikini-style black underpants. It seemed like a strange wardrobe choice for a near-stranger's house, but that was the least of my concerns.

I wanted to let her keep sleeping—hell, I wanted to crawl into my *own* bed—but I had already put off breaking the news for way too long.

She didn't stir as I came into the living room and sat down on the coffee table in front of her. Dopey lifted her head to look at me, yawned, and settled back onto her front paws, the tip of her pink tongue sticking out from between her teeth. She gazed at me with perfect contentment from on top of the werewolf, and I wondered for the millionth time how the little dog had gone this long without being picked off by natural selection.

"Mary," I said softly. Neither of them moved.

I tried sitting on the empty corner of the couch next to Mary's head, resting a hand lightly on her shoulder. "Mary," I said again, and this time her eyes opened.

She craned her head back to look at me and said bleakly, "He's dead, isn't he?"

I didn't ask how she had known. It was probably all over my body language or my scent or something. "Yes. I'm so sorry."

Mary curled her legs in and sat up, displacing an unoffended Dopey, who hopped down to the floor and trotted off to sniff the bookshelf with great interest. "How?" Mary asked.

I told her about the bridge, and the damage to the Forester's locking mechanisms. Although I didn't say the words *he was murdered*, I could see the understanding break across her face. It was painful to watch.

Given what Maven had told us about werewolves, I sort of expected her to lash out physically, and I tensed my body, ready to spring away. To my utter astonishment, though, Mary collapsed across my lap, curled into herself even tighter, and began to cry.

I patted her shoulder awkwardly, feeling a little ashamed of myself. There was also a part of my brain that thought, *Huh*. Dogs huddled for comfort, and sought touch as a way of communicating. This was probably a werewolf thing. God, there was still so much I didn't know about them.

I had no idea what I could say that might help, so I just let her cry for a long time. Eventually, she seemed to be winding down, and I said—partly to break her out of it, and partly because . . . well, I really wanted to know—"Hey, Mary? Why aren't you wearing pants?"

She sniffed and sat up, pulling up the neck of her T-shirt to wipe her face, exposing a flat, muscled stomach. "I don't like having anything on my legs if I can help it. It feels too restrictive." She said it with the practiced tone of someone who's had to repeat an explanation many times.

"Oh." When I thought about it, I realized that I'd *never* seen her wear pants. "Uh, okay."

"What's going to happen now?" she asked me.

I didn't know if she meant with the werewolf pack, or with the overall situation in the Old World, but the answer was the same either way. "I don't really know," I admitted. "Can you think of anyone who would want Dunn dead?"

She arched a single eyebrow, as though I was being annoyingly coy. "The witches, of course. They're still pissed about Trask."

I blinked. I hadn't actually gotten that far in my own reasoning. "Was Dunn on Trask's side during the war?" As far as I knew, Maven had killed Trask and all his lieutenants, but his pack had been enormous. She probably wouldn't have been able to dispatch every single one of them.

Mary shook her head. "Dunn lived in Oregon until . . . six or eight years ago? Most of the Cheyenne pack is new."

Which was probably why Maven had wanted to work with them. "What about the Ventimiglias?"

"They moved to Cheyenne after Dunn did."

Well, there went the witch theory. "I can't see the Colorado witches coming up with this elaborate murder plot just to get revenge on a werewolf who wasn't even involved in the previous war," I pointed out.

Mary scowled at me. "Who else could it be?" she snapped.

Without waiting for an answer, she jumped off the couch, impossibly fluid and graceful, and began pacing back and forth in front of me.

It wasn't like a human pacing. Earlier, when I'd practically walked a hole in the floor at the coffee shop, I had been moving to get rid of angry energy. Mary's pacing, on the other hand, was a controlled, anticipatory lope, like a caged predator eager to get out and tear into something. "I thought it might have been Maven," she said, "but if anything, this makes her look bad, like she's either incompetent or intentionally deceiving the witches. It could be someone *wanting* to make Maven look bad, but that leads me back to the witches too." She stopped and turned to face me, jabbing a finger. "It *has* to be one of the clans."

Her reasoning made sense . . . but she was leaving out an entire species of suspects. Very carefully, I said, "I'd be curious to see which of your pack members becomes alpha now."

Mary actually bared her teeth, and to my surprise, Dopey let out a whimper and scuttled out of the room. Apparently even she had *some* survival instinct. "Don't even think about it," Mary snarled. "A werewolf would never do this."

"Why not?" I argued. "Someone wanting to be alpha, wanting control of the pack—"

"Would either challenge Dunn or leave the area to start their own pack," she snapped. Her feet were planted, her hands balled into fists. "Despite what you might think, we're not savages. There *are* peaceful ways of gaining power."

That hadn't really been my experience, but there was no need to get into that. Before I could answer, I felt my cell phone vibrating in my pocket. I pulled it out, glanced at the screen. Quinn.

When I looked up at Mary, she had crossed her arms over her chest, obviously not going anywhere. And, of course, she had super werewolf hearing. I sighed and answered the phone. "Hi, Quinn. I'm here with Mary."

A two-second pause, then he said, "Okay. I'm in Cheyenne, and the werewolves are gone."

Chapter 12

Mary's eyes widened. "Gone?" I said, confused. "You mean they're missing?"

"Not exactly. I took a quick look at a couple of their places, and their toiletries are missing, drawers left open. They must have seen the news and decided to make themselves scarce."

I was watching Mary as Quinn spoke, and I saw a slight relaxing of her shoulders when he mentioned the missing items, like now everything made sense to her. "Let me call you back," I said to Quinn.

When I put the phone back in my pocket, Mary's expression was defiant. "Where did they go?" I demanded.

She shrugged. "I honestly don't know. That's the whole point."

"The whole point of what?"

"The . . . oh, what's the word?" She stared at the ceiling for a moment, then snapped her fingers. "Protocol. Dunn set up a protocol years ago, when he first became alpha. If the pack as a whole is threatened by an enemy we can't see or overpower, we're supposed to disappear for a few days to give him a chance to either work it out or find us a new territory. It's like a, what do you call it, a doomsday protocol. One of the other pack members must have activated it."

"Was it you?"

She shook her head. "I checked in briefly on the phone on the drive back, but only to warn them that Dunn was missing. Someone else must have decided the protocol was necessary."

"Who?" I asked. "Which pack member has the power to make that call?"

She shrugged. "If you asked me yesterday, I would have said only Ryan or Matt. But now they're dead, and someone decided that was enough of a threat to warrant the quick disappearance."

She might have been lying to protect the other werewolves, but I couldn't tell. And either way, this was getting us nowhere.

I flopped back down onto the couch, and Mary perched on the edge of the chair. We sat there regarding each other for a long moment, until finally I scrubbed my face with my hands and said, "Okay, look. Someone found out about Matt and Cammie's trip to the Dunes. They used that knowledge to set up a way to kill Ryan Dunn in Maven's territory. We need to know *exactly* who knew about the trip."

"Which of the witches, you mean," she retorted.

I threw up my hands. "Goddammit, Mary, I'm trying to help you here!"

"Really?" she said sarcastically. "Because you care so much about me and the other werewolves?" She tapped her nose. "I can smell the silver in that gun, you know. I'm not a fucking idiot."

Crap. The revolver was in a pancake holster at the small of my back. I was so used to having a weapon that I had genuinely forgotten about it, but Mary probably wouldn't believe that. I sure wouldn't if I were her.

I made myself pause for a slow, deep breath. When I was ready, I said in a quiet voice, "Look, Mary. Dunn was your alpha, and he was in Colorado under my protection." It hurt to say it out loud again, but I made myself do it. "He got killed on my watch. We both want to find out who killed him, and we both agree it wasn't my boss. Right?"

She gave me a tight nod, then added, "But you have loyalties to the witch clan, too."

Was *that* what this was about? "No," I said slowly, "I have loyalties to Simon and Lily Pellar. *They* are my friends. The rest of Clan Pellar hates and fears me." Vampires knew if someone was telling the truth by how their scent and pulse changed; now I hoped werewolves had similar abilities. "I know you haven't spent much time with them, but in your gut, do you think Simon or Lily was responsible for this?"

Mary hesitated, but she had to concede. "No."

"Then, like I said, we want the same thing. But I need to know who in your pack knew about Matt and Cammie's trip."

Mary chewed on her lower lip for a long moment, looking at me. "We all did," she admitted finally, leaning forward and resting her elbows on her knees. "The pack voted on where we wanted to go with the next weekend pass, and we all knew Matt and Cammie would be the scout team." She shrugged. "The exact date and time wasn't common knowledge, but anyone could have just asked Cammie and she probably would have told them." Her face softened. "Cammie wasn't a suspicious person."

I nodded. It was my turn to share information. "Quinn and Maven were the only vampires who knew, and neither of them told anyone," I told her. "Not even me. The witches didn't know."

"You *think* they didn't, but they could have found out without being told," she argued. "Someone in a witch clan might have seen the Ventimiglias at a gas station or rest stop. If someone's been keeping tabs on us, they could have been spotted."

I sighed. "I suppose you're right. But that leaves us pretty much where we started." I needed another way to come at this problem, but aside from figuring out who'd known about the trip and who might have held a grudge against Dunn, I had no idea where to start. Quinn was the former detective. I was just hired muscle who could talk to ghosts.

At that moment, I heard Mary's stomach growl audibly. She glanced down at herself with a look of exasperation. "We need to eat a lot," she told me, rolling her eyes. "Can we order a pizza or something?"

I was just kind of spinning my wheels, and it would be more than an hour before Quinn got back and we could talk through the turn of events. "Sure."

I used my phone to order online—wisely getting an entire meat lover's just for Mary and a small cheese pizza for myself. While we waited for the food, Mary took a shower, and I went and took care of the herd, making sure the dogs got to go outside and everyone had food and water. The big dogs—my lab mixes, Chip and Cody, and Stitch, the new foster—didn't seem as manic as I had feared, and I guessed that Jake had taken them for a hike. I sent him a text to say thank you and let him know I was home.

Inside, I set out paper plates and napkins, my thoughts on the werewolf pack. Despite what Mary had said, I was itching to go through the files Maven had given me, to see if anything about the remaining pack members stood out as suspicious. I couldn't do it in front of Mary, but I couldn't exactly send her away either, not when Maven had told us to keep her safe.

The shower was still running, so I went out to the car and retrieved the files, spreading the stack on the kitchen table. There were ten folders, but I left Ryan's, Matt's, and Cammie's files alone for the moment, focusing on the seven surviving werewolves. I smiled when I saw one of the names: Tobias Leine. I'd met Tobias years ago, back when he was voluntarily living as a wolf at a preserve in Wyoming. Trask had tortured him psychologically for years, and when I'd forced Tobias to become human and talk to me, he was barely coherent.

There shouldn't have been much anyone could do for Tobias, but because the ley lines near Boulder had experienced a brief surge in power, my friend Sashi had been able to heal some of his psychological damage. I took a quick glance at the file and saw he was now a regular, healthy member of the wolf pack. So at least one good thing had come out of that disaster.

The doorbell rang, so I stacked the files and shoved them into a kitchen drawer. I pulled some cash out of my wallet and trudged toward the front door. Damn, my body was tired. From the back hallway I could hear the guest shower turn off. A few seconds later, the hair dryer started. I wondered if Mary would bother putting on a shirt before she came out.

I was absently considering tactful ways to ask someone to put on clothes as I swung open the front door—and an angry blur tackled me to the floor.

Chapter 13

He wasn't big, but he was bigger than me, with onion breath and a snarl on his ruddy face. And he was *heavy*—not fat, but the kind of beefy Midwestern muscle that somehow seems denser than it should. His momentum drove me backward so fast I landed flat on my back. The force of the attack—especially from a standing position—was breathtaking. I'd encountered this kind of strength in only two kinds of people, and I would have known if he were a vampire. I would have been able to press him.

Werewolf.

At least this time I didn't get the wind knocked out of me. Instead, my spine pressed painfully against the revolver in the small of my back.

"Who the hell—" I gasped, struggling to sit up. He got a palm on each of my shoulders and pushed down hard enough to make me clunk my head on the floor. He straddled my chest and kept the pressure on my shoulders, pinning me down.

"Where is she?" he hissed, his face two inches from my own.

I fought to roll sideways, just enough to get my hand to the gun, but he had moved his weight to the sides of my body, pinning me easily to the floor. Using all my strength, I barely even rocked him. "Where?" he demanded.

"Where is who?"

His lips twisted with renewed anger. Whoops. Wrong question. "Where is Mary Hollis?" He shouted it in my face this time, his hot breath stinking of burgers, onions, and rot. This was not a flosser.

Fear bubbled up inside me. I couldn't beat a werewolf, not with physical strength, and I couldn't press him. This must be the killer, and now he was here for the person I was trying to protect.

I needed to buy time, and to get him off me so I could get to the revolver still digging into my back.

Shit. This was going to hurt.

I fluttered my eyelids a little, like I was on the verge of passing out. "She . . ." I whispered something unintelligible.

"What?" Without thinking, the werewolf leaned closer to my face to hear better.

With as much speed and strength as I could possibly muster, I drove my forehead into his nose.

Head-butts might be popular in movies, but in real life, they're a last resort. Even under the best possible circumstances, they hurt like hell, and if you don't do it just right, you can cause yourself as much pain as the person you're hitting.

I did it just right, but my forehead still felt like I'd been clobbered with a Louisville Slugger. The floor seemed to tilt for a moment and my vision blurred—but at least I was ready for it. The werewolf, on the other hand, immediately leaped backward, his hands cupped to his broken nose, and began to wail with pain.

Ignoring the intense ache in my forehead, I rolled sideways and got my revolver. By the time my attacker lowered his bloody hands enough to look at me, I was sitting up and had the barrel pointed right at his chest, safety off.

"What the fuck is going on out here?" Mary's irritated voice came from the doorway to the living room. I didn't want to take my eyes off my assailant, but I risked a quick glance. She was standing there with her hands on her hips, wearing my favorite green T-shirt and a pair of

Quinn's boxer shorts, rolled at the waist. She didn't look the least bit afraid. "Keith! What are you doing?"

"Mary!" The other werewolf began to run toward her.

"Don't!" I ordered, sliding my finger over the trigger.

He stopped, but didn't take his eyes off Mary. "I thought she was holding you against your will!"

My forehead throbbed. I wanted to rub it, but I wasn't ready to put my gun away yet. "Why would I do that?"

"Why do you have silver bullets?" he countered, finally looking over to glare at me.

That argument wasn't going to go anywhere, so I spoke to Mary. "I take it you know this guy? And does *every* werewolf in the country know where I live?"

"He's in my pack. His name is Keith Zimmerman," Mary said, sounding tired. I noticed she didn't address my second question. "You don't need the gun. Keith is harmless. You've met him before."

He hadn't seemed very harmless to me—or to my throbbing forehead—but now that I could look without fearing for my life, I realized I *had* seen him before. Keith was one of the werewolves Dunn had brought to help hunt the sandworm three years earlier. We'd split up into teams, and Keith had gone with Quinn, while I had gone to the hot springs with Dunn, Mary, and Jamie. I'd never actually gotten his name.

Warily, I stood up, put the safety on the revolver, and went to the freezer, pulling out a massive, high-quality ice pack. I don't spend much money on clothes or shoes, but my ice packs are top-of-the-line.

After a moment's hesitation, I offered one to Keith, who had walked over to Mary.

"No thanks," he said distractedly. "It's almost healed."

I could feel the goose egg forming on my forehead and had to swallow my resentment. I leaned against the counter with the cold pack pressed to my head and watched Keith look over Mary like a mother examining her child's muddy clothes.

"You're really okay? We all saw the news. I thought you'd call."

Mary tilted her head at me. "Her idea. She was afraid someone going after werewolves would come after me, too."

I expected Keith to object to that, but he just nodded, helping himself to a seat at my counter. Mary sat down too, but left an empty seat between the two of them.

"That's exactly why we decided to disappear," he told her. "So they couldn't come after us."

"Or so the werewolf responsible for the murders wouldn't have to face Maven," I interrupted.

Both of them looked at me with shock. Keith's expression quickly morphed into hurt, while Mary's turned to anger.

"We've been through all that," she snapped.

I sighed. We hadn't actually settled anything, but going around in the same circles wasn't going to get us anywhere. "Never mind," I mumbled, checking my watch. Quinn should be getting back soon. I hoped he had some ideas, because I was at an impasse. "It's almost one o'clock," I said to the werewolves. "You guys should stick around for tonight. We can make a plan in the morning." After I'd had a chance to talk through this with Quinn.

Mary chewed on her lower lip for a moment, then said, "If we stay here, your dogs are going to lose their minds. It's not fair to them."

That surprised me, but she wasn't wrong. "Let me call Simon," I told her. She seemed to at least sort of trust him. "His apartment has an extra bedroom. We've used it as a safe house before."

The two werewolves exchanged a glance that I couldn't interpret, and then Mary nodded. "Call him."

I picked up my phone and started for the hallway to my bedroom. "You guys can watch TV or something," I offered. "Pizza's on its way, and you can eat whatever's in the fridge."

Keith reached for the remote control.

I closed my bedroom door behind me, not wanting to be overheard. Simon's phone rang and rang, which surprised me. I'd seen him only an hour or two earlier, and he'd obviously been on his way to his mom's place. Maybe he'd decided to go home and go to bed instead.

Down the hall, the werewolves had turned the television up loud, though I didn't know if they were giving me privacy or trying to cover their own conversation. I hated to wake Simon, but I dialed the phone again anyway, and this time he answered after four rings.

As soon as the connection opened up, I heard a multitude of arguing voices, then Simon's raised voice came through above the others. "This is my teaching assistant Emily; I have to give her instructions." I could hear the tension in his voice, like he was right on the edge of losing his temper. Had I ever even seen Simon lose his temper?

Into the phone, he said, "Hang on a second, Emily, let me get somewhere quiet."

I didn't speak, not wanting to give anything away. The quality of the background noise became muted, as though he'd put his thumb over the microphone, but I could still make out the sound of a door closing firmly, and the noise finally cut off. In a low voice, Simon said, "I can't talk, Lex, unless this is life or death."

I instinctively paused, waiting for him to make a joke about death and the boundary witch. It didn't come. "What's going on, Simon?"

"I can't talk—"

"If you don't tell me, I'm coming over there right fucking now," I broke in. I'd had a long day.

Deep sigh. "Look . . . a bunch of the other clan leaders are here. And they're pissed."

"Because of the weekend passes?"

"Among other things." A loud banging began in the background and Simon yelled, "One minute!" To me, he added, "I need to go. They're going to take my phone away until we figure this out."

Take his phone away? It should have sounded a little funny, like someone was threatening to ground him, but Simon's voice was so grave it chilled me. "Are you guys in danger?"

He let out a choked laugh. "Not physically, no."

"What's going to happen when one of them looks at your phone and it says 'Lex'?"

"You've been listed as 'Emily-TA' in my phone for the last six months."

God, he was smart. "Then why do you sound scared?"

A beat, then Simon admitted, "One of the other clan leaders got in Lily's face. She . . . reacted badly."

"Reacted how?"

"She zapped the woman."

"*Shit.*" As part of her original deal with the witches, Maven had cut off the Colorado clans' access to the most powerful level of witchcraft—apex magic, which included Lily's favorite trick of turning into a human Taser. Maven had restored Clan Pellar's magic so Simon and Lily could help me stop the sandworm. We'd all kind of hoped no one would notice.

"We knew this could get out, though, right?" I said, hoping they'd had a contingency plan. "If you just explain about the sandworm—"

"Oh, we're way past that." Simon sounded weary. "It's the timing, Lex."

"What does that mean?"

He started to answer, but I heard another knock on his end, then Simon's voice explaining very calmly that he had to tell Emily how to proctor the exam and he'd be done in a minute.

While he was speaking, I jerked a hand frantically through my hair, yanking at the tangles. This was getting worse and worse. When Simon finally came back on the line, I blurted, "Maybe if I come over and tell them about the sandworm—"

The same choked laugh, this time with an edge of desperation. "*Don't.* Your name has already come up, and not in a good way.

Somehow the other clans found out that we've been helping you with your side project, and . . . you know."

My heart sank. Most of the witches I'd met considered boundary witches the next best thing to the Antichrist. No wonder they didn't want him calling me. I might use my evil powers to corrupt him further.

I knew I should apologize for making a bad situation worse, but instead my mouth decided to double down. "What's so wrong with helping me lay ghosts?" I asked defensively. "It's not like you and Lily are sacrificing goats and worshiping the angel of death."

Heavy sigh. "Lex—"

I kicked at my bedsprings, hating myself. "I know. I'm sorry, Si." My voice came out thicker than I'd expected. "Before you go, please just tell me. How worried do I need to be? What's the worst-case scenario, here?"

There was another pause, and I could practically feel him trying to decide how to downplay the situation. "Don't you *dare* lie to me, Simon Pellar," I snapped.

More silence. Then, finally: "Fine. Worst-case scenario? The other clan leaders bring in help from outside the state, and they'll . . ." His voice broke for a moment. "They'll take away our access to magic."

"What? They can't do that! It's in your blood." You couldn't take magic out of someone's *blood* . . . right?

"Oh, it would still be there, but if the other witches decide that Clan Pellar has turned against witches, they can bind our access to all magic, the same way Maven already bound part of it." His voice was raw with pain. "No more spells, no more connection to Wicca or the earth or our religion. They can wipe away our whole way of life. It's the worst thing you can do to a witch, short of death."

"Oh, Simon . . ." I couldn't think of a single thing to say, other than, "I'm not going to let that happen."

There was another loud bang in the background, like a door slamming, and Simon cursed. There was a muffled sound and Hazel Pellar's annoyed voice came on the line. "Who is this?"

Crap. "It's me. Lex."

Simon was talking to her in the background, but Hazel ignored him, snapping, "Do you have any idea the danger you're bringing to my children by calling here? Or the danger you've already brought them by dragging them into your messes?"

I swallowed hard. Hazel and I were never going to exchange Christmas cards, but I respected her, and I knew that, with me, she at least *tried* to overcome her lifelong conditioning against boundary magic. It was more than I could say for most of the witches in Colorado. "I'm starting to see that, yes," I said in a small voice. "What can I do to help?"

Hazel sighed. "Maybe the hardest thing there is," she said, sounding suddenly exhausted. "Nothing. You have to stay away from this whole thing. You'll only make it worse."

"I'm sorry—" I began, but I realized she had already hung up.

I stood there for a long moment, staring at my phone in disbelief.

Intellectually, I had always known that Simon and Lily might get in trouble for helping me, or even just for being my friends. But we'd been getting away with it for so long now that I'd taken our security for granted.

There had to be something I could do, but if I had to stay away from the Pellars, what did that leave? Even if Quinn and I found the person who'd killed the werewolves, it wouldn't undo any of the problems I'd created for Simon and Lily.

Feeling shitty, I stuffed the phone in my pocket and opened the bedroom door, relieved to see that Mary and Keith weren't eavesdropping right on the other side.

"Hello?" I called, heading down the hallway. "Mary? Is the pizza here?"

I turned into the living room, where a sitcom rerun was playing loudly on the television—to an empty room. "Oh no."

I ran through the kitchen to the door that led to the garage, flinging it open. The Ventimiglias' truck was there, right where Mary had left it.

I felt an instant of relief; then I hit the button to raise the garage door. It opened slowly, revealing a dark night with a drift of snowflakes beginning to settle on the empty driveway.

They had stolen my fucking car.

Chapter 14

"What do you mean, Mary's *gone?*"

Quinn didn't look angry so much as confused. The poor guy had returned from a fruitless trip to Wyoming to find his girlfriend wild-eyed with anger and worry—and sporting a goose egg in the middle of her forehead. I'd pretty much met him at the door with invisible steam coming out of my ears.

His nostrils flared briefly, and he pulled down the collar of the clean T-shirt I had put on, exposing a few drops of dried blood I'd somehow missed. "That isn't yours," he said. He was trying to sound calm, but having to work at it. "You head-butted Mary? Is that why she left?"

"No," I said, touching the lump on my head. The ice pack had helped the swelling a little, but it had already started turning bright purple and blue. "This wasn't her. Come in, let me tell you the whole thing." I went over to the sofa and sat down stiffly, one of my knees jiggling wildly. I was still angry about Quinn keeping shit from me, but this was business and he needed to know.

No dummy, Quinn perched cautiously on the ottoman instead of joining me the couch. I told him about Keith arriving, and the misunderstanding where both of us thought the other was there to hurt Mary. "Then I needed to call Simon to ask if the werewolves could hide out in the lab, and I didn't want them to overhear the call. In case . . . you know."

Quinn nodded, understanding. In case Simon was worried about sleeping down the hall from a strange werewolf. I thought he kind of trusted Mary, but I couldn't vouch for Keith.

"But why would they take your car?" Quinn asked, practically. "They must know you could report it stolen."

I sighed. "Yeah, but Mary probably figured it was better to steal mine than get caught driving a vehicle belonging to a murdered couple who are all over the news." And she was betting that I wouldn't bring the police into Old World business. She was right.

"True." Quinn wasn't a pacer—vampires didn't feel the impulse to walk away nervous energy—but he had the same distant look in his eyes that Maven got when she was thinking. "You could call Elise, see if she can find it quietly," he suggested.

I shook my head. "You know she'll ask a hundred follow-up questions." My cousin Elise was a cop, but she was also human. I couldn't exactly call her and say that I had lost my car to werewolf frenemies and could she please hunt it down without telling anyone or speaking to the thieves? It was already hard enough to keep the Old World hidden from her. I slumped back into the couch cushions, feeling exhausted.

Quinn crossed the space between us and sat down next to me, lifting my legs and pulling them into his lap so I was facing sideways. He did it gently, slowly, so that I could easily pull away at any time. What can I say? The man got me.

"Would it make you feel better," he said quietly, "if you yelled at me some more?"

I considered this for a minute. "It might," I said, "if I really understood what I'm upset about. I'm still . . . sorting through it."

He nodded.

"How about we turn our full attention to this werewolf thing, but I reserve the right to reopen this fight at a later date, when I know exactly what horrible thing you've done to piss me off?"

Quinn smiled, as I'd hoped. "Sounds fair."

It really wasn't, but we did need to move on. "There's more," I said. I told him about Simon and the witches and the very real threat of having their connection to magic stripped away. Quinn's eyes widened with worry, which for him was the equivalent of screaming "holy shit!"

"Jesus," he breathed. "Losing magic would *kill* Lily. Simon might get over it eventually, with his work, but Lily . . ."

I shook my head. "Simon has spent his entire life examining connections between science and magic. If he lost half of that, it'd be like losing half of himself. I practically heard it in his voice."

"But they don't want you to get involved." This was a statement, but there was also a hint of a question in his tone, like he was worried I wasn't going to listen.

"Technically," I said, "they just told me to stay *away* from the problem. One could interpret that geographically."

Quinn started to protest, and I held up a hand. "Don't worry. Right now, the witches are just talking. From what I understand, binding another witch's magic would require help from out of state, and that takes time. I'm not going to do anything crazy tonight."

He relaxed a little, but said, "You know we have to go fill Maven in on all of this, right?"

"Yeah." I checked my watch: one thirty in the morning. Driving *back* into Boulder wasn't exactly appealing after so many hours in the car, but Maven had a thing about discussing sensitive stuff on the phone. I thought she was a little paranoid, but Quinn had once pointed out that she'd been around when telephones were first invented—and when the only way to talk was on a party line.

I looked down at myself and wrinkled my nose. "I'd like to clean up first, though, so I don't stink of werewolf blood."

"Good idea." His voice was carefully mild, but he was obviously relieved I'd suggested it first. Men.

"I also haven't had a chance to look at those files Maven sent."

He nodded. "Why don't I go talk to Maven, and you stay and look at the files? If she needs time to think, I'll just come back here. If she has something else for us tonight, you can meet me in town."

"We only have one car here." He'd driven Maven's Jeep. Since I wasn't about to drive the dead couple's vehicle either, it was the only vehicle I could use.

He grinned. "I'll take the bike."

Quinn had spent most of his spare time over the summer restoring an old BMW motorcycle—there were advantages to months with no Old World violence—which now resided in my garage. We'd gone for a few leisurely rides during the warmer months, but it was way too cold for me to take it anywhere now.

Vampires weren't bothered by low temperatures, though, and the idea clearly appealed to him. "Wear gloves," I warned him. "And your helmet."

Quinn wrinkled his nose. "I know," I said before he could argue, "you can survive a crash. But riding bareheaded on a motorcycle when it's twenty degrees outside does not scream 'I'm passing as a normal human.'"

He smiled. "You're not wrong."

After Quinn left for the coffee shop, I went back into the bathroom, took off my shirt and sports bra, and scrubbed off every speck of red I could find with a washcloth. I didn't find any blood on my jeans, but I changed into a new pair just in case, taking care to replace the holster at the small of my back and secure the revolver. I wasn't going anywhere without silver bullets until we figured out who had killed Dunn and the others.

Back in the kitchen, I held a fresh ice pack to my forehead as I pulled the files out of the drawer. I spread them over the table, choosing

Keith Zimmerman's folder first. There was a photo of him attached to the inside of the cover, and it looked like an employee ID photo: Keith smiling a little awkwardly, wearing a red polo shirt embroidered with the logo of a shipping company. Keith, I read, was currently middle management at Sierra Trading Post, a Cheyenne-based retailer for outdoor gear and exercise equipment. Before that, he'd been an engineer with the Wyoming Department of Transportation. It seemed like an odd career change, but as I understood it, a lot of werewolves had to switch jobs after being turned. Something to do with the change in their temperament.

Scanning the file, I found several typed pages of biography, a few more photos, and a newspaper article about an attack on a campsite near Yellowstone—probably how he had been turned into a werewolf. I had once asked Maven how Trask had built up his pack so quickly, and she'd said soberly that in addition to absorbing existing packs, he and his people "recruited" at popular public campgrounds. Becoming a werewolf was an excruciating, life-altering event that left you reliant on the pack for physical, emotional, and often financial support. An unscrupulous alpha could target anyone he wanted and they would be entirely dependent on him.

According to the article, Keith had been turned only five years earlier, so he would never have met Trask. It wouldn't surprise me if some of Trask's people were still engaging in his "recruitment" methods in Wyoming. There just wasn't much I could do about it.

Other than that, there wasn't a lot to the file, and I found myself setting it aside. Keith had no history of violence or conflict within the pack. In the file—and when I'd met him—he came off as a boring middle manager who'd adopted the same position in the pack as he filled in life. It made sense that he'd come looking for Mary, a more dominant wolf, after she'd slipped off the radar. I was still pissed about him attacking me in my home, but it was probably the bravest thing he'd ever done.

It didn't take long to skim through the rest of the files. Finn Barlow was the newest pack member, a huge, muscular man who looked like he'd been rejected from the WWE for scaring the other wrestlers. When I read through the bio, though, I saw that he was also an ex-marine, a friend of Dunn's from Minnesota. Barlow had been diagnosed with fast-progressing ALS before he was forty. There was a Minneapolis police report of a suicide attempt; then he'd seemingly left his home state, turning up in Cheyenne a few months later as a healthy man who'd received a false diagnosis.

It was so easy to read between the lines that Maven's investigator hadn't bothered to spell it out: Dunn had changed Barlow to save his life. I frowned. That didn't mesh well with the theory that he'd murdered the alpha . . . unless maybe the werewolf magic had driven him insane? He was big enough to take out the Ventimiglias, and trained in combat, vehicle mechanics, and weapons. Was it possible he'd arranged things this way so the rest of the pack wouldn't know he had betrayed the alpha?

I set that folder to one side to show Quinn and flipped through the rest. None of the other pack members seemed to scream "murder suspect." Alex Elliott was the other person I had seen, but not officially met, during the sandworm incident. Alex was nonbinary, an accountant for Dunn's construction company. The included photo showed a cool, assessing gaze, and once again, their bio spoke of infinite loyalty to Ryan Dunn. Alex was not a great candidate either.

The last two pack members, Nicolette Wan and Lindsay Magner, had been brand-new werewolves at the time of the sandworm attack, so they hadn't accompanied the others to Boulder. They were both twenty-year-old college students at the University of Wyoming who'd been turned while on a mission trip to Costa Rica. After taking two years off to adjust, both women were now trying to finish their degrees, although Lindsay had switched from animal studies to ecosystem science, probably because most animals would be terrified of her. Nicolette and Lindsay were sharing an apartment in Cheyenne, commuting to classes in Laramie. If either of them had killed Dunn, I would eat the stack of files.

Which left Mary. I still didn't think she could have anything to do with the murders, but I took a look at her file anyway, out of simple curiosity. Mary had moved to Wyoming from Houston, where she'd spent her early twenties partying and experimenting with drugs. As a human, she had a few arrests for possession, and there were photos of her copied from another arrest record—the werewolf boyfriend who'd regularly beaten the shit out of her.

Mary's story just got worse from there, and even under current circumstances I felt guilty about reading her file. On the other hand, I thought I might now understand why Mary had taken a liking to Simon, enough to save him from the sandworm. He was the spitting image of her brother, who'd died trying to save her from her abuser.

There was nothing in the file to make me think Mary had the slightest interest in hurting Dunn, though.

I picked up my cell to call Quinn, but before I could even unlock the phone, the dogs abruptly went nuts—barking furiously and swarming the front door. I stood up and started toward them, in no particular hurry—they freaked out several times a day over squirrels, and vampires or werewolves were capable of sneaking up on them. "Guys, come on—" I began, but then I saw a folded piece of neon-green paper slide under the door.

Chapter 15

Without looking at the note, I waded through the dogs, flipped on the exterior light, and flung the door open. Big wet snowflakes were still falling, so all I could really see was a dark outline moving quickly away from the house. "Stop!" I yelled, pushing open the exterior door so I could follow. I made a belated effort to block the dogs, but four of them nearly trampled each other to race outside after the intruder. I cursed and sprinted after them, my bare feet instantly freezing on the fresh snow. I was fast, but the dogs were faster, and in seconds I heard a girlish scream as they overtook the trespasser.

"*No!*" The figure stopped and held up their hands like this was a gunfight on television. The gesture only excited the dogs, who thought they were being offered a treat. Tails wagging frantically, they began to jump up on the newcomer, trying to reach the raised hands. The revolver was in my hand, but I kept it pointed at the ground, my finger out of the trigger guard. The dogs would have reacted very differently if the intruder were a werewolf.

"*Please,*" a woman's voice begged. "Call them off. I give up!"

She sounded so terrified that I actually felt sorry for her—and I wanted to get the hell back inside the house and get some shoes. "Chip, Cody!" I shouted, skidding to a halt twenty feet away. "Come here!" The two lab mixes were the ringleaders when it came to security.

A little begrudgingly, the two big dogs turned and trotted back toward me. Pongo, my black-and-white mutt, gave the woman's legs one last sniff and followed the others back toward me. "Now turn around," I yelled, trying to look dignified while hopping from one foot to the other. Holy *crap*, my feet were cold.

She pivoted slowly, but I still couldn't make out her features. Her head was tilted toward the ground, where Stitch, the enormous new foster, remained at her side, gazing up at her with his tail wagging happily.

"Is it going to bite me?" she asked fearfully.

"Of course not," I said, a little exasperated. "Put your hands down; he thinks you've got a treat." I didn't actually say *you idiot*, but it was kind of implied.

"Oh." Sheepishly, she crossed her arms protectively over her chest. Without being told, she began trudging back toward me. Stitch danced at her side, his tongue lolling out one side of his mouth.

The voice hadn't been familiar, but when she reached the glow of the front security light, I could see that she was petite and Chinese-American, dressed in an expensive knee-length quilted coat. Her glossy black hair flowed out from under a snow-dotted ski cap that perfectly complemented the coat.

And I knew her.

"*Tracy?*" I asked, genuinely shocked. The young witch was a member of Clan Pellar—and Simon's ex-girlfriend. In the years since I'd learned about the Old World, we'd probably exchanged twenty words, all of them variations on "hello." I'd gotten the impression that she was frightened of me. Now she was on my doorstep in a burgundy winter parka, looking like she was about to cry. "It's two thirty in the morning. What are you doing here?" I asked, holstering the revolver. This woman was not going to hurt me.

"I was just trying to stay out of it," she told me, her voice trembling. Stitch began enthusiastically licking the hem of her coat.

I sighed. "You better come inside."

I led Tracy through the entrance and into the living room, the dogs clustered around our legs like a vanguard. They tracked fresh snow into the house and shook even more of it off their backs, but I was too relieved to be back inside to care. I rubbed my own wet, frozen feet on the carpet, trying to warm them up.

Tracy followed me with wide eyes, looking around as though she'd entered the lair of a boogeyman and couldn't believe he had comfy furniture.

"Sit down," I said, more sternly than I'd meant to, and Tracy dropped onto the sofa without unzipping her coat. The dogs crowded around her again, and she pulled her arms around her body. I considered shutting them in the back bedroom again, but when it became obvious that Tracy wasn't going to pet anyone, they all got bored and wandered away—except for Stitch, who dropped his butt down on Tracy's feet and panted at me happily. He probably looked like he was preventing her escape, but his expression said *what a fun adventure we're having*.

I had snagged the neon paper on the way back into the house and now I unfolded it. It was a sort of fancy flyer, the letters all in calligraphy, advertising a town hall meeting Friday night to discuss new leadership for the witch clans.

"What is this?" I asked, looking up at Tracy. She seemed to be trying to figure out a way to get Stitch off her feet without actually touching him or moving in any way.

Her eyes lifted to me. "You heard about what happened at the Pellars' tonight?"

"A little," I said cautiously. The last thing I wanted to do was get Simon in more trouble for talking to me. "I heard that some other witches showed up to talk to Hazel."

Tracy snorted, showing a little defiance for the first time. "That's one way to put it. It was more like an impromptu trial." She looked down again, playing with the pull tie on her zipper. "People are saying she let werewolves back into the state in exchange for access to apex magic."

"Oh *shit*," I blurted. That's what Simon had meant about the timing. All these things happening at once had to look terrible. Not for me—I was a boundary witch, and therefore everyone expected me to do evil shit. But I'd dragged the Pellar family name through the mud. "But that's not what happened," I said. "Come on, Tracy. You *know* Hazel isn't for sale."

Tracy shook her head. "I thought I did, but . . . I don't know. I don't know anything anymore."

Her voice and body language were despondent, and Stitch turned around to lick her hand. Belatedly, I remembered Lily telling me that Simon's ex worshipped Hazel, wanted to be just like her. Crap. No wonder she was so shaken.

I felt a rush of sympathy. I understood the idea of disillusionment with an authority you believed in, though I knew Hazel hadn't been bought, at least not for power or money. She'd bartered for the safety of her daughter. It was probably the most selfish thing she'd ever done, and it was for her kid.

I would do a hell of a lot worse for Charlie. If I hadn't already.

"Tracy," I said more gently, "what happened tonight? What was decided?"

A small shrug. "Nothing was decided. Yet. Hazel called a witch congress."

Her voice was reverent, but I didn't get it. "What's that?"

She blinked at me, a look I'd seen many times from Simon and Lily. The *how do you not know our customs?* face. "A meeting of all the clan leaders in the state. They haven't done that since Trask started killing people."

A meeting? "That . . . actually doesn't sound too bad," I said, relieved. "When is it?"

"Saturday morning. To give the clan leaders a chance to get to Boulder."

And, probably, to give everyone a little time to cool down. It was, impossibly, only Thursday night now, so that would give everyone more than a day. "The other witches agreed to that?"

Tracy's expression soured. "Yes, but only if the Pellars stay put at the farm until then."

"They're under *house arrest*?"

"More or less, yes. Hazel, Simon, Lily, and Sybil, anyway. The rest of the clan got to go home for tonight." She pointed at the paper in my hand. "But then this was in my car when I went to leave. In most of the other cars, too."

"*Inside* the car?" I repeated, getting sidetracked. "Didn't you lock it?"

She gave me a pitying look. "We're witches?"

Oh. Right. I was so used to magic that dealt with death; I often forgot there were plenty of perfectly ordinary spells that made life convenient for others.

I looked at the sheet again. *New leadership.* "Someone wants to usurp Hazel? Why wouldn't they just start their own clan?"

Tracy had always struck me as very polite, and now I could see her struggling not to roll her eyes at my ignorance. When she spoke, her voice was very slow and measured. "First of all, this isn't about being leader of Clan Pellar. It's about being the witches' representative to Maven. The person who's effectively in charge of all Colorado witches."

"Okay. And second?"

She opened and closed her hands for a moment, searching for words. "This is . . . I'm not sure how to explain it. The clan system in Colorado is old—really old. Most of the clan leaders are over sixty. Some of the younger witches think they're too . . . um . . . compliant, I guess. That's been building for a long time."

"Ah." Simon and Lily talked about this sometimes—the old-versus-new tension within the witch clans. They were always trying to figure out how to balance modernization with the old traditions.

Whenever they talked about future plans, though, they made it sound like everyone was sort of waiting out the treaty before they did anything. I'd figured there were three more years before I had to worry about it.

If the treaty was broken, though . . .

I looked down at the flyer. "So, Hazel is meeting with the clan leaders, but whoever sent this is targeting the younger witches? The ones who want change?"

Tracy had abandoned the zipper pull and was picking nervously at her cuticles. "I think so. And at the moment, pretty much everyone outside Clan Pellar wants to punish Hazel and choose a new liaison to Maven. It's a mess."

I rattled the paper. "Who sent the flyer?"

"I honestly don't know," she said, spreading her hands. "But look at the address for the meeting."

I squinted at the small print on the bottom of the page. "Tie Siding, Wyoming? Where is that?"

"I looked it up. It's just over the state line, on the way to Laramie. The town is so small they don't even count it in the census, but there's this big rustic barn that rents out for weddings and parties and stuff."

Wyoming. I felt a fresh jolt of worry. Renegade witches wanted a meeting outside of Maven's territory, where Maven and Hazel had no power. And the Pellars were all under house arrest. This could not be good.

I needed to get this to Maven as quickly as possible. I folded the piece of paper and put it carefully in my pocket. "Are you going to this meeting?"

Tracy shook her head. "I'm out of it. I don't know what I . . . no. I'm not going."

I blinked. She sounded conflicted as hell. "If you're trying to stay out of it, why bring this to me?" I asked.

For the first time, Tracy reached down and tentatively touched Stitch on the head. The dog panted happily at her, and she scratched his ears a little. "Because I feel like someone is herding all of us in a direction, you know? It has to stop before people get hurt."

People had already been *killed*, but there was no point in making that argument to Tracy. I wasn't sure the witches would even consider werewolves people. Hell, before I'd met Dunn and his pack, *I* hadn't really considered them people either.

Tracy stood up. "I need to go. If anyone finds out I came here, they might bind my magic, too." She gave me a worried look. "You're a witch, and you work for Maven. Please, fix this."

Chapter 16

The snow had stopped by the time I pulled the Jeep out of the driveway, making tire tracks in the inch of fresh powder. The night was crisp and cold and refreshingly clear of ghosts—the route between my home and Magic Beans was the first section of Boulder I had cleared, with Simon and Lily's help.

My thoughts spun as I drove back into downtown Boulder, the flyer tucked safely in an inner jacket pocket. Could this entire thing be a plan to unseat Hazel Pellar? That sounded crazy, and it *felt* crazy. If that was all you wanted, and you were willing to go as far as murder, why not just come after Hazel and Lily directly? That would leave the Pellars without a leader, creating an opening in the witch community. And it was a hell of a lot easier than killing werewolves.

Of course, anyone who hurt Lily would have me to deal with . . . but in a roundabout way, that was the outcome now anyway. I shook my head. None of this made any sense. I just hoped Maven would have some idea of what to do.

I didn't partake in Christmas decorations, other than a fresh wreath on the door and a small, live tree in one corner of my living room, but plenty of homes and businesses along my route had set out twinkling lights, including Magic Beans. Maven had strung the gutters with white icicle lights, which were flickering in a repeating pattern as I pulled up. I parked in the slot behind the building specifically reserved for the Jeep. That was one advantage to having my car stolen, I guess.

My shoes crunched on the snow as I walked inside, and I figured every vampire in the building would know I was arriving.

I had texted Quinn to tell him I was coming, and when I hurried in, he and Maven were both waiting for me in Maven's office. I didn't like the small, cramped room, but it was soundproof, and I suspected that Maven had it regularly checked for magical or electronic listening devices.

Conscious of my claustrophobia, Quinn had thoughtfully turned my chair sort of sideways so I could see him, Maven, and the door at the same time. He also handed me a large white coffee cup without comment, and I sent him a grateful look. The nightmare-fueled catnap at the hotel had done nothing to fight off my exhaustion.

"I wasn't expecting you back so soon," Maven said, looking concerned. "Did something happen? Were you attacked?"

I shook my head. "Not attacked, no, but I did get a visitor. A local witch who doesn't want to get involved in the . . . whatever you'd call it, the power struggle in the witch clans." I sipped the coffee.

Quinn's face sparked with comprehension. "Was it Tracy? Simon's ex?"

I was naturally uncomfortable about exposing her, but Tracy hadn't really done anything wrong, by Maven's standards. "Well . . . yeah. How did you know?"

He shrugged. "Just a guess, based on what Simon's told me about her. Why come to you?"

"She wanted to give me this." I unzipped my pocket and dug out the paper, standing up so I could hand it across Maven's desk.

Maven unfolded it and frowned, looking back up at me. "Lex, this is blank."

"What?" I stood up again so I could see over the edge of the desk. The writing was plain as day. I pointed to it. "Right there, see? It's calligraphy."

Maven raised her eyebrows at me, bemused. "What color is the ink, Lex?"

The question was jarring, but I was too confused to do anything but answer. "Black? No, wait." I peered closely at it. "Very dark red, maybe."

"Ah." She handed it back to me. Quinn held out his hand and I automatically passed the paper to him.

He glanced at it and shook his head. "I can't see anything either."

"That's because the ink is mixed with witchblood," Maven told us. "There's a little charm on the blood to keep it from being viewed by anyone without active magic. I've seen this before."

Quinn held the paper under his nose and sniffed deeply. He nodded. "I can smell it. Just a little. They must have added some sort of sealant or powder over the ink."

"Wait. *Wait.* How is that possible?" My voice came out a lot louder than I'd intended. "When I met you-all, the *first* thing everyone said is that magic doesn't work against itself. So how the hell can there be magical ink that's invisible to vampires?"

Quinn's eyes slid to Maven; he was obviously worried that I was being insubordinate. But Maven simply said, "Lex, when we first met you, you received a rudimentary explanation of our world, the most basic details. And on that primary level, no, magic doesn't work against itself. I could never turn you into a vampire. You cannot cast a spell that will cure a werewolf. The fundamental rules of how we function are unbreakable." She paused, as if to make sure I wasn't going to argue that. "But there are nuances, spaces in between the rules."

Quinn spoke up. "Like illusions." Maven and I both looked at him. "Simon can make illusions that work on me," he said, looking somehow . . . guilty. I raised my eyebrows, and he grimaced. "There have been some . . . uh . . . pranks."

I had to grin at that, and even Maven smiled a little. "Yes, illusions are a good example," she said, "especially if you don't know they're there.

Witches can bend light, move air, disturb water—and those things affect our bodies, which are made to function in ways that are similar to humans. By the same token, we can get physical sustenance from witch or werewolf blood, but we can't press them to forget about it."

"Nuances," I grumbled. It seemed like every time I thought I had a handle on the way things worked in the Old World, I got blindsided.

I looked down at the flyer in Quinn's hand. "So the ink is like an illusion spell?"

"Something like that. Perhaps," Maven said, with the infinite patience of vampires, "you could read it to us."

"Oh, right. Sorry." I took the flyer back from Quinn. "Your presence is requested at a public forum to discuss the state of our community in Colorado. The time has come for new leadership. All clan witches are welcome. Please join us at the Meadowlark Ranch Barn, Friday at 4:00 p.m., Tie Siding, Wyoming."

"Wyoming." Maven looked pensive. "And the Pellars are being forced to stay at the farm. Someone wants to wrest power away from Hazel Pellar, and they don't want me to be able to stop it."

"Couldn't you anyway?" I asked. Both Maven and Quinn gave me surprised looks, and I shrugged. "You told me there's no cardinal vampire in Wyoming, right?"

"Correct. Wyoming's entire population is smaller than that of Denver, and they're spread across nearly a hundred thousand square miles. The state is all wrong for vampires."

"So why couldn't you fuck up a meeting?" I replied. She wouldn't go herself—the sun didn't set until four thirty—but she could send someone. Sending a boundary witch would probably be too antagonistic, but she had plenty of people working for her. She could even press someone in Wyoming, like the police. For a second, I entertained a little fantasy where the anti-Pellar witch club got busted by the cops.

"I can't," Maven said calmly, bringing me back to the present, "because if I take aggressive public action in Wyoming, I'm claiming it as my territory. And I don't have the resources to hold an enormous amount of undesirable land. Especially right now."

I started to ask what that meant, but Quinn spoke over me. "My question is, did whoever set up this meeting—I'm assuming it's a she, because of the witchblood—recognize an opportunity and throw this together quickly, or did she kill the werewolves to set this in motion? Because it seems like an awful lot of trouble to go to, when you could just kill Hazel and Lily," Quinn remarked. Then he winced and met my eyes. "Sorry."

I waved it off. "No, I had the exact same thought. If all you wanted was to take those two people off the board, it's ridiculously convoluted."

"Although," Maven mused, "Quinn mentioned that the entire clan is being threatened with magical binding. If *that* was the goal, perhaps it isn't so convoluted."

I shook my head. "Honestly, I just can't see it—or at least, that can't be the whole picture. Maybe if it was personal, like if Dunn or the Ventimiglias had been involved with Trask, but all three of them were new to Wyoming."

"At any rate," Quinn said, looking at Maven, "what do you want us to do?"

She looked at me, the force of her attention cresting against me like a tide. I'd gotten better at bracing myself, but sometimes being near her made me feel like I was being pulled in by her personal gravity. "I want you at that witch meeting," she told me.

I blinked a few times to make sure I hadn't accidentally started hallucinating. "But you just said—"

"As a spy," she interrupted. She gestured at the flyer. "The meeting is before sunset, so I can't send any of my people."

"You have human employees—" I began, but she interrupted.

"If they're this serious about security, Lex, they'll likely set up wards to block anyone without witchblood. Don't worry. All you have to do is stand in the back and listen, then return here to report."

A spy? The walls of Maven's little office seemed closer than they had just a moment ago. I was not the person you called for an undercover mission. I was the person you called when you needed to either punch someone or talk to ghosts.

Trying to make my voice even, I said, "I'm not a clan witch."

"No," Maven replied, "but you're my *only* witch. The Pellars are unavailable, and I can't trust anyone else in the state."

I wished that was because she was so sure of my loyalty, but we both knew Maven also had fantastic leverage on me. If I ever turned against her, Charlie would pay the price.

"Still," I insisted, "if they invited Tracy, they invited other members of Clan Pellar. Someone there will recognize me."

A smile spread across Maven's face, and it was one I did not like at all. A thousand-year-old vampire should not look mischievous. "I believe I can help with that."

Quinn raised an eyebrow. "A disguise?"

"Exactly."

"I'm not . . . that's not my kind of thing," I sputtered, panic clawing inside my chest. "Give me a security problem, a safety issue—"

"Lex," Maven interrupted, "why is this bothering you so much? Haven't you been wanting more to do?"

I cut my eyes to Quinn, who was sitting there with a perfectly blank face. Had he told Maven I was unhappy and bored? No, he wouldn't do that. She'd probably just worked it out based on the tiny amount of work she had been giving me.

They were both looking at me curiously, so I swallowed hard. "Ma'am," I said, as calmly as I could manage, "I was a soldier. That's my skill set. I'm not an actor or an undercover cop. If they figure out I'm there, knowing I work for you . . . it will make everything worse."

Maven folded her hands in her lap. "I see no other course of action, Lex." Her voice had hardened, just a little bit. On the desk in front of her, her cell phone began to vibrate, and she glanced at the screen. "I should get this."

I stood up abruptly. "Would you excuse me for a moment? I'd like to get some air."

Maven nodded, picking up the phone, and I fled through the exit.

Chapter 17

Quinn found me crouched on the other side of the emergency exit door, my back planted against the building. It was way too cold to be leaning against a brick wall, but I barely noticed.

"Lex?" He sat down next to me, close but not touching. "What is it? I haven't seen you this shaken in years."

I shook my head, unable to explain. The trip across the sand dunes had unnerved me enough to bring back the Iraq nightmares, but . . . he was right. It had been ages since I'd freaked out like this. It took me a few more minutes before I was sure I could speak.

"If I fuck this up," I whispered, "Simon and Lily will lose their magic for sure. The entire Old World relationship in the state could collapse."

It sounded unnecessarily dramatic when I said it out loud like that, but we both knew I wasn't wrong. Quinn scooted a little closer and put his arm around me. He didn't emit any warmth, but at least it blocked the chill from the bricks.

"Why is she making me do this?" I mumbled. "She hasn't had much use for me in months, and now she wants an undercover op?"

There was a long pause, longer than I would expect even from my taciturn boyfriend. "I don't know all her plans," he said at last. "But I know you can do this."

I turned my head to look him in the eye. "How? How do you know?"

"Because you have to," he said simply.

That wasn't very inspiring. I leaned my head against the cold building again, watching the icicle lights twinkle. Maven had set them up all the way around the building, even though only a handful of people ever came through the back door. "Why did she say she doesn't have the resources, *especially right now?*"

He shook his head. "I honestly don't know. Something's going on, but I'm not in the loop . . . yet. She'll tell us when she's ready."

I just gazed at him for a minute. He sounded so calm. Sure, vampires were generally pretty patient, but could I trust him to tell me the truth about this? He hadn't told me about the weekend pass, and he'd been evasive about his reasons. I couldn't tell if he'd kept quiet on Maven's orders, or if he'd done it to protect me. And asking him would be pointless, because if Maven had ordered him to lie to me, he'd have to obey her.

I didn't like this feeling of not knowing whether I could trust my boyfriend. I thought of Sam's words from earlier. *You're not all the way in or all the way out.* Was this what it meant to be all the way in? Pretending to be a clan witch, in a room full of clan witches?

Why did I get the niggling feeling that Maven was testing me? That was nuts, right? Surely I'd proven my loyalty, many times over.

I wished I could talk to Lily about it, or Simon. Or Sam. The moment I had that thought, I really, really wanted my sister, and not in a half-assed psychic connection way.

I scrubbed the back of one cold hand across my eyes. It would have been nice to sit there and feel sorry for myself awhile longer, but Quinn was right about one thing: I had to do this. I stood up. "Let's go back in."

When we got back to her office, Maven was off the phone, and she didn't say anything about my little time-out. Instead, she just asked Quinn to contact Opal.

"Why Opal?" I asked, looking back and forth between them. Opal was one of Maven's most loyal vampires and had once saved my ass in a fight—but I knew very little about her outside of that context.

Quinn had already pulled out his phone and begun texting, but Maven answered me. "In life, she was a hairstylist and makeup artist. She helps all of us with our appearances when a change is required." She smiled again, in a kind way. "Or did you think I was born with orange hair?"

"I never really thought about it," I admitted. I'd known that the vampires had a complex system to change their legal identities every decade or so, but I hadn't really considered that they'd also need to change their appearance. It . . . made a lot of sense, actually.

Opal arrived twenty minutes later, slinking into the big concrete-floored space with a pricey backpack over her shoulders. She appeared to be about twenty, a white woman with streaks of electric pink in her shoulder-length black hair. While we were waiting Quinn had explained that she lived nearby—like many of the young-looking Boulder vampires, she hung out in the university area, where she blended in perfectly with the students.

When she walked through the door, she seemed subdued and stressed, like any other college kid worrying about finals. As soon as the door closed behind her, though, she trotted to the open office door and leaned in with a shy smile. "Someone call for a makeover?" she asked.

Quinn and Maven both pointed at me. "Shit," I muttered.

Maven gave Opal a general explanation of the situation: they needed me to sneak into a witch meeting this afternoon, but no one could know it was me. That sounded like a completely impossible problem to my ears, but Opal just nodded thoughtfully, looking me over. "Can you stand up, please?" she asked.

I liked Opal well enough, but I had serious trepidation as she took my hand and pulled me gently into the concert space, walking around me in a circle. She asked how tall I was and what size shoes and pants I wore. "Is all of this really necessary?" I asked desperately. "Can't you just loan me a wig or something?"

Maven was already shaking her head, but Opal answered first. "You're underestimating women," she said. "There are plenty of women who notice things like brands, fit, body type. And wigs."

"Come on," I protested. "Nobody pays that much attention to what other people are wearing."

Opal gave me a sympathetic smile. "Lex, I've seen you in person maybe ten times, and you were wearing the same shoes seven of those times." She pointed to my beat-up waterproof Merrells. "I'm betting you own two, maybe three pairs of jeans, and not one of them is less than three years old. That increases the chances of them being recognizable in some way."

I gaped at her for a second, struggling to recover. "Fine, I'll change my clothes."

"Plus hair and makeup," she said, as though this were obvious. "How do you feel about facial piercings?"

Piercings? In my *face*? I looked desperately at Quinn, who read my expression and moved toward me vampire-fast. The two of us never did PDA, preferring to keep our relationship as quiet as possible, but now he took my face in his hands, stepping into my personal space. In my peripheral vision, I saw Opal's eyes widen. She hadn't known about us.

"Opal is kidding about the piercings," Quinn said, his eyes locked on me. "And I'm sure she won't do anything that can't be undone. Right, Opal?"

"I *wasn't* kidding," she corrected, "but I didn't mean I wanted to actually pierce you, just that I would get some fakes. They make great magnetic nose rings now. And yeah, I can use a hair color that will wash out."

I relaxed, finally. "I'll bring you some stuff," she said, checking her watch. She frowned and looked up at Maven. "Timing is going to be a problem."

Maven nodded. "I don't suppose you can stay up between now and the witch meeting?" she asked me lightly.

God help me, I actually considered the question. It was already after three a.m., though, and I was exhausted. I shook my head. "Physically, I could manage it, with caffeine pills and energy drinks. But I'd be jittery and slow-witted. Not exactly what you look for in a spy."

Maven regarded me for a moment. "Can we use Charlie?" she asked softly.

Opal's face lit up, but she didn't speak, her eyes flicking back and forth between Maven and me like a kid who's been invited to a sleepover but needs Mom's approval. Some vampires hated the notion of being made human—and vulnerable—around a null, and some, especially the newer ones, loved it.

I blinked, opening my mouth to say no, but I forced myself to stop and think. I'd always been hell-bent on keeping Charlie out of everything related to the Old World, but after she turned eighteen, my niece would almost certainly have the supernatural as a part of her life. Simon had often suggested that it would be good for her to start learning about what she could do. Besides, Opal was an ally, and Charlie could probably use more allies who knew what she was.

I couldn't see the harm—as long as I understood what Maven was asking. "To be clear, Opal comes to my cabin before sunrise and hides out in Quinn's spot, then Charlie wakes her up long enough to do the makeover and Opal goes back to sleep at my place. Is that what we're saying?" I asked.

Maven nodded, but the paranoid aunt in me had to be sure. "No fighting, no meetings, no feeding. Right?"

"Lex," Maven said, a little exasperated.

"Okay." I sighed. "I'll call John. If he says yes, we'll do it."

I stepped out into the dim parking lot to give myself at least the pretense of privacy and called my brother-in-law. Waking him up two nights in a row made me feel like an asshole, but at least I wasn't going to show up at his house this time.

"'Lo?" he said groggily. "Allie? What's wrong now?"

"Actually, nothing," I said, deciding to forgive his use of my old name. Just this once. "No crisis or anything, I just want to ask a minor favor, but I need an answer before sunrise. Can you sit up and put your feet on the floor so I know you'll remember?"

There was an audible yawn and a shuffling noise, and when John came back, his voice was much clearer. "You know me too well," he said.

I explained the problem the same way we'd explained it to Opal: I needed to go to a witch meeting in disguise, but the person who could help was a vampire. Would he bring Charlie over from noon to two so she could be nearby during a makeover?

Yeah. It sounded stupid to me, too.

"You want me to introduce my four-year-old to a vampire?" John sounded plenty awake now.

"*Another* vampire," I corrected. "She already knows Clara and Quinn. And I trust Opal. She saved my life once, when she didn't have to."

John knew me well enough to know what that meant to me. "Are you sure about this, Lex?" he asked, sounding dubious.

"I am. It really won't be a big deal. You guys can come over, and Charlie can watch a movie while Opal puts makeup on me."

"All right." But he still sounded unsure.

"John . . . I think it would be good for her to meet a few more of the local good guys." I did *not* say "in case she's kidnapped again," but we were both thinking it.

"Okay," he said, more firmly this time. "I'll pick up Charlie and take a long lunch break. See you around noon."

I drove the Jeep home, and Opal followed in her own car, an unremarkable—and untraceable—Chevy Malibu. It was registered under one of her aliases, and I would drive it to the witch meeting, since Maven's big, specially altered Jeep wasn't exactly incognito.

When we arrived at the cabin, I was too tired for an official tour, so I simply grabbed some clean sheets from the hall closet and took Opal downstairs to the lightless room Quinn had built for himself in the basement. Actually, the word "room" was a little generous—it was more like a really dark alcove—but Opal just thanked me and took the sheets from my hands. "You should get to bed," she said. "Big day tomorrow and all that."

"Yeah." I waved a hand in the direction of the stairs. "If you want to watch TV or anything, help yourself."

Upstairs, I did the bare minimum required for the animals, most of whom were in the back bedroom, hiding from the strange new vampire. When I finally climbed into my own bed, it was with a gratitude that almost made me dizzy. "I love you, pillow," I mumbled.

I expected to be out before I could pull up the blankets properly, but I found myself staring at the ceiling for a while, thinking about Simon and Lily and my own contributions to their situation. The farm was beautiful, and I was pretty sure they weren't being mistreated, but I hated the whole idea of house arrest, especially since they were mostly in this mess for helping me. I wished I could call or text to apologize—or, better yet, sneak over to the farm and bust them out of there.

But I wouldn't do it—at least, not yet. My friends were still trying to repair the rift in their clan, which was the cornerstone of their entire lives. The least I could do was stay out of the way while they tried.

My last thought before I finally drifted off, near 5:00 a.m., was that Lily would have loved to be there for my makeover.

Chapter 18

When I opened my eyes, I was in my old bedroom, on the twin bed I'd slept in for all of high school.

Unlike in real life, where my mom had long since redecorated, everything was the same: the posters on the wall, the comforters, our backpacks stuffed with textbooks. I sat up and looked to the other side of the room, where my twin sister was sitting cross-legged on her own bed, facing me.

"Sam!" She looked as she had the last time I saw her in life: my own bright blue eyes on a pixie face and more petite frame. She wore black leggings and a long turquoise shirt that draped past her hips.

She smiled at me in great relief, like she'd worried we wouldn't find each other. "Hey, Allie. It's good to see you."

I folded my own legs to mirror her position. We had spent hundreds of nights like this in our teens, discussing homework and boys and our futures. Despite all those hours of speculation, neither of us had ever guessed that Sam would die young from a werewolf attack and I would become the witch that other witches feared.

A big part of me longed to talk to her about Quinn, about my fears for our relationship, but that seemed like a selfish use of our limited time together. "Did I call you, or did you call me?" I asked.

Her smile faded, replaced by a small frown. "A little of both, I think. Strange things are afoot at the circle K, babe."

"What do you mean? Have you been following this thing with the murdered werewolves?"

"I have, and it's not—" she began, then tilted her head for a moment, like she was listening to a voice I couldn't hear. I waited, unsurprised. Sam and I were on opposite sides of a bridge; there were things she could see that I couldn't, and she wasn't supposed to tell me about all of them. As I understood it, she could advise me a little, point me in certain directions, but she wasn't allowed to give away too much, especially about the future.

Although all that was pretty much just a guess, since explaining it would fall under the *things Lex is not allowed to know* heading.

Sam tried again. "A lot is getting stirred up right now, babe. Old grudges. Old hurts."

I rolled my eyes. "Yes, I know that much, Captain Cryptic. Is there anything you can tell me that will help?"

She met my eyes. "It's bigger than you're going to think it is, Lex."

Bigger than . . . ? For some reason my thoughts flashed to Maven's recent preoccupation. What wasn't she telling me?

"Sam, what the hell's going on?"

Her lips were pressed in a tight line. It was her *I want to tell you but I can't* face. There was something in her eyes that I hadn't seen since we'd begun talking together in this space, shortly after I came into my powers: worry. Sam, who was dead and well beyond such things, was actually worried. She hadn't even looked like this when Charlie was kidnapped, because she was so certain I'd be able to save her.

"What is it?" I asked, alarmed. "Charlie? Is something going to happen to Charlie?"

She gave a little headshake. "All I can tell you is, this thing you've got going on, the bigger thing? A lot depends on how you handle it. The decisions you make on this one are going to create some big-ass ripples, and not just in Boulder."

I sighed. "That's not very helpful, Samantha."

She gave me a pointed look. "Think about everything you've done in the last couple of days. There's a question you should ask me."

I stopped myself from pointing out that she could just *tell* me the answer. I knew how much her restrictions were probably driving her nuts. Instead, I nodded and took a slow breath, in and out, thinking about everything that had happened since the werewolves showed up at my door. Wait, no. Sam had suggested I think about everything *I'd* done, not everything that had happened. I tried to trace my steps backward. Tracy . . . the werewolves . . . Dunn's car on the bridge . . . the sand dunes . . .

The ghosts. I opened my eyes. Once I saw it, I felt like an idiot for not considering it sooner. I sat up straight. "Sammy," I said, trying to choose my words carefully, "when vampires and werewolves die, can they leave ghosts behind?"

She slumped her shoulders a tiny bit in relief. I was on the right track. "It's rare," she said calmly, "especially for the older ones. When they reach a certain age, they start to expect a violent death, maybe even welcome it."

"But it's possible."

"Yes."

"I've met ghosts that died of suicide," I pointed out. "They also welcomed their deaths, but it still made a psychic imprint."

Sam shrugged. "Ghost-leaving isn't a science—it's a complex set of emotional reverberations. It involves gravitational magic, but it can also be affected by the witch magic you're used to." She still had an expectant look. I was missing something.

I thought about that for a second. "But when vampires or werewolves die, the magic leaves their bodies. The corpse becomes just an empty physical shell, like any human's. So why would they be any more or less likely to leave a ghost?"

Sam chewed on the inside of her cheek for a second. I knew my sister's expressions well enough to know that I wasn't taking the conversation in the exact direction she wanted. "What?" I said, frustrated.

"Look, do you remember what Maven said when she first told you about the wraiths?"

I searched my memory. "She said there are as many types of ghosts as there are witches."

"Right. You and your friends have been categorizing ghosts, but you've been focused on humans, and especially on *places*. Ghosts aren't only tethered to places."

I'd never considered it like that, but she was right: all the ghosts I'd laid to rest in Boulder had been tethered to a specific location. "What do you mean?" I asked. "How are there ghosts that don't tie to a place?"

"You have to ask—" Sam began, but she was cut off. Tilting her head again, she began to argue with someone I couldn't see. "But she's going to use them against her, and I just want her to be prepared—"

My alarm went off.

"Goddammit!" I yelled before I'd even fully opened my eyes. I turned off the alarm on my phone and rolled over onto my back, looking at the dogs crowded around me on the bed. They had all lifted their heads and were staring at me with confusion.

"Yeah, I know. Getting pissed won't change anything," I said, scratching Pongo's head. I heaved a sigh, lay there for one more minute so I could sulk, then hauled my ass out of bed.

I had set my alarm for ten thirty, which wasn't nearly enough sleep, but it gave me time to take the big dogs for a run, feed and water all the animals, and shower. I had to admit, I felt miles better than the day before. The swelling on my forehead had gone down, and although my muscles were still sore from the hike through the dunes, it was nothing I couldn't handle with a couple of ibuprofen.

I was still toweling off my hair when the dogs, always thrilled to have something to get worked up about, abruptly ran for the front door, barking enthusiastically. I followed them, tossing the towel in the laundry room on the way. Through the door glass I saw John pulling my four-year-old niece out of her car seat, and the dogs' barks changed to a delighted whining accompanied by bruising tail wags. Charlie was a great favorite of theirs, mostly because she was usually sticky with some kind of food, and whatever she had left she was happy to share. Unfortunately, this meant they had a tendency to crowd her—even knocking her down a few times.

John and Charlie came up the front steps hand in hand, Charlie chatting about something with great animation. "Be cool, guys," I warned the dogs as I reached for the doorknob.

The dogs were not cool.

John, who was used to this routine, simply picked Charlie up and carried her inside, while four mutts did their best to jump up to her level—all except Dopey, who was in the opposite doorway, toward my bedroom, turning in tight, happy circles. John saw this and laughed. "That dog should be studied," he said, leaning down to kiss my cheek. "Hey, Lex."

"You got an owie," Charlie said as her dad set her on a stool. She pointed at my forehead.

"That's true, I did," I agreed. I'd expected the question. "I was picking up something on the floor in front of the door when the big dogs crashed through it."

Charlie wrinkled her nose. "Ouch." She rubbed her own forehead in solidarity. "I have an owie too, look." She pulled up her pant leg to show me the tiniest little red mark on one shin. Her face was very grave.

"See? It hurted a lot. I couldn't even walk on it, but now my body is healing it all by itself."

"Makes perfect sense," I told her, suppressing a smile.

Charlie let her pant leg fall down again, and John looked at me, a little nervous now. "You ready to do this?"

I nodded.

"Daddy says I get to watch Jack Skellington," Charlie announced, looking at me eagerly. "And if Aunt Lex has popcorn I get to eat it all up!"

I smiled. "You sure do. But before we do that, would you come help me wake up my friend? She's fast asleep downstairs."

Her eyes widened. Charlie wasn't usually allowed to go in the basement, because the stairs were old and there was nothing down there but exercise equipment and laundry machines. Oh, and a vampire hideout.

"I go downstairs?"

"Yes, you can, Charlie-bug." I stood up and held out my hand, which she took happily.

With her dad just behind us, Charlie happily tromped down the steps, chatting continuously about why triceratops had three horns. Well, "chatting" implies a two-way conversation; this was more like a long, adorable lecture.

"Ooh," Charlie said when we got to the bottom of the steps and I turned on the basement lights. "It's like a cave for aminals."

Well, kind of. "My friend is over there," I said, pointing to the long, boxy protrusion in the back corner of the basement. Quinn had built it by nailing two-by-fours at right angles and attaching the resulting structure to the wall in the corner. Thick plywood boards were added to the top and side to form a tunnel, and caulk and sealant made it lightproof. Finally, he'd painted it the same color as the concrete walls, so it looked like a part of the building, as though it had been added on to hide a cumbersome water heater or electrical works.

A door wasn't really required, since the basement's high windows were angled wrong for the sun to ever reach the opening, but he'd used a nail gun to add a thick leather flap over the entrance.

One nice thing about hanging out with little kids is that benignly odd things don't really faze them. It never occurred to Charlie to question why my friend might be sleeping in a horizontal closet in the cold basement instead of one of my two guest bedrooms. Instead, she was delighted. "It's a cave! It's a wolf den!" She gave a little wolfish howl to the basement rafters, and despite my current werewolf troubles, I couldn't help but laugh, and John was smiling too.

"You're right. I think we should call it a den from now on," I told her.

"Can I climb on the top?" she asked.

I hesitated, but I knew how solidly Quinn had reinforced the top of the hideout. I doubted the tunnel would collapse if the whole house fell down on top of it. "Sure."

I helped Charlie climb up, so she was sitting more or less above Opal's midsection. With John hovering behind me, I crouched at the opening and said, "Opal? Can you wake up?"

There was a gasping sound, then a cough. Charlie looked at me in alarm. "Is she sick?"

"No," Opal's voice said between coughs. "Just not used to . . . breathing . . ."

She crawled out of the hidey-hole and leaned against the wall for a moment to catch her breath. Her face was a little red, and she'd lost some of the unnatural glow I associated with vampires.

Charlie looked at her with curiosity. "You feel weird. Like Uncle Quinn."

Opal smiled, unoffended. "Hello. You must be Charlie."

"And I'm John." My brother-in-law stepped forward and held out his hand. Opal shook it with some amusement. Vampires didn't usually shake hands with humans, because why would you exchange pleasantries with your food source? But she read the protective look on John's face and was smart enough to play nice.

"Miss Charlie," Opal said then, looking at my niece. "Would you maybe hold my hand on the stairs? I get a little scared sometimes."

Charlie puffed up with importance, holding out her hand. And that was that.

Chapter 19

John helped Opal carry up two suspiciously large bags of supplies. I'd set out my card table and a folding chair in the living room again, and we spent a few minutes getting Charlie set up with her DVD and snacks. By the time Opal was spreading a protective hairstylist cape around my shoulders, my niece was seriously engrossed in *The Nightmare Before Christmas*. John, who had probably been forced to watch the movie about two hundred times since Halloween, sat down in my armchair with a Longmire novel and one wary eye on Opal.

The vampire, for her part, began by fussing with my hair. It was still a little damp from my shower, but she spritzed on a bit more water and picked up a very professional-looking set of shears. Since all I cared about was keeping it long enough to pull into a ponytail, I agreed to let her trim two inches off my hair and add in some layers. When she finished, handing me a mirror the size of a clipboard, I had to admit it looked kind of good.

"Thank you," she said with a little bow. Then uncertainty crossed her face, and she glanced at Charlie with a look of longing. "Do you think I could, um . . . try some of those fish-shaped crackers?"

John looked up, raising an eyebrow. "She doesn't usually get to eat . . . uh . . . people food," I explained. The previous year, when Scarlett Bernard had made an appearance in Boulder, I'd seen how much Maven and Quinn enjoyed getting to try different pastries at the coffee shop. "Would you mind going to the kitchen and putting a plate together for her?"

John gave me a look that clearly said *You really want me to leave my kid with the vampire?* but he dutifully got up and headed into the kitchen. He returned with a plate of baby carrots, a peanut butter and jelly sandwich, more goldfish crackers, and two of the organic Oreos I kept for when my cousins' kids came to visit. He also had two juice boxes—but he had to help Opal with her straw. Charlie happened to look up from the movie long enough to see this, and she told Opal confidentially, "I think they're tricky, too."

After her snack—which Opal ate with much "mmm"-ing and smacking of lips—she announced that it was time to do my hair. She'd brought along a sort of gel that contained color—in this case, a bright gold—and would, she promised me, wash right out. She put on surgical gloves and began to squirt it onto my hair in chunks, combing it through with a special brush.

When the gel covered my hair, she began plaiting it on either side, tying it off with rubber bands. When she finally snapped off her gloves and handed me the mirror, I had two bright gold French braid pigtails.

"It looks so . . . cute," I complained.

John glanced up and started snickering, and from her spot on the floor, Charlie looked up at me, her eyes practically bulging with surprise. "You look so pretty, Aunt Lex!"

"Thanks, honey," I said in a near grumble. I always looked younger than my years, thanks to boundary magic, but now I could pass for about eighteen. "I was kind of expecting you to go with neon green or something. This almost looks natural."

Opal took the mirror away and set it back on the shelf, out of my reach. "That's the idea," she told me in a low voice. Charlie had gone back to her movie. "A neon color would stand out too much, even in a group of hippie witches. It would make everyone take a second look at you, and that's the last thing we want."

I sighed, but nodded. She had a point. It might not have been as eye-catching, but this hair still didn't look like something Allison Luther would ever, *ever* do. I tilted my head to see the bottom of the pigtails, but the braid was so tight that they were only a couple of inches long—hard for anyone to grab in a fight. It would do.

I narrowed my eyes at Opal. "Wait a minute—if you were planning to braid it, why did you cut it first?"

"Your split ends were driving me nuts," she said, deadpan. John broke into a laugh. I glowered at both of them, but I'm sure the effect was ruined by my adorable hairdo.

Makeup took over an *hour*, and required more brushes, sponges, and powders than I could possibly keep track of. The entire top of the card table was eventually covered in jars and pots and compacts. Opal even put a tiny bit of putty on my nose to change the shape. When she was finally finished, she helped me put in a magnetic nose ring and handed me the mirror again.

I gasped at my reflection. "What the *hell*?" I almost dropped the mirror.

"Language," John said, looking up from his book. He gaped at me, then blurted, "Holy shit!"

I looked like a complete stranger, with different cheekbones and coloring. The small amount of putty Opal had applied gave me an entirely different nose, and even though she hadn't added any to my chin, somehow that shape also looked different. I wouldn't have recognized a picture of myself like this.

"Daddy," Charlie said, gazing at her father. "You gotta put a quarter in the jar."

"You're right, sweetheart, but just look at Aunt Lex's makeup."

Charlie's head swiveled toward me. A look of complete shock came over her face; then her lower lip trembled.

"Charlie-bug? You okay?" I asked.

"I don't like it!" she wailed. "You don't look like you!"

"It's okay, honey, it all comes off," Opal promised her. "It's a costume, like Halloween."

Charlie's eyes instantly went to the TV screen, where Sally was trying to save Santa from Oogie Boogie, then shifted back to me. "But it's not Halloween anymore."

"I have to go to a costume party tonight," I explained. "Tomorrow I'll look like me again."

"Good," Charlie grumbled, and went back to watching the movie.

Opal stepped back and surveyed me thoughtfully. "Okay, last thing before we change your clothes. Have you worn contacts before?"

"Once, in high school," I admitted. John snorted without looking up from his book. Sam had talked John and me into volunteering for a haunted house fund-raiser for our high school. She and I had dressed as the twins from *The Shining*. John got to be Jack Torrance, and no matter how much I begged, he refused to trade costumes. He did help me destroy all the pictures my mother had taken, though.

"All right," Opal said. "Same principles apply."

It took a few tries, but I got the brown contacts in and put on the trendy, rectangular glasses she handed me. Then I went into my bedroom and changed into the ridiculous outfit she had put together: a long jersey skirt with a slit up the back for movement, a skintight camisole, and a delicate pink sweater that "brought out the roses in my cheeks," according to Opal. Knee-high socks and actual clogs, which were easy to walk in but ugly as hell. I particularly hated the sweater, which belonged on the female lead in a teen romantic comedy. I had to admit, though, everything was the exact right size for me.

When I walked back into the living room, I expected John to start laughing, but instead his jaw dropped open.

"Well," he said, when he'd gathered his wits. "Charlie's right. You certainly don't look like you."

Opal glanced at him. "You've known her a long time, right? Do you think you would recognize her on the street?"

John shook his head, still looking shocked. "No way. You're really good at this." He glanced at Charlie, who was watching the screen a little pointedly now. She didn't want to look at me, and I couldn't blame her.

"Thank you." Opal gave him a curtsy. She reached into her reusable shopping bag and pulled out a thick denim jacket lined with shearling. It looked broken-in and comfortable, and fit me perfectly. It was the only item I was wearing that I might actually have chosen for myself. "Thanks," I told her.

"Check the pockets," she suggested. I reached in and found a pair of gloves in one side, and a burner phone in the other. "The phone is from Quinn," she explained. "He dropped it off last night after you went to bed."

I nodded, turning it over in my hands. I had used this model before—Quinn favored it because it looked a lot like an iPhone. It had navigation, too, so I would be able to use it to get to the meeting. I turned the phone on and saw that Quinn had even filled the contacts with fake numbers.

Opal snapped her fingers. "That reminds me. He said to tell you he went out to the farm to check on your witch friends last night, and they're fine."

Something in my chest loosened. I really wished Opal had told me that the moment she woke up. I reminded myself that she had no way of knowing how worried I'd been. "Did he talk to either of them?" I asked.

She frowned. "I don't think so. But he saw them both through the windows, and he said they're not being hurt or starved or anything; they just have to hang around the house with no phones. There are a couple of witches there too, making sure they don't try to contact anyone. So if you call them or whatever . . . it would be a whole thing."

I nodded again, not needing to ask how Quinn had managed to check on the Pellars without alerting the "guards." If there was one thing vampires could do well, it was sneak around in the night.

"Which reminds me," Opal added. "Try not to talk much at the meeting. Your voice is the one thing I can't change."

"Got it." I hesitated for a moment. I wanted to ask if I could wear my birth mother's bloodstone—I wasn't planning to use boundary magic, but I felt vulnerable without it, like a kid without their favorite teddy bear. But I knew the answer was no. Anyone who might recognize me by sight could conceivably recognize the bloodstone necklace.

Charlie's movie ended. She was still clearly uncomfortable with my appearance, so John suggested the two of them walk Opal back down to the basement den, giving me a chance to take care of the dogs one more time before I left.

As they walked down the stairs, I overheard Charlie say in an awed voice, "You have to take *two* naps? Wow. I haven't had to do that since I was a baby."

Chapter 20

By the time Opal went back downstairs, it was nearly two p.m., time for me to leave for Wyoming. I said goodbye to John and Charlie and drove to a café to pick up a massive coffee and a vegetarian burrito. Then I began the drive north to Wyoming.

Boulder to Wyoming isn't a particularly interesting drive, but at least it was daytime, when I didn't have to worry about ghosts distracting me from the road. The glare of sunlight off the snow was a little blinding, so I put on sunglasses and a podcast and let my thoughts drift. I wondered if I should come up with some sort of backstory, in case I was questioned, but in the end I tried to put the undercover mission out of my mind. I was still nervous enough that the burrito felt like a rock in my stomach.

I drove through Fort Collins, where I'd spent plenty of time in my youth, and crossed the state line just after three. This part of the country was known as the high plains, and it was easy to see why: snow-powdered hills rolled along on either side of the road, interrupted by the occasional ranch building or gas station covered in Christmas lights. The elevation here was even greater than in Boulder, and I hoped it wouldn't affect my breathing if I needed to run. Then I just hoped I wouldn't need to run.

As I got closer I began to worry the "rustic barn" would be too rural for the burner phone's GPS, but to my relief it guided me down several long country roads surrounded by clumps of forest, and right to the parking lot for the Meadowlark Ranch Barn. I drove by slowly once, and found the location was exactly as advertised: the biggest barn I'd ever seen, sitting next to an enormous parking lot that was already more than half-full.

I did a three-point turn and went back, deciding to leave the car on the edge of the road instead of parking in the lot. I knew it was paranoid, but I wanted to be able to make a quick exit if necessary.

It took a while to walk through the parking lot and to the front entrance, and as I joined the stream of witches—mostly women, but a handful of men, too—heading inside, I snuck glances at them, trying to look casual while simultaneously not tripping on the long hem of my skirt. Opal had been spot-on in her wardrobe choices: long skirts and delicate sweaters were everywhere, and I blended right in—as long as I didn't fidget with my hair too much. I knew from the car mirrors that it appeared fine, but it felt, and probably sounded, crunchy to the touch.

When we approached the cluster of people at the front entrance, I noticed that they were grouped in loose lines. A buffet-style table had been set up on either side of the double doors, with two women sitting behind each one. As each person reached the head of the line, they bent and spoke to one of the women, who waved them toward the barn entrance. Two more people, a man and a woman dressed in generic private security uniforms, stood on either side of the double doors. As I watched, a black-haired witch approached the female guard, who waved a portable metal detector over her. When it didn't go off, she glanced at something in the witch's hand and waved her on.

Well, it was good that I'd left my weapons in the car. But what had the witch shown the guard? For a second, I imagined her flashing some sort of witch ID card, and I pressed my lips tight to keep in a nervous laugh. I assumed they must have set a humans-go-away spell on the building itself, and the sun was still up, which excluded vampires . . .

but there must be some sort of final screening process to keep were-wolves out, and I had no idea what that could be.

Not knowing what else to do, I joined the back of a line, my stomach in knots. I didn't like crowds under the best of circumstances, and this was a crowd of potentially hostile witches. What if they figured out I was a boundary witch? I didn't know of anything that could detect my boundary witchblood, but that wasn't really comforting, given how little I knew about trades magic. I wished I could just call Simon and ask him. The unfamiliar braids felt tight and itchy, and I fought the urge to fuss with my hair, not wanting the color to come off on my hands.

Antsy, I took out my new phone, intending to make sure I remembered how to use the functions—but the screen was dark. I frowned and pushed the power button. Nothing happened.

"Ooh, did they kill your phone?" said a witch right behind me. She was a red-haired woman in her late fifties, with an enormous purse the size of a duffel bag. She dug her own phone out and glanced at it, then pulled out a Kindle and looked at that too. "Yep. They've shut down the electronics." She shook her head with a little whistle. "I'd heard there's a hex for phones now, but I don't know anybody who's used it."

"Is it like an EMP?" I asked without thinking. "The phone is destroyed?"

"Oh no, honey, they wouldn't do that. It'll work again once you get outside the wards."

Great. That was assuming I made it outside the wards.

The woman patted me gently on the shoulder, and I had to work hard to suppress a flinch. The crowd was making me nervous, and not having a weapon made it worse. She pointed toward the table. "Look, honey, it's your turn."

I stepped up to the table. There were two women sitting behind it, each wearing surgical gloves and a professional-grade smile. They were dressed in street clothes, but something about them immediately made me think of nurses. "Hand?" the woman in front of me asked.

Stomach rolling with nerves, I began to extend my hand. She made an impatient noise and grabbed it. "Come on now, it's just a quick poke." She was holding a tiny plastic box that looked familiar, but before I could remember where I'd seen it before, she was jamming it onto my right index finger. I felt a quick, sharp stick; then she released me, revealing a drop of bright red blood on my finger. The little box was a disposable needle poke, the kind diabetics used to draw enough blood to test their blood sugar.

"See? Nothing to worry about." Clearly impatient, she waved me off with one hand while the other reached down to toss the little box in a plastic garbage pail. "Next!"

Shuffling to the side, out of the way, I almost laughed. Werewolves could heal very quickly from non-silver wounds, but witches didn't have that ability. *That* was how you made sure only witches got in: a simple humans-go-away ward and a finger poke. I'd been lucky she was in a hurry. If she had seen the calluses on my fingers from laying ghosts, the conversation could have gone very differently.

Keeping the rest of my fingers curled up, I joined the throng of witches filing into the huge building. The male guard waved the metal detector over me and checked my finger to make sure the little needle mark was still fresh, and I was in.

In Colorado, and probably Wyoming, too, the word "rustic" is thrown around a lot, and it can mean anything from "cheap and shitty" to "handmade and priceless." In this case, however, the word actually felt right for the space. The inside of the barn was a massive single room filled with oak pillars and natural light that pooled down from skylights in the barn ceiling. I suspected there was some sort of electrical lighting hidden in the shadows of the rafters, but it wasn't necessary yet. Other than some discreet outlets, exit signs, and a thermostat, the whole place felt like it could have been made at the turn of the last century. Except I doubted they'd ever made barns this big. Or with skylights.

You had to go down a few steps to get to the main floor, but I paused for a moment to survey the massive room. Most of it was packed with rows and rows of what looked to be Amish-made wooden chairs. They were pointed at a rectangular stage, maybe twenty feet long, at the far end of the barn, partially hidden by ivory-colored lace curtains. Presumably, there was another exit somewhere behind them.

As soon as I'd taken in the building's layout and exits, I was struck by the size of the crowd: there had to be hundreds and hundreds of witches already settling into their seats. I'd arrived a few minutes early, but the neat rows of wooden chairs had already been filled, and the extra chairs someone had haphazardly added were nearly filled too. Even more people were standing around behind the chairs, sometimes four or five deep, and I suspected we were violating at least a few different fire codes.

I went down the steps and moved to one side, where I spent a few minutes scanning the crowd as if I were trying to find my friends. I couldn't have looked through the entire room without being obvious, but I managed to spot four different members of Clan Pellar just in my line of vision, which was troubling. I'd assumed most of Simon and Lily's clan would be loyal to Hazel, or at least to the family overall, but apparently they were interested enough to have shown up.

I didn't see any open seats, which was fine—I'd much rather stand if it meant I could be near an exit, both for strategic and claustrophobic reasons. I took a position at the very back of the room, a few feet from one of the fire exits, and settled against the wall to wait.

Four o'clock came and went, and although the room buzzed with anticipation, the small stage at the front of the hall remained empty. Finally, at twenty after four, a single spotlight blazed down from the rafters, illuminating the stage and making me realize how dark the room had gotten while we waited.

A witch in her midtwenties emerged from behind the ivory curtain, pushing a podium in front of her. She was wearing a headset, her eyes lowered and shoulders hunched. She practically projected the words "don't look at me." When the podium was centered onstage, she immediately hurried back through the curtain, passing another woman on her way out. The newcomer was short, attractive, and maternal-looking, and as she stepped into the spotlight she smiled, throwing out her arms in a welcoming gesture.

And then my heart stopped, because it was Morgan fucking Pellar.

Chapter 21

The last time I'd seen Simon and Lily's eldest sister, she had knocked John unconscious and threatened Charlie with a Sig Sauer.

I used to lose sleep wondering what Morgan was up to and whether she'd come back, but eventually I figured she'd settled down to be an asshole somewhere else. But nope, the bitch was back—and smart enough to stay out of Maven's territory.

Maybe you're wrong, I told myself in a daze. I hadn't seen Morgan in nearly three years and I was in the back of an enormous hall. I was tired. Maybe this was someone else, who just looked a little like a Pellar. This woman *was* muscular where Morgan had been plump, and she had short, natural hair where Morgan had had long, straightened locks. She wasn't wearing one of the feminine dresses Morgan used to favor, but brown corduroy pants and a cream-colored sweater that looked like it had been knit on a Scottish moor.

Before I could lie to myself any further, the woman leaned into the microphone. "Witches of Colorado," she began, smiling demurely. "My name is Morgan Pellar, and I thank you for coming."

An anxious murmur went through the crowd, and my composure snapped. My vision narrowed to a pinprick of rage, and I was already stepping forward when I felt a hand on my upper arm. "Steady," a familiar voice whispered.

My head jerked sideways. *"Katia?"*

My biological aunt, the younger sister of my birth mother, had sidled up beside me. She was also in disguise: instead of her usual clinically cold, expensive clothes, she was wearing soft beige leggings and a blue cowl-neck sweater under a quilted jacket. Her hair was braided so it circled the top of her forehead, with tendrils floating loose in a romantic style. I could count on one hand the number of times I'd seen her hair in anything but a practical low bun.

I had never been so happy to see a familiar face, but I couldn't help but say, "What are you doing here?" She wasn't supposed to come to Colorado until a couple of days before Christmas, and that was still weeks away.

Also, we were in Wyoming.

I had been too surprised to lower my voice, but the whole audience was still buzzing and no one even glanced at us. Onstage, Morgan had taken a tiny step back from the podium to give them a moment, smiling patiently.

"I heard you could use some backup," Katia said quietly.

"Did Quinn call you?" I whispered, not sure how I felt about the idea.

Katia smiled, showing her teeth. "No. Valerya did. She suggested I might enjoy a visit to Wyoming. Immediately."

Ah. I nodded, understanding. Valerya was my dead birth mother, Katia's sister. She could contact Katia in her sleep the same way Sam could contact me—at least, when I wasn't having the Iraq nightmare. I didn't know why we had links across the life-death boundary, and I'd never really made an effort to find out. Talking to my dead twin was only just starting to feel natural, and I'd been doing it for years now.

"What about work?"

She shrugged. "There will be other jobs."

Well, there went my Christmas present. My nose itched, and I remembered my disguise. "You recognized me?" I asked, a little worried.

Katia grinned, a rare sight from her. "No," she said. "When I was nearly to Boulder, I tried your phone, then Lily's, and finally John's. He described your new look."

I nodded. My brother-in-law had met Katia many times, back when she was staying with me in Boulder. He knew that I trusted her.

I wanted to ask more questions, but Morgan was stepping back to the podium now, holding up her hand. I still wanted to charge the stage and beat the snot out of her, but Katia's arrival had shocked me out of the worst of my anger. Which was probably the point.

"Please," Morgan said placatingly, "I have no doubt that you have all heard terrible things about me, but if you'll bear with me for just a moment, I will explain everything."

The crowd settled down a little at that, though I saw a number of witches take out their phones, only to frown with disappointment when they couldn't call or text anyone. I sympathized. This was big news. Big, horrifying news.

"As you know," Morgan said, "the past eighteen years have been a difficult time for witches. We were unable to prevent the mongrels from wreaking havoc across the state, and lives were lost." She paused with a sad smile, probably to remind everyone that her own father had been killed. God, I hated her. "Then my mother, Hazel Pellar, made a Faustian bargain with a vampire, and our people have suffered ever since. Our magic was restricted, and our leadership, well . . ." She heaved a great sigh. "I truly believe my mother tried her best, at first, but she was unable to perform the balancing act required to serve all of your diverse interests. And over time, I'm afraid she became corrupted."

It was dead silent in the great hall then, but I could see heads turning to glance at one another—including two of the Pellar witches in the back row. "Three years ago," Morgan continued, "I began to suspect that my mother was no longer pushing for the best interests of witches. She was far too complacent, too deferential to the vampire. But the last straw was when she welcomed a *boundary witch* into the clan, at Maven's request."

She said "boundary witch" the same way anyone else would say "flesh-eating virus." Boundary witches had done some very creepy, very evil things during the Inquisition, and if there was one thing the entire Old World was good at, it was holding a grudge. It shouldn't have shocked me to hear myself mentioned, but my head was still spinning.

And Morgan was just getting started. "I knew I had to do something, before anyone else in my clan could be corrupted by Maven's influence. But what could I do? How could I stop an ancient cardinal vampire?" She held up her hands, a helpless expression on her sweet-looking face. I clenched my teeth. "Oh, she is *good*," Katia whispered, so quietly I could barely hear her.

Morgan summoned a look of great sadness. "Some of what you've heard about me *is* true: I did stir up the ley lines in Boulder. My intent was to use the power boost to take my mother's place as clan leader, and save my clan, including my own brother and sisters, from Maven's influence."

"Bullshit," I muttered. Morgan was making herself sound like a crusader for good, but Hazel hadn't done anything wrong, except raise a daughter who would make such a callous power grab. True, she had allowed me at a few clan functions, but I'd hardly been "welcomed."

Morgan heaved a sigh. "Unfortunately, this was a mistake. There was no way I could have known that activating the ley lines would awaken a hungry creature. Or that innocent people would be killed." She hung her head, and even rested her right hand over her heart. "For the rest of my life, I will carry the weight of those deaths. But because of my efforts to right a wrong, I was excommunicated from my clan and banished from my home. From my *children*."

This time the crowd's murmur held a note of sympathy. "That's not how it happened!" I protested to Katia, feeling the anger building in my chest. "She's spinning everything!"

A few of the nearby witches glanced my way and Katia made a shushing motion with the flat of her hand. Onstage, Morgan said solemnly, "At the time, I thought a death sentence would have been better. You have no idea how hard it's been to leave every person I've ever loved, including my own babies."

She actually paused to wipe tears from her eyes with a quick swipe of her fingers, and Katia must have sensed my urge to scoff, because she shot me a warning glance. "But I kept an ear to the ground," Morgan went on. "When I heard that Maven was allowing the mongrels to run amok in Colorado, practically parading their crimes under your noses, I knew it was time for me to step forward again."

That was it. I was absolutely certain Morgan had orchestrated all this, and I wasn't about to let her get away with this *bullshit*. My temper flared, and I started to step forward—but Katia was waiting for it. She grabbed my arm and dragged me back through the entryway before I could regain my balance.

"Hey!" I protested. Behind her, I could see that Morgan was still talking, though a bunch of witches in the back snuck curious glances at us. "Let me go. I have to *tell* them—"

"What?" she hissed, so quietly that I could barely make out the word. "That Morgan is lying? The first thing they'll say is 'well, how do you know?' Then what will you do? Tell them you were there, because you're Lex Luther the infamous *boundary witch*?" She mimicked Morgan's disgusted tone.

"No," I said, although I hadn't actually gotten that far. Part of me knew she was right, but this was *Morgan Pellar*, who had seduced John and threatened Charlie and broken Simon and Lily's hearts, not to mention Hazel's. My chest burned with anger, and I *really* wanted to punch something. Well, some*one*. "Maybe I'll just beat the shit out of her onstage and leave it at that. She can't lie with a broken jaw."

"There are a thousand of them and two of us," she whispered matter-of-factly. "And any one of them can throw you through a skylight."

That brought me up short. "I . . ." She was right. I just *really* didn't want her to be right.

"You can't be here anymore," Katia pronounced, reading my face. "I'll listen to the rest of it and meet you at your place in a few hours."

"But—"

"Go."

Reluctantly, I allowed Katia to push me through the double doors, where the two guards were now sitting with the table attendants, all of them chatting amiably. They looked up when I stumbled outside, and for a second I really wanted them to rush me. I was just aching for a fight.

"Everything okay?" the female guard said, sounding concerned. "You look a little pale. Do you need to sit down? Do you want some water?"

Well . . . shit. Where's a rude, aggressive asshole when you really want one? The anger began to leak out of me like a balloon with a pinhole. "No," I said, trying not to sound sullen. "I think I'm getting a migraine. I'm heading out early."

They nodded, and as I began to walk toward the darkened parking area, the male guard actually called, "Feel better, miss!"

Leaving the annoyingly friendly guards behind, I stalked past the rows and rows of cars, fuming to myself. Morgan fucking Pellar. I wondered how she'd managed to set all this up. It would have cost a ton of money to rent this space and hire guards. To say nothing of the difficulty of arranging the deaths of three werewolves.

Katia had been right, though. I needed to calm the hell down and think it through before I did anything. I took a deep lungful of the crisp winter air, slowing my pace. Passing the last row of cars, I reached the end of the massive lot and turned onto the road. The sun was already down, and the remaining light was fading quickly, so I had to squint to pick out Opal's sedan. Ten or fifteen cars were lined up behind it now—people who'd arrived after the lot was full.

I didn't really want to trudge through the ditch in the near darkness, so I checked for cars, then began walking right down the middle of the road.

Something caught my eye, and I paused for a moment. Had I just seen movement? I looked around, wondering if someone else had left the meeting early, but I didn't see anything in the twilight. I noticed that the vehicle next to me was the same make and model Subaru as Ryan Dunn's, and I felt a pang of heartache as I remembered those claw marks. I couldn't help but picture Dunn, frantic and half-changed, scrabbling wildly at the reinforced glass. I had agreed to be his escort through Colorado, and I had blown it.

I stood there staring dully at the Subaru, and that moment of melancholy probably saved my life. In my peripheral vision, I saw the shadows between the cars shift, and I managed to get my arms up and shift my weight properly just before the werewolf leaped out and attacked me.

Chapter 22

That was twice in two days that I'd been tackled by a werewolf. It wasn't any more fun the second time.

The woman was about my height and weight, but faster—*too* fast, which was how some part of my brain immediately processed what she was. The rest of me was busy reacting. When she ran at me, I had just enough time to bend forward at the waist, letting her momentum roll her over my back and onto the road. Unbalanced, I dropped to my hands and knees.

My glasses fell off, but I wasn't hurt. I could hear, rather than see, the werewolf's body scrape on the asphalt, and a yelp of pain followed. It was getting dark quickly now, but werewolves could see perfectly well with just a little bit of moonlight. My only chance was to end this fight fast, and for that I needed weapons.

I kicked off the clogs and managed to take about one step toward Opal's car before the werewolf sprang up, spitting mad—and spitting gravel. Then she was running toward me again, her fingers curled like claws and a low growl coming from her throat. In the dimming light I could just barely make out scrapes on her face and a trickle of blood running into one eye. They would heal quickly, but it gave me an idea.

She charged me again. I managed to dodge her, but barely—she was just so *fast*. I wasn't going to be able to get out of the way a third time, so I pivoted as quickly as I could on one heel, like a basketball player.

When she slammed into the car behind me, an old minivan, I got a fistful of her long hair, planted my feet, and slammed her head into the window once, twice, three times, spiderwebbing the glass.

I would happily have kept going, but she twisted toward me, wrenching around far enough to land a clumsy haymaker that hit me with the force of a baseball bat.

I let go of her hair, staggering backward as pain exploded in my cheekbone—but it had worked: I had opened more cuts in her forehead. She was momentarily blinded from the blood running into her eyes, and she smeared at it with her hands, letting out a cry of rage.

I rushed around her and sprinted for Opal's Malibu without looking back. If she recovered in time to catch me, I was dead. Seeing it coming wouldn't make any difference.

Thank God I had Opal's car instead of my own ancient Subaru. It recognized the key fob in my pocket and unlocked as I ran up. I yanked the door open, dropped to my knees, and was digging under the seat for my weapons when the werewolf reached me.

She could have killed me pretty easily right then by slamming the door against my spine, but instead she yanked on my waistband, dragging me out of the car. I rolled onto my back with the revolver in my hands and saw that she had a weapon too: a three-inch blade.

What the hell? Since when did werewolves need pocketknives?

"Stop," I warned, releasing the safety on my weapon. "Drop the knife."

She grinned at me with bloody teeth. Her face was a mask of red, but the cuts had stopped bleeding, and the whites of her eyes seemed to glow. "That won't kill me," she said, stepping forward.

"Silver bullets," I snapped.

She froze, frowning with uncertainty. "You're bluffing," she said.

"You're downwind. Do I *smell* like I'm bluffing?"

"All I smell right now is blood." She licked the blood off her lips, sticking her tongue all the way out to reach as much as possible. It was disgusting, but I figured she was trying to unnerve me and said nothing. She sniffed the air and her eyes widened with fear. Like Keith, she'd caught the smell of silver. She took a step back.

"Drop the knife," I said again. This time she did it. I stood up slowly, pulling the burner phone out of my pocket and activating the flashlight so I could see her properly.

She was short, white, and muscular, with cropped black hair, wearing expensive hiking boots over jeans, and a soft-looking flannel shirt. It didn't look like she'd planned to turn into a wolf anytime soon. "What's your name?" I asked her.

"Heather." She bared her bloody teeth in a parody of a grin.

"Are you out here alone?" I asked.

"For now. Others are coming."

"How many?"

She didn't answer me. "Do you really want me to shoot you in the leg to get you to talk?" I asked. "I'd hate to think what might happen if the bullet doesn't go all the way through." As I understood it, a werewolf could heal from a through-and-through at roughly the same speed as a human, but they could die from silver poisoning if the bullet was left inside.

The smug look fell off Heather's face, and she answered in a sullen voice, "Two more. They'll be here any second."

"Why did you attack me?" I demanded.

She shrugged. "Nothing personal."

I realized, with a shock, that she actually meant that. In all the excitement I'd forgotten my disguise, but this woman seemed to have no idea who I was. Which meant I hadn't been specifically targeted. "Get out your phone," I ordered. "Slowly."

She did as I asked, producing an iPhone in a protective case. "Text your friends," I instructed. "Write this exactly: 'Don't come; the whole thing is off.' If you add anything else, I will shoot you. Then I will wait here with my silver bullets, and ambush your pals as they pull up."

Heather didn't have much of a poker face. I could pretty much see the wheels turning in her head: she and her friends had been expecting a bunch of weak, fragile witches; silver bullets changed the rules of engagement. "All right," she said finally. "I'll call them off."

I wasn't going to come any closer, considering how fast she was, so I made her turn slightly so I could see her unlock the phone and start typing. She sent the text, but before I could tell her to toss me the phone, she lifted her arm and slammed it down like a football, spiking it into the asphalt.

Even with the case, the phone seemed to explode into pieces. I guess the manufacturer hadn't factored in werewolf strength. I cursed loudly, but I didn't move, not wanting to give her an opening. "Good luck getting information off that," she said smugly.

I gritted my teeth with frustration, but I was running out of time. "Why are you killing witches?" I asked.

She shrugged. "Don't know. Don't care."

"Who are you working for?"

"Same answer."

Ugh. "How many were you supposed to kill?"

"As many as we could cull from the herd without getting caught." She lifted her chin in defiance, glaring at me over the light. "We get a bonus for every corpse."

The *herd*? I'd met a few werewolves now, but none of them had talked as if humans, or witches, were their prey. On a wild hunch, I said, "You were with Trask's pack, weren't you?"

Her face darkened, but she didn't answer. "That's a yes," I said.

"Well—" she began, and then she lunged at me.

If she'd turned and run away, into the darkness, I probably wouldn't have been able to catch her. She couldn't afford to let me get away, though, and she was hoping I'd be too startled to react quickly.

I wasn't startled, but I wasn't nearly as fast as her, and she was smart enough to go for my arm first, pushing the sidearm into the air.

Her fingers tightened on mine, and I pulled the trigger, letting off one deafening shot. The werewolf squeezed my fingers upward like she was squeezing yogurt out of one of those tubes, and at last I cried out and let go, the revolver tumbling to the ground. She gave it one fierce kick in the direction of the barn, then hooked my leg and toppled me over, her body pressing onto my chest. The burner phone flew out of my other hand, and I heard an alarming *crack* as it landed on the asphalt and the flashlight winked out.

I tried to throw my weight sideways to pitch her off, but she hit me, a lazy slap across the same cheekbone she'd punched earlier. Pinpricks of light danced in front of me. I beat my fists against her as hard as I could, but she just snarled, absorbing the impact.

Then she was wriggling around, and I realized belatedly that she was pulling something from one of her boots, probably a weapon.

I blinked hard, trying to clear the lights, trying to think of something—then the werewolf gasped and arched up, and almost simultaneously I heard the gunshot.

Chapter 23

The silver bullet must have hit something important in the werewolf's back, because she went limp almost immediately, her body slumping on top of me.

I swore, shoving the werewolf to the side and rolling free. I came up on my knees, and a different phone flashlight flicked on. In the screen's illumination, Katia was peering down at me, perfectly calm. "Thanks," I said in a gasp.

"You're welcome. Is she dead?"

"I think so." I knelt beside the body, trying to avoid the blood, and checked her pulse—already gone.

"Will they come to investigate the gunshots?" Katia asked.

"In Wyoming? I doubt it. There's plenty of hunting around here." I flexed the hand she'd squeezed. It was sore, but I didn't think any of the bones were broken.

When I looked up, Katia was frowning thoughtfully at the body. "Should we leave her?"

I followed her gaze down to the werewolf. In death, she had lost the glow of health and sense of barely contained energy that I'd come to associate with werewolves. Without magic, her body now looked . . . well, like a dead human's. "We can't leave her," I told Katia. "If one of the witches finds the body, they'll assume she was a witch too. They'll start looking for a murderer." They would probably also call the police, since there was nothing apparently supernatural about the cause of death.

Another nod. "How did you know to come after me?" I asked Katia.

She shrugged. "I started thinking that Valerya wouldn't have told me to come here just to listen to the witches talk. I was supposed to come here for you, so I should stick with you." She tilted her head at the werewolf as if to say, *and that's why.*

I said a silent thank-you to my dead birth mother. "Okay. Hang on a minute."

While Katia leaned casually against the nearest car, I went and checked the burner phone. It was useless—the battery had detached from the phone, and the mechanism that usually held them together had broken off. I stuck both pieces in my jacket pocket, and Katia held up her light while I went back to search the werewolf.

Along with the knives, she had been carrying a set of keys, a crumpled gas receipt, a money clip with two hundred dollars in cash, some gum wrappers, and a thick wad of industrial-strength, gallon-sized ziplock bags. I frowned at those for a second, flipping them around in the beam of light. They were completely empty. Why the hell would—

Then I realized what the baggies meant, and that we needed to move a lot faster. I looked at Katia. "Where did you park?"

She pointed toward the back of the lot. "Last row, on the east end."

"Okay. Do me a favor? Go back to the meeting and pull the fire alarm in"—I checked my watch—"ten minutes. I'll meet you at your car after."

She raised her eyebrows, but when I didn't offer an explanation, she gave a little shrug and handed me the revolver. Then she turned around, sauntering back toward the building.

I picked up the werewolf under her arms, hoisting her into the trunk of the Malibu. In my sock feet, I padded back down the road until I nearly tripped over the clogs I'd stepped out of. I put them back on and stood there for a moment, debating with myself. First things first: I needed to hide the car. But where? It was too dark to see anything except the road I was standing on. If I ran the car off the road, some Good Samaritan might see it, which would eventually lead to someone checking the trunk. There was a patch of forest nearby, but the car didn't have four-wheel drive, and trying to make it to the tree line would probably just mean ending up in the ditch.

You're a witch, dummy. Use what you've got.

"That's not helpful, *Samantha*," I said out loud, but my sister had a point. I closed my eyes and forced myself to relax into what Simon called my boundary mindset.

Most witches had a way to see magic. Lily envisioned a third eye she could switch on and off. Simon perceived magic as a sort of density in the air. As a boundary witch, I didn't get that useful set of skills: I could only see a creature's life essence—or their death-essence. That was Simon's term for it, anyway. Lily called it the soul, and I sometimes thought of it as human-being extract. Whatever you wanted to call it, I could look at the world as though I were wearing thermal-imaging goggles, and living or dead things would light up.

I was hoping to see signs of lots of tiny life nearby: a forested area or deep ravine where the car could disappear. Instead, I lucked out. My eyes popped open again, and I got inside the car and turned on the headlights.

The side of the road had a lot of tall yellowed grass, partially flattened by a dusting of snow, but a few hundred feet ahead, I could just make out a flat area with no grass. A driveway.

I started the engine, creeping forward so I could take the turn. It led into a patch of trees, and just past the tree line I could see the blackened, charred bones of what had probably once been a pretty nice summer cabin. Parts of the structure still stood, like a bunch of broken spider legs, but they didn't keep me from seeing the three separate ghosts hovering inside. I was too far away to make out the details, but two of them were large and one very small, maybe a child of three or four. I had no way of knowing how long they'd been haunting the cabin's remains.

The owners had dug out a single, car-sized turnout, directly on my left, and I parked Opal's sedan there and quickly wiped it down with one of the gloves she'd put in my jacket pocket. I checked the clock before I got out of the car: it had been about five minutes since Katia had shot the werewolf.

I wanted to lay the ghosts, but there just wasn't time. Regretfully, I left the sedan and jogged clumsily back to the road, past the line of parked cars, and through the parking lot to Katia's car. By the time I got there, the alarm was just beginning to blare, and a swarm of witches burst through the doors.

Katia had thoughtfully unlocked the Equinox as she'd gone back inside, so I was able to open the door and climb onto the running board, watching the stampede of witches. They came out in a hurry, but most looked wary, as if they half expected a trap of some kind. Good. I wanted to get everyone out in case Heather's friends decided to show up after all, but sowing seeds of mistrust against Morgan was a nice side benefit.

In the confusion, Katia had been able to disappear into the crowd, and with her disguise I wasn't able to pick her out until she was nearly at the driver's-side door. I didn't drop down from my perch right away, though, because as the crowd fled into the parking lot, Morgan Pellar appeared in the doorway, wringing her hands. "Everyone stay calm!" she called, her microphone still booming through the interior speakers. She looked genuinely pissed at the turn of events, which made me happy. "I'm sure it's a false alarm. We can continue this here in the parking lot!"

Nearly all the witches ignored her. Only a handful of them clustered around her to talk, and those were probably the ones she'd already won over.

I stepped down and got myself buckled into the Equinox. Katia arched an eyebrow at me as she started the ignition. "Where to?" she asked.

"Back to Boulder," I told my aunt. "Fast as you can."

Chapter 24

Katia followed the line of other cars back toward the highway. I turned to watch as we went by, but none of the other drivers seemed the least bit interested in the turnout where I'd left Opal's car.

I settled back in my seat. "Can I use your phone?"

She dug her cell out of her pocket and held it out to me, saying, "I trust you will explain what's happening?"

"Promise. But I need to warn some people first."

The road was currently empty, but I automatically took my usual ghost precautions, flipping the sun visor down as far as it would go and scooting myself up in the seat to block out as much of the windshield as possible. Katia didn't comment. This wasn't the first time she'd driven me after dark.

I called Quinn first, but there was no answer. At this hour, I realized, he was probably out feeding. Vampires turned their phones off or left them behind while they fed, mostly because it was really annoying to fully hypnotize someone, then have it break down when your pocket started playing ringtones. I left a message for him to call Katia's phone and tried the coffee shop.

"Hello, Magic Beans, this is Sharona," came a bored-sounding voice. She was one of the human baristas Maven employed until about eleven p.m., when the shift became mainly vampires.

"Sharona, it's Lex. Is Maven around?"

My ear filled with the sound of gum snapping. "Nuh-uh, she's not in yet. She said six, though, and it's only quarter to."

Right. Quinn and Maven usually fed right after they woke. It was rare for them to be gone at the same time, but they probably thought I was still in the witch meeting—and that there might be trouble later tonight. "You wanna leave a message?" Sharona asked, in a voice that betrayed her lack of enthusiasm.

"No, I'll call back. Thanks."

I hung up the phone and Katia looked over at me, a tiny worry-crease between her eyebrows. "One more," I promised. I knew John's number by heart, but Katia had it in her contacts too.

My brother-in-law answered on the second ring. "Let me guess," he said good-naturedly. "You're in the middle of a crisis, and you'd like me to let your dogs out."

"No—well actually, yes, but it's bigger than that. John, Morgan is making some kind of play."

There was a long moment of silence.

Two years ago, with Maven's permission, I'd told John about the Old World, and filled him in on some of the problems I'd been dealing with since Charlie's first kidnapping—including the fact that the woman he'd dated for months was a witch who'd wanted to use Charlie to kill my boss. It had been . . . awkward.

"Is she here?" John asked. His voice was hard with anger. "In Boulder?"

"Not yet. So far she's staying out of Colorado, but to make a long story short, she's planning something, and she knows what Charlie can do. This would be a really great week to take Charlie to Disneyland." John and Sam had lived in LA for a few years, and he had plenty of friends they could stay with there.

John sighed. "I've already taken so much time off this year . . ."

"I know." John worked in the graphic design department at Luther Shoes, my dad's company. He wasn't really arguing with me—we both knew Charlie's safety took priority over his job. He was just worried.

"Okay," he said after a moment, sounding resigned. "Do we need to go right now?"

"No, I think you're fine tonight. First thing tomorrow?"

"Yeah."

He sounded unhappy, and I had an idea. "If you want, I could put you in touch with Scarlett while you're there. I know you had more questions for her." Scarlett Bernard was an adult null, and there was a lot John wanted to ask her about her life. She'd spent a few hours in Colorado this spring, but he hadn't gotten a proper chance to talk to her.

His voice brightened immediately. "Do you think she'd be okay with that?"

"Probably." I did some mental calculations. "She's something like eight months pregnant right now. She's probably bored out of her skull."

Beside me, Katia started, and I realized I'd forgotten to tell her about Scarlett's baby. Whoops.

John and I talked about the details for a few minutes—his vehicle had been outfitted so he could travel with Clara, who would continue to play bodyguard at night. She could also help with driving, which was a bonus.

Then I had to ask, "Are you good for money?"

Just the briefest hesitation. "Yeah. Yeah, I'll make it work."

We said goodbye, and as I placed Katia's phone in the cup holder, she glanced my way. "Scarlett is having a baby?"

"Yep. Apparently if it's two nulls, it's a thing."

"Hmm." Katia nodded to herself, processing that, then moved on. "So that woman tonight, Morgan, she is Lily's older sister, yes?" Katia didn't have an accent, but she had picked up the occasional strange syntax, the result of being born in the Ukraine and more or less owned by an evil vampire who traveled a lot.

"Her oldest sister, yes. Morgan was supposed to be the heir to Clan Pellar, but she disagreed with her mother's policies and decided she couldn't wait around for Hazel to retire."

"And John?"

I sighed. "He dated her, before I was allowed to tell him about the Old World. She almost used Charlie to kill Maven."

"Which is why you're getting them out of town," Katia said, nodding again.

But John and Charlie weren't the only ones in danger from Morgan, I realized, checking the dashboard clock. Hazel was planning her witch town hall for tomorrow morning, and she had no idea that half her clan had just met to discuss a possible mutiny. More importantly, she wouldn't know who was behind it.

"Hang on a second." I stared blankly out the windshield for a moment, weighing the risks, then picked up the cell again. "I need to warn Simon and Lily."

"Are you sure that is wise?" Katia asked. "If Morgan has people monitoring their phones, they could recognize your voice."

"She'll have someone watching them, but it won't be anyone from Clan Pellar," I insisted. "Morgan wouldn't risk sending anyone who might be even a little bit sympathetic to Hazel. And the Clan Pellar witches are the only ones who know what I look and sound like."

Just to be on the safe side, I searched for the number for Pellar Farm, and dialed the landline. I didn't think it had caller ID.

"Hello?" The voice was wary, female, and completely unfamiliar.

Drawing on years of working retail, where I'd waited on CU's finest, I channeled my best uncertain college girl. "Hi, um, I'm looking for Professor Pellar? I'm Emily, one of his TAs?" Beside me, Katia's lips twitched with amusement.

A beat, then the voice said, "Simon Pellar isn't available to talk right now, Emily. You can leave a message for him at his office."

"Wait!" I said quickly, before she could hang up. "This is like, *super* important. I have this emergency family issue and I can't proctor his exam, and if he doesn't find someone else in a hurry it's going to screw up the whole semester of grades. Then he's gonna get in trouble, and *I'll* be in trouble, and I just don't know what to do!" I did my best to wail, hoping it wasn't too much.

Annoyed now, she said, "Hang on a minute. I'll see if I can get him, but you'll need to make it quick."

"Ohmigod, thank you *so* much!"

There was a pause, then some shuffling around; then a confused-sounding Simon came on the line. "Uh, hello?"

I toned down the irritating voice. "Hi, Professor Pellar? This is Emily, your TA."

To Simon's credit, it took him only about a second and a half to catch on. "Oh, hello, Emily. What's going on?" There was a tightness in his voice that suggested someone else was listening in.

"I'm supposed to proctor your exam, but I've got this emergency family problem."

"Oh?"

Shit, how was I going to phrase this? "Yeah, remember I told you about my older sister, the one who, like, disappeared for a while? We thought she was in a psychiatric facility or something, but it turns out she's not. She's on her way home, and it's causing all this family drama. My parents want me to come home right away."

"I see." Simon's voice was still perfectly even. "Thanks for letting me know, Emily. Are you on your way home now?"

"Yes." I checked the clock. "I'll be there in two hours."

"Safe travels. I'll find someone else to proctor the exam."

Damn, Simon was smooth. "Thank you, Professor. Have a good holiday."

"You too."

When I hung up, Katia raised both eyebrows. "Do you think that will be enough?"

I exhaled, leaning back in the seat. "I hope so. Simon's pretty smart. At any rate, that's the best I can do without completely giving him away."

Katia nodded. We drove for a few minutes in silence, her letting me catch my breath. When I glanced over at her face, illuminated in the dashboard lights, I was struck by how much she looked like Sam and me. My aunt was only six years older than me, in her late thirties. She aged slowly because of boundary magic, but I aged even *more* slowly, a shitty souvenir from my shitty birth father's powerful bloodline. When all the math was said and done, Katia looked twenty-eight or so, and I still got carded regularly. Eventually, I was going to need to leave Boulder and my human family behind, but I wasn't going to worry about that until Charlie turned eighteen.

"Okay," I began, "here's what's going on."

I walked Katia through the events of the last few days, starting with the night the werewolves had shown up at my door. I didn't leave out anything, including my discussion with Sam. As close as I was to Quinn, Lily, and Simon, they all got a little weirded out when I talked about my conversations with my dead sister. I suspected they believed I just had really vivid dreams about her, and they were too polite to break the news to me. Katia was one of the few people on the planet who didn't find my conversations with Sam the least bit odd—because she did the same thing with Valerya.

When I mentioned the part about ghosts not being tied to places, I asked Katia if she had any idea what Sam had meant. She shook her head. "As you know, I experience ghosts differently," she said, frowning. "For me all ghosts are a faint glow in the air, like a charged mist, the size of a person. I never get details like you do, and I don't have a sense of ghost . . . levels. Types." She waved a hand. "Whatever you call it."

I nodded, but I was a little disappointed. My aunt had used boundary magic since she was a teenager, but she wasn't as strong as I was. With Katia, I sometimes felt like a big, clumsy Newfoundland trotting along with a sleek greyhound. She was efficient at using everything she had, and half the time I was barely in control of myself. "All right. Anyway, that's how I ended up at the meeting."

She nodded, processing. "So if I am understanding this correctly, you tried to return a favor to this alpha werewolf, and accidentally stumbled into Morgan Pellar's plan to poach the Colorado witches from her own mother?"

"Yes. No, wait. What do you mean by 'poach'?"

Just then, Katia's cell phone rang, and Quinn's name appeared on the screen. I found the button on her dashboard to send the call to the car speaker. "Quinn?"

"Lex." That one word was full of relief. "You're okay?"

"I'm fine." I didn't expect him to get all mushy, but just in case, I added, "You're on speaker with Katia, by the way."

"Right." He sounded just the tiniest bit embarrassed, like he'd been caught professing his undying love. "I'm going to put you on speaker, too, so Maven can talk. We're in her office."

Which was safe, and which Maven regularly swept for listening devices. There was a tiny *beep* as he sent the call to a Bluetooth speaker; then Maven's voice came on the line. "Katia," she said pleasantly, but I knew her well enough to hear the thread of anger in her voice. Every single Old World resident in Colorado had declared loyalty to Maven in one form or another, but my aunt was stubbornly determined to remain independent—which was how she had ended up having to move away. "You're in my state again."

"You said I could visit for the Christmas holiday," Katia reminded her. "You didn't say when that would start."

There was a pause, and then to my surprise, Maven let out a begrudging chuckle. "You know what, you're right, I didn't. I will not be making that mistake again. *Ever.*"

"Katia came here to help me," I told Maven. "I needed the backup."

"All right," Maven acknowledged. "Now, will you explain what's going on?"

"Morgan Pellar was at the witch meeting," I began. "She's trying to . . ." I trailed off and looked at my aunt, realizing I was fuzzy on Morgan's actual plan. "Wait, what were you saying about poaching?"

"She wants all the witches in Colorado to move to Wyoming," Katia said bluntly. "She's offering them access to their apex magic, plus financial assistance to help find housing and jobs. She plans to declare herself the witch queen of Wyoming and establish the state as a safe haven for witches."

There was a moment of silence, and I could practically feel Quinn and Maven looking at each other. That was a huge move—and an unwieldy one. Making herself the leader of Wyoming *did* sound like Morgan, but asking everyone to move? All the witch clans had deep roots in Colorado—they would look at every available option before they considered pulling them up. Besides, where would Morgan get the money to offer financial assistance?

"I don't think that's what she's really doing," I said after a moment of thought. "I left the meeting early, and on the way out I was attacked by a werewolf. She didn't actually recognize *me*. I was just the first one to come out of the building."

"Are you injured?" Quinn broke in.

"Katia got there in time to save me. I've just got a few scrapes." And a throbbing cheekbone from being punched, but it wasn't like it was my first time. "Although I did leave Opal's car there, with a dead body in the trunk, so maybe someone could get that?"

"Yes, we'll take care of it," Maven said quickly. "Go on."

"Right. Anyway, the werewolf came at me with a knife, and she had a bunch of heavy-duty ziplock bags with her."

"What time was this?" Maven said sharply. She had made the same connection I had—only a lot faster.

"Just after the sun went down, before it was really dark. She said she was early, and her friends were coming to help."

Katia's brow furrowed. I was about to explain, but Maven got there first. "She's trying to frame me for murder."

Chapter 25

I had reached the same conclusion. If whoever had hired the were-wolves just wanted to kill witches, the woman would have attacked in wolf form. Most vampires now carried a small blade to cut, rather than bite, their victims. The baggies suggested the wolf had planned to bleed me to death, then carry the blood away to make it look like a vampire attack. It would appear as though Maven had sent her people into Wyoming to break up the meeting. Violently. As plans go, it was smart as hell—and that scared me.

"All right, Lex," Maven said next. "You've got all the pieces of this thing. Walk us through her plan."

What she was really saying was *convince me you get this.* Katia shot me a look of sympathy, and I took a deep breath. "Okay. Morgan knows there are only three years left before the treaty between you and the witches is over, which means you'll be negotiating a new one soon. You said yourself that you've sort of already started, by grooming the Cheyenne pack to come into the state. That—the weekend pass—gave her a way in. She made sure the werewolves were killed in a big, public way—so there was no chance it *wouldn't* make the news. That sent all the witches in the state to Hazel Pellar's door, and I'm guessing Morgan still has people loyal to her."

I paused, then added, "I also think she got one of them to goad Lily until she used her apex magic." I hadn't wanted to reveal Lily's slip, but

Maven needed to understand the scale of this thing. I wished I could see her face, to gauge if she was upset with Lily, but all she said over the phone was, "Go on."

So I did. "While Hazel was distracted and off-balance, Morgan got the witches to come to Wyoming so she could persuade them that she'd been the victim all along. I think the moving offer is a sham. During and after the meeting, the werewolves were supposed to kill the witches and make it look like a vampire attack, a sentence I never thought I'd say out loud." The Colorado witches were already distrustful of Maven, and anyone who didn't understand vampire politics and resources would find it perfectly believable that Maven would send her people into Wyoming—hell, *I* had believed she could do that, before she'd explained it to me.

"And what would she accomplish by framing me?" Maven's voice was calm, and I figured I was doing okay, but now we were getting to the guessing part.

"If the werewolves had succeeded in killing witches, Morgan would have had someone in Clan Pellar propose a change in leadership in Colorado rather than a move to Wyoming." Morgan wouldn't make the suggestion herself—that might put suspicion on her, or at least make it look like she was taking advantage of the hypothetical murders. But if someone *else* suggested it, and all the witches in Colorado believed it . . .

And they probably would. After all, in their eyes, Maven had already broken the witches' arrangement with her by letting werewolves into the state. They didn't know that Hazel had agreed to the weekend pass in order to save *Morgan's* life.

The whole plan was infuriating, but that was the part that bothered me most. Morgan had backed Hazel into an impossible position, forcing her to choose between professional compromise or her child's life. Hazel had chosen to save Morgan, and her daughter had repaid her by using it against her.

"Good," Maven said, her tone approving. "I think you're correct on all counts. But you have thrown a wrench into her plan, at least for the moment."

Yeah . . . by accident, I thought but did not say. It scared me how close I'd come to leaving the witch meeting without stopping the werewolves. If Heather hadn't chosen to attack early, or if Katia hadn't come out to save me, the outcome could have been very different.

Quinn spoke up. "I don't mean to be a downer, but the last time Morgan made a play, she had a backup plan established and ready—using John to get to Charlie. She's gotta have contingencies."

"I agree, but I don't know what she might be planning," I told him.

"I think perhaps the werewolves are the key to all this," Maven said thoughtfully. "Was the woman who attacked you part of Dunn's pack?"

"No, she wasn't in the files. But I got the distinct impression she was one of Trask's people." I told them how Heather had reacted when I'd brought up Trask's name.

"All right," Maven said. "We need to locate the rest of the Cheyenne pack, starting with Mary and this Keith."

Katia and I exchanged a look, and in the dashboard light I could see that she was thinking the same thing I was. Even if we could find them—and that was a big *if*, since they'd had enough time to be just about anywhere in the three surrounding states—why would we want to piss off the witches even more by bringing werewolves back into this?

"Uh . . . to what end?" I asked Maven, keeping my tone polite. "The clans still hate the werewolves—maybe even more than they did before this mess started."

"True," Maven replied. "But Morgan Pellar is using werewolves, and that changes things. We need allies—or at the very least, we need to make sure our former allies haven't signed up with the enemy."

I thought about that for a moment. Maven had a point—if the Cheyenne wolves were allies, we could use them to help us find the other pack, and if they were secretly our enemies, we needed to know that. My gut feeling was that Mary would never work for Morgan Pellar, under any circumstances. But that was just a hunch. "When we find Mary and Keith, what do you want us to do?"

"Either bring them onboard or get them off the board," she said. I opened my mouth, but she was already adding, "No, I'm not saying you should kill them, if you can avoid it. But if we can't trust them, I don't want them anywhere near my state."

That sounded next to impossible. Mary would want to find Dunn's killer, and if she insisted on getting involved, was there really any way I could stop her? My magic didn't work on them, and I didn't exactly have a silver cage sitting in my basement. How could I possibly keep a couple of werewolves out of a mess I didn't fully understand yet?

I started to say as much, but Katia shot me a look, shaking her head, and I closed my mouth as I realized her meaning. If I asked Maven for specifics, I would have to do whatever she ordered. As long as she was vague, I had wiggle room to get creative.

"All right," I said instead. We would come up with something. "Meanwhile, do you want Katia and me back at the coffee shop?"

"No. Actually, I want you to stay away from here tonight. You too, Quinn."

"Why?" he asked.

"Because whatever Morgan is planning, she'll expect us to be here. We need to be unpredictable."

I agreed, and made plans to meet Quinn at Simon's laboratory-slash-apartment. It was our safest bet, since Simon hadn't moved in until well after Morgan was kicked out of Colorado. He'd kept its location from the rest of the witches—he hadn't wanted them to know he was doing hard-core research for Maven—so Morgan's spies wouldn't know where to find it either.

I gave them our ETA, but before I could hang up, Katia abruptly said, "Maven . . . is it true that little Charlie helped a vampire with Lex's disguise today?"

I shot her a look, but she was pointedly keeping her eyes on the road.

"Yes," Maven answered.

"And both Lex and the vampire were acting on your orders?"

A pause, then: "Yes. Where are you going with this, Katia?"

"Charlie should be paid a consultant's fee," Katia said evenly. "Your current arrangement, to protect Charlie until she is eighteen, does not include her services. And her father now has to pay for the two of them to leave town, even though you are supposed to be protecting them. Charlie deserves compensation."

I sat there with my mouth open, blinking at her. Maven recovered way before I did. "You know, Katia, you're right. I should have thought of it myself. Lex, can you get me John's banking information so I can make a deposit?"

"I—uh—sure. Yes," I sputtered.

When we hung up a moment later, Katia was looking a bit smug. "I didn't even think of that," I admitted.

"That is because of how your mind works," she replied. "You think in terms of service, sacrifice, the greater good. But in the Old World, nobody does anything for free. Maven knows this."

"Huh," was all I could say.

I got the banking information, and Katia and I made a quick stop for food; then we spent the rest of the drive brainstorming about Morgan's possible backup plans. My aunt had led a strange and difficult life—she'd run away from an abusive foster father as a teen, only to become the property of a truly evil vampire pimp named Oskar. Though Katia wasn't as powerful as I was in many respects, she had a gift for pressing vampires, and her job had been to keep the prostitutes calm and complacent. That sounds bad, and it was, but Katia had thought—or maybe just hoped—she was helping them get through a horrible situation.

Oskar was dead now, and Katia had to deal with not just what she'd done, but the fact that she had spent twenty years out of time, trapped in one of the seedy, barbaric pockets of the Old World. Over the last year she'd worked hard to get her GED and put together some sort of life, but she had a unique perspective on things. She could think like a criminal because she'd spent so long serving one.

"Perhaps Morgan will try to kill Hazel," was one of her suggestions. "If she makes it look like a vampire kill, surely the witches will ask her to be in charge."

I shook my head. "It's a good thought, but a) I'm not sure even Morgan is ready to kill her own mother, and b) her whole plan so far has been built on the message that Hazel's been corrupted and is in cahoots with Maven. If the witches believe Maven has completely rejected any peace with them, they really *will* want to leave for Wyoming, and even if she does have the resources, I think Morgan is too arrogant to actually go through with that. She wants what was promised to her: to be witch leader of Colorado."

Katia considered this for a moment. "You seem to understand her very well," she remarked. From someone else, this might have been a dig, but I knew Katia meant it as a simple observation. And, a little bit, as a question to me.

"I understand roots," I replied. "Morgan was born here, and she grew up thinking she'd spend her whole life here, and that she'd eventually inherit a great deal of power."

"Like you?" Katia asked. "If you hadn't joined the army?"

I smiled in the darkness. Katia was always curious about the Luthers. She couldn't quite understand our family dynamic, because she had no frame of reference. "Not really. My family is all here—the Luther part, I mean—but even if I'd gone to college and come back to Boulder, I wouldn't have taken over Luther Shoes. My dad never expected either of us to want the family business. Morgan, on the other hand, has been told her whole life that clan leader is her birthright."

"Then why didn't she wait to inherit the position?"

"Because of me," I admitted. I didn't like to think about it, but Morgan herself had told me that Hazel's decision to allow a boundary witch in her town had been the catalyst for her would-be revolution. "Morgan is of the *all boundary witches need to be destroyed* school of thinking."

"Ah," was all Katia said. She had encountered this attitude plenty of times.

"Still. If it hadn't been me, something else would probably have set her off," I added. "I think Morgan's marriage was falling apart, and her life hadn't turned out like she thought, and she just kind of snapped."

There was another moment of silence in the car while we both thought about that. Finally, I shook my head. "I don't think we're going to figure out what she's planning. I might be able to understand Morgan's reasoning, but she's also good at being unpredictable."

Katia tilted her head for a second, reminding me of Sam. "What?" I asked. "What would you do?"

"I would drive back to Wyoming and kill her," she said quietly. "I know it isn't how you do things, but she nearly killed you before, and she *would* have killed innocents tonight. If she is dead, the problem is solved."

She had hunched her shoulders a little, worried that I would judge her. But I'd had the same thought myself—though I wasn't sure if I'd be able to go through with killing Morgan in cold blood, if for no other reason than because she was my best friends' sister.

"At this point, I'm not sure Morgan's death would be the end of things," I remarked, in a tone that showed I was unoffended by the suggestion. "She's gotten the witches and werewolves so riled up that killing her would make her look like a martyr. And it's not what Lily and Simon would want. Besides," I added, "Maven would have to send someone to Wyoming to do it, and that would break her rules of engagement."

Katia turned to give me a faint smile. "Always the soldier."

We crossed the state line again, lapsing into a comfortable silence. A few minutes later, I felt Katia glance at me, and she said guardedly, "And how is Quinn?"

My aunt had nothing against Quinn personally, but she did have plenty of reason to dislike vampires. I had the distinct impression that she didn't like that I was dating a vampire—but she still made an effort to be polite. "Oh, you know. The same."

She choked out a little laugh at that, which made me happy. Then I thought about our argument the night before. "I don't think he's telling me everything," I admitted. I knew Katia probably wasn't the right person for this conversation, but Lily wasn't available, and I was worried.

"Things about his history?" Katia asked, in the same careful tone.

"No, more like . . . Maven's orders to him. I think something is going on with Maven, something kind of big. Quinn says he doesn't know, but . . ." I shrugged. "Sometimes I get paranoid. He's sworn troth to her, so if Maven really ordered him not to tell me something, he'd have to listen."

Katia nodded. "That is a tricky situation," she ventured. "Probably especially tricky for Quinn. Are you certain that he loves you?"

"Yes," I answered, surprised by the question.

"Then you know that if he could tell you, he would," she said simply.

"True."

She eyed me. "Do you think that can be enough for you?"

"I . . . struggle with it," I confessed. Katia simply nodded, her eyes back on the road.

"What about you?" I asked, trying to keep my voice light. Katia hadn't dated anyone in the year I'd known her. "Any prospects in Albuquerque?"

I couldn't resist a quick sideways glance. My aunt looked surprised. "Me? No. There is . . . there was—someone of interest, but . . . no," she sputtered.

Now it was my turn to raise an eyebrow at her. Katia was squirming in her seat, which was entertaining in itself. "Do not ask me, please," she said. "I had an interest, but it was . . . unrequited. I believe that's the word."

"Okay," I said, but my thoughts were engaged in this interesting new distraction. Katia had a crush? That was so . . . normal of her.

We spent the rest of the drive talking about Charlie and the rest of my Luther family. Katia adored Charlie, and although she found the Luthers a bit sheltered and naive—even for humans—she had enjoyed hanging out with my cousins in the past, and was interested in updates.

As I talked about the people I loved, I found myself really relaxing for the first time since the werewolves had shown up at my door, and I wondered if Katia was doing it on purpose. I decided not to ask.

Chapter 26

Maven owned an apartment building just off Longbow that featured several basement units, including the one where Simon lived. It had started out as sort of his private research lab, but he'd moved in a couple of years earlier, after breaking up with Tracy. I think it was just easier than going through the hassle of finding a new place.

I didn't have my keys with me, but I saw Quinn's sedan in the parking lot and knew he'd beaten us there. He buzzed us through the outer door, and I led Katia into the basement hallway, moving slowly. I didn't expect trouble, but I still had my revolver, and had given Katia my silver knife, just in case.

I knocked gently on the door and Quinn answered it instantly, a smile on his face. The smile twitched a little when he saw me—he'd forgotten about the disguise. "Hey," he said, and over my shoulder: "Hello, Katia. Thanks for helping Lex tonight."

"Of course," she said brusquely, moving past him into the apartment.

"I've got a surprise for you," Quinn said as I followed my aunt into the apartment.

"Oh?"

Just then, I heard a crash from the kitchen, and my hand flew to my sidearm. Katia had her knife out just as quickly. "No, it's just—" Quinn began, but then a familiar figure stepped into the doorway.

"Lily!" I cried.

"I dropped a plate," my friend explained, looking back and forth between the three of us. I had automatically moved forward to hug her, but Lily took a step backward. "Who is this?" she asked Quinn, seeming bewildered.

He laughed.

"It's me, dummy," I said, reaching up and jerking the magnetic nose ring and putty off my face. "I'm in disguise for the witch meeting."

"Oh, *Lex!*" Looking sheepish, she darted forward to embrace me. When she stepped back, she reached out to touch the tip of one of my pigtails. I made a face. "That is *wild,*" she marveled.

"Quinn *could* have warned you I was dressed like this," I said, cutting my eyes to him.

"But then Quinn would have missed the stunned look on her face," Quinn said, grinning.

Lily flung out an arm to smack him, but of course he was too fast for her.

Katia was standing with her hands in her jacket pockets. "Hello, Lily," she said awkwardly. "It's good to see you again."

"Kat! Didn't mean to be rude, I was just kind of thrown." Lily went over and hugged her, too, which prompted a look of surprise from Katia. Lily was the only one who got away with calling her Kat. It hadn't occurred to the rest of us to try.

When Lily pulled back, she touched the braid encircling Katia's head. "I love your hair. Did you do it yourself? Can you teach me?"

Katia actually blushed, and Quinn and I exchanged an amused look. "Yes, and yes," she mumbled.

"By the way," Lily said to me, "Simon is pissed that you haven't been answering the walkie-talkie."

I actually smacked my head with the palm of one hand, like in a cartoon. I'd been so focused on the witches taking away Simon's and

Lily's phones, it hadn't occurred to me that I'd had a way of communicating with the Pellar farm all along. "I'm an idiot." If I had taken one minute to think it through at any point in the last few days, it should have been obvious. "I'll grab it next time I stop at the cabin for sure. I don't suppose you have yours?"

She shook her head, a little embarrassed. "I left in such a hurry, I forgot too. I don't even have my phone, since it was confiscated."

"Yeah, about that . . . how are you here?" I asked, checking my watch. "I'm thrilled to see you, but I thought you were still under house arrest."

Lily's happy expression fell. "Come on, let's sit. I just made tea." She ushered us into the kitchen, where a steaming cup was waiting at her usual spot at the table. We all sat down. "After you called the farm, Simon and I had a talk with Mom." A look of worry flashed over her face.

"How is Hazel holding up?" I asked.

"She's putting on a good show of indignation and strength, but she's my mother. I can tell this has devastated her." Lily's eyes filled with tears, which she swiped at distractedly. "Mom has dealt with a lot of shit, but the double blow of having her loyalty questioned and what Morgan's done . . ." Lily trailed off, not knowing how to finish that thought.

"I'm sorry, Lil," I said quietly. I couldn't imagine how she must be feeling.

She gave me a quick nod and went on. "Anyway, Mom snuck me out. They'll figure it out in the morning when I don't show up to the meeting, but that's part of the plan. Mom thought I should distance myself from the witch congress, as a . . . mmm . . ." She paused to take a sip of tea, thinking over the right word. "Well, a plan B, I guess. She'll tell everyone that I didn't feel well, but Si will get a rumor out there that I disagreed with how she's handling this whole mess."

"So if Morgan convinces everyone to turn against Hazel, they'll have another option," I said.

She gave me a tiny smile that held more sadness than mirth. "I don't like looking like I'm betraying Mom—she hasn't done anything wrong—but this at least gives us some room to maneuver."

Her eyes shone with the tears she was fighting. I reached over and covered her hand with mine for a moment. "It was the right call," I told her.

"That's what I said," Quinn added mildly.

Lily patted my hand absently, then raised her mug to her lips again, both hands clutching it like she needed the warmth.

"What is your mother going to say to the other clans tomorrow?" I asked.

"To stay the course, more or less. She'll tell them the truth about Morgan and the weekend passes, for one thing, and Maven has agreed to restore their apex magic—if they'll finish out the three years in peace."

"Well, that's something," I said, my hopes lifting a little for the first time since the witches had found out about the weekend pass. It was smart of Maven to make a concession, but I didn't know if Hazel would be able to convince the others to go for it, after everything that had happened already. "Did Quinn fill you in on everything else?"

Lily nodded, but her expression was troubled. "Yes."

Something was bothering her, more than just the general situation. "What?" I asked.

She shook her head a little. "I just . . . I can't believe my sister paid werewolves to kill witches. I know it's silly to focus on that one small part, given the enormity of the situation, but . . . still." Her face darkened. "After Dad, and all this baggage between us and the wolves . . . I just can't believe she's so far gone."

"I'm sorry, Lil," I said, feeling like a broken record. I meant it, though. Lily and I had talked about Morgan's actions before. She'd been of the opinion that her sister was . . . well, maybe not redeemable, but Lily'd felt some sympathy for the combination of fear and rage that had driven Morgan to do what she did. This was something else. Hiring werewolves—probably even the same wolves who had helped Trask—to bring down the clan was well past a line she had never imagined Morgan would be capable of crossing.

"Anyway." Lily made a quick swipe under her eyes and looked at me. "There's something else you need to know. You're thinking Morgan killed those werewolves?"

"Yes. She must have snuck into the state. Maybe an illusion spell?"

Lily was shaking her head. "That's the thing, Lex. Morgan literally *can't* come into Colorado. Tonight Mom told us that when we all got our apex magic back, she went to the four corners of the state and set up a ward, using her own blood. Morgan cannot break the circle."

I gaped at her. I knew about protection circles, but only around single buildings. "That's . . . that's possible? A ward that big?"

My friend wrinkled her nose. "For me? No. Not yet, anyway," she said wryly. "But my mom's on another level. She goes back once a year to renew the wards. Remember her trip in September?"

"You said she was going on vacation."

"Yeah, because that's what she told Si and me. Mom didn't want to tell us it was to keep Morgan away. I think . . ." Lily shrugged. "I think she was just too sad that it's come to this."

Quinn and I looked at each other. "Well, we know Morgan had at least three accomplices in Wyoming," I offered. "Maybe she hired those same werewolves to tamper with the car."

Quinn shook his head. "It's possible, but I doubt it. When Maven kicked Trask's people out of the state, she put the fear of God into them. Taking mercenary work in Wyoming is one thing, but I doubt even Trask's old pack members would cross Maven just for a payday."

"What about the Cheyenne pack?" Lily asked. "Could one of them have snuck into the state?"

"It's possible," I admitted. "I looked through the information she collected on the pack, but nothing really jumped out at me. That's why Maven wants us to find Mary and Keith. Hopefully they'll have a way to get in touch with the rest of the pack, and we can start eliminating suspects."

Katia was listening to all this very attentively, like she was waiting for a chance to be useful. "Morgan may also have a spy in the witch clan," she suggested.

Lily looked back and forth between us, her expression mournful. "You think someone else in our clan betrayed Mom?"

"I honestly don't know," I told her. "There were a bunch of Clan Pellar witches at Morgan's little meeting."

She sighed. "That part doesn't surprise me, all things considered. Si said he told you about how the younger witches have been frustrated. I don't want to think they'd actually work for Morgan, though."

She looked uncertain, and I felt a rush of sympathy. Lily had grown up with those witches, kind of like me and my cousins. Even if it hadn't been her own mother being accused, this had to feel like a betrayal.

"Well, what exactly did the accomplice need to do?" Katia asked, pragmatic as usual. "How much involvement are we talking about?"

I thought about it, my eyes unfocused on the ceiling. I was picking up habits from Maven. "Go out on the dunes and shoot Matt and Cammie with silver bullets. Bury them in the sand—that would require some strength. Then, while we were out searching the dunes, sabotage Dunn's car so the doors wouldn't open from the inside."

"And wait on the bridge to ram his vehicle into the water," Quinn added.

I nodded. "Plus, distribute the flyers at Hazel's house—although, honestly, that could have been someone else."

"I wouldn't be surprised if it was," Lily put in. "*That* was almost certainly a witch, but they might not have known where the flyers originated."

"Okay, so the murders of the Ventimiglias and Dunn," I summarized. "Does all of that sound like something a witch could do?"

Lily shrugged. "Everything except the car. It's too . . . surgical? There are hexes that will disable a vehicle entirely, but I've never heard of a spell that can alter one small interior mechanism and leave everything else functional."

"It sounds more like someone experienced with cars arranged that," Quinn agreed. "That could be anyone."

"Finn Barlow, the newest member of Dunn's pack, trained as a mechanic in the marines," I offered, remembering the file I'd read. "That's not really proof, though."

"It's means," Quinn pointed out, brightening a little. "Now we just need motive and opportunity."

"Which will be really challenging, since we have no idea where the werewolves are," I grumbled.

"There's something else," Katia said suddenly, looking over at me with sudden fierceness. "Did any of the werewolves actually *see* their murderer?"

It was a strange question, but I thought it through and shook my head. "Matt and Cammie were killed from some distance, and their attacker probably wore lots of layers to disguise their scent, which would make them hard to identify." Hell, Simon and I had been unrecognizable out on the dunes, and we hadn't even tried to hide our identities. "And Dunn's car was tampered with while he was out on the dunes with us. Why do you ask?"

Katia folded her hands in front of her. "I think perhaps the killer knew you would get involved," she said to me, looking uncomfortable. "Which points back to someone in Colorado. A witch."

"Wait, what do you mean?" Lily asked. "Why do you think the killer knew about Lex?"

"Because if any of the three victims had seen their murderer," Katia said, gesturing at me, "Lex could just bring them back and ask who killed them."

Chapter 27

Whoa.

When Simon and Lily had first explained boundary magic to me, they had mentioned that raising the dead was possible. Since then, though, we'd rarely discussed it, much less considered it as an option.

Quinn, Lily, and I all shifted a little. The whole idea of raising the dead was just . . . unnerving. After an awkward silence, Lily ventured, "That's . . . that's really possible?"

Katia looked surprised. "Of course. My mother's people talked about it sometimes. I had a great-aunt who would raise people for money, so their loved ones could say goodbye." She shrugged. "I am not strong enough to do it myself, at least not without supplies and several days of preparation. But Lex is."

"Wouldn't she have to sacrifice another person to do it?" Quinn asked. "Like with Simon?"

That was how I'd saved Simon's life. I'd stolen the life force from a very bad man and pushed it into my friend. I hadn't really understood what I was doing, though—and besides, the guy had already been dying. I didn't lose sleep over it.

"If she wanted the victim to *stay* alive, yes. That, I would not recommend," she added, looking at me. "It would draw too much attention.

But if she simply wanted to have a conversation with the victim, she could sacrifice an animal. Chickens are popular."

Lily looked disgusted, and I suddenly wanted to throw up. I was a vegetarian, for crying out loud. I didn't want to personally hand-murder an animal.

I had no idea what to say, but luckily Katia added, "Anyway. It doesn't matter, if none of the dead saw their killer. I'm simply suggesting that whoever killed them knew that a powerful boundary witch would get involved."

"Morgan knows what Lex is," Lily said thoughtfully, "but none of us ever learned all that much about boundary magic. Our parents kept it from us."

"We don't know where Morgan has been or what she's been doing," Quinn reminded us. "Maven's people lost track of her eighteen months ago. That's plenty of time to do research."

"And make plans." Lily looked glum.

I sighed. "Okay, one thing at a time. We need to find Mary and Keith." I shifted in my seat, and was instantly reminded of the restricting skirt. "And I need to get the hell out of this outfit," I added.

Quinn pointed to a familiar duffel bag sitting on the carpet where the dining area turned into the small living room. "I brought you a change of clothes, your cell phone, and your keys."

"I love you," I told him with great sincerity. "Did you bring my bloodstone?"

He winced. "Sorry; didn't think of it."

"Wait, you brought keys?" Lily brightened. "You said those were-wolves stole your car, right?" I nodded. When she'd stolen my car, Mary had at least had the decency to use the spare key, which I'd left on a convenient hook near the garage door. "If you have your key, like an actual physical key that fits into the ignition, I can find it for you. It's a simple finding spell, like-for-like magic."

My car was an ancient Subaru. It had never heard of LoJack or key fobs. "Lily," I said solemnly. "I love you too."

"Well, that cheapens it," Quinn grumbled.

Lily got to work on her spell, and I went into the bathroom, where I foolishly glanced in the mirror. My disguise was a mess, with makeup smeared around my nose like my face had started to melt. A dark bruise had already appeared on my cheekbone where Heather had hit me, and the bump on my forehead was visible through the smudged concealer.

I popped out the brown contact lenses, yanked the rubber bands off the damned pigtails, and got in the shower. When I was finally satisfied that I'd shampooed away all the gold hair dye, I dried off and put on the clothes Quinn had brought me—jeans, a simple scoop-neck tee, and a soft flannel shirt with long sleeves. This time, when I checked the mirror, I actually recognized myself, bruises and all.

I went back out to the dining room, where Lily had spread a map of Colorado over the table. Quinn had a laptop open beside it, while Katia was in the kitchen fussing with the tea kettle. "Did you find them?" I asked.

"Yes." Lily looked up at me. "Well, I found your *car*," she corrected herself. "It's just outside Allenspark."

"Really?"

Quinn spun the laptop around so I could see the screen. "It's here," he said, pointing to the words "Longs Peak Campground" on the border of Rocky Mountain National Park.

"Huh." The werewolves had stayed in Colorado, which I hadn't expected. Then again, there were plenty of problems in Wyoming now, too. "Isn't it a little cold for camping?" I asked.

Lily and Quinn exchanged a glance. "We were just talking about that," Quinn said. "Mary's no idiot. She wants us to think they're either at the campground or in the park, and we could lose weeks trying to track them down. But—" He tapped the keys to zoom in, showing me a tiny building about a half mile from the campground. "I think they might be here."

"Mike's Mountain Inn," I read. I glanced back up at Quinn. "Is it even open, this time of year?"

"It's not," he replied, "which is why I think they're there. Mike's does the occasional winter retreat for cross-country skiers, which means they have heat, but their website says the whole place is closed until after the holidays."

"So Mary and Keith could break in and hole up for a while," I mused. Katia came over and set a steaming cup of tea in front of me. She'd added milk, no sugar, the way I like it. I shot her a smile. "Thank you." Then I looked at Lily, whose lips were pursed. "Lil?"

She shrugged. "I'm not totally convinced. I mean, it's basically a guess."

"I know, but it's what I would do," Quinn insisted. "The full moon is coming up. If Mary and Keith are planning to stay there, they'll have great access to the national park when they need to change."

Lily tilted her head, conceding.

"They're scared because their alpha was killed," I reasoned. "It makes sense that they'd try to hide out until this mess blows over."

I couldn't even really blame them. I sort of wished *I* could hole up until everything was solved—but then I thought of Ryan Dunn and the scratches on his windows, and I set my shoulders. "Let's go talk to Mary," I said to Quinn.

Katia wanted to come along and help in case there was trouble, but I pulled her aside and asked her to stay with Lily. "She may end up being the only chance of keeping peace within the witch clans," I said softly. "If I know that, Morgan sure as hell does too. I don't *think* she would kill her own sister, but . . ." I didn't bother to finish the sentence. I didn't need to.

Katia nodded. "All right," she said reluctantly. "I will stay with her."

"You still have that silver knife?"

She gave me an insulted look, and I held up my hands. "I withdraw the question."

I kept my eyes closed for most of the hour-long ride, to avoid dealing with the ghosts that would be lining the highway. We didn't talk much, although now and then I could feel Quinn's eyes on me.

Eventually the Jeep slowed, and Quinn reached over to touch my hand. "There's your car," he said softly, and I opened my eyes to see the Subaru in an empty parking lot. I breathed a sigh of relief—not just for the car, but for the fact that there were no ghosts nearby to distract me. "Any sign of Mary and Keith?" I asked. I was looking, too, but his night vision was better.

"Nope," he said, scanning the darkness. "The campground looks deserted. It's too cold for fragile human bodies." He shot me a grin, trying to break the tension.

"To the motel?"

"Yes."

We decided to drive past the place first and look for signs of occupancy. Quinn drove slowly the whole way from the campground, so we weren't obviously slowing down as we approached the motel.

Mike's Mountain Inn was identical to any number of mom-and-pop motels around the state: a two-story log building in an L shape, with eight rooms on each floor and a big community room on the end where large parties could gather. These kinds of motels had been replaced by big chains in most parts of the country, but they were still viable businesses in Colorado, because they could open and close with the seasons, and because they catered to the kind of people who wouldn't be comfortable in a generic Holiday Inn—what my dad fondly referred to as the three Hs of Colorado: hippies, hunters, and hooligans.

Unfortunately, those were the same kinds of people who often left ghosts, and even without my boundary mindset, I could see four or five translucent shapes moving at the windows. I didn't spot any sign of the living, though. A single streetlight lit the parking lot, more for security than anything else.

"Did you see that?" Quinn asked abruptly, craning his neck to look back as we went past.

"What?"

"In the big room on the end—I saw a lit fireplace."

I turned in my seat to look. I couldn't see anything, but I trusted his enhanced vision. "Let's go check it out."

Ordinarily we would have parked a few blocks away and crept in on foot, but we had no chance of sneaking up on two werewolves. Instead, Quinn did a blatant U-turn and pulled the Jeep up in front of the party room, the headlights beaming inside. Or they would have beamed inside, but the interior windows had been covered with something. Quinn and I exchanged a look and got out of the car.

"Mary?" I called, looking at the building. "It's Lex and Quinn. We just want to talk." I had a hand on my revolver, but kept it in the holster.

One moment Quinn was standing next to me, and the next instant he'd whipped around to face the other direction. "What is it?" I asked, glancing over my shoulder.

"Don't run," he said softly; then the wolf stepped out of the shadows, into the streetlight.

The sandy-brown werewolf was the biggest I'd seen yet, easily reaching my waist. Its teeth were bared, and as it closed in I could hear a low growl from the back of its throat. "Back slowly toward the Jeep," Quinn murmured.

"That's not Mary," I said under my breath. And this wolf was way too big to be Keith. Had Mary and Keith been attacked? Or could they have met up with someone else from their pack?

Quinn's head jerked sideways again, and a second, mostly gray wolf came at us from the direction of the road, snarling softly. Long ropes of saliva dripped from its mouth, and I could see blood on its muzzle. The revolver was already in my hand, but I didn't know who to target first. In seconds the gray wolf would be between us and the Jeep, but the brown wolf was bigger and closer. I pointed the weapon at him. Quinn and I had stopped moving now, but the wolves were advancing on both sides.

"Make a run for the building?" I whispered, but then I caught movement in the corner of my eye and cursed under my breath. "Second floor," I said, and Quinn's eyes jumped to the snow-white wolf prowling along the upper balcony, headed for the stairs. I took an involuntary step backward, bumping into Quinn, and the white wolf crouched and then leaped over the railing toward us.

Chapter 28

The white wolf landed gracefully about four feet away from my shoes. Close enough for me to see green eyes and enormous claws. I aimed the weapon at her, but just in case, I yelled as loud as I could, "*Mary!* I really don't want to shoot this guy!"

The door to the lodge's common room slammed open. I glanced up, expecting Mary, but saw another, equally familiar, face.

"*Stop,*" Tobias called, his hands going out in front of him. "She's a friend!"

The three wolves swung their heads to face him for a moment, then looked back at me. It was eerie, and I didn't put my revolver away just yet. "Tobias?" I said. "What's going on? Where's Mary?"

His attention was focused completely on the wolves. "I know her! She won't hurt you unless you hurt her," he said urgently. "But that gun has silver; you can smell it. Back down, *please.*"

The three wolves' postures shifted as they began to relax. Then, one by one, they turned and trotted back to wherever they'd come from. The white wolf that had leaped from the balcony loped toward the stairs to resume her position, and I realized she faded completely into the white walls on the second story. Smart.

Tobias lowered his arms and grinned at me. He was skinny and on the tall side with an easy smile and college-kid features, though he was probably close to my age. He wore jeans and a flannel shirt that was too cool for the weather, but wolves rarely got cold. "Hey, silver girl. How've you been?"

"Tobias." I holstered the gun and stepped forward, letting him throw his arms around me. Werewolves were into touching. He smelled like woodsmoke and marshmallow, and there was a telltale white smear on his collar. "Were you . . . making s'mores?"

"Yep," he said cheerfully. "Sorry if those guys scared you. That was Finn, Nicolette, and Lindsay. They don't know you yet. We're all a little on edge, and you smell kinda angry."

I probably smelled pretty fucking scared too, but Tobias was too polite to mention it.

Finn had to be the enormous brown wolf. "The gray wolf had blood on her muzzle," I said.

"Nicki? Yeah, we've been going to *town* on the local rabbit population." He gave me a wolfish grin, and I couldn't help but smile back.

"Where's Mary?" I asked.

"Behind the building." He pointed with a thumb. "She was in four legs, doing a scout. She'll be done with her shift soon. You guys want to come in?"

Quinn glanced at me, questioning. I took a deep breath, trying to swallow the rest of my flight-or-fight response, and nodded.

We followed Tobias into the lodge's gathering room, a big space with an open ceiling and faded red carpets that had seen many pairs of rough hiking boots. Benches lined the walls, but the space was dominated by a massive fireplace right in the middle of the room, with a bricks-and-mortar ledge all around it so people could sit and warm up.

There was a person curled up on one of the benches against the wall in the back corner, now sitting up and looking at us sleepily. I recognized them from Maven's files, though it took me a second to remember the right name: Alex.

Keith was asleep on the bench opposite Alex's, right next to the emergency exit, and he didn't even stir despite all the noise. His mouth was wide open, a low snore audible over the crackling fire. I noticed there was a ghost in the same corner, a very faint one.

"You guys want a s'more?" Tobias asked cheerfully. Then he shot an apologetic look at Quinn. "Sorry, dude. Forgot about the vampire thing for a second. Lex? S'more?"

"No thank you." If I was being honest, a s'more sounded great, but I wasn't certain we were out of danger, and I didn't want to be covered in sticky marshmallow goo if there was a fight.

"Hey, how's Sashi?" he asked. "Is she good? Can you say hi for me?"

"Sure. She's—"

At that moment the emergency exit opened—they must have taped it so it could be opened from either side—and Mary prowled into the room in a long-sleeved black dress made of some kind of sweatshirt material. Her hair was disheveled and her feet were bare, but she moved toward us like she was stalking across a dance floor on stilettos. "Lex," she said with a small frown. "How did you find us?"

"Locating spell," I said, crossing my arms. "What the hell, Mary? I tried to protect you, and you stole my fucking car."

Quinn gave me a sideways glance—*you sure you want to do this?*—but I didn't back down. I was pissed, and apparently unable to hide it. Might as well clear the air. "Tell me again about that run-and-hide protocol?"

She abruptly stopped walking, opened her mouth. Closed it again. Then, to my surprise, her shoulders drooped slightly and her eyes went to the floor in front of me. "I'm sorry," she said quietly. "I wasn't lying—there is a protocol—but it involves regrouping at one of our safe locations." She looked around the room. "This is the one our pack used to have in Colorado, years and years ago."

"You could have just told me."

She straightened up. "I wasn't sure who to trust."

"Have I done something to make you think you couldn't trust me?"

Her eyes narrowed. "You mean besides swear loyalty to Maven?"

Walked right into that one. Her voice was sharp, and beside me, Quinn shifted his weight. I could feel Alex's gaze from the corner of the room, but they hadn't risen from the bench.

Tobias, meanwhile, was looking back and forth between Mary and me like a crestfallen puppy. "You guys . . . Lex is here to help." He gave me a hopeful look. "Right?" Before I could answer, he added to Mary, "That's what she does. She helps."

I blinked at Tobias for a second. His dedication to Sashi wasn't surprising, but I hadn't realized he thought so highly of me.

"Why don't we all sit?" Quinn suggested. "It's been a long day."

It wasn't like he got tired from standing, but I understood the gesture and allowed Mary to lead us to the empty benches at the opposite side of the room from Alex and Keith. She probably wanted to let them rest, but it came off as a small gesture of trust. Or maybe just a sign that she didn't find me physically threatening in the least.

"Why are you here?" Mary said once we were settled. "To kick us out of the state?"

I glanced at Quinn, who gave a tiny nod, his cue that I should do the talking. I was less affiliated with Maven than he was, and he could always step in and be the bad cop if I was too permissive. "Believe it or not," I said to Mary, "we don't currently give a shit about you guys hiding out here. Bigger fish and all that."

Mary glanced at Quinn, then back to me as if she couldn't quite believe it. "What do you mean?"

"Do you know a werewolf named Heather?" I asked. "White, about my height, short black hair, unnecessarily violent?"

Mary shook her head, but Tobias spoke up. "Heather Macrone," he said, shrinking into himself a little. "She was one of Trask's favorites."

Which meant she'd probably participated in tormenting Tobias. Mary immediately wrapped an arm around the taller man, which should have looked clumsy, but he leaned into her. "Tobias," I said quietly, "I killed her. She's very, very dead." I didn't feel the need to bring up Katia. I didn't think any of these werewolves knew about her, and I preferred to keep her off their radar just in case.

Tobias straightened up a little, his eyebrows lifting. "Really?"

"I promise," I assured him.

"Where was this?" Mary asked.

"In Wyoming."

"Yellowstone?" she asked, searching my face. "There are a bunch of asshole wolves at Yellowstone. We steer clear of them."

"No, this was just outside Tie Siding."

Mary's face twisted into a snarl. "Shit. That's supposed to be our territory."

"Tobias," I said, focusing on him, "do you have any idea what Heather has been doing since the war?"

He shook his head. "I was . . . away."

At the wolf preserve. I'd figured as much.

"What's all this about?" Mary asked me.

"Morgan Pellar is trying to use werewolves to start another war, this time between the witches and Maven."

Mary stood up so fast that Tobias had to put his hand on the bench to keep from being knocked over. *"What?"*

Chapter 29

I told them about the witch meeting, leaving out only Katia's involvement. This wasn't her fight, and I didn't want my aunt to get any blowback if Finn or one of the others really was involved somehow. During my explanation Alex came over to our side of the room and took a spot on the bench next to Mary.

When I was finished, Mary gave me a hard look. "What is it you want from us?" she demanded.

I glanced at Quinn. His expression was impassive to anyone but me. "We want your help," I told Mary. "Again."

She scowled at me. "Because the other side has werewolves, so you figure you need some too?"

"No." Well, kind of. "Look, we could use some help, period, and it wouldn't hurt to show the witches that not all werewolves are . . . um . . ."

I searched for a diplomatic word, but Tobias broke in with a grin. "Psycho killers," he said cheerfully, sending an impish grin toward Mary. Her scowl lightened a little but didn't go away.

"Well, yeah," I admitted. "Besides, the bad guys killed three of your people. Helping us comes with the great side benefit of revenge."

She looked dubious. "But there's no guarantee that you'll figure out who actually did this. You really want us to risk our lives for a PR campaign and the *possibility* of some payback?"

"And territory in Colorado," Quinn said softly.

Immediately, every conscious werewolf in the room turned their complete attention to him. Both Alex and Tobias had longing expressions. "What makes you think we'd even want that?" Mary demanded. At least *she* had a poker face.

"Because that's what Dunn was working on with Maven," Quinn said. "That was his long-term plan."

Alex, who had been quiet through my entire explanation, now snorted loudly. "I can assure you that being subservient to a vampire was *not* one of Ryan Dunn's plans."

"No one said anything about being subservient," I told them. Before Alex could answer, I turned back to Mary. "Colorado is a big state. When the treaty is up in three years, werewolves are going to come back in—"

"Unless Maven just kills everyone who tries," Alex snapped.

I blinked, looking back and forth between Mary and Alex. "She wouldn't—"

Alex interrupted with a harsh laugh. "Of *course* she would. Do you know how many wolves she killed during the war? Do you think *all* of them were loyal to Trask?"

The question was rhetorical, of course, but I still didn't know how to respond. I'd spent only a few minutes with Alex's file: they weren't a particularly strong werewolf, and had turned down all opportunities for leadership. They didn't seem to have any motive for killing Dunn or the Ventimiglias.

"We all lost friends," Alex said through clenched teeth. "Good people who were too powerless to stand up to Trask."

My eyes slid to Tobias, who was making himself as small as possible on the bench. He and Alex had both lived in Colorado before the war, although only Tobias had been part of Trask's pack. "Is that true?" I asked softly.

Tobias cringed even more, as if to hide from my words. "Yes. When Trask began to absorb the other Colorado packs, I wasn't the only one who opposed it. I was too weak to resist him, but there were lots of Colorado wolves who ran away to avoid being recruited. They hid out in the mountains . . ." He trailed off, looking miserable.

Alex lifted their chin. "Some of us ran north or west, leaving behind everything and everyone we knew. And we were *lucky*. The ones who stayed in hiding were . . ." They waved a hand, struggling to think of a word.

"Caught in the cross fire," Mary finished gently. She put her arm around Tobias again, letting him lean into her again.

Quinn and I looked at each other, and I caught his tiny headshake. He hadn't known about this either. Quinn had moved to Colorado after the war was over.

Now came the part I didn't want to do, but Maven needed to know if this pack was involved. I looked straight at Alex. "It sounds like you have a pretty good motive to stir up shit in Colorado."

Alex's eyes bulged with outrage. "You think I . . . you think I could hurt *Dunn*?"

Mary put a hand on their shoulder, and Alex seemed to calm under her touch. To me, she said in a surprisingly controlled voice, "We've been through this. My pack would not hurt our own. Certainly not out of revenge for a twenty-year-old crime."

I realized, watching Alex calming down from their anger, that Mary was right: the werewolves ran hot, and struggled to control their impulses. If Alex had wanted to attack Maven, they wouldn't do it after all this time, and probably not in such a roundabout way.

"I believe you," I said to them. "But Colorado was your home once. You could come back. Things could be different."

Alex glared at me. "Until they're not. Until Maven decides we're an inconvenience after all."

"And do you speak for the whole pack?" I asked.

It was like I'd flipped a switch. Alex flinched back, and their eyes and shoulders immediately turned toward Mary. Interesting. "Do you?" I asked her.

Mary nibbled on her lower lip. "We haven't really figured that out yet."

There was the tiniest sound from the back of Tobias's throat. If I could hear it, with my lousy human hearing, everyone else in the room certainly could too. I raised an eyebrow at him. "Was that . . . a *snort*?"

His eyes darted to Mary, then back to me. "No," he squeaked.

I couldn't help but smile at him. "Tobias? You snorted, buddy. What's up?"

"It's just . . ." Another desperate look at Mary. "Can't you feel it?" he said to her, his voice pleading.

She turned her head to frown at him. "Feel what?"

Tobias squirmed, and I understood he couldn't challenge her, even in this. "Mary," I said gently. "You're the alpha."

"What? No, I'm not." But she didn't sound convincing, and she wouldn't meet my eyes.

"Then who is? Alex? Barlow?"

Now she looked at me, her eyes narrowing. "No."

I pushed her. "Keith, then? Maybe one of those new college kids?"

"Shut up," she snapped at me.

If only I could. "Mary . . . ordinarily, I would be happy to let the pack mourn and make adjustments in your own time. But Colorado is under attack. Morgan Pellar is using werewolves to kill witches in Wyoming."

"Leave us alone," she snarled, standing up. On either side of her, Alex and Tobias visibly flinched. "We haven't even been able to bury our dead. Dunn—"

"Is *gone*." I knew I was probably pushing too hard, but I was so tired, and sick of Old World politics. I stood up, putting myself toe to toe with Mary. "And you're going to have to step up and pick a side."

"Fuck you!" Mary's hands were clenched into fists, and her face was twisted up with grief and rage. Tears began coursing down her cheeks, and I took an involuntary step back. She wasn't acting like someone who was avoiding responsibility, or a lieutenant struggling with a decision.

My confusion must have been obvious, because she began, "Ryan . . . he . . ." But Mary choked on the words.

"*Oh,*" I said, finally understanding. "Oh, Mary, I'm so sorry."

Alex tilted their head in confusion, eyes flashing between us. "What?"

I pressed my lips together, but I saw Mary decide to answer. "I loved him," she said, her eyes still on me. "Ryan. I was in love with him."

Alex's eyes widened, but Tobias looked like he wanted to disappear into the bench. He had known, or at least suspected, Mary's feelings.

Alex, with all the tact of blunt people everywhere, blurted, "Did he love you back?"

Mary sank down onto the very edge of the bench, folding her arms across her stomach. "I don't know. I think . . . we were . . . we were talking."

I studied her for a moment, and even I could see she was on the verge of a breakdown in front of the pack.

This was my fault. I had cornered a werewolf when she was already vulnerable. The fact that I hadn't known how she felt about Dunn wasn't really an excuse. If anything, it made my actions worse, because I'd just forced her to reveal her deepest feelings.

"I'm sorry, Mary," I said quietly, standing up and heading toward the door. "Come on, Quinn."

"We're not finished here," he said, a question on his face. If we couldn't recruit the werewolves, our orders were to run them out of town.

"Yes, we are," I told him.

He got up and followed me. At the door, I paused and turned around. "Our plate is pretty full tonight," I said to Mary. "We probably won't get around to telling Maven your location until tomorrow."

I felt Quinn's eyes on me. That was a direct violation of what she'd told us to do with the werewolves, and he knew it—but, God love him, he didn't correct me. He nodded to show me he was willing to back my play.

Mary brushed at her cheeks and squared her shoulders. "Sorry I stole your car," she said in a subdued voice.

"Sorry I pushed you." I hesitated for three heartbeats, trying to decide if I should take one last shot at persuading her to help—but I'd burned that bridge, at least for tonight. "You've got my number," I said at last. "Feel free to use it."

Quinn drove back to the parking lot and pulled up to my car. The temperature had dropped down into the teens, and knowing the slow response time of the Subaru's heater, I wished I'd brought my gloves and hat.

I started to climb out of the Jeep, but he laid a hand gently on my forearm. "We might not be able to find them again," he said, looking troubled.

"I know. And I know I put you in a bad spot. But I don't have it in me to rub Mary's face in her grief."

He looked over his shoulder, in the direction of Mike's Mountain Lodge, debating. Quinn had sworn an oath to Maven; it was practically fighting his nature to go against her wishes.

"Mary is not working for Morgan," I said, certain now. "And they're hurting. If Maven wants us to come back tomorrow night and throw them out of the state, I'm game. But . . . please."

My voice cracked at the end, and he reached over to touch my face, drawing me closer for a kiss. Afterward, he rested his forehead against mine. It hurt a little—we'd both forgotten about the bump from my ill-advised head-butt—but I didn't care.

"I think we can probably consider them off the board," Quinn said softly.

I smiled, and in that moment I realized that in all the ways that really mattered, I trusted him.

We had to drive back separately but agreed to meet up at Magic Beans. Back in my Subaru, finally, I turned the radio off and drove home slowly, doing my best to keep my eyes on the road just in front of my headlights, ignoring the remnants that occasionally appeared in my line of vision. My cheek and forehead still ached, and I was exhausted, but there was no chance of my falling asleep at the wheel. I was too busy berating myself for how I'd handled things with Mary.

I'd tried to manipulate her, like the vampires and many of the witches did, and it had backfired. And now I'd defied Maven's order. "What a spectacular fuckup," I said out loud. Part of me sort of hoped Sam's voice would chime in, even just to agree with me, but she stayed out of it. She probably didn't want to kick me while I was down.

When I reached the outskirts of Boulder, I tried to rehearse what I was going to say to Maven. I really had nothing. We hadn't learned anything about Morgan's contingency plans, and I'd failed to recruit more help.

As I pulled into a parking spot on the street near Magic Beans, I tried Katia's cell, just to check on her and Lily, but the call went straight to voice mail. That felt off to me—Katia was too security-conscious to let her battery die, and I knew she got reception at Simon's place.

I got out of the Subaru and met Quinn at the back of the building. "I can't reach—" I began, but then my phone buzzed in my hand. "Oh, hang on." I checked the screen, expecting to see Katia's name—but it was an incoming video call from Charlie. She probably thought I was home and wanted to see the new foster dog. It was past 11:30, but this wouldn't be the first time she'd woken up in the night and decided she'd rather chat with me than be put back to bed by John. Served him right for teaching her how to use FaceTime. I smiled to myself, then glanced up at Quinn. "Let me just say goodnight to her, okay?"

"Of course. I'll meet you inside."

He turned and began walking to the coffee shop's back entrance— he had a key—while I answered the phone. "Hi, Charlie-bug . . ." My voice faltered, and I squinted down at the screen. The call had connected, but the video feed was nearly black, much darker than Charlie's room with its twin night-lights should be. There was just enough illumination for me to make out the outline of her face, but not her expression. "Charlie, where are you?"

In my peripheral vision I saw that Quinn had paused, turning back around, but my eyes were fixed on the screen. "Aunt Lex," came her voice in a trembling whisper. "There's someone bad here."

All my muscles tensed, like I might somehow teleport myself to her if I tried hard enough. Quinn was suddenly by my side. "Charlie, baby, what happened? Where's your daddy?"

"He's downstairs with—with—with—" I couldn't see her face, but the tears were obvious in her voice.

"It's okay, baby. Take a real deep breath for me and try again."

She sucked in a breath, pushed it out hard. "With Clara," she finished. "There was fighting."

I struggled to keep my face calm. "Daddy and Clara were fighting?"

"No! Bad guys hurt Clara!" Her voice had risen to a wail.

"Hang on, baby." I looked at Quinn, who nodded grimly, pointing toward the Jeep. I ran around to the passenger side and climbed in. Juggling the phone while I buckled my seat belt, I said very softly, "Charlie, Quinn and I are coming *right now*. Are you hiding?"

The outline of her head moved in a nod. "In the basket," she whispered. "In my room."

I knew exactly what she was talking about—the wicker hamper was a favorite choice during hide-and-seek. "Okay, baby, that's a great spot. And you're doing exactly the right thing. That's just what your daddy would want you to be doing."

"Will you be here soon?"

The pleading in her voice wrenched at my heart. "Of course I will. I'm going to be there in—" I looked stupidly at Quinn, as though I hadn't made the drive between Magic Beans and John's house a hundred times. He mouthed *less than five*. "Five minutes. Just five short minutes, okay? And I'm going to stay right here on your screen until I get there . . . but let's be real quiet so nobody knows where you're hiding."

A sniffle. "'Kay."

And so I sat there staring at the nearly dark screen, trying to look reassuring instead of terrified and guilt stricken. I had told John they would be safe until the morning. I'd known Morgan would move on to another plan, but since *she* couldn't come into Colorado it hadn't occurred to me that John and Charlie were at risk. Stupid—I'd been so *stupid*.

I braced my arm for when Quinn made wild, sharp turns with the Jeep, but I didn't put the phone down or look away from the screen until the tires screeched and we lurched to a stop. "I'm coming, baby," I promised.

Chapter 30

I bolted out of the car, but Quinn was already out and around the hood before I made it to the sidewalk. "Don't wait for me," I told him, and he blurred away without another word. I'd never seen him move that fast.

I ran up the sidewalk to the house, revolver in one hand. I had no idea what to expect, but even after all this time, the sidearm felt more comfortable to me than the shredder, so I went with it.

The foyer was dark, but before I could pick a direction, I heard Quinn's voice calling urgently from the living room. "Lex, in here."

I ran into the room—and into a horror movie. Huge splotches of bright red blood had been sprayed on every surface, and three dead bodies lay discarded on the carpet: two men and a woman, none of whom I recognized.

But I barely glanced at any of that. Clara and John were both lying spread-eagled on the floor, and John's eyes were closed. They were covered in blood, and bloody footsteps led out of the room.

Ripping off my winter coat, I dropped to my knees beside John, half-afraid to touch him. "Is he—"

"He's alive," Quinn reported. "But his pulse is fading quickly."

There was so much blood that I couldn't find the wound. My fingers danced over his blood-soaked T-shirt, looking for a tear, until I found the gouge on his right forearm, a long, deep gash made by something sharp. It was still pumping blood. I hissed and clamped my hands on it, sealing the wound as best I could. "Clara?" I said to Quinn.

"She's not decaying," he pointed out, which I should have thought of. Her face was pale and waxy, and she wasn't even blinking as far as I could tell, but if she were truly dead, her body would be reverting. There was a heavy iron poker on the floor next to her, blood spreading out on the carpet around it.

"Charlie!" I shouted toward the ceiling. "Are you okay?"

Her voice came back after a moment, but I had to strain to hear her. "I'm fine. Can I get out now?" She was still in the hamper.

There was no way I could let her see this carnage. I looked at Quinn. "Anyone else in the house?"

He shook his head. To Charlie, I called, "Yes, but stay in your room 'til I'm sure it's safe!"

I turned my attention back to my brother-in-law, feeling his blood seeping out through my fingers. Quinn was bent over him too, and I could see his nostrils flaring, his jaw clamped shut. *Shit.* Being around this much blood would be hard for him, and I couldn't deal with that right now. "Call an ambulance, then follow the blood trail," I barked at him. "I'll handle this."

"Fine." Quinn disappeared, and it felt like most of my calm went with him. This wasn't enough; I wasn't doing *enough.*

"Sam, I could really use an idea right now," I muttered, looking at John's terrifying pallor.

For once, her reply was immediate. *I can't help you with this.* Her voice was anguished and worried, and it made me want to cry, because now there was nobody left to help and I still didn't know what to do.

Then, without really thinking about it, I fell into my magic.

Like all humans', John's living essence usually looked to me like a warm blue glow in thermal-imaging goggles—but tonight was different. The blue was giving way to a dull yellow-gold that I recognized as death-essence. Soon it would start to seep out between my fingers, just like the blood; then John would die.

Panic clawed at me, but I fought to stay calm, to think. What did I have? What could I do? In that moment I would have given anything for thaumaturge magic, or even a trades witch spell that could close the wound or get help here faster. All I had was my stupid *useless* boundary magic, made for death. *I* was made for death.

"Think, you idiot," I mumbled. Magic. I'd used boundary magic to save Simon . . . but it had worked only because I'd pushed another man's life essence into him. This was a totally different situation.

Still in my mindset, I tried to focus on the part of his life essence that corresponded with the wound—which meant I was watching when it ruptured and began to leak yellow death-essence in earnest.

"No no no no . . ." I pressed down even harder with my hands, hoping to close the fissure, but magic didn't work that way. I couldn't use my real hands to interact with what I could see only in my boundary mindset.

Real hands. That gave me an idea, and I visualized ghostly blue hands coming from my griffin tattoos; the same way I usually performed boundary magic. I'd spent so many months using my magic only to lay ghosts that I felt rusty, but I had done this sort of thing before, hadn't I?

Not for fine motor work, though. When I tried to pinch off the leak, my ghost-fingers were too big and thick for such a delicate maneuver. And John was losing blood quickly.

Blood.

My blood was filled with boundary magic; boundary magic wouldn't allow death. Would that work? It was the only idea I had, so I released my mindset, my regular vision returning. I reached for the metal poker, but then I spotted the handle of a small penknife under John's right arm and grabbed that instead. It was already covered in blood, and my fingers were slippery, but I managed to cut the base of my right hand, dragging the blade through the meat harder than I'd intended. Then I pressed it to John's injury.

After a few seconds, I dropped into my boundary mindset again to look at John's death-essence. It wasn't leaking anymore, but it didn't look any better either. I held my hand to the wound, praying as hard as I could, pressing that prayer into John. *Live, live, live, live.*

I don't know how much time passed like this, but the next thing I was aware of was Quinn's voice at my ear. "That's enough. Lex, that's *enough.*"

I felt him pulling my hand away from John, then tying the wound up tight with a ripped piece of fabric. I had no idea where he'd gotten it. I was light-headed, but I managed to focus on his face. There was a tiny spatter of blood near his chin, and his skin was a little flushed. He must have fed—vampires could get sustenance from witch or werewolf blood, although they couldn't press them—because the sight and smell of my blood didn't seem to bother him. "Did you find more of them?"

He nodded, grim. "Two werewolves and a witch. There were six total. Clara took out three of them."

So the dead bodies on the floor had probably been werewolves too. Vampires would have decayed, and witches or humans would have been easy for Clara to dispatch. "Did you kill them?" I asked, my voice distant.

"Only the werewolves. The witch is still alive, for now." He cocked his head. "The ambulance is almost here."

A second later, I heard the siren too. "The EMTs—" I began.

"I'll press them," Quinn said firmly. "You should go check on Charlie."

"Right . . . right."

"Maybe take off your flannel shirt?"

I looked down at myself and saw the blood that coated my sleeves and the front of my shirt. "Right."

I tried to unbutton my shirt, but my hands were clumsy with the bandage, and eventually Quinn reached over and did it for me. "Thanks," I mumbled, checking the rest of me. My T-shirt looked okay, and the few smears on my jeans could have been any number of things. Good enough. I staggered to my feet and headed for the stairs. There were no bloody footprints on the wooden steps, and I realized with remote satisfaction that no one had come close to Charlie.

I traipsed up the steps and down the hallway toward Charlie's room, my head spinning. Morgan had sent people after Charlie. *Morgan had sent people after Charlie.* Now that the danger was more or less stalled, I felt the anger building inside me, and my steps quickened. I would *kill* Morgan for this.

Then I reached Charlie's doorway, and the dark cloud of rage and fear began to lift. Charlie had that effect on me—or perhaps Charlie being a null had that effect on my boundary magic.

Either way, I pushed open the door and saw my niece, fast asleep on her stomach, on the rug in front of the hamper. Her arm was wrapped around her favorite stuffy, the teddy bear that Sam had given her when she was born. I felt my whole body go slack with relief.

Since Charlie was all right, I took a moment in the hall bathroom to scrub my hands and forearms free of John's blood, working carefully around the makeshift bandage.

When I went back into Charlie's room, the ambulance had parked outside, and red and white lights were pounding through her windows and reflecting off the ceiling. As I got close to her, I saw that the short, hard-foam sword that she used to play pirates was lying next to her other arm. My breath caught in my throat.

She was *four*, goddammit.

Her eyelids fluttered open. "Hi, Charlie-bug," I whispered, not sure if she was really awake. I went and sat down next to her.

"Aunt Lex." Abandoning the sword, she got a firm grip on her bear and crawled into my lap. The siren cut off, though I could still see the flashes of red light playing on Charlie's ceiling. "Is Daddy okay?"

"He got hurt, baby, but I think he'll be okay," I told her, praying I wasn't lying. I pulled her into a hug with my heart against hers, the same way I carried her to bed sometimes. "He's going to go to the hospital. We'll visit him tomorrow."

She smiled and nestled her head on my shoulder. "'Kay." Her eyes closed again.

I'm not sure how long we sat there, with Charlie fast asleep and me vacillating between agonizing over John's status and marveling at my niece's perfection. It had been such a close call. If Charlie hadn't called me . . .

From downstairs, I could make out the sound of urgent voices and some running around, but in my cowardice, I didn't go check on my brother-in-law. Some stupid, superstitious part of me imagined going down the stairs just in time to see the life leave his body. Eventually the lights began moving away from the house, and the siren started up again, which I took as a good sign—lights and sirens weren't necessary for dead people.

A moment later, Quinn appeared in the doorway, holding a small backpack. He looked at us for a moment and smiled. "She's getting so big."

Relief blossomed in me. He wouldn't look at me like that if John were dead. Still, I said, "He's alive?"

Quinn nodded. "The paramedics don't really know how. They said his heart should have stopped, with that much blood loss. They're doing a transfusion right away."

"Is he—" My voice caught, but Quinn understood.

"I don't know, sweetheart," he said softly. "The EMTs couldn't believe he made it this far. Whatever you did to him . . . he's got a chance."

I nodded, feeling numb. Quinn came over and sat down next to me, dropping the backpack so he could smooth Charlie's hair. If John died, I would become her legal guardian, and I wasn't ready for that. There was no way I could take care of her and still work for Maven, which meant . . . what? Maven could start using Charlie for Old World stuff? No. I'd have to give her to my parents or to one of my cousins to raise, and I wouldn't be able to tell them about what Charlie was. My family would get pulled further into all this, and they wouldn't be able to defend themselves.

I should never have agreed to guardianship, but I'd always assumed John would outlive me.

Quinn reached for the backpack and I realized dimly that it was the heavy-duty first aid kit we kept in the Jeep. He gently took my wounded hand, peeling back the bloodied scrap of cloth still wrapped around it. "This needs stitches," he said quietly.

I shook my head. "Just do the glue."

Our first aid kid was serious; it included some of the skin adhesive ER docs used on small wounds, similar to Super Glue. Quinn uncapped the bottle and began sealing my wound.

Hot tears started to slide down my face. "I told John they could wait until tomorrow to leave," I whispered. "I said it was safe."

Quinn didn't tell me it wasn't my fault. He knew me too well, and he'd been a soldier once too. You made your best call in the moment, and you took responsibility if it fell apart. He just finished gluing the wound and kissed my forehead. "Don't worry," he said, very calmly. "We're going to destroy her for this."

See? He *did* know me.

While Quinn rebandaged my hand, I leaned back against the wall and looked down at the sleeping little girl cuddled against my chest. I would have to take her somewhere safe—my first thought, of course, was my family. I tried to remember if John had introduced anyone else in my family to Morgan when they'd dated. Could she know where the others lived? Could I take that risk?

"Katia," I said, my brain finally beginning to work again. Charlie knew Katia; they'd spent time together before my aunt moved south. "Katia can take Charlie to a hotel tonight. I won't let her tell me where they're going. But John . . ." My voice faltered. Half of me wanted to be at his hospital bed, waiting to be there when he woke up. After all, he'd done it for me.

The other half was ready to tear out Morgan's insides.

"You'll need to call your family," Quinn said. "We'll come up with a story. I can arrange to have the house cleaned—" His voice broke off for a second, and I remembered that his usual cleaning team was a bunch of Hazel's witches. Maven paid them—very well—to get rid of bloodstains when necessary, but I doubted they'd be working for him tonight.

He shrugged. "We'll figure it out. Right now, we need to get Charlie safe and to get this witch talking."

"Right." I perked up a little. Nothing lifts your spirits quite like remembering you have a hostage. I figured Quinn had come up with a way to restrain her, but I didn't need the details just yet.

There was so much to do. I rested my cheek lightly on Charlie's head, wishing I could just stay right there with her. My injured hand ached, but I didn't want to move. "She fell asleep with her sword," I told Quinn.

"Well, of course she did." He grinned, wide and sweet. "She's yours, isn't she?"

Then I began to cry in earnest.

Chapter 31

When I was sure I could talk without sobbing, I called my parents, who still kept a landline next to the bed in case there was an emergency in the night.

Unfortunately, my mother, the eternal worrier, answered first. I briefly ran through the story Quinn and I had concocted and asked if she and my father would go to the hospital to be with John. She agreed, of course—I could already hear them hurrying around in the background—and even offered to call John's mother, Blossom. My mother knew I was intimidated by the old woman, and wanted to spare me the conversation. That small gesture almost made me cry again.

After I hung up, Quinn offered to carry Charlie downstairs for me, but I declined—less because I wanted to prove I was strong enough to do it myself, and more because I wanted the simple reassurance of her weight in my arms as long as I could have it.

So Quinn carried the teddy bear down the stairs ahead of us, and I followed slowly, checking each step for toys before I put my foot down. I felt like I was carrying delicate china.

We rounded the corner into the living room, and I stopped short. A young woman stood near Clara, surveying the carnage. She faced away from us, wearing black pants and a bland gray coat, her hands tucked into the coat pockets. I instantly shifted Charlie so I could reach for the revolver. I had it halfway up before the woman turned, and I realized with a shock that it was Maven. Maven with brown hair and conservative horn-rimmed glasses with a slight yellowish tint.

"Whoa," I mumbled, replacing the revolver in its holster. "Uh . . . hi," I added, hearing how dumb it sounded. I'd seen Maven away from Magic Beans only a handful of times, and although I knew she wore different clothes when she went hunting, I'd never seen her change her look so completely. She wasn't even wearing any costume jewelry.

She read the surprise on my face and gave me a faint smile. "It's a wig, Lex."

Oh. "What are you doing here?" I blurted. Not a great recovery. At least I stopped myself from asking how she'd gotten in. Vampires do have to get permission before entering a private home, thanks to gravitational magic, but Charlie's null abilities negated that. Her house wasn't protected from vampires, although of course they stopped being vampires if they got too close to her.

"Quinn texted me." Maven crouched down near Clara, putting one hand on the floor for a second to steady herself. It was so odd seeing her without vampire grace. "Don't bring her any closer, please," she said to me, holding up a hand. I realized my mistake and retreated a few steps with Charlie, dropping down onto the edge of a rocking chair. Maven seemed to glow with sudden health, and she gave me a nod.

"Clara's not healing?" I asked.

"She is, but it's slow." Maven looked up into Quinn's eyes. "Did you tell her?"

He shook his head.

"Tell me what?" I asked him.

Quinn winced, eyeing Clara for a moment. "Quinn," was all I said, and I made sure my voice was level. I wasn't going to flip out, and I wasn't going to wake Charlie, goddammit.

He rested a hand on my shoulder. "The people who broke in, they weren't the ones who hurt John. It was Clara."

I gaped. "What?"

Maven picked up the knife I'd found and sniffed the handle. She gave a little headshake. "I don't think Clara used it."

I forced myself to take a deep breath, nodding. "She was wounded fighting off the werewolves, and John gave her blood to save her."

"She might have pressed him to donate," Quinn said quietly.

Maven looked grave, and I realized for the first time what we were actually talking about: whether or not Clara would need to be punished for what had happened here. Vampires were not allowed to kill humans in the state of Colorado, by Maven's own law. If John didn't make it . . .

Clara was my responsibility. She was under my protection.

"No," I said firmly, searching for the right words. "Clara and John respected each other. She wouldn't do that to him. And I know John. He would have been happy to help the person who'd saved Charlie. He must have cut too deep by mistake."

Maven and Quinn exchanged another look, then Maven tilted her head to one side, acquiescing. "Let's drop it for now," she said. She lifted an eyebrow. "I'm assuming you want to call your friend?"

For the space of a heartbeat, I thought she meant Scarlett Bernard, for some reason. Then my thoughts cleared. "Sashi!"

"I'll pay her bill," Maven said calmly.

"I'm a fucking moron," I muttered as I freed one hand to dig in my pocket for my phone. Why hadn't I thought of that immediately? True, it had been a couple of years since I'd needed her magic, but we talked once or twice a week. It should have been obvious. Sashi was a healing witch who worked on humans, and John was human.

Not to mention Sashi's ex.

I perched on the edge of the couch—there was blood on the backrest, but the seat was clear—which freed up my uninjured hand to scroll through my contacts for her name. Quinn and Maven, meanwhile, picked up Clara and took her out the back way, presumably to get her bagged blood—somewhere far away from my null niece.

The phone rang only twice before Sashi answered. She was semi-nocturnal, like me. "Hey, Lex," came her warm voice over the phone. "How are things? Has Grace said anything about—"

"Sashi," I interrupted. "It's John. He's hurt."

Three seconds of silence, and when she responded, her voice was businesslike. "How bad?"

"Pretty bad." My voice quavered, which I hated. "Some wolves attacked him trying to get to Charlie. Clara was hurt and John got cut."

That was more detail than she really needed, but Sashi absorbed it quickly. "He wasn't bitten?" she asked.

Jesus, it hadn't even occurred to me. But I was sure Quinn would have mentioned if there'd been a bite, and from the little I knew about werewolves, his symptoms would be different. "I don't think so," I said into the phone. "It's mostly the blood loss."

"Okay," Sashi said. "We'll be on the next flight. Call you when I get there."

She hung up the phone. I stared at it for a moment, taken aback. "We?" I said to myself.

Quinn was coming back into the room and overheard me. "She's bringing the new boyfriend?"

"Apparently." I shrugged and put the phone away. "John wasn't bitten by one of the werewolves, was he?"

Quinn shook his head. "I would have been able to smell it."

"Okay, good." I looked at Maven. "I need to get Charlie to Katia."

She nodded. "Of course. Make the arrangements for your family situation. Quinn and I will speak to the witch he captured." She gave me a smile that was all bared teeth, and the word "predator" flashed through my mind in huge neon letters.

Then her words caught up with me. "Wait a minute," I blurted. I held up a finger in a *let me think* gesture, which made Maven raise an eyebrow, but she waved a hand to say *be my guest.*

Why would Morgan send a witch with the werewolves?

She knew about Clara, who'd taken her down the night she'd tried to use Charlie, but witches weren't great in a fight against vampires—at least, not compared with five werewolves. So what was the point of sending one?

Maven and Quinn were still looking at me expectantly. Vampires were very good at waiting. "Quinn, can you take her for a minute?" I asked. Without hesitating, Quinn came over and lifted Charlie out of my arms with a tiny *oof*.

I had to smile. "Not so strong without your magic powers, huh?" He rolled his eyes at me.

"Maven, would you please move the bodies?" I asked my boss. I could drag them around if I really needed to, but I could lift weights for twelve hours a day and never be half as strong as a vampire.

She just looked at me for a moment, eyebrows raised. "I need five minutes to follow a hunch," I promised. "I want to check their pockets."

"All right."

Quinn retreated into the foyer so Maven could scoop up the dead werewolves. Matter-of-factly, she picked up each body and held it as I searched the clothing.

Nothing there.

Maven moved all three bodies through the kitchen and stacked them near the back door. While she was doing that, I squatted down and duck-walked around the living room, scrutinizing the floor for anything out of the ordinary. I could periodically feel Maven's eyes on me from the doorway, but my five minutes weren't up yet, and she didn't comment.

I found it under the edge of the armchair: a tiny vial made out of hard plastic with a screw-on top. The liquid inside was brownish-yellow and had flakes of something suspended in it. I held it up to the light, shaking it slightly.

Fuck. Me.

"Quinn!" I called, and he came back into the doorway, carrying Charlie on one hip. His eyes widened when he saw the vial I was holding. "The witch you found," I said before he could ask. Maven watched us with interest. "What does she look like?"

He gave a tiny shrug. "I wasn't paying attention, to be honest. She was fighting like a whirlwind, so I just grabbed her and threw her in the trunk."

"Did she smell like the Pellar farm?"

"Well, yeah, but I thought half the witches in the state were out there in the last couple of days . . . why?"

"Because this just got even more complicated." I sighed. "You better go get her and bring her back in here. Don't hurt her," I added, though Quinn wasn't the type for callous violence.

"You know who she is," Maven said. A statement, not a question.

"That's what I'm afraid of."

Quinn laid Charlie on the padded bench in the foyer, and after a few moments he came in through the back door with a woman slung over one shoulder. He had taken a roll of duct tape from John's kitchen with him, and when he plopped her down on the couch I saw that he'd wound it around her ankles and wrists enough times to stop a rampaging werewolf. A shorter piece of tape was plastered over her mouth. She glared at each of us in turn, then her eyes narrowed on me, specifically. "Hello, Sybil," I said tiredly.

Chapter 32

I didn't know Sybil Pellar very well, mostly because she hated me. Most witches did, of course, but with Sybil I didn't take it personally. From what Simon and Lily had told me, their next-older sister was universally very good with plants, and very bad with people. The few times we had actually interacted, she'd struck me as a sour, resentful woman who was angry about how her life had turned out.

Back when Morgan was the golden child, Sybil had been jealous, but she'd also idolized her older sister, which Morgan had used to her own advantage. On the night that Quinn and I had hunted the sandworm, Morgan knew we were closing in on her, so she'd sent Sybil to Chautauqua Park to perform the complex magical ceremony that would boost the ley lines.

It was supposed to distract us, and it worked—but Morgan threw Sybil under the bus, and if Maven hadn't been such a careful leader, Sybil might have taken the fall for the entire thing. I wasn't surprised that Morgan was trying a similar play here—but I *was* surprised that Sybil was going along with it. Again.

When Quinn stepped back after dropping her on John's blood-stained sofa, I saw that she was painfully thin, with cheekbones like blades and hungry eyes that made me think of a starved crow. She reached up with her bound hands—Quinn had left her fingers free—and carefully peeled off the tape over her mouth. I let it happen, figuring we were going to need to have a conversation, but before I could say anything, Sybil muttered something under her breath and made a flicking motion at me.

I flew backward into the wall.

The back of my head hit the drywall and everything went loud and dizzy for a moment, while I struggled to get my legs back under me. I could vaguely hear someone talking, but I couldn't make out any words. A moment later, Maven's hand was on my shoulder. "Lex. Can you hear me?" I got the feeling it wasn't the first time she'd asked.

"I'm fine," I mumbled, blinking away tears of pain. Damn. Sybil could pack a wallop. Maven nodded and retreated to the foyer to keep an eye on my sleeping niece. While Quinn was fetching Sybil from the car, Maven and I had agreed that I would do the talking. Adding the cardinal vampire of the state to the situation would only make it more complicated; using me to negotiate gave us more room to maneuver.

By the couch, Quinn was stepping back from taping down her fingers, surveying his handiwork. "I don't know if you can do that without your fingers," he told Sybil, his voice so cold and flat that I felt my own eyes widen. "But I doubt you can do it without a tongue. You got me?"

Sybil paled, and though the anger didn't lift from her eyes, she nodded.

I went over and sat down on the couch beside her. Quinn stayed where he was, right behind her, where he could play vampire lie detector. We'd done this before and it wasn't foolproof—if the suspect had enough drugs or alcohol in their system, or was a complete sociopath, they could fool him. But I didn't think Sybil fell into any of those categories.

"So," I said, trying to sound calmer than I felt, "you're the inside man."

Sybil didn't answer, but to be fair, it hadn't been a question. I tried again, starting with something easy. "Did you hand out flyers for Morgan at your mother's house?"

Sybil lifted her chin, defiant. "Yes."

I felt myself relax an inch. She was talking. "Why?"

A blink. "Because the witches of Colorado deserve a chance to hear her out and make their decision."

Well, *that* sounded like a line Morgan had fed her. "And what about the werewolves you helped her kill? Did *they* deserve *that*?"

Confusion flickered over her face for a minute, but she recovered fast. "Probably. But I didn't do anything to any werewolves."

Quinn and I exchanged a look. He nodded. She was telling the truth. "How long have you been in touch with Morgan?" I asked, trying to throw her off guard a little.

"A couple of months."

"That's a lie," Quinn said lazily.

"Wanna try again?" I said to Sybil.

Her shoulders hunched. "Fine. The whole time. I give her updates on Saffron and Sebastian. She's their *mother*. And I'm not breaking any Old World laws."

This was true—Maven hadn't forbidden communication with Morgan, probably realizing it would only make some witches more inclined to contact her. Hazel, on the other hand, had told her own clan not to speak to Morgan, but apparently Sybil wasn't afraid of her mother's punishment. "You'd do that, even after she set you up?"

Sybil sneered at me. "She didn't *set me up*. She just asked me to do a spell on the ley lines. I'm the one who didn't ask more questions."

"Morgan knew we would conclude that you were involved in raising the sandworm," I pointed out. "And she knew Maven would come for you."

"And that *they* can tell when we're lying," Sybil countered, jerking her head at Quinn. I had to give her credit, she didn't seem the least bit unnerved to have a vampire at her back, which was more that I could say for myself in the same situation. "Morgan made sure I didn't know anything, because she knew Maven wouldn't hurt me without questioning me first. My sister was protecting me."

Quinn and I exchanged another look, this one of disbelief. I didn't know a lot about Stockholm syndrome, but that's what this sounded like. In Sybil's eyes, we were relentlessly hunting her sister, who was trying to bring democratic changes to the witch clan system. Fuck.

"I've answered your questions," Sybil spat at me, still seething. "Now *where* is my *sister?*"

I stared at her in confusion. "Morgan? I have no idea. That's what I was going to ask you."

"Not Morgan," she dismissed. "She's in Wyoming. Where is *Lily?*"

Quinn looked as puzzled as I felt. "Lily is at Simon's apartment," I told Sybil.

Now it was her turn to look surprised, like she hadn't expected me to answer. "What did you do to her?" she demanded.

"I . . . nothing. She's hanging out with Katia; I think they were going to play gin rummy. Why?"

"Morgan said—" Sybil began, but she caught herself.

"What? What did Morgan say?"

Sybil pressed her lips together—which was Quinn's cue to rest his hands lightly on her shoulders. He wasn't hurting her, but Sybil suddenly looked scared.

Morgan had probably told her we were violent psychopaths. I wouldn't *really* torture Simon and Lily's big sister, but I had no moral problem with trickery.

"*You* took Lily," she squeaked. "You kidnapped her so Morgan would back off. That's why . . ." She trailed off, but her eyes flicked to the doorway to the foyer.

"That's why you came for Charlie," I finished for her. "Morgan said she was going to trade her for Lily."

Sybil didn't actually nod, but the confirmation was all over her face.

"What was the potion for?" I asked, holding up the little plastic vial. "It wouldn't work on Charlie." My niece was susceptible to anything nonmagical that might affect a human, like sleeping pills or, God help me, poison—but Sybil's spells were infused with actual magic, which wouldn't work on a null.

"For Charlie's dad," she said, sullen. "It was my idea, to make him forget. Morgan doesn't have any vampires working for her in Colorado, so she couldn't press him."

Quinn and I exchanged a look over her head, and I could see him thinking the same thing I was: Morgan Pellar was so goddamned sneaky. Maven had literal control over every vampire in the state. Sending vampires into Colorado to undermine her would be the equivalent of Maven sending her people into Wyoming: a declaration of war. So she'd sent werewolves instead, knowing if they got caught, she had deniability.

Still, it would have been easier for Morgan to just kill John. Sybil, in her stupid Sybil way, had been trying to spare him. She might have even saved his life.

Shit. This made things even more complicated. Sybil was gullible and small-minded, but not exactly an architect of evil.

"Your mother sent Lily away from the farmhouse," I told her, trying to sound calm. "If all the Colorado witch clans turn against Hazel, she wants Lily to present herself as an alternative."

"That's what Morgan said you'd say," Sybil muttered, but she looked uncertain.

"Lily is fine," I assured her, pulling out my cell phone. "Here, we can call her." I dialed Katia's phone and put the call on speaker, so Sybil would know it was not a trick.

The phone went straight to voice mail. Sybil looked a little smug, but I frowned and tried it again. Straight to voice mail again.

In my hurry to get to Charlie, I had completely forgotten about Katia not answering earlier. Katia wouldn't turn her phone off during a crisis.

I looked at Quinn. "Something's wrong."

Chapter 33

It still took another five minutes of planning before we could leave, because we'd need to split up. Maven left first: she would run out to the farmhouse to check on Simon and Hazel and make sure Lily and Katia hadn't gone back there for some reason. I wasn't sure how Maven would deal with any wards the witches might have set up, but I had no doubt she could stay undetected. She was a thousand frickin' years old.

Quinn loaded Charlie's car seat into the Jeep, and I got the sleeping child secured inside. We considered making Sybil ride in the vampire compartment, but in the end Quinn just picked her up in her duct tape and buckled her into the back seat next to the window. Neither of us really thought she was a threat anymore. "I won't tape your mouth, as a sign of good faith," I warned her. "Don't make me regret it."

Sybil just gave me a tight nod. She'd gone quiet, and I could tell the wheels in her head were turning. She didn't really believe us about Lily, but probably realized I wasn't a good enough actor to fake this much concern. She was willing to let this play out a little.

"I need to blindfold you for the first part of the drive," I told her. Sybil glared and opened her mouth to protest, but I overrode her. "We have to drop off Charlie, and I don't want you to know where. This is not negotiable. If you want to argue with me, you can ride in the portable coffin."

I could see Quinn suppressing a snort, but Sybil just gave me a dark look and conceded. I put one of John's ski caps on her head and pulled it down over her eyes and part of her nose. "Leave it on," I ordered.

Quinn drove us straight to Elise's duplex in Lafayette, which was more or less on the way to Simon's apartment. He parked on the street and I jumped out, rushing around to unbuckle Charlie and grab her bear. I hoisted her onto my hip and hurried up the driveway.

The security light flicked on, bright enough to make Charlie mumble and bury her head in my neck. I leaned on the doorbell, peering into the glass on the front door.

The lights began to flick on throughout the house, and a moment later Elise came hurrying down the hall. My cousin had the honey-blonde hair and brown eyes that were the Luther trademark, but her cropped hair was currently standing up at all angles. She was wearing a ratty old robe thrown on over a Boulder PD T-shirt, and her right arm was tucked along her side, probably to hide her service weapon. Of all my family members, Elise was the most naturally suspicious—and the most well armed.

Her confused irritation turned to just plain confusion when she saw me through the window. She unlocked and opened the door. "What hap—"

I held a finger to my lips, then pointed at Charlie. Elise nodded. "What the hell happened?" she said in a loud whisper. "What time is it? What happened to your face?"

Dammit, even half-asleep she was good. I had nearly forgotten about the bruises on my forehead and cheekbone. "It's late. John's had an accident. Can you watch Charlie for tonight?"

Elise had reached up to rub her eyes, but now she froze. "*What?*" She was already opening the door wider to let us in. "What happened to John?"

Quinn had offered to go up first and press Elise, but I'd demurred. We were using a story with my parents anyway, and I didn't want to mess with *anyone's* thoughts unless there was no other option. Instead, Quinn had moved to the passenger side and was slumped down with his head in his hands, looking miserable. If Elise glanced outside, she would see him looking badly shaken.

"I was watching Charlie tonight," I told Elise, as calmly as I could. Human or not, my cousin could practically smell a lie. "John and Quinn were using Quinn's bandsaw, and John cut his arm. He lost a lot of blood. The ambulance took him to BCH; Mom and Dad are already on their way."

"Okay." I saw Elise processing that, knew she was about to ask why *I* couldn't keep Charlie. "Was Quinn hurt?"

"No, but the EMTs think he had some kind of minor heart incident—myocardial . . . something." I was keeping it vague on purpose. "He didn't want to ride in the ambulance, so I need to take him to get checked out. Can you please take her just until tomorrow morning?"

Elise frowned, in a mildly insulted way. "Of course I can." She opened her arms, and I handed Charlie over carefully. It was a relief to give up the weight—I had been getting overheated, still in my winter coat in the foyer—but I immediately felt less grounded.

"Jesus, the two of you get in more accidents," Elise grumbled, hoisting Charlie higher on her hip. Then she paused. "Wait—Quinn has a bandsaw?"

"He just got it. Where's Natalie?" I asked, mainly just to change the subject. Elise's soon-to-be wife was a medical examiner in Denver.

"Sleeping like a log. She just got off a double shift."

"Okay. I gotta go. I'll call you first thing in the morning, promise. Maybe we can take Charlie to breakfast, then visit John." It seemed absurd as soon as I said it—how could this mess possibly be over by then?—but as I'd hoped, the words seemed to normalize the situation for Elise. "Okay." She took a step back, already starting to turn toward the stairs. "When we get up, I'll call the hospital and check in too."

"Night," I said, and hurried back out the way I'd come.

• • •

When we were a couple of miles away from Elise's place, Maven texted—she was already at the farmhouse, and there was no sign of Lily or Katia. Hazel and Simon both seemed fine. She would wait around for an hour or so to make sure nothing happened.

I took the ski cap off Sybil, who immediately started shaking her head and rubbing her bound hands against her face. "Goddess, that was itchy." To me, she added in a subdued voice, "Is your niece okay?"

"She's fine. Now we need to get to Simon's." Beside me, Quinn pressed down hard on the accelerator. With Charlie out of the car, he was willing to use Maven's arrangement with Boulder PD to do some serious speeding. I approved.

We were only a minute away from the apartment building when Sybil said, "I'm going in with you."

Quinn and I exchanged a look. "It's safer if you stay out here," I told her.

"Safer for whom?" she shot back. "And isn't that *exactly* what you'd say if you were responsible for Lily disappearing?"

I sighed.

"I'm coming in," Sybil insisted. "Are you going to make me hop?"

We didn't have time for this. I nodded at Quinn, who got out his pocketknife, leaned between the seats, and sliced along the duct tape binding her legs. I knew he'd be careful, but Sybil complained the whole time anyway. Typical. "It's gonna look awfully weird if I walk in with my arms covered in duct tape," Sybil pointed out when he was done.

"Don't push it," Quinn told her.

"There's a blanket in the back," I told him. "We can throw it over her hands."

That's exactly what we did. I parked in the lot—Maven owned this building, and kept a few spots reserved for Old World business—and the three of us hurried inside.

I expected Sybil to complain the whole way about her legs going to sleep or her wrists being tied, but she looked as grim and worried as

I felt. Inside the main doors, we took the stairs down to the basement, and Sybil was moving so fast that I had to put a hand on her elbow to keep her from pitching down the steps. That was when I realized she believed me about Lily—or at least about something being very wrong.

At Simon's door, Quinn jerked Sybil's arm so they were standing to one side of the doorframe. He held a finger to his lips. I went to the other side, turning my body just enough to fit my key in the lock. I turned the key as quietly as I could, checked Quinn to make sure he was ready, and kicked in the door, rushing in with the revolver in one hand and a shredder in the other.

The main room, a combination dining-kitchen area, was empty—but it looked like there had been a hell of a fight. The kitchen floor was strewn with cast-iron frying pans and playing cards, and the floor-length cupboard where Simon kept the trash was dented inward. I nodded at Quinn, who planted Sybil against the wall and indicated that she should stay there. He and I moved down the hall then, checking the rooms. He disappeared into Simon's bedroom while I went on to clear the bathroom, the closet, and the spare room. Quinn hadn't come out, so I rushed back to the bedroom to check on him.

He was kneeling next to Simon's bed, gently shaking the covers. A person-sized lump was huddled under the blankets. "We're clear," I said, moving closer. "Who is that?"

In answer, he said loudly, "Lily. *Lily!*"

I ran forward, dropping to my knees beside him. Lily looked asleep, but even when he shook her hard, she didn't move, didn't make a sound.

My heart plummeted, and I made myself say the words. "Is she—"

"She's breathing," he said shortly. I could hear Sybil's footsteps in the hall. Quinn looked around, saw a glass of water on the nightstand, and upended it on Lily's face. Nothing happened.

"Get out of the way," Sybil snapped, hurrying to her sister's bedside. Quinn backed up so Sybil could check Lily's pulse, then lift her eyelids.

Sybil looked up at me. "She's been drugged."

"I thought your little potions didn't work on people with witch-blood," I countered, feeling inexplicably angry at her.

"They don't. This isn't magic. It's regular, nonmagical belladonna," she snapped. "Someone used a *precision* dose to knock her out without killing her. That's very difficult. She'll be out for . . ." She narrowed her eyes speculatively. "Maybe twelve to eighteen hours."

Long enough to miss the witch congress. If Sybil said Lily would live, though, I believed her. "Where's Katia?" I demanded.

"*I* don't know!"

"Okay," Quinn broke in, holding up his hands. "Who would know how to dose Lily like this?"

"Me." Sybil thought for a moment. "Other than that, I can only think of Morgan and my mother. And Ardie Atwood, but nobody's heard from her for a couple of years."

I very carefully did not look at Quinn when she said that last part. Ardie, her husband, and their kids had disappeared from Colorado shortly after Ardie had participated in an attempt to kill Maven. I was certain my boss wouldn't have hurt the children, so I figured their father had moved them out of state. I had no idea if Ardie had been alive to go with them. I didn't really care.

"Morgan could do this?" I repeated.

"Yes, but not in person. She can't come into Colorado, unless . . ." Sybil trailed off, thinking.

"Unless what?" I asked.

"Unless the witch congress decides to take away my mother's magic," Sybil said, looking up at me. One hand was still on her sister, like she was afraid someone would steal Lily away. "That would destroy any of her active spells. But they don't meet until tomorrow." She shrugged, looking at her sister with a miserable expression. "Morgan could have sent the dose with someone else."

I looked at Quinn. "I don't like this. Whoever came here must have arrived at almost the same time as Sybil and the werewolves hit John's house. She's attacking on multiple fronts at once." God, I hated her.

"A blitzkrieg," Quinn muttered under his breath.

Anyone who deals with military tactics learns the concept of *blitzkrieg*: a series of fast, concentrated attacks using more than one channel. The idea was to unbalance the enemy and make it impossible for them to adjust quickly enough to save themselves.

"And it's working," I said. We weren't adjusting fast enough. We were too busy reacting.

Quinn nodded, looking grim . . . and a little pissed. I rarely saw Quinn actually get angry—he was usually the cool one, the detached investigator. But Morgan had attacked Katia and Lily, people who were important to me. That was enough to make even Quinn mad.

He turned narrowed eyes onto Sybil. "Where is Morgan hiding?"

"I don't know," she whined. "Somewhere in Wyoming. I haven't visited her in person."

"Who *would* know?" I asked. "Who else is working for her?"

Sybil's lower lip trembled, but she was thinking. "There's a whole pack of werewolves," she said slowly. "I don't know any of them, though. The ones I was with . . . I just met them tonight."

"That's not all of you," I said. "She has other witches, doesn't she?"

Sybil swallowed hard. "I only know of two. Marissa Shaw is from Clan Shaw, down in Pueblo. She was at the farmhouse keeping an eye on us. And Joanna Green used to be in Clan Pellar, but she left when Morgan did."

"What do they look like?"

Sybil did her best to describe them. I didn't think I'd met Shaw, but I was pretty sure Joanna Green was the timid woman who'd brought out the podium at Morgan's big meeting. That didn't really get us anywhere, though.

Sybil stroked Lily's hair.

"You're sure she's going to be okay?" I heard myself asking.

"Mostly sure. In the Middle Ages belladonna was used as anesthetic during surgery; in theory it shouldn't do any lasting harm." She was frowning. "But there's always the possibility of complications."

"Is there an antidote?" Quinn asked.

"Yes, but I don't have it with me. It's at the farmhouse."

I looked at Quinn. "We should—"

The trilling *brrrrrrrrring* of an old-fashioned telephone erupted from the kitchen, cutting me off. I went out there, the other two at my heels, and found a small black burner phone on the counter, tucked against the fridge. "Is it Katia's?" Quinn said, frowning.

"No." I went over to the counter and looked at the screen. The caller ID had been blocked.

"Should you answer it?" Sybil said.

"I think I have to." I picked up the phone and hit the "Talk" button. "Hello?"

"Lex?" Katia's voice was raw and weak.

My stomach contracted. I'd never heard her sound like that. "I'm here, Aunt Katia. What's going on?"

"I need . . . I need you to get somewhere you can't be overheard. By anyone."

Quinn and I locked eyes. He gave a tiny headshake—*don't do it*—but I couldn't take the risk. "Hold on."

I walked briskly out of the apartment, the phone pressed to my ear, and closed the door behind me. I put twenty more feet of hallway between me and the door, then said, "Okay. I'm alone."

"Excellent," a new voice purred. Fear erupted inside me like an explosion of adrenaline.

"Hello, Morgan."

Chapter 34

"Did you find Lily yet?" she asked, as though I had lost a shoe.

"Yes. Nice way to treat your own sister."

"She's alive, isn't she?" Morgan said, unperturbed. "She'll wake up tomorrow night with a headache."

"What the hell is *wrong* with you?" I blurted.

A sigh. "You still don't get it. It's not your fault, really: you're out-clan, and a black witch on top of it. You don't know any better."

"Oh yeah, I'm clearly in the wrong on this whole drugging-and-kidnapping issue," I said sarcastically.

"Lex." Morgan was using the patronizing tone of a kindergarten teacher, which made me even angrier. "At some point you're going to realize that there was never anything wrong with *me*. I'm just the only one not brainwashed by that scheming vampire bitch and her corpse-loving lackey. No offense, of course," she added.

It was a near thing, but I held my temper. Yelling at Morgan could have consequences for Katia. "Tell me what you want."

Her voice hardened. "All right. It's very simple: bring Charlie to Wyoming."

I blinked. "You think I'm going to deliver my four-year-old niece to you? Did you get brain damage?"

"I didn't say bring her to *me*." Morgan sounded impatient. "I said bring her to Wyoming. If she travels across the state line, she'll break my mother's ward. You can even pick up Katia while you're here."

Her tone suggested she was being very generous. "And then what will you do?" I asked.

"That's not your concern," she said primly. "But I told you once before: I have no interest in hurting children. I won't lay a hand on Charlie; you have my word."

I was too busy trying to think ahead to snort at the concept of Morgan's *word*. "You're going to crash your mother's congress, aren't you? Turn the witches against her? Or maybe you'll try to find Maven during the day, when she's vulnerable." A worse thought occurred to me. "You've had your people following her, haven't you? You think you already know where to find her."

"*Lex.*" Her voice was sharp now. "You're making this harder than it needs to be. And what exactly is your loyalty to Maven, anyway? She can't keep your niece safe—I've personally proven that for you. Twice. And she's been neglecting you for months. What have you been doing lately? *Errands?*"

I took a step back toward the apartment. I was sure it had been silent, but Morgan seemed to read my mind. "If you tell Quinn or Maven, I *will* kill Katia," she said. "I've been doing a little experimenting. I think I've figured out how to make a boundary witch stay dead."

I froze, both from fear for Katia and paranoia for myself. Was she watching me? Could she have planted recording devices in the apartment?

Of course she could have. With a bunch of werewolves and several witches working for her, there wasn't much she couldn't get away with.

"You make some interesting points," I said, my voice sounding strangled.

"Good," she replied. "Now, I'll leave Katia with one of my employees at the Depot in downtown Cheyenne. Nice and public. But you should know," she added, "if you arrive without Charlie, I've taken steps to make sure you and Katia will both die."

"Charlie's not with me," I said quickly. "I'll need to go get her."

A pause, like she was checking a watch. "It's two thirty now. I'll give you three hours. That's *more* than enough time."

"Wait—" I began.

"See you soon, Lex."

And then she was gone.

I stood there for a long moment, completely still, my thoughts churning. I was absolutely certain of one thing: I was not going to get Charlie. She wouldn't be involved in this in any way. But that meant I had to come up with another plan.

And I had no time to waste.

I marched back to Simon's apartment. Quinn and Sybil were sitting at the kitchen table. Quinn had sliced the rest of the tape off the Pellar witch, and they were both sitting there with their hands folded.

I paused. They were awfully close to the door. I looked at Quinn. "Did you overhear that?" I asked.

He shook his head. "I couldn't make out any words."

I looked at Sybil. "Can you go sit with Lily, please?"

I was a little surprised when she quietly rose from her seat and went into Simon's room without a word. My face was probably pretty scary at the moment.

"Lex?" Quinn said, looking worried. "What's going on?"

I blew out a breath. "This part you can overhear." I pulled out my own phone and called Maven.

She answered in a low voice. "Hello, Lex."

"Maven," I said, as clearly as possible, "I'm calling to resign."

Quinn's eyes widened, and he stood up and came over to me. In my ear, Maven said, "Excuse me?"

"Our deal is not working out," I told her. "I quit."

I enunciated very clearly. There was going to be no confusion about this.

Maven paused for a long moment, then said, "Of course, you can leave my employ whenever you want. But Charlie will no longer be under my protection. Nor will you."

"To be fair," I said, a little testily, "we haven't been feeling a whole lot of protection lately."

Quinn flinched. I might have gone a little too far, but it was too late to take it back.

Another pause from Maven, then: "All right, Lex. I release you from my employ. I hope you know what you're doing."

Me too. "I ask you for one parting favor," I said, accidentally picking up on her formal language. "May I please borrow your Jeep tonight? Just as a friendly gesture."

Her voice had a touch more warmth as she replied, "Of course. No strings attached. Please return it to Magic Beans anytime tomorrow."

I hung up the phone. Quinn immediately began to speak, but I held up my hand. "Don't," I warned.

"Why—" he began, but I threw my arms around him, hugging him tight. I breathed in his familiar scent, taking comfort in it. I didn't say anything. If I told him what I was planning, he'd never let me leave alone. And Katia would die.

When I stepped back, his eyes were troubled. He wouldn't look at me, and with a jolt I realized why: he was afraid I would press him.

I'd done it once before, under circumstances not so different from these . . . but I'd sworn that I never would again. My cheeks flared red with shame. I'd worried that I couldn't trust him, but maybe he felt the exact same way.

"I wouldn't," I told him, my voice cracking. "I made a promise."

Quinn finally risked a glance at me, his eyes sad. "And I know that it means nothing next to the promise you made Sam," he said frankly. "You'd do anything to protect Charlie, and I don't blame you. But if you quit Maven's service . . ." He gave me a helpless look. "You're sidelining me again."

"This isn't—that's not—" I sputtered, but I knew he wasn't wrong. All of a sudden Katia wasn't the only person I could lose tonight. "Please," I said at last. "Please, Quinn, trust me."

I held up a hand to touch his face; he turned his head to plant a kiss on my palm. I could see what it was costing him, but he nodded. "All right," he said at last. "Go."

I started to turn away, stopped. "If you can get away tonight, please go watch that place we stopped earlier." I gave him a pointed look and then sent my gaze around the room, to indicate that someone could be listening. "Or send Clara, if she recovers."

To his credit, Quinn picked it up quickly and nodded. "I will." He brushed my hair back from my face. "I love you."

My throat seemed to close up, so I brushed a kiss across his lips and exchanged my personal cell phone for the Jeep keys on the table. I kept the burner Morgan had left for me.

On my way out the door, I heard Quinn's cell phone start ringing, heard him answer it. "Hello, Maven."

A couple of years earlier, Maven had paid a lot of money to get her Jeep tricked out. It had bullet-resistant windows, a lightproof storage area where vampires could hide during the day, and one other cool feature that most people didn't know about: you could turn the GPS tracking on and off with the touch of a button. As soon as I got in the Jeep, I turned the tracking feature off. I couldn't risk being followed.

I drove home first. The roads weren't slick, so I went as fast as I dared, especially on the back roads. It was well after dark, but Simon, Lily, and I had cleared this route of ghosts. For better or worse, I was able to concentrate on what I needed to do.

At the cabin, the dogs immediately began their frantic chorus of barking. I waded through them and opened the back door, allowing them to race out into the fenced-in backyard. Then I hurried to my bedroom and dug through a pile of clothes until I found the backpack with my ghost-laying supplies. I tore things out of it, tossing them aside, until I found the encrypted walkie-talkie.

The walkie-talkies had a range of about fifty miles, more than enough to contact Simon out at the farm. I switched on the handset and found the button that made a single beep. I hit it three times very quickly, our code for "Anyone there?"

I waited for two minutes, all I could afford, and tried again. This time there was a crackle of static; then Simon's voice exploded over the line. "About fucking time! This is Phoenix; what the hell's going on?"

I almost cried. Suddenly code names didn't seem so silly. "Phoenix, this is Griffin. Can you talk?"

"Can I *talk*? I've been sitting next to this thing in my room for the past two days!" I gave him a second, and he said in a calmer voice, "Yes, I'm alone."

"Okay, listen, because I don't have much time." As I spoke, I stood up and began darting around my room, throwing stuff into the backpack. The first thing I grabbed was Valerya's bloodstone, from the dish by the window where I kept my assorted crystals. It was on a cord, which I put over my head with one hand, settling the bloodstone against my chest. I immediately felt better. "Katia is in trouble. I know you guys have been trying to play fair with the witch clans, but I'm asking you to blow it all up and come help me."

I held my breath. I could have given him more information, of course, or tried to plead my case, but I knew what I was asking. I wouldn't manipulate him into it.

Simon paused for only a heartbeat before answering. "Tell me what you need."

Chapter 35

"Well, *that* was satisfying," Simon said half an hour later as he climbed into the Jeep. We were a quarter of a mile from the Pellar farmhouse, and he was a little breathless from running. He'd dressed in dark clothes and carried his favorite messenger bag, which functioned as sort of a witch emergency kit. He half stood to deposit a cardboard box on the back seat, and when he settled back down his coat pocket gaped enough for me to see the outline of a pistol. Jeez. He was ready for war.

"What'd you do?" I asked as I put the Jeep in Drive.

"I threw Marissa Shaw into a wall and zapped her unconscious." He was positively gleeful. "I know apex magic has gotten us in trouble, but *damn*, that felt good."

Despite the circumstances, I couldn't help but glance over and smile at him. Then I looked at the box in my rearview mirror. There were holes punched in the top. "So you brought . . ."

"Yeah. I gave her a sedative, though."

"Thank you," I said sincerely.

"It's okay . . . but what exactly are we doing?" he asked.

My smile faded. "Morgan has Katia. She wants me to use Charlie to break your mother's ward."

"*What?!*"

I gave him the short version of events, including Quinn's comment about the blitzkrieg. "Morgan's right. Maven won't be able to put out all the fires fast enough to stop Morgan from crashing your mom's meeting tomorrow," I concluded. "Lily's off the board, too, so she won't be able to be your mom's plan B."

Simon groaned. "So you're saying my evil sister is using Sybil and Charlie to get what she wants. Again."

"Yes." I pressed down hard on the accelerator, causing Simon to brace himself on the dash. He didn't say anything about my speed.

"Okay, so what are we doing?"

I told him. I was concentrating on the road at the time—I hadn't cleared this path yet, and it's hard to speed with ghosts popping in and out of sight—but his tone was wary when he answered. "Lex . . . I don't know about this."

"Really?" I risked a sideways glance. Simon looked pale. Shit. "I figured you of all people would be . . . interested."

"You know all those books and movies about what happens when science goes too far? They exist for a reason. Are you sure you want to cross this line?"

"No, I'm not," I admitted. "But I'm not putting Charlie at risk, and we don't have time to do this the normal way. If you've got another idea, I'm all ears, but otherwise . . . this is my only chance to save Katia."

My voice broke a little at the end. I was trying very hard not to think about the way my aunt had sounded on the phone. It wasn't just that she'd clearly been hurt. It was that she sounded resigned to it.

"Still." Simon was stubborn. "The risks—"

"Are mine," I interrupted. "I'm sorry, but I'll do this with or without you, Simon. If it goes wrong, though, I'd rather you were there to zap me unconscious." Simon knew the same "human Taser" spell that Lily favored, and it would be able to affect my biological systems. Thank you, nuances.

Simon sighed. "All right."

• • •

We drove first to John's house, where I went through the house and opened the garage door. I backed John's car out so Simon could back the Jeep in. He waited for me to come inside before he pressed the button to lower the garage door, smiling a little wistfully. "Doesn't it seem like we were just hanging out in John's garage, talking shoe sizes?" he said with a little smile.

"Honestly? That feels like a month ago."

When we got to the living room, Simon's jaw dropped at the sight of all the blood. "I can't believe he's still alive," he blurted, then winced and glanced at me. "Sorry."

"It's okay. Besides, most of this"—I gestured at the walls—"was Clara tearing up some werewolves."

He let out a low whistle. "Remind me not to piss her off."

We stepped carefully around the bloodstains—I felt a little like I was following those old-fashioned footprints they used to use to teach people how to dance—until we reached the kitchen. I gestured at the back door, where three bodies were still stacked in a wobbly pile. "There. No one has had time to do anything about them. And it's not like John's coming home from the hospital tonight." My voice cracked, dammit. Simon laid a hand on my shoulder. His other hand was already holding a pair of surgical gloves. "Do you want to call and check in?" he asked kindly. "I can handle this part myself."

I raised an eyebrow. "You can?"

"Hey," he said defensively. "I've been working out!"

I smiled and went to the kitchen landline, which John insisted on keeping. I boosted myself up onto the counter to sit, and dialed my father's cell phone. He would be honest with me, where my mom might try to sugarcoat things.

"Hello?" came my dad's gruff voice.

"It's me. How is he?"

"In surgery." There was a heaviness in his tone that frightened me. "Dad?"

"We just got an update. They . . . well, they can't believe he's alive, honey. Apparently his heart stopped on the table, and they barely managed to get it beating again." My stomach sank. Whatever power I'd lent John with my blood had worn off. "They're doing everything they can to stabilize him, but they found some other injuries."

Shit. I had been so distracted by John's blood loss, I hadn't checked him thoroughly. "What other injuries?"

"He's got a hema . . . hema-something, I don't remember the name, but it's blood in his kidneys, like he was hit." My dad sounded worried. "Did he and Quinn get in a fight or something?"

"No, no . . ." *Shit*. One of the werewolves must have hit John while Clara was busy. Why hadn't I thought to ask Sybil about the fight? I was losing control of the situation. "I don't know how it happened. Maybe he fell or something before we were hanging out tonight."

"Well, ordinarily it wouldn't be life-threatening, but with the blood loss . . ." His voice was heavy. "They're doing everything they can," he repeated. "Blossom is on her way, and I've called Pastor Sean to come too."

I felt like my insides were being run through an industrial shredder. My parents had invited their pastor to the hospital to pray over John. They wouldn't do that unless they were really worried he could die. "Blossom's not going to like that," I said without thinking.

"She'll have to deal with it," he said a little sternly. "Prayers won't hurt anyone, whatever you believe."

I made myself take a breath. "Listen, Dad . . . I sent for Sashi." I was pleased at how clear I sounded.

My dad grunted, startled. "To . . . say goodbye?"

"Oh, *no*," I hurried to say. "No, she's a trauma specialist, remember? I told her what happened, and she's coming."

There was a much longer pause this time, and I knew my dad was thinking it through. From his perspective, Sashi wouldn't be able to do anything for John that wasn't already being done, but he wasn't going to say that, since calling her had obviously made me feel better. "If you think that's best," he said finally. "You know we love Sashi. We'll make sure she gets in to see him. How's Quinn?"

"Better. His doctor thought it was just, um, some kind of panic attack. Not a heart attack."

My dad made a hmph noise. "Just make sure he takes it seriously. I know he's young, but he should get a full cardio workup when he gets a chance."

That would be a very interesting day for some hapless doctor. "I'll tell him, Dad. I'm having a little trouble with my cell phone, but I'll call back to check in, okay?"

"We'll be here."

Simon came back into the kitchen, pulling off the surgical gloves. He stopped when he saw my face. "Is he . . ."

"Alive? For now." If I talked about it, I was going to cry again, so I hopped off the counter. "Come on, let's go."

Simon followed me without a word.

Chapter 36

It should have been at least a forty-five-minute drive from Boulder to Denver, but there was no traffic at three thirty in the morning and I decided to push Maven's deal with the police as far as I could. Luckily for me, our route passed through the main streets in Boulder, which I had already cleared of distracting ghosts. We made it to the Denver city limits in less than a half hour, but then I did need to slow down so I could navigate through the remnants.

It was even more difficult than usual, since I felt like my brain was full of skittering bugs. John could die. Katia could die. I'd burned my relationship with Maven, possibly forever. And I was about to do something I'd never thought I'd even consider.

"Lex?" Simon had asked me something, obviously more than once.

"Sorry, what?"

"I said, did you bring that stone?"

"Oh. Yes. It's in my backpack, in a drawstring bag."

Simon leaned between the seats to dig through my backpack and emerged with a simple cotton bag the size of a cell phone. "Can I touch it?" he asked.

"You're going to have to, for it to work."

Simon upended the bag into one hand, exposing a chunk of cassiterite as big as his thumb on a black silk cord.

Crystals were powered by gravitational magic, which often clashed with the magic used by witches. I didn't really know why some stones worked for witches and others didn't, but I was happy to use the ones I knew about: labradorite, obsidian, bloodstone, amethyst, a few others. Cassiterite was a threshold stone, and I'd found that it could work as a sort of telephone to ghosts.

The first time I'd used it to talk to a ghost during the day, I'd gotten a small, store-bought rock. This piece of cassiterite was bigger and of better quality than the first, purchased from a grumbling Blossom Wheaton, who'd become my reluctant—and price-inflating—source of high-quality crystals.

"What do I do?" Simon said uncertainly. He wasn't used to being on the student side of our student-teacher relationship.

"Um . . ." I hadn't really tried to verbalize how I used the crystals, and I struggled for the right words. "Well, when I use it, I kind of hold it in both hands and concentrate on seeing with my magic. It's gravitational magic, and you're a different kind of witch than me, so I suppose it might not work for you at all. But it's worth a try."

Simon looked thoughtful. "Okay. I can try a few things. Anything else I should know?"

I pursed my lips for a moment. "Well . . . she's probably going to be kind of pissy. I haven't been visiting."

"Really?" He sounded surprised.

I rolled my eyes over to him. "She's not actually my family, you know. I used to come in exchange for information, but nothing's been going on." I shrugged. "Our last deal was up six months ago. So she's either going to be pissed or desperate, or some combination of the two."

"Great," Simon said dryly. "How could that go wrong?"

Finally, we reached the commercial area around Market Street. In the nineteenth century, Denver had a booming red-light district near what is now Coors Field. I have no idea how many brothels existed in that era, but I know one of them was owned by a boundary witch named Nellie Evans. Nellie had gotten into a disagreement with Maven and "killed" her, only to discover Maven was an extremely powerful vampire. Maven hadn't been very forgiving, and she'd put an end to Nellie's life by cutting off her head.

Nellie hadn't moved on, either because she couldn't or because she'd chosen not to. As it turned out, boundary witches left fully sentient ghosts, and Nellie was willing to give me information on boundary magic—for a price. She would not, however, go into detail about her family's history, or explain why she preferred being a bored ghost in a run-down old brothel to moving on. She also did not want to discuss how she had failed to notice that Maven was a vampire when she was alive, though I'd asked.

Dealing with Nellie was a hassle, and I had been perfectly happy to take a break from it while things were slow in Boulder. But now I was back.

It was not even four in the morning, so we had no trouble finding street parking just off Market, in front of Nellie's brothel. It was a shabby, derelict building on a street that had been dramatically gentrified in the last twenty years to entice tourists and Rockies fans. It was situated between a club and a vegan pizza place, and despite frequent attempts over the years, no one had yet managed to turn Nellie's eyesore into something pretty. I sort of respected that about her.

"Jeez, it's not hard to figure out which building, is it," Simon muttered as he looked up at the old, paint-splintered façade. The door that faced the street was heavily boarded, and even in the streetlight you could see rust on the nails. "It's like the Addams family moved in next to adult Disneyland."

"Don't let Nellie hear you say that," I warned. "Can you do that security camera hex thing?"

"Sure."

I wasn't worried about a humans-go-away ward here—Nellie's brothel seemed to discourage visitors without any additional intervention. I figured the security camera hex was worth the extra two minutes, though.

When he had finished, Simon joined me at the back of the Jeep, where I was lifting out the bundle we'd brought from John's house. "How are we going to get in?" he asked, pointing at the old boards over the entrance.

"The real entrance is in back," I told him. "Apparently it's a brothel thing. We go through that alley."

Simon looked over my shoulder at the dark passage between the club and the brothel. There were no lights down there—the club kept trying to install them, but they always mysteriously shorted out. "Oh," he said, looking a little nervous. His eyes dropped to the bundle in my arms. "Here, why don't I get that. You can grab the box from up front and lead the way with the light."

A moment later, I had balanced the box on my hip with my bandaged hand so I could guide us with a flashlight. We started down the alley, picking our way around the trash from the club. I occasionally called over my shoulder to warn Simon so he wouldn't step on anything. "They've never heard of security lights?" Simon grumbled as he narrowly avoided slipping on a slick of dried vomit.

"I think Nellie blows them out," I told him.

"She has control over the physical environment?" Simon sounded interested now.

"A little—cold spots and minor power outages, mainly. That's how she's kept this place from being torn down for the last hundred-some years."

"Hmm. Is she restricted to this building?"

I stepped around an overflowing recycling bin. "Yes . . . but I guess I don't know if that's by choice or not," I admitted. I hadn't thought to ask. I had a feeling Simon was going to have a lot of questions I hadn't thought to ask.

I pushed open the door—I'd broken the lock years ago, and no one but me ever seemed to come here. I wasn't sure if Nellie had a way to actively discourage humans from entering, or if people had just sort of forgotten about this building, after so many years of trying to ignore it. Maybe it was both.

I walked in without thinking much about it, but Simon was more cautious, entering slowly and dropping the bundle just inside the door so he could look around. The back door opened onto a sort of grand entrance—a massive staircase curved up to the second story, where a balcony railing would have once allowed the women to make their appearance. On previous visits Nellie was always waiting for me at the entrance, impatient and complaining. "Nellie? Are you here?" I called, feeling a little ridiculous. Where else would she be?

My voice echoed in the empty space. The building *felt* empty, and I began to worry in earnest. "Could she have . . . moved on?" Simon asked, sounding as nervous as I felt.

"I don't know. It seems silly, but the only thing I can think to do is look in all the rooms." I gestured upstairs. "There are bedrooms up there, and downstairs has a kitchen and parlor and stuff. I haven't spent much time in any of them."

"Okay. Are the stairs safe?"

"Yeah, I've gone up there before, to check for drunks and rats."

"Charming." Simon turned on his cell phone flashlight. "I'll try up there, if you want to look down here."

He started up the creaky steps, and I headed to the left of the staircase, still calling Nellie's name. I'd taken only a few steps out of the main foyer when I heard Simon call down the stairs.

"Lex? Something seems . . . weird."

Weird? That didn't sound like my friend the scientist. I turned and went back into the entrance hall, tilting my head back to see the second floor. Simon was paused on the next-to-the-top step, half-turned so he faced the railing. The glow from his phone's screen illuminated his face enough for me to see his frown. He squinted down at me.

"What is it?" I asked.

"I don't know—I'm wearing the stone under my shirt, but I just feel . . ." He put one hand on the railing to steady himself.

I saw it then, in the phone's glow—his breath was fogging. "Si, maybe you should—"

Then Nellie burst into view an inch and a half from his face.

I'd seen Nellie change her clothes and hair plenty of times, but I'd never seen this particular look on her: filthy, moth-eaten rags and long tangled hair that screamed "corpse." She looked straight out of a horror movie, but terrifyingly real—and as vivid as I'd ever seen her, even when Morgan had been boosting the ley lines. Simon cried out and instinctively stumbled back. I was already running toward them, but way too late—his back foot skidded off the edge of the step and he tumbled down the stairs.

Chapter 37

"No!"

I ran up the steps, the beam of my light bobbing wildly so that all I saw was flashes of pinwheeling limbs. I was moving as fast as I'd ever moved in my life, but he was already two-thirds of the way down before I reached him. I had just enough time to drop the flashlight and grab the banister *hard* as he bowled into my midsection.

An *oomph* burst out of me, but I managed to grab hold of Simon's shirt with my free hand. My left arm wrenched as his momentum tried to carry him straight through me, and I heard the banister creak dangerously. It held, though, and so did my shoulder.

"Simon? Simon!" He didn't answer. His body was limp, draped across the steps.

Nellie had winked out again, and my flashlight had tumbled down the stairs and rolled away toward the door, leaving us in almost complete darkness. I released the banister and felt around his chest until I found his neck. He had a pulse.

I was off-balance; I needed to get us off the fucking steps before anything else happened. I eased his body down the rest of the stairs to the floor. When I touched his head, one of my hands came away wet, and I fought not to sob. I scrambled to my feet and ran after the flashlight, a sturdy Maglite that would probably survive a fall off the building, much less the stairs. As I grabbed it, I caught sight of my hand—it was bright, jarring red.

I bolted back to Simon. He still wasn't moving, and I had a horrifying flashback to Lily's limp body only an hour and a half earlier. Being my friend was costing the Pellars way too much tonight.

I panned the light over him, trying to find the source of the bleeding without jostling him any further. There was a small cut on the back of his head, which was probably what had knocked him out. His cheekbone was already puffing up, and one wrist was obviously broken, judging by the grotesque angle. He had probably tried to catch himself on it. I'd done the same thing before.

Suddenly one of his legs shifted, and he let out a small moan. I flicked my wrist to train the light on his ankle, using my other hand to gently pull up the leg of his jeans. It was red and already swelling—a sprain or a hairline fracture, probably. I stood up, stepping back from him. "Nellie," I yelled. "Get your ass out here!"

There was a pause; then her sullen voice rang down from the direction of the second floor, though she still wasn't visible. "I weren't trying to hurt 'im."

I ignored that for now. "Listen to me, Nellie Evans," I called. "I'm going out to the car for a first aid kit. If you so much as *look* at him funny while I'm gone, I will make you regret it for every second of this life."

As fast as I could, I jogged out to the Jeep and scooped up the backpack with all the first aid gear, ignoring the ache in my own shoulder. When I got back inside, Simon hadn't moved, and his eyes were closed again. There was no sign of Nellie, so I dropped the backpack next to Simon and knelt down to deal with his injuries.

I had a simple plastic-and-Velcro splint that would stabilize his broken wrist; best to do that first, while he was still unconscious. I slipped his hand into the loops, slid it slowly into place, and, holding my breath, gently repositioned the broken bone so it would connect again. Simon made a little noise of pain, finally opening his eyes.

"Simon? Can you hear me?"

His eyes rolled to me. "Lex . . . what happened? Did we win?"

I choked on a laugh. "Not yet. Hold on, this is gonna hurt." I pulled the Velcro straps tight, wincing as Simon cried out in pain.

Through gritted teeth, he asked me, "How long was I out?"

"Maybe three minutes? We just got here."

There was no reply. His eyes were closing. I scooted to his face. "Hey! Simon!"

He didn't respond. I didn't want to risk jarring his head injury, so I took his face gently in my hands, being careful with the puffy cheekbone. "Simon," I said softly. "Please wake up."

Simon opened his eyes, and I was suddenly aware of how close together we were. "Your hands are cold," he whispered.

I began to pull back, but his good hand floated off the floor and settled on my elbow, holding me in place. I had dropped my guard, and for a moment I felt the connection between us as though it were a palpable thing, a cord that looped around us. Simon's eyes widened. "I'm sorry," he said softly.

"For what?"

"I never . . ." His voice drifted off for a moment, his gaze losing focus. When his eyes returned to mine, he just said, "Lex? I don't feel so good."

"I think you have a concussion," I told him. "I've got a little emergency supply of morphine—"

He started to shake his head, grimaced, and said, "No. I can handle it."

I would have said the same thing in his position—in fact, I *had*, more than once—so I didn't argue. "Then just rest here for a minute, okay?"

"'Kay."

I stood up and backed a few feet away from him, turning to face the room. "Nellie Evans," I shouted. "Show yourself."

Nothing happened. There was no movement in the dark entryway.

"Nellie!" My voice was threaded with rage.

Her voice floated down from above. "I was just having a bit of fun. I dinna mean to hurt anyone."

"Bullshit," I spat. "You were pissed at me, and you thought you'd hurt my friend to put me in my place."

Silence.

"No more lies, Nellie." I put the warning in my voice. "Come out where I can see you."

Nothing happened.

I did not have time for this. "Okay, fine. You want to play games? I can play too."

I pulled my pocketknife out of my jeans and squatted down in the flashlight beam. Gritting my teeth, I dragged the blade across the meat of my uninjured thumb, careful not to cut too deeply this time. I didn't want to mess around with the skin adhesive again.

Nellie popped up across from me as I was drawing a circle on the floor with my blood. The horror movie getup was gone, replaced by her standard look: a pinup-style polka-dotted crop top and short-shorts, complete with bright red lipstick and black hair in those fancy curls. Very Bettie Page, if Bettie were a leathery forty-year-old who looked like she knew her way around a knife fight. "What are you doing?" she demanded.

I didn't look up. "I'm sending you across the bridge."

"No!" Nellie disappeared, reappeared next to me. She was burning up a lot of energy tonight—but then, she probably hadn't needed to become visible in months. Maybe she could store up her strength. It would have been an interesting thought, if I'd had time to care. "I said I was sorry!" She sounded desperate.

"Yeah, but you didn't mean it." I took a moment to fuss with the circle, filling in every gap so it was complete.

"Goddammit, Lex!"

I finished the circle and touched the tips of my tattoos to the line of blood, willing it to open. *Door.*

"Don't you do this!" She was pleading now, her voice practically a sob.

I sat back on my heels, regarding her coldly. "I came here in good faith, owing you nothing, and you tried to kill my friend."

"I didn't—"

I overrode her. "I told you once that I had no interest in banishing you if you weren't hurting anyone." I pointed at Simon. "What do you call that?"

"Please," she begged. "I'll do anything you want."

I cocked my head at her. I could feel the magic of my circle begin to build up inside me, the door pulling at my attention. We were running out of time in more ways than one, but I still drew out the moment for another five seconds.

"*Please*, Lex!"

I shrugged, scuffing the line of blood. The door vanished. "I want information, right now, no more games or tricks."

"Ask. Ask me anything."

I pointed through the entryway, toward the body rolled up in John's cheap IKEA living room rug. "Tell me how to raise the dead."

Chapter 38

I had expected an argument, and I got one. "Do you have any idea what you're askin' me?" Nellie didn't sound angry, just scared and worried. "That's the strongest magic we have—deep and dark. If you—"

"I have *no time*," I snapped. "My friend needs a hospital. You have two minutes to explain it to me before I decide to cut my losses with you." I twirled the pocketknife, a little theatrically.

We stared at each other for a long moment, but Nellie saw something in my face and sagged. "You need a sacrifice," she finally grumbled. "Life for life, death for death. I'm assuming you didn't bring your boyfriend here just to kill him."

"He's not my boyfriend," I corrected, but I got up and went over to the box I'd brought in with us. I peeled back the top flaps slowly, but the chicken was still fast asleep, thanks to Simon's sedation.

Nellie had manifested next to me, her color the normal, translucent level I was used to. She peered into the box. "That could work," she said, begrudging. "For a few minutes. Maybe ten."

"How do I do it?"

Nellie didn't need to breathe air, as far as I could tell, but she still made a point of sighing. "Lex-girl . . . don't do this. Once you raise the dead . . . they'll begin to call to you."

I could have asked her what she meant. I should have. But I had ninety minutes until I was supposed to be in Cheyenne, and I was afraid to know. "I have to. Tell me how."

So Nellie explained.

I'm not sure what I expected for a ritual to raise the dead, but it was actually fairly simple, if gross: I needed to exsanguinate the chicken on top of the corpse. As the blood rushed out, so would its life. I had to use my mindset to guide the chicken's life force into the werewolf and hold it there while I asked my questions.

The container for life force—the werewolf's *soul*, for lack of a better term—was gone, so whatever I poured into the body wouldn't stay long. Since I wasn't about to kill another human and steal their soul, the chicken's life force would start seeping from my fingers almost immediately, and I would have to let it go.

"What happens if I don't?" I asked, trying to keep the nervousness out of my voice.

Nellie gave me a frank look, then glanced at Simon. "Your magic will start taking life out of the next weakest soul it can find."

My eyes hardened. "He's a witch."

"Really?" Nellie's ghostly eyes widened, then narrowed with calculation. "Interesting. You don't see many men witches, at least not back in my day."

"Focus, Nellie." My stomach roiled with nerves, but I didn't have time for second thoughts. "We're running out of time."

Nellie looked uneasy. "Listen . . ." she began. "Is there anything I can say that will talk you away from this?"

I met her eyes. I had learned how to look at the surface of them, rather than let my gaze drift through. I had never seen Nellie's face look so devoid of calculation. If I didn't know better, I would have believed she was actually worried for me. I softened a little. "No, there isn't." I took a breath, moving the flashlight so I could check on Simon. His eyes were open, and he'd turned his head sideways so he could watch me. I kept the light out of his eyes, and when he saw me looking, he shot me a weak smile. "It's okay," he said softly. "We'll be okay."

I nodded. It was time to begin.

Killing the chicken was the worst part. I had to slice her throat, but at least the poor thing was still sedated and I don't think she felt much. I stood over the dead woman, one foot on either side of her waist, and made the cut as quick and deep as I could. When the blood began to pour out of the chicken, running onto the werewolf's chest, I switched into my boundary magic mindset, feeling the steadying presence of my mother's bloodstone over my heart.

It was just as Nellie had said—the blood was like a weak, yellowish cascade of gossamer, pooling onto the dead werewolf's chest. I extended ghostly fingers with my free hand and cupped them over the heart, trying to keep the pool together. When the bleeding stopped, I dropped the chicken, crouched, and used my other hand to help hold the small accumulation of life in place. Then I shifted to a kneeling position and pressed down, like I was doing chest compressions.

The body began to spasm.

Startled, I blinked out of the boundary mindset, seeing the corpse clearly now. Behind me, both of the lower legs were convulsing, and the knowledge that I was straddling a dead body suddenly crashed into me. I started to swing one leg off her, but realized that if I moved, her spasming legs might cause me to let go of the chicken's essence. I clenched my jaw and stayed put.

Nellie's quiet voice came to me from a few feet away. "Now, call her back."

Through gritted teeth, I pushed my words into the body—the same way I pressed vampires, or opened the gate to lay ghosts. *"Come back."*

Slowly, the woman's eyelids dragged their way upward, fighting against the beginning of rigor mortis, which had already started in her face. Her pupils were as dilated as any I'd ever seen, and her eyes ticked around on the ceiling like her muscles had already forgotten what to do. I struggled to keep my magic working at her chest without actually dropping into my mindset. I needed to see her face.

Her legs had stopped convulsing, but my position was too precarious to move away. "Ask her a question," Nellie instructed, as though I were an idiot. "Your clock is ticking."

"What's your name?" I blurted.

The ticking eyes finally found mine, though she seemed to stare right through to my soul. "Kelly," she said, her voice a mechanical croak.

"Why were you working for Morgan Pellar, Kelly?"

"Why doesn't it hurt?"

That confused me, and I almost lost my grip on her chest. I could already feel the stolen life force trying to seep out through my fingers. "Why doesn't what hurt?"

Kelly's dead hand slowly rose, scratching lightly at her chest just above where I sat. "The wolf. There's no itching. No hunger."

"You brought me a dead *werewolf*?" Nellie complained.

I ignored her. To Kelly, I said, "You died, Kelly. The werewolf magic won't bother you ever again. After you answer my questions, you can rest."

Her hand relaxed back down to her side. "Okay."

I had about a thousand questions, but I skipped to the most important one. "Where is Morgan Pellar?"

"In the tunnels," Kelly rasped without hesitation.

"Where are the tunnels?"

"Beneath Cheyenne."

I glanced up, past Nellie to Simon. He looked as baffled as I was. But the chicken's life force was already slipping away; it was like trying to hold down steam. "Where is the tunnel entrance?"

Her eyes ticked away, then back, a human gesture for trying to remember. "There are lots of them." Her eyelids began to sink down.

I dropped into my mindset to check the yellow life force. There was so little left. "Kelly! Which entrance is the closest?" I burst out.

The eyes didn't open any farther. "Central and Lincolnway."

I was already losing her. Nellie had said I'd have a few minutes, but maybe it worked differently if the sacrifice was sedated, or maybe I was just too new at this. I could feel the gossamer sliding away from me and I wished I'd prioritized my questions. There was so much I still didn't understand.

"Why were you helping Morgan?" I asked, desperate.

"Money," Kelly's voice was still mechanical, but very quiet now. "Our pack needed money."

Simon's voice rang out from behind Nellie. "Ask her where Morgan got the money!"

He'd startled me; I almost lost it, struggled, got control again. "Where did Morgan get the money?" I demanded.

"He gave it to her."

"Who did?"

The last of the life bled out through my hands, but I was so focused on my question that I barely noticed. Then something very small gave way to my right, collapsing. Then another. And another. I dropped into my mindset and saw small drifts of yellow worming through the walls toward me.

I'd killed something.

"Let go, you damn fool!" Nellie hissed. She must have been able to see it too.

I wasn't sure how to disconnect, so I threw myself sideways, ripping my tattoos and my focus away from Kelly. When I looked back, her body seemed to have hardened into wax.

Nellie disappeared for a moment, then blinked back. "You killed rats," she announced. "Four of them."

Relief flooded me, but I could only nod. Then I turned my head sideways, away from the body, and puked. A lot.

Nellie began to curse, using words I'd never heard—or at least never considered as fuel for expletives. It would have been impressive if I weren't busy dry-heaving. I caught the words, "This is my son-of-a-bitchin' *home*!"

There was nothing else in my body to come up, but I didn't respond. I could feel a bit of the boundary magic still inside me—I'd stolen more life from the rats than I'd pushed into Kelly. I had to do something with it, or I would get magic-drunk.

So I put both hands on the floor and whispered the cleaning spell Simon had taught me. It did come in handy. The vomit disappeared—along with all the dirt, cobwebs, dust bunnies, and blood spatters from the chicken. The room was still old and shabby, but it was spotless.

Nellie's mouth fell open in shock, and for the first time since I'd met her, she was rendered speechless.

"Time to disappear, Nellie," I said, wishing my voice were stronger. "I'm calling an ambulance. You *will* allow them to come take my friend away without interference."

Her face tightened as she finally remembered herself. "The deal was to help you raise the dead, and I did that. You never said nothin' about allowing humans in here."

"I have no. Fucking. Time for this," I snapped. "I will come back and talk to you this week, but right now, get the hell out of my face."

Whatever she saw in my eyes convinced her, because Nellie blinked away immediately. I turned and crawled over to Simon. He had gotten paler, his olive skin an unnerving shade of green, and sweat had broken out over his face. The pain had to be pretty serious. I checked his fore-head—not feverish, but clammy.

"Are you okay?" he asked me.

I had to smile. "I'll be fine. Just a little nausea. Did your cell phone survive the fall?"

"No idea."

I stood up and shone the flashlight around until I found Simon's phone, which had tumbled down the stairs with him. There was a shallow crack on the screen, but the heavy-duty case seemed to have protected it from serious damage. I handed it to Simon, who unlocked it and handed it back.

I went to his contacts and called Quinn.

"Simon?" he answered, sounding worried. "What's going on now?"

"It's me," I began, but he broke in before I could go on.

"Lex! Where are you? What the hell is—"

"Quinn, listen: I'm going to call an ambulance to come to Nellie's brothel and pick up Simon. I need you to get a vampire here to press the EMTs." I glanced down at the floor. "Oh, and get rid of a werewolf body."

There was a pause of one heartbeat, and then my boyfriend exploded with questions. I had to practically shout him down. "There's no time! Did you check on Charlie?"

"Yes—Maven got Clara back on her feet; she's outside Elise's house. And Sashi called your cell. She's in Boulder on her way to the hospital to help John." He recited this quickly, sounding pissed. "Now, what happened to Simon?"

"He fell down the stairs. Broken wrist, and I think a bad ankle sprain." I thought of John's injuries. "Possible internal damage. Go see him at the hospital; he can explain. I love you."

I hung up the phone. Simon opened his mouth, but I held up a finger, dialing 911. I gave the dispatcher the address and told her to send the paramedics around the back. Then I hung up on her, too, and handed the phone back to Simon.

He gave me another wobbly smile. "What are you going to do?"

"As soon as your ambulance gets here, I'm going to go up to Cheyenne to get Katia." Morgan had said my aunt would be waiting at the Depot, but I knew she wouldn't risk that I'd show up without Charlie. One of her employees was probably stationed there as a trap.

"Oh." Simon's eyes widened with understanding. "I'm an idiot. That's why you quit Maven's service."

I nodded. "If I don't work for her, she's not liable for my actions, in Wyoming or anywhere else."

He looked at me silently for a long moment. "You're going to kill Morgan, aren't you?"

I didn't answer. Morgan was expecting me to go along with her plan, so she would likely still be in Cheyenne when I got there. The odds that she'd let Katia go without a fight seemed pretty much nonexistent.

My plan had been to send Simon to the meeting point at the Depot as a diversion, while I approached Morgan wherever she was hiding. But I was on my own now, and I wasn't playing around.

Simon saw most of this in my face. "I'm coming with you," he said, struggling to sit up.

"Whoa, hey." He got even paler when he was sitting, but I helped him scoot back to the wall, stretching his legs out in front of him. "You can't come with me, Si. You can barely sit up."

"She's my sister," he insisted.

"She's killing people, Si," I said heavily. "Or sending them to be killed."

I glanced back at the dead werewolf. *Why doesn't it hurt?* I didn't know anything about Kelly, and I wasn't sorry that Clara had killed her to protect Charlie. But somewhere along the line, Kelly had been a victim too.

"You think I don't know that?" Simon released my hand so he could swipe at his eyes. "But she wasn't always like this. She taught me how to swim . . ."

"Oh, Simon." I couldn't hug him without hurting him, so I scooted to sit next to him and rested my head on his shoulder. He and Lily had been through a lot in the last few days, and so much of it had been for me. None of this was fair to them.

"Wait, listen," he said, his voice suddenly hopeful, "maybe we can convince the witches at the congress to bind her magic. Like Morgan's been trying to do to all of us."

I lifted my head to look at him, considering it. "Is that possible?"

"It's expensive, and it will probably take a couple of days. They'll have to find someone from out of state who can perform the ritual, and get at least a full coven to back them up, but . . . yeah, it's possible."

I bit my lip, thinking. "Okay," I said at last. "If you and Hazel can work on Maven, I will try to capture her instead of killing her."

He tilted his head back so he could study my face. "Promise me."

My heart sank. What were the chances that I could free Katia, capture Morgan without one of us dying, *and* get her all the way back to Boulder alive?

Even if I managed it, I sort of doubted that Maven would let Morgan live a second time. She would have to face the consequences of her actions, and by bringing her to Maven in Colorado, I would more or less be delivering her to her executioner.

But I wouldn't *be* the executioner. Maybe that was cowardly, or splitting hairs, but I did not want to kill my friends' sister. I was still messed up about werewolves because *one* werewolf had killed Sam.

I took a deep breath. "You have my word that I will do everything in my power to bring your sister back alive."

"Thank you." I'd rarely heard him sound this intense.

"If I can, you'll need to talk your mother into dropping the ward, so I can bring her back to Maven," I pointed out.

"I can do that," he said fiercely. "But I'll wait for your call." Then: "What time is it?"

I checked my watch. "Four twenty-five."

"Lex, you gotta go," he said. "I'll be fine. I've got my phone."

I wanted to argue, but he was right. Even if I got on the road right now, I'd need to drive like a bat out of hell to get there in time.

"Okay. Do me a favor? See what you can find online about tunnels in Cheyenne?" I asked, standing up. "Maps or blueprints or whatever?"

I felt bad about giving him work while he was hurt, but if anything, he looked relieved to have something to do. "You got it."

"There's some extra burner phones in the back of the Jeep. I'll call you from the road."

I was nearly to the door when Simon called after me. I turned around. "Tunnels," he said, his forehead wrinkled. "You're claustrophobic."

I sighed. "I know."

Chapter 39

The last time I'd been to Cheyenne was about a year and a half earlier, when Charlie had become obsessed with a television show called *Daniel Tiger's Neighborhood*.

The program was about a young tiger who rides around on a trolley visiting his friends, learning lessons about friendship, and being neighborly. I had watched many hours of it with Charlie, and for a few months it was the only thing she wanted to play, watch, or talk about.

That spring my parents had gone on a vacation, and I'd taken care of Charlie for a week while John was at work. After a few days of visiting our favorite Boulder spots, I started casting about for something new to do—and discovered that Cheyenne has a trolley tour.

When Morgan had instructed me to meet her at the historic depot, I'd known exactly where that was, because I'd been there with my niece. The people of Cheyenne—or at least the nice folks who ran the trolley tours—were crazy about the Depot, because it showcased Cheyenne's whole reason for existing: the railroads. Cheyenne had been chosen as a major stop on the First Transcontinental Railroad, which was a big deal in this part of the west.

It was cold, but there was no snow or ice on the roads, so I drove the big Jeep pretty recklessly all the way to the state line, doing my best to ignore the remnants. There are always plenty of ghosts on the highways, but I forced myself to blow right through them, absorbing the occasional emotional impact when one of them actually touched me. It was unsettling as hell, and I wished I'd thought to bring my mahogany obsidian, which protected me from psychic attacks. The remnants would still have been visible, but they wouldn't have been able to get inside my head. I'd never gotten in the practice of carrying the obsidian, though, because it also blocked Sam's voice. So I gritted my teeth and concentrated on not swerving the Jeep.

As I passed the rock formations and big metal bison silhouette that marked the border to Wyoming, I finally had to slow down. Maven didn't have any pull with the police in Wyoming. I had, I realized, gotten very used to Maven's support and protection. Even when I'd gone alone to face Lysander, an insanely powerful conduit, I'd done so with the reassurance that I had Maven's name behind me. Now I was on my own, and I couldn't even call my friends for help without causing political problems.

This sucked.

When I was about ten miles outside Cheyenne, driving within the speed limit now, I called Simon's cell with one of the burner phones.

"Hello?" Simon was talking loudly to be heard over what sounded like hospital noises. Part of me relaxed a little. I hadn't liked leaving him alone in Nellie's brothel.

"Hey, it's me. What did the doctor say?"

"Lex!" Simon sounded relieved too. "Hey. They think it's just the sprained ankle and broken wrist, but they're gonna do a scan—hey! I'm talking to—ow!"

There was a small commotion, and then Lily's voice came on the line. "Lex? What the hell is going on?"

"Lily!" I felt myself smiling like an idiot. It was so good to hear her voice. "Are you okay?"

"*No*, I'm not okay!" She sounded furious. "I feel like crap! A bunch of asshole goons showed up at Si's place and beat the shit out of Katia, and they held a gun on her until I drank fuckin' *belladonna*, and apparently it was all orchestrated by my own fucking *sister*—"

"Lily," I broke in. I was approaching the Cheyenne exits. "I'm really glad you're awake, but Simon has information that I need, and I'm out of time here."

"Ugh. Fine." She grumbled, but gave Simon the phone again. He came back on the line and said, "Okay, the tunnels are kind of a weird situation. A bunch of conspiracy-type websites suggest there are tunnels underneath much of downtown, built at the same time as the railroad. They might have just been transportation in the winter, but my guess is that they're steam tunnels, which used the waste steam from the railroad boilers to heat parts of downtown Cheyenne. Plenty of cities used to do something similar: Milwaukee, DC—"

I cut him off before he could get rolling. "Okay, so what's the weird part?"

"There's no official information on the tunnels anywhere online, and I haven't found a single photograph. A lot of sources suggest the whole existence of tunnels is just a rumor. It's like they're ashamed of them or something."

I frowned. "That's weird." Colorado was littered with tunnels, both the legitimate ones built for mining and the illegal ones built for illicit activities. A hundred-some years ago, a brothel like Nellie's would probably have had an underground entrance, for example, and bored miners had built plenty of secret tunnels during Prohibition to smuggle booze around. There were times when I was shocked that the entire state hadn't collapsed down a hundred feet.

But in Colorado, all that was celebrated public knowledge. There was a whole industry built around the shady parts of the state's past, and you could pay to take tours of many of those old tunnels. Some of them were too dangerous to visit, of course, but it struck me as odd that Cheyenne denied the tunnels' existence altogether.

"Yeah, well, I think there's something fishy there, like a humans-go-away spell, or some kind of payoff to city officials to keep the tunnels out of the public eye," Simon went on, his voice lowered. He sounded frustrated. "If I had more time, I could probably come up with some primary sources, but the bottom line is that I can't get you any maps or anything. Assuming the tunnels are real, you're going in blind."

Shit.

"Lex," he continued, pain in his voice, "maybe this is a bad idea."

"You think I should just let her kill Katia?"

"Of course not," he replied with irritation. "But maybe you should just go to the meeting spot at the Depot. Morgan might be willing to negotiate."

I had to doubt that. Morgan wanted me to use Charlie. If I wasn't going to do that, and I no longer had Maven's authority, what was there to negotiate? Even if she really did send Katia to the meeting with a guard, the guard could shoot Katia in the head the moment they realized Charlie wasn't with me, and take me as a hostage instead.

Trying to sound more confident than I felt, I replied, "I'll figure it out. Is Quinn with you?"

"No. He called, though. He's busy finding a new daytime hideout for Maven."

"Ah. Smart," was all I said. Sunrise was in an hour and a half. If I failed, or Morgan Pellar found some other way into Colorado, Maven would need to be somewhere Morgan couldn't find her.

"Oh, one more—" Simon began, but he was cut off by another small commotion in the background. He returned after a moment, his voice pitched even lower. "Lex, I gotta go. Quinn's guy is here, and so are the police."

"Okay, bye."

I hung up the phone, feeling nervous. From the moment Kelly had said the word "tunnels," I'd pictured myself in something the size of a subway tunnel, holding a map . . . which would somehow point to a single big spacious underground room, which would be Morgan's obvious hiding place.

But how much room would you really need for a steam tunnel? And if a lot of downtown Cheyenne had these underground tunnels, I might get lost down there forever.

The heat was on in the Jeep, but I found myself shivering. Could I even do this? What if I climbed down into one of the tunnels and just . . . froze? What if I got lost down there?

I didn't have any answers, but now I was entering the downtown area, and it was 5:27.

Downtown Cheyenne had a big public parking garage where tourists could leave their vehicles all day. I dumped the Jeep there, grabbed the backpack of supplies, and quickly checked my weapons. I had two shredder stakes, the Smith & Wesson revolver with its .357 silver bullets, and a Glock 21 that held ten rounds of .45 ammunition. After a moment of thought, I put the Glock in a pancake holster at my back and dropped the revolver into the Western-style holster on my left hip, where I was strongest. I rarely wore the hip holster in cities—it made me look like a day player in one of those cheesy Wild West shows—but my thigh-length parka hid it easily. It was only twenty degrees out, but I left the coat unzipped. It would still be tricky to draw the Glock from my back, but I figured if I needed a second gun I was probably already in trouble.

Cheyenne's downtown wasn't all that big, and the parking garage was only a couple of blocks from the tunnel entrance on Lincolnway. I jogged the two blocks, my breath fogging in front of me as I ran through it. The sky would begin to lighten soon, but for now I was just running from streetlight to streetlight, on the lookout for any kind of movement that would indicate I was being watched.

From the moment I'd talked to Morgan, I had expected a trap—but I didn't know what *kind* of trap. There were several times when I thought I saw something—a hint of movement, a glint off a glass window—but I was nearly late to the meeting. I wasn't stopping unless someone stepped into my path.

At first, the intersection of Central Ave and East Lincolnway seemed completely unremarkable. The northern half had buildings on each side, and the southern half was a small public lawn bordering parking lots. Given the choice, I turned north, toward the buildings. On the northeast corner of the intersection, the building's twin façades were broken up by a short alley, probably a place for vehicles to park and make deliveries. Along one side of the alley was a rickety-looking wrought iron railing with a narrow gate. When I got closer, I saw that the gate led to a set of concrete stairs. The stairs and the pavement next to them were littered with cigarette butts—probably a favorite smoking spot for the employees.

I switched on my flashlight and shone it down the stairs, exposing a heavy brick door at the very bottom. Even from here I could see a weathered silver padlock the size of my fist secured to the door. Shit. I had a small multitool in the backpack, but why hadn't I thought to bring a bolt cutter?

I jumped the gate, which was only hip-high, and descended the stairs slowly, leaving the relative safety of the streetlights. When I reached the door at the bottom, I tested the padlock. It was thicker than it had looked from the top of the steps. Even the bolt cutters I had at home wouldn't cut through that monster.

Anxious now, I felt around the iron metalwork that the bolt secured, hoping I might be able to break it or pry it open with the multitool, but despite its obvious age, it was sturdy. Fighting panic, I ran my gloved fingers over the top of the doorframe and along the seams, hoping for a hidden key. There was nothing.

Which meant I was screwed.

"Shit!" I smacked one fist against the bricks at face level and imme-diately had to shake out my hand from the pain. Now I had no choice but to go to the meeting and try to kill Morgan's lackey before he or she could kill Katia. I had *raised the dead* for nothing.

Something dropped past my ear, and there was a metallic tinkling sound at my feet.

Quick as I could, I pulled the revolver and raised the weapon and the flashlight toward the top of the staircase, then ran the light along the railing. Nothing there.

I dropped the light to my feet and saw a bronze key on a cheap key ring. I squatted down to look closer, not touching it. The key chain was a smiling cartoon animal with a mischievous grin.

A wolf.

I flashed the light up again. "Who's there?"

A familiar face popped over the railing above my head, smiling down at me. Then another. And then a couple of snouts pointed through the bars, and a big-ass brown wolf appeared above the gate at the top of the stairs, leaning on his front paws.

"Hey, Lex," Mary said with great satisfaction. "You know, it helps if you have a key."

Chapter 40

There were five werewolves total, though only Mary and Keith were in human form. It was Keith who pushed the little gate open—not even slowing down as he snapped the thin metal lock holding it closed. A sand-colored wolf with a white undercoat and bright blue eyes trotted past the others and down the stairs, where he reared up to put his front paws on my shoulders, licking my cheek with a warm pink tongue. "Tobias," I said, laughing a little. "Gross. Get down."

He dropped to all fours, still doggie-grinning up at me with his tail and ears high. I looked up at Mary, who had come around the railing and started down the stairs, her long legs bare under a hip-length parka. "What are you doing here?" I asked.

"Got a voice mail from Simon. He said you could use some help."

That was what Simon had been about to say on the phone—that he'd told Mary I was coming. I eyed her. "You must have already been back in Cheyenne, to get here so fast."

She blew out a breath, taking the last step. I tilted the flashlight down so I wouldn't blind anyone. "Yeah, well. I thought about what you said. We all did." She glanced behind her, up at the rest of the group, then looked at me again. "I'm the alpha," she said simply. "And if we're going to be a pack, we needed to come back to Cheyenne."

I bent and picked up the key, holding it up to show her. "And how do you have this?"

Her face hardened. "Because," she said with a little heat, "this is our fucking town, and those are *our* fucking tunnels." She lifted her chin. "Ryan Dunn discovered them almost twenty years ago, and figured they'd be a good emergency place for werewolves to change if we ever got stuck in Cheyenne during the full moon. Our pack has spent years exploring the tunnels in both forms—not to mention finding creative ways to keep humans away."

Which was why no one in Cheyenne wanted to talk about them. I nodded. "And when Morgan Pellar killed three of your wolves—"

"She effectively broke up the pack so someone else could come in and take our territory," Mary said flatly. "We've checked all four of our entrances tonight, and they all smell like strange wolves."

I looked down at the key in my hand. "How did *they* get in?"

Mary gave me a smile that was all teeth and hostility. "That's exactly what I'm planning to ask them."

I wondered if the flashes of movement I'd seen had been the wolves, but it wasn't really important. "Wait, you've been scouting downtown? Did you see anyone at the Depot?"

Keith started to shake his head, but Mary said, "Yes. There are two werewolves waiting on a bench, a male and a female. The female has a blanket over most of her."

"Crap." Morgan had sent a decoy to the meeting point in case I didn't bring Charlie. I took no particular satisfaction from being right. "Okay, well, I'm already late, and it sounds like there's a lot of ground to cover. We should go in and start searching."

She shook her head. "That won't be necessary. We're pretty sure we know where Morgan is holed up."

I brightened. "Really?" That would save me so much time.

Mary nodded. "These tunnels are just a grid, with a few old maintenance closets—but at the southeast corner there is a natural offshoot leading toward Holliday Park."

I tried to pull up my mental map of Cheyenne. "What's at Holliday Park?"

"What's *beneath* Holliday Park," she corrected. Her smile was grim. "It's a cave." She gestured at the key. "Come on, let's get moving."

With the werewolves keeping watch, I unlocked the heavy door, pushing hard to swing it open. To my surprise, it was warm inside. Mary was already unzipping her parka. "We're going to run, so you might want to leave your coat here," she told me, dropping her own on the floor of the tunnel, just inside the door. Beneath it, she was wearing an athletic tank and short-shorts.

I shrugged out of my coat, exposing the hip holster. Nobody in the tunnels was going to care if I was armed. Keith's jacket was no more than a windbreaker, but he took it off and dropped it on top of Mary's coat and mine.

"Why is it so warm? I thought these tunnels weren't being used."

She shrugged. "Dunn knew more about how it works, but I think a small amount of heat still leaks into the tunnels from the depot."

"Okay." I pointed the flashlight into the tunnel. It was perfectly round, with two huge pipes running along the right side at waist height. The walls were stone or concrete, with metal-caged utility lights every hundred feet or so. Most of the lights seemed to have blown out, and I had no hope of navigating without the flashlight.

I had been expecting lots of moisture, for some reason, but it was dry and silent. "Finn, Tobias, and I will go ahead of you," Mary said, stepping backward without looking, going deeper into the tunnel. "Alex and Keith will bring up the rear."

She saw me shifting my weight from one foot to the other and stopped moving. "What?"

"Nothing." I glanced at the round walls, my chest already tightening, and Mary followed my gaze. I realized the beam of my flashlight was shaking slightly. She marched back to me.

"You're claustrophobic," she stated, hands on her hips.

I winced, not bothering to deny it. "I'll be fine."

Mary sighed and put a hand on each of my shoulders. "Look at me," she said, her voice low and calm.

I tore my gaze away from the cramped space and met her eyes. "It's a *tunnel*," she emphasized. "It goes on and on. You will *not* be trapped."

I just nodded, because what else could I do? I had to go in, and I had to be okay.

You can do this, Allie, came Sam's voice in my head. *This isn't the Humvee, or the hole in the desert. There's plenty of space.*

Mary looked at me for another moment, then looked at Tobias, who was sitting next to me. "Tobias, stay with her," Mary commanded. "If she panics, get my attention."

Tobias ducked his head in compliance, then shoved his head under my hand. I scratched behind his ears a little absently, taking comfort in his canine presence. I didn't really understand why Tobias liked me so much, but at the moment I was grateful for it.

"Okay," Mary said, nodding at Finn, the biggest wolf. My eyes narrowed at him, but it wasn't exactly the right moment to bring up how someone with mechanical experience had tampered with Dunn's car. At least he was going up front, where I could keep an eye on him. "Let's go," Mary said.

And we began to run.

In either form, I discovered, werewolves are basically made of stamina.

I was in very good shape—and I'd spent a lot of time running while carrying weapons—but I was exhausted and sore and fighting claustrophobia. Running through the tunnels with werewolves, some of whom I wasn't sure I could trust, felt like slogging through warm water, and I had to push hard to keep up.

To distract myself, I thought about what Mary had told me. I had a hard time picturing Morgan Pellar holed up in a cave. It wasn't that she was too sophisticated and worldly—she'd grown up on a farm, after all, and like all the Pellars, Morgan had definitely leaned in to the "hippie-Wiccan" vibe. But her whole thing was about power, and hiding in a cave wasn't a power move. Of all the places in Wyoming, why would she choose this one? And how would she even know about it? From what Simon had told me, the Cheyenne tunnels were now kind of an urban legend.

She didn't just know *about the tunnels.* Sam's voice sounded thoughtful. *She had a key.*

"Good point," I panted. Finn and Tobias both overheard me and glanced over their shoulders, but I gave a little headshake to show I was fine.

It occurred to me that Sam had talked to me twice in the last ten minutes, but not at all for hours before that, when I'd been in the middle of some scary stuff. She hadn't had a single comment about me *raising the dead*, which seemed . . . troubling. That was the kind of life-altering decision Sam would usually weigh in on. Was she not allowed to talk about it, the way she hadn't been allowed to help me save John?

I puzzled over that for a while, but we were approaching the southeast corner of the tunnel grid before I figured out any answers. By then I was breathing hard, and my heart felt like it was pounding out of my body. I'd scraped my arm against the pipe twice, creating a small cut that was trickling blood. But at least I hadn't freaked out . . . yet.

Ahead of me, Mary's pale, churning legs slowed to a walk and finally stopped. Turning toward me as I caught up, she pointed to a bend in the tunnel just ahead. "Just around that corner, there's a small sandstone offshoot that opens into the cave," she whispered. "The cave's plenty big, so you should be okay, but if she has wolves or bloodsuckers in there they probably already know we're here."

I nodded and clicked off my flashlight to keep the light from bouncing around the corner where someone might see it. Then I shoved the light in my pants pocket, trying to keep my hands from shaking.

I kept the revolver with silver bullets in my left hand, which would take care of werewolves, but I had no idea what I was going to do about Morgan. My magic was basically useless against other Old World people.

But Katia was in there, and I was losing time. "I'll go in first," I said to Mary. "If Morgan throws me into a wall, try to overpower her. Do not kill her unless absolutely necessary."

Her eyes narrowed at that, but I didn't stop to explain. Instead, I turned the corner—and saw them.

The tunnel in front of me was filled with ghosts. They were packed in like sardines, some even seeming to overlap each other. Most were remnants, but a few had the angry, glowing definition of wraiths.

And every single one of them appeared to be on fire.

Chapter 41

As I stood there with my mouth open, they all seemed to catch the scent of my blood at once, turning toward me with curiosity on their pain-twisted features.

"Lex? What's the matter?" Mary had stepped up beside me, and looked from me to the tunnel in confusion. She couldn't see them.

The wraiths began to move toward me and I took an instinctive step backward, nearly dropping my revolver. At my side, Tobias pressed his body into mine, baring his teeth at the invisible threat.

"Shit, shit, shit," I hissed, backing away farther.

"*What?*"

"Ghosts." My mouth was instantly dry, and I was having a hard time speaking. "There was a fire down here. Lots of people died."

"Oh." Mary looked at the hall again, squinting like that would help. "Is it a problem?"

I almost laughed. "Yes." The closest wraith, a man about my height, was only a few feet away now, and he stretched out one arm to touch me. It was on fire, and though I could feel no heat, his face was gnarled with agony and anger. I backed up until my spine hit the wall.

Something bumped my shoulder, and I realized distantly that it was Keith.

"What's going on?"

He and Mary started talking, but I couldn't listen anymore, because they were *so close*. I could move sideways, back around the corner, but then I wouldn't be able to see the ghosts, and that was somehow scarier. My pulse was going so fast I wondered dimly if I was having a heart attack.

Think, Lex, Sam's voice screamed in my head. *You can lay ghosts!*

Right. I may not have had the obsidian, but Valerya's bloodstone pressed against my chest, solid and comforting. I crouched down, set the revolver on the tunnel floor, and squeezed the cut on my arm, too freaked out to feel the pain. The wraith was only two feet away, and there were two more behind him.

I hadn't bled enough for a full circle, so I touched the smear of blood and drew a line across the tunnel floor as quickly as I could. Thank God the little stone offshoot was rectangular instead of circular. I pressed the tips of my tattoos on the line, and though I'd never actually done this before, my bloodstone helped me figure out what to say. *Wall.*

The wraith's outstretched hand hit an invisible barrier and confusion crossed his features. But he had stopped. I hugged my knees to my chest, scooting my body into the corner.

Mary finished her conversation with Keith and squatted down next to me, resting one bare knee on the tunnel floor. "What just happened?"

I tore my eyes away from the trapped wraiths and made myself look at her. "I know why Morgan picked this place, and I know why she set the meeting for before sunrise." I gestured toward the line of blood. "If I cross that, the wraiths—the stronger ghosts—will try to tear me apart."

Keith had edged up along the side of the tunnel, and now he peeked around the corner, trying to figure out what I was seeing. Maybe it was my imagination, but the ghosts seemed to reach for him too.

Mary's brow furrowed. "What if you run through real fast?"

I shook my head. "When I touch one of them—*any* one of them— I'll feel the psychic imprint of their death. It's—" I tried again to swallow, despite my dry mouth. The sight of the livid, burning wraiths pounding silently against my barrier was unnerving as hell. I forced my eyes away again. "It's rough," I finished. "They all burned to death. I wouldn't make it to the cave entrance."

She pursed her lips. "Can't you, like, get rid of the ghosts?"

I almost laughed. "I've never even *tried* laying a wraith, and to lay any one of them, I'd need to be able to concentrate. To relax."

"Huh." She glanced up at the tunnel again, her face sort of admiring. "You have to admit, it's a hell of an obstacle."

I think I nodded, but I wasn't really sure. "How about we go in there and drag Morgan out?" she asked.

"That could work," I admitted. "But we have no idea what she has in there."

"It doesn't matter," Mary said frankly. "If it's the only way to end this, we need to go in."

"I'm afraid I can't let you do that," Keith said.

I was so distracted that I barely heard him speak, and by the time I registered the words and turned my head, he had pushed Mary into the tunnel wall and was raising the barrel of my gun to shoot Finn in the chest.

He moved the barrel toward the other wolves. I shoved Tobias away from me, back the way we'd come. Keith had the gun pointed at Alex. "Run!" I screamed, and then I tackled Keith, aiming sideways so I wouldn't fall across the line of blood.

With everyone off-balance and moving, Keith's second shot went wide. I heard either Tobias or Alex yelp, a terrible pained sound, but they both kept running.

Keith flung me away easily. It was all I could do to throw up my arms and keep my head from hitting the rock wall. My elbow smacked into it instead, sending reverberations all the way into my shoulder. The pain made me dizzy for a moment.

I could hear growls and a scuffling of feet as Mary attacked Keith, but by the time I turned around, he had the revolver jammed under her chin and she had gone very still, her eyes huge.

He pressed up with the barrel, forcing her to her tiptoes, her teeth bared in rage.

"You," I said stupidly, clutching my elbow and leaning against the rock. I had forgotten my claustrophobia, even forgot to look at the wraiths trapped a few feet away.

"Me," Keith said, his gaze never leaving Mary's. I looked down at the enormous brown wolf. A pool of blood was spreading away from his body. There was a shimmer that I couldn't quite focus on in the dim light, and then the wolf was gone, replaced by the corpse of an enormous nude man.

"No," Mary choked. Her eyes were full of tears.

I let go of my sore elbow and slowly drew my left arm behind me, going for the pancake holster. "Stop moving, Lex," Keith snapped.

Mary had to speak through gritted teeth. "Why?"

Keith reached up with his free hand and smoothed the hair away from her face. "I don't know where to begin," he said simply.

A tear rolled down Mary's cheek. "Ryan. Matt. Cammie."

Keith sighed. I was watching carefully, but he never let up pressure on that gun. "Matt would have made a shitty alpha. And you and Ryan were getting too close," he said, as though that explained every single thing he'd done.

"You have a thing for me." Mary's voice was bitter. "You cowardly little fuckwit."

"Enough," rang a familiar voice. I turned my head back to the wraiths—and saw Morgan Pellar come striding through the middle of them, swinging something around her finger. It was hard to get details through all the remnants.

She stepped carefully over the line of my blood, closing in on us. I wasn't going to get a better moment.

I pivoted on my heel, driving my left fist at her with everything I had . . . which wasn't a whole lot, thanks to the shoulder I'd wrenched earlier. Morgan took the haymaker on her cheekbone, her head whipping sideways. She stumbled a step, leaning on the wall next to Keith. I raised my other fist and stepped closer to hit her again, but to my surprise she calmly took the gun from Keith and shot Mary through the meat of her upper arm.

Mary howled with pain, and I froze. Morgan gave me a very severe look, like I was a naughty toddler. "That was *your* fault. I hope that punch was worth it."

She handed the gun back to a disgruntled-looking Keith and spun Mary around, pushing her face into the stone wall as she snapped something around her wrists. Mary screamed with pain again, and I realized that Morgan had locked her into a pair of silver handcuffs.

"Stop!" I cried, reaching for the cuffs. Keith pointed the revolver at my forehead, and I backed up again. "Take them off her."

Mary was taking short, shallow breaths now, trying to bear up against the pain of burning silver. Two lines of blood, from the entry and exit wounds, ran down her arm, converging into a dark worm of red. She still managed to mumble, "Hit the bitch again."

Keith pulled a pair of gloves out of his pocket and began putting them on.

"What about the two that got away?" Morgan asked him.

Keith snorted. "Those two won't be a problem." Wearing the gloves, he grabbed the handcuffs and wrenched Mary's manacled hands up behind her back. She sobbed with pain as he marched her deeper into the hall, right through the wall-to-wall ghosts.

I was so distracted by them walking right through my own personal nightmare that I failed to notice Morgan wrapping a zip tie around my own wrists, in front of me, until she pulled it tight enough to bite into my skin. I gave serious thought to another head-butt, which Morgan apparently read on my face. "Touch me again and Mary will pay for it," she promised. "Silver heals human-slow. How many holes before she bleeds out?"

I dropped back, eyeing the gauntlet of wraiths over her shoulder, and Morgan coolly thrust one fist into my stomach. I hadn't been ready for it, and I doubled over. Before I could recover, Morgan had looped another zip tie around the first, making a sort of handle. She reached out one polished leather boot and scuffed away the line of my blood.

"No!" I yelled, but of course I was too late. Morgan yanked the zip tie and dragged me right into the crowd of burning wraiths.

No, oh God, no, Jeannie, I love you so much . . .
    Make it stop! Somebody just bloody shoot me!
    It hurts it hurts it hurts it hurts—
    WHY WHY WHY WHY WHY—

It went on and on.

As I was yanked through ghost after ghost, my mind was barraged with fragments of their last moments, as though for a second, I became each person. Most of them couldn't form a coherent thought through their terrible pain, the worst I'd ever felt. I had been cut up, shot, and broken, but none of it compared to the sensation of being burned alive. It was like being tattooed over every inch of your body simultaneously. Only worse. Many of their final thoughts were just endless screaming.

The wraiths hurt the most—they didn't just exude pain; they were full of rage and malevolence and a hatred so powerful that it sucked the breath out of my lungs. They tore at my psyche, trying to take something from me—my life force? My magic? Blood? I didn't know what they wanted, and I didn't know how to fight them. After some time—a few seconds? Hours?—I sagged down, unable to control my body enough to keep my feet under me. Morgan began to drag me, but the psychic attack didn't let up, and then I lost some time.

I know I screamed. I screamed and fought as long as I could, but eventually I couldn't keep myself together enough for either. I might have fainted, or maybe my brain just sort of short-circuited; I don't really know. Everything faded away into a distant blur, followed by darkness.

Chapter 42

The next thing I was aware of was an icy-cold shock, as a pail of near-frozen water was dumped over my head.

"What—what—" I sputtered, sitting up so fast I got dizzy. I'd been lying on my back in a massive underground chamber—the cave Mary had told me about. My hands were still zip-tied, and I realized that my ankles had been secured as well. Great. Someone had removed the sidearm from the holster at my back, and when I lifted my bound hands to touch my chest, Valerya's bloodstone was gone.

"Oh good, you're awake," Morgan said cheerfully. She was standing over me swinging an empty five-gallon bucket.

I lifted my bound hands to push wet hair out of my face and glared up at her—but I was distracted by my surroundings. This was the cave Mary had told me about. The egg-shaped sandstone chamber was as tall as a two-story house, and about half as wide. I had pictured moisture running down the walls and active stalactites, but it was dry and pretty, lit by yellowish camp lanterns that gave it a soft, comforting glow. Natural rock formations turned the walls into wavy, eclectic works of art, and the room was even warm, thanks to a small generator and some strategically placed space heaters. I spotted two exits, at more or less opposite sides of the room, one at my nine o'clock and one at my four o'clock.

I looked farther up. There was a ledge going most of the way around the dome, six feet from the top. A werewolf I'd never seen before was lying on the ledge at an angle, watching me lazily with its head resting on its enormous front paws.

"Pretty, isn't it?" Morgan looked around with obvious pride. "I was skeptical at first, but it's really come together."

I snorted. "A cave lair, really? Did you watch too many Bond movies as a child?"

Her smile didn't waver. She tilted her head toward the exit on my left. "If you don't like it, we could go back down to the hallway."

That exit must lead to the wraith tunnel. I closed my mouth. The ghosts hadn't been able to follow us in here—they were apparently limited to the area where they'd died—but the memory of their pain was fresh in my head, and I had a feeling it would be a long time before it faded from memory. Shuddering, I pulled my knees close to my chest and tucked them between my bound arms. I felt weak and achy. Was it possible to get a psychic hangover? Or some sort of brain flu?

Morgan sighed down at me, shaking her head. "Why do you do this to yourself?"

I said nothing.

"All you had to do was run an errand with your niece," she said with exaggerated patience. "I'm not a vindictive person; I was willing to let go of everything that happened between us in the past. But you just couldn't be a grown-up, could you?"

"How long was I out?" I asked, hoping it was past sunrise. I never saw ghosts during the day, not even wraiths.

Morgan smiled, reading my thoughts. "Only about fifteen minutes. Still plenty of ghosts in the hall, if you'd like to run the gauntlet again."

I blocked the thought, trying to stay focused. "Why am I not dead?"

"Because," she said pleasantly, "there's something Keith would like from you first." Her eyes flicked sideways. "We had hoped your aunt might be able to help us, but she either doesn't know how or is too stubborn."

"What do you want?"

"Why, for you to lay the ghosts, of course." Morgan pointed to the other side of the chamber, and I followed her gaze to a waist-high hole in the stone. "They're right on the other side of that." She made a little disgusted noise. "I thought you would do it the moment you saw them, but apparently I overestimated your resolve in the face of *tunnels*."

"*That's* what this was all about? Laying ghosts?"

Morgan shrugged. "I *did* want you to bring Charlie. It would have made things so much easier later this morning. But I can find another way in. A deal is a deal, and Keith wants those ghosts laid to rest."

"Why?"

She pressed her lips together and crossed her arms over her chest, her message clear: I was just the help. The help didn't require details.

"Knowing what happened might affect whether I can lay them," I told her. I was counting on her not knowing anything about boundary magic.

"Do I really have to spell it out?" she said impatiently. "He killed them."

I stared at her for a moment. "He was an engineer," I said slowly, "for the department of transportation."

She waved a hand in a circle. "Yes, yes, there was a terrible accident, the city hushed it up, you get the idea. He says they haunt him in his sleep, whatever that means."

Ghosts aren't only tethered to places. When Keith had been asleep at the lodge, I'd seen a ghost practically on top of him.

The people Keith had killed were anchored to the tunnel, but somehow they were also haunting him, and not in a metaphorical way. I lifted my head to the ceiling, not caring who heard me. "Goddammit, Sam," I said loudly. "Thanks for all the *no help*."

Morgan was bending down, taking hold of the zip-tie handle again and pulling me up. "Come on, now, we're running out of time. Sunrise is in forty minutes, then you'll be of no use to me."

"Just kill me," I said tiredly. I'd like to say I was being brave against a hostile combatant, but mainly I was terrified of trying to lay the wraiths. If Morgan was going to kill me either way, I'd rather she just got on with it.

Morgan stood again, throwing up her hands. "See, this is exactly what I'm talking about! You're so *pointlessly* obstinate!" Raising her voice, she added, "Keith! You'll have to bring them in!"

There was another shuffling noise, this time coming from the exit at my four o'clock. It was a short, narrow gap that would require a human to turn and crab-walk at an angle. There was some grunting and snarling, but then Mary edged into the room sideways, her hair mussed and wild. She was still wearing the silver handcuffs behind her back, and I thought I could *smell* the skin on her wrists burning. When she was all the way in the room, she fell to her knees, her teeth gritted against the pain.

There were more noises, and then a body was shoved through the gap behind Mary, instantly crumpling onto the cave floor. At first I thought it was a dead stranger, but then I recognized the hairdo. Parts of the braid were still holding together.

"Katia!"

I tried to army-crawl over to her with my hands and ankles bound, but Morgan said impatiently, "Oh, for God's sake, this could take all day. Just bring her over."

Keith, who had shoved Katia's body through, emerged from the gap and grabbed her by the waistband of her pants, hauling her easily toward me. When they were still four feet away, he tossed her, and she slid across the rough sandstone floor to rest at my side.

I looked right into his eyes. "I will *kill* you for this," I said coldly.

Keith swallowed, his eyes darting to Morgan. From the floor, I heard Mary's soft, pained voice, forced through her teeth. "Get . . . in . . . line."

Katia groaned softly and I scooted closer, shocked that she was still alive. Her arms were bare, and her torn shirt had ridden up, so scraping against the floor must have hurt like hell. Awkwardly, I rolled her over so I could see her face. It was puffy and swollen, her lower lip the size of a banana.

Mary had been watching all this, and she knee-walked closer, meeting my eyes. "Pulse and breathing are strong," she muttered, trying to look as though she weren't in agonizing pain. "I think . . . mostly cosmetic injuries. To upset you."

"Well, it worked," I said through gritted teeth. Rage erupted in my chest.

I glared up at Keith again and he actually flinched. "Let them go," I snapped. "Let them both go."

Morgan sighed. "Here we go again," she said to the heavens. Then she dropped her head to look down at me. "Don't be so dramatic. No one's going anywhere. After you perform your little ritual, I'll send her to the ER." She gestured at Katia. "You'll stay here until my mother drops the barrier to Colorado, and for a full day afterward. Then you're free to go."

Now it was my turn to roll my eyes. "Yeah, right."

"I'm serious," Morgan insisted. "I'm still willing to deal, Lex. I was *always* willing to deal. I heard you quit working for Maven, which means I've done absolutely nothing to her or her people." She allowed herself a tiny smile. "Certainly nothing anyone can prove."

I was suddenly really proud of the punch I'd managed to land on Morgan earlier. "Why would you let me go?" I asked.

She shrugged. "Despite your efforts, I'm still confident I can convince the Colorado witches to put their trust in me."

"That's why you didn't take Lily hostage until your mom dropped the ward," I said, understanding. "You still want all the witches to love you."

Her eyes narrowed, but she didn't deny it. "As I was saying, once I'm leader, Maven will have no choice but to work with me. And you'll have to either leave the state or beg for your job back. Either way, you won't be a threat to me."

"Morgan, you tedious bitch," I said conversationally, "I will *always* be a threat to you."

As if I hadn't spoken, she sashayed over and crouched in front of me again, resting her elbows on her knees. She smiled at me and confided, "Personally, I hope you decide to run. There would be a delicious poetic justice to you being forced away from *your* home, cut off from *your* family." She flipped her hands, palms up. "But I'm good either way."

I tried to keep my expression level, but Keith said to Morgan, "Her pulse is picking up."

"And Mary?" I said to Morgan. "What happens to her?"

Morgan stood up, waving a hand as though Mary were an inconvenient rash. "Mary will stay with Keith until she learns some manners."

It probably seems silly, after everything Morgan had already done, but this actually startled me. "You're just . . . *giving* her to him?" I said. "I knew you were twisted, Morgan, but I didn't think that included selling other women to be sex slaves."

Keith began to protest, but Morgan waved him away. "She's just stalling for time," she told him. "Go get the supplies we discussed."

He looked unhappy, but he bobbed his head and disappeared through the opposite exit.

Morgan eyed me imperiously. She was definitely getting a kick out of looming over me. "They're werewolves, you twit," she said, in a low voice filled with disgust. "They're not even people. At *best*, they're tools."

I raised my eyes to the ledge above her head. "Did you hear that?" I called up to the wolf on guard duty. "She called you a tool."

He or she—I couldn't tell from this angle—actually opened their mouth and yawned, displaying twin rows of teeth, each one nearly as long as my fingers. For some reason, it was the whiteness of the teeth that creeped me out most—natural wolves didn't have that.

"Oh, Declan?" Morgan said, looking up at the wolf. "Declan is *very* well paid, aren't you?" Without waiting for a response, she looked back at me and added, "He's also quite strong, I'm told. And very willing to recruit new followers and send them into battle. We have an understanding."

I thought of Simon wanting to ask the dead werewolf where Morgan was getting her money. *From him.* I opened my mouth to ask, but at that moment Keith came edging back into the room, holding a plastic grocery bag weighed down by something. He tossed it at my feet, keeping a few feet between us. "There you go."

I looked in the bag and found my pocketknife, a stick of chalk, a few votive candles, and a plastic safety lighter. There were also a few vials of herbs I was probably supposed to recognize, and a plastic camp lantern.

"What's this crap?" I asked Morgan.

"I wasn't sure what you use for spells." She pointed to the waist-high hole. "Better get started. You're running out of time, and the longer it takes you to lay the ghosts, the longer Katia will suffer."

"I need my bloodstone," I told her.

She looked at Keith, who dug Valerya's stone out of his pocket and tossed it at me. I made a panicked fumble, but managed to catch the priceless crystal without letting it hit the floor. I put the cord over my head again.

"You'll have to untie me," I said, holding up my wrists. I could have gotten the pocketknife out and done it myself, but it would have taken longer.

"Keith," Morgan said, and on cue, the werewolf pulled my Glock from the back of his pants, squatted down, and pressed it to Katia's thigh.

"Ever had a broken femur?" Morgan said casually, as she pulled a blade from the pocketknife and sawed apart the zip ties. "I've heard it's very painful, and it takes forever to heal."

I got the message—don't try to hurt Morgan.

I climbed to my feet. I was a little wobbly, and my clothes were still wet, but I could manage. "Keith," I said to the sneering werewolf, "I just want you to know, you're a whiny little bitch and no one likes you. You'll never be an alpha wolf."

Keith flinched back as if I'd stung him, but his lips tightened and he pressed the gun harder into Katia's leg, making her stir. "Say the word," he said to Morgan.

Morgan raised her eyebrows at me. "Last chance."

"Fine, I'll do it." I plucked the knife from her hand, ignoring the rest of the "supplies." "If Keith only sees them in his sleep, how will you confirm that I really did what I said I would?"

Morgan smiled, as though the question was a sign of my compliance. "Keith will sleep."

I sighed. "There's a faster way. I can get started, but I need one of your people to grab something out of the backpack in the back of my Jeep," I told her. I described the cassiterite that I'd brought along for Simon to use with Nellie. I'd tossed it in the back with the first aid kit when I'd left the brothel.

Morgan looked skeptical. "And this will enable one or both of us to see these ghosts?"

I shrugged. "If you run water over it in the moonlight, cleansing the crystal, it should."

"Fine," Morgan said dismissively. She obviously didn't really care about the ghost-laying part of the project, but wanted to keep Keith as an asset. "I can get it myself. I wouldn't mind some fresh air. In the meantime, Keith, why don't you show our other guests to their accommodations?" Her smile was creepy, and I had a bad feeling about anything that would make her this happy.

"What does that mean?" I asked, but Keith was already putting on a single leather glove. He picked up the limp Katia with his uncovered hand, and with the gloved hand he grabbed Mary's handcuffs. She had been unusually silent during the whole conversation, but I could tell she was struggling with the pain of the handcuffs. She let out a short scream as Keith forced her to stand.

"What are you doing?" I had started toward the wraith tunnel, but now I doubled back, hovering. No one answered me, which somehow made it worse.

Keith carried the women toward the sideways exit, but instead of trying to push through it, he veered right, behind where I'd originally woken up. It just seemed like an empty stretch of cave wall.

"This chamber comes with a built-in jail," Morgan remarked, and she allowed me to follow a few feet behind Keith until I finally saw it: a long, narrow hole in the floor itself, partially hidden by the cave wall. You had to be at just the right angle to even see it.

"You're not going to stuff them down there!" I cried, appalled.

"Relax, Lex," Morgan said. "It's more than ten feet deep. There's plenty of room for both of them."

"No! You can't do that!" The thought of my injured aunt trapped in a dark hole was terrifying. Actually, the thought of anyone trapped down there was terrifying.

"You want them out?" Morgan countered. "Do the spell."

I stood there with my hands balled into fists for a moment, but there was nothing I could do. The only weapon I had was a pocketknife, and Morgan alone could toss me into a wall. Declan could pounce on me, and even Keith would be able to overpower me. I had no chance against all three of them. Goddamn werewolves. Goddamn boundary magic. Sucking the life out of people might have sounded scary, but it didn't do shit against anyone with their own magic.

"Fine." I turned on my heel and stalked over to the wraith tunnel exit, pausing only to grab the camp lantern as I went by. I turned it on, and saw that the floor of the main room dropped down. I sat down cautiously, peering into the tunnel. It was three feet below this room, and the wraiths were trapped a little way farther down. So at least they wouldn't get me the moment I started.

I gripped the wall, preparing to slide down to the tunnel floor. "By the way," I said over my shoulder, "your brother and sister are both in the hospital right now. Because of you."

Her voice hardened. "You're lying."

"No, she isn't," Keith said quietly. He'd returned from shoving human beings into a fucking hole in the ground.

"Letting other people pay for your crimes is kind of your thing, though, right?" I added to Morgan, and ducked down through the hole in the floor.

I was not above enjoying the last word.

Chapter 43

The moment I dropped into the hallway, the temperature fell about thirty degrees. My stomach seemed to have stayed in the upper chamber. I flicked on the lantern to get my bearings, since I'd been unconscious by the time Morgan, or whoever, had dragged me up into the chamber.

Ahead of me lay about twenty feet of clear tunnel, and beyond that milled the ghosts. I couldn't tell how many there were, or how far back they went.

I was no longer bleeding, but I caught their attention anyway, possibly just because I was the only living thing there. They watched me come closer, and although only the wraiths seemed to project malevolence, all the ghosts still danced with flames. Looking at any one of them was terrifying.

I swallowed hard, fighting the hysteria that seemed to be affecting my breathing. I stopped ten feet away from them, unable to make myself go any closer. Wraiths. Wraiths stood between me and the way out. I would never run without Katia and Mary, of course, but a primal sense of self-preservation was screaming at me in total panic. Usually I was pretty good at pushing away panic—or at least, I'd had tons of practice—but the memory of being dragged through all those burning ghosts was pounding against any mental walls I might have built up.

I squeezed my eyes shut, held on to the wall with one hand, and reached for my sister.

I thought about Sam all the time, of course, not just when I spoke to her. But I wasn't sure I had ever called for her like this while I was awake, certainly not so forcefully. And she answered.

Sammy!

I'm here, Allie. What's the matter?

I don't know what to do.

Yes, you do.

I know, I need to stop Morgan, but I don't know how.

Sam's voice was patient. *Babe, she says she's going to cut a deal, but she could do that from Wyoming. She's going after Maven, and she'll try to use Charlie to do it. You* know *all this.*

The wraiths . . .

Are just fucking ghosts, babe. Who you gonna call?

I cannot believe you just said that.

Allie. Forget Morgan for the moment. There's only one choice right in front of you. Stop feeling sorry for yourself and get it done. Glorious purpose, remember?

I hate you.

You love me.

I opened my eyes. Nothing had changed—the ghosts still crowded ten feet away from me, staring at me with flames dancing over their skin. I pushed out a breath, stuffed the bloodstone into my bra, against my skin, and picked up the pocketknife.

Most of the ghosts I'd encountered were tethered to the place where they'd died, and these were no different—I could call them away from there with my blood, just as I had with the two little girls playing in the road.

I set the lantern to one side, cut my finger, and made a circle of blood that took up the entire width of the hallway, so there was no chance of any wraiths going around it to get to me. When I was sure the circle was perfect, I sat back on my heels and looked up at them. "All right, guys," I said softly. "I'm sorry for what happened to you. I'm sorry you died the way you did. But it's time for you to move on now." I pressed my palms against the circle and focused. *"Door."*

The ghosts in the lead took experimental steps toward me, and then the whole burning mass of them was moving down the hall. When they reached the opposite edge of my circle, I gave a small nod. One by one, the regular remnants dropped down through the doorway I'd created, on their way to their next destination, whatever that was. I counted nineteen of them, making eye contact with each one as he went.

Part of this process was the feeling that it was my duty to witness them. To let them know I saw them and their pain.

Then they were gone, and five wraiths stood on the other side of my door, their anger blazing at me.

I pointed toward the door. "Go. Be at peace."

They didn't move, not a single one. They didn't blink, or breathe. They just stood there radiating malice and burning, always burning.

It was an effort, but I forced myself to keep my shoulders back and my head high, like the army had taught me. One of the wraiths, a white guy in his fifties with a pug face and sagging jowls, stood a little in front of the others. I focused on him. "Can you understand me?"

Again, there was no response. "If you can understand me, raise your right hand," I said in my most commanding tone.

The wraiths' expressions didn't change, but the leader lifted his right arm, as though he were about to take a pledge.

Interesting. They had some sort of sentience. There was still so much I didn't understand about my magic. Had he answered of his own volition, or did they have to obey my orders?

I jabbed a finger at the doorway. "Go through the door."

None of them moved. Well, it had been worth a shot.

I didn't like leaving the door open like that, but I was afraid to break the circle, because I was pretty sure these guys would still do everything in their power to destroy me, and I doubted I could survive another impact with their psyches tonight. So I left it where it was, for protection, and tried to figure out what to do.

I knew of a boundary witch who could trap active wraiths in crystal, but the only crystal I had with me was my mother's bloodstone, and I wouldn't taint it by stuffing psychotic ghosts inside. Even if I could find something else as a receptacle, I had no idea how to imprison the wraiths, and a single false step would end with another trip into their psyche. *All roads lead to spectral insanity*, I thought, then wondered if I was losing it.

I chewed on my lip for a moment, trying to focus. The longer I knelt there looking at them . . . well, they didn't become less terrifying, but it became a little easier to think. "Would it help," I finally asked them, "if I brought you the man responsible for your deaths?"

The pug-faced man's eyes were permanently trapped in a glare, but they seemed to narrow even more as he very slowly raised his right hand again.

Now we were getting somewhere. "Okay," I said, looking at all of them, "here's what we're going to do."

In my head, I added, *Sammy, I need a favor* . . .

A few moments later, without really taking my eyes off the wraiths, I stood and shuffled backward ten feet so I could raise my head into the cave entrance. I could see one of Declan's paws still hanging from his perch, where he was probably on guard duty, but the others weren't visible. "Keith!" I called.

He stepped into my sight line, holding my revolver loosely by his side. He must have been standing near the cave's side wall. "Is it done?" he demanded, a tremble in his voice. "Did you exorcise them?"

"Where's Morgan?"

He flapped a hand. "Upstairs, talking on her phone. No reception here. What about my ghosts?"

"They need you to apologize," I said flatly.

"What?"

I chose my words carefully, and kept my voice as even as I could. I needed to sell this, because Keith would likely be able to tell if I outright lied. "Most of them moved on, but five of them aren't regular ghosts—they're wraiths. I don't really know how to explain it, but they're superpowerful and full of hate and anger. My theory is that they'll only move on if you get involved." There, that was actually the truth. "I want you to come down here and apologize. You have to mean it, though," I added.

Keith stared down at me, and I could tell he was having a hard time figuring out if I was messing with him. "You're joking."

I sighed. "Look, I've never tried to lay a wraith before. I think this will work, but if I'm wrong, what have you lost?" I asked. I wanted to change the subject before he could think it through, so I went on, "Did Morgan get the cassiterite I asked for?" I wasn't sure how long I'd been talking to the ghosts, but I estimated about ten or fifteen minutes.

I didn't have much time before sunrise. I was not going to let them leave Katia and Mary in a hole for a full day.

"Yeah . . ." Keith fished in his pocket and pulled out the chunk of cassiterite. "Will it work on me?"

"I'm not sure, but it might—it's gravitational magic, not witch magic," I said. "Theoretically anyone could do it."

Keith tilted his head, thinking, and finally said, "Throw the knife up here."

"One second." I went back to where I'd made the circle, the wraiths still watching me from the other side, and picked up my pocketknife. I tossed it up through the hole.

"Now back away," Keith demanded. I obediently backed away from the entrance, scuffling my feet to make noise. I stopped about five feet away from the circle.

After a moment, Keith's head finally appeared in the hole. I glanced over my shoulder and saw that the wraiths were already going nuts—snarling silently, their lips moving as if cursing him out.

Turning back to Keith, I held up my empty hands to show I was unarmed. He still looked suspicious, but he hopped down and approached me. No sign of my gun, but he had the chunk of crystal with him.

I showed him how to open and close his hands several times to activate his chakra, then had him hold the cassiterite with both hands. I wasn't sure why I felt like this was important—maybe to close a loop, like with electricity. I was sort of going with intuition here.

Keith suddenly went very quiet. "Did it work?" I asked, but he didn't answer. I couldn't see his face with the camp lantern just behind him, so I went over and picked it up, half expecting him to warn me away. He was silent. When I moved next to him and lifted the lantern, I saw that he'd gone completely white, his eyes wide. His lips moved, but if he was actually speaking I couldn't hear it.

I followed his gaze to the wraiths. They paced the short distance of the barrier, silently snarling at him. Every few seconds one of them would throw himself against their side of the circle, but it held strong.

"I think they recognize you," I said mildly.

Next to me, Keith's head jerked up and down. I eased him a few steps closer to the wraiths. "They can't cross the circle of blood," I told him, honestly. "Tell them what you came to tell them."

"It wasn't my fault," Keith blurted, eyes fixed on the wraiths. "I didn't know there was a gas line there!"

I wouldn't have thought it possible, but the wraiths seemed to get more agitated. "I'm sorry you died!" Keith wailed. "But I got my punishment, don't you see? I'm stuck being a werewolf forever. You got your justice, so just . . . move on!"

Wow. I'd thought I hated this guy before. "You think being a werewolf is the same thing as *burning to death*?" I said in disbelief.

His head snapped toward me. "*You* don't know! You have no idea what it's like, feeling this itching inside your head, like the wolf is pawing at the door twenty-four seven. Nobody takes me seriously—*Mary* doesn't take me seriously—and I'm just . . . stuck! No one deserves this!"

"The wraiths don't seem to agree."

Keith turned his whole body toward me, flinging the chunk of cassiterite down the dark tunnel. "I did what you asked! Now get rid of them!"

This was my only chance. As much as I disliked Keith, I didn't feel good about this. But if I wanted to stop Morgan, it was the only play I had.

I put my hands up in surrender. "Okay. You win. I'll get them to cross over."

"How?"

"Well," I began, taking one tiny step forward—then shoved him as hard as I could toward the circle and the still-open doorway within it.

Chapter 44

I had never put a living person through a blood circle—it hadn't even occurred to me to try—so I didn't really know what would happen. It was perfectly possible that Keith would stumble over the circle, come through on the other side, and turn around to attack me. Or that his feet would scuff up my blood circle and the wraiths would be able to rush past it and get to me.

At the same time, I sort of . . . had a feeling. The wraiths wanted me, but they wanted Keith more. One way or another, this seemed like my only chance.

Keith stumbled into the curling smoke of my doorway, and he automatically reared his upper body backward to avoid the wraiths, which left him standing inside my circle. Acting on instinct, I quickly went into my boundary mindset—just in time to see the glow of Keith's life essence abruptly . . . drop.

I came out of my mindset, trying to process what was happening. Keith's body was in the process of crumpling to the ground. He landed with a sickening slap on the cold floor. His arms and legs flopped over the edge of my circle, but it didn't seem to matter.

I looked at the wraiths, who were staring at the circle with indescribable rage. "Well?" I asked.

The pug-faced leader looked up just long enough to snarl silently at me.

"Yeah, I know. You want me, but you want him more. Right?"

I held my breath. After one more moment of indecision, the leader crouched like an Olympic diver and dove into the doorway, the others crowding each other to follow him.

The second the last wraith disappeared, I scrubbed my foot against the blood line, breaking the circle. The door vanished, and I collapsed against the side of the tunnel, panting. I'd been tired and achy before, but I suddenly felt winded. I'd never held a door open for that long.

When I could move again, I reached over and touched Keith's wrist, just to be sure. No pulse. I patted him down, but he'd been smart enough not to bring my revolver with him. Crap. Then the rush of using boundary magic hit me, flooding me with adrenaline and exhilaration, and I jumped to my feet.

"Sammy, do it now," I muttered under my breath.

I vaulted back into the main chamber and ran toward the hole where Katia and Mary were being kept—but a two-hundred-pound wolf touched down six feet in front of me. Declan had leaped down from the shelf, probably to investigate why Keith's heartbeat had abruptly vanished.

I skidded to a halt on the dirt floor. I'd hoped to make it to Mary and Katia before he got between us, but he'd reacted faster than expected. He crept toward me, teeth bared, a low growl thrumming from his chest.

He was big, as big as Barlow had been. His head was taller than my waist, and he moved with the same tireless grace I'd seen in the other werewolves. It was menacing in a way that triggered hopelessness, like he would never tire, never stop, never get too hurt to keep coming. I swallowed, feeling my fear spike and knowing he would be able to smell it. That really pissed me off.

"Nice doggie," I said. "You know you're not supposed to kill me if I don't do anything." I held out my hands to show they were empty.

The werewolf intentionally looked past me to the waist-high exit. I made a show of following his gaze. "Oh, Keith? He's fine. He decided to go for a walk." I lowered my voice. "I think he didn't want you to see him crying."

Declan obviously didn't believe me, but he hesitated, uncertain. There was no blood on me, and I had touched only Keith's clothes, so I wouldn't smell like him either. Declan couldn't go look for Keith without leaving his post, and he couldn't do anything to me without evidence that I'd actually done something wrong.

Then, behind him, there were two terrible *crunch* sounds, one right after another, and a short scream of pain. Declan reared around, loping back across the room toward the hole. "Lex!" came Katia's hoarse voice, and a second later two silver handcuffs, no longer connected to each other by a silver chain, came sliding between Declan's paws, headed straight for me.

Through Sam and Valerya, Katia had gotten my message.

I pounced on the broken handcuffs, and although he was miles faster than me, Declan was slow to respond, probably nervous about getting too close to the silver. I winced when I saw that the cuffs were smeared with blood—Mary had lost some skin when Katia had broken her thumbs to get them off—but I picked them up anyway, looping one over each fist and clicking them closed until I had a nice double set of silver knuckles.

Ignoring the pain in my shoulder and elbow, I got my hands up, boxer-style, and let out a little whistle. "Here, doggie," I said. "Come here, boy."

Declan turned to snarl at me then, and I had his full attention. I needed to keep it, so I continued to taunt him. "Nice puppy," I said. "Sit."

The werewolf began to circle me, probably wary of the silver. I let him circle, but kept my body turned toward him. I had never fought a werewolf before, and I had a feeling I wasn't going to enjoy the experience. But I didn't have to win—I just had to stay alive long enough for my backup to heal her broken thumbs.

Okay, that sounded bad.

Real wolves, I knew, tended to attack their prey's extremities. They often bit a deer or even a buffalo on the leg, then simply waited for it to bleed out. So I dropped into a boxer's crouch, which put us almost at eye level, and waited for him to attack.

When he lunged for my right leg, I was ready—but I still wasn't fast enough to stop him. He got his teeth around my calf in a shallow bite. I immediately hammered my silver-clad fists on his snout, and he yelped and backed off.

I gave my leg a quick glance and saw a few puncture wounds, but nothing that would even require stitches. Good.

The wolf was already circling again, but the space was too small for him to make a big enough circle to flank me. I backed toward the nearest wall, intending to get myself in a better defensive position. He didn't like that, though, and he made another lunge, this time for my face.

Silver knuckles or not, there wasn't a lot I could do about his momentum, and when his paws hit my shoulders, the weight knocked me onto my butt. I let it happen so I could concentrate on keeping my hands up.

When you take self-defense classes, or do military combat training, they often teach you to shove something into an attacking dog's mouth to prevent him from biting. In the absolute worst-case scenario, you can theoretically use your fist, if the dog's mouth is big enough.

This particular canine had the biggest mouth I'd ever seen. When he opened it, I crammed my fist with the silver handcuff down his throat. He let out another yelping noise, trying to release me and back off, but I bent my wrist so it formed a hook, making sure the silver stayed in contact with him.

Then he raked his claws against my shoulder and upper arm, and I had to release him. Declan backed away from me, pawing at his muzzle. The silver had burned his esophagus. Good.

"Mary," I yelled. "How's it coming over there?"

"Soon . . ." Her voice was ragged, but sounded stronger than the last time I'd heard her speak.

Declan snarled, but his circling had put me between him and Mary. His feet shuffled a little in frustration. There were burns on his nose from the silver, and I noticed with satisfaction that they weren't healing well. "Not used to an even playing field, are you?" I said.

Then Morgan edged into the cave through the narrow entrance. She took in my bloody leg and the silver handcuffs, and Declan shaking his head back and forth like the pain in his throat was an annoying gnat he could shake off. "What's going on?" she demanded.

"Uh . . . your guard dog attacked me?"

I saw Morgan's lips move and tried to duck, but the spell hit me anyway, catapulting me backward. I was too far from the wall to actually hit it, but I landed on my back, which hurt like a motherfucker. I groaned, and Declan trotted over to me, his fangs bared. He put his two front paws on my chest and just stood there, his muzzle dripping saliva and a little blood.

Morgan stalked over to us and crouched down near my face. "I'll ask again," she said, annoyed now. "What the hell is going on?"

"Keith attacked Declan," I wheezed. It was hard to breathe with two hundred pounds of werewolf compressing your lungs. "For . . . alpha. Keith is hurt. He's in the hallway."

Declan snarled again, pissed now, but Morgan held up a palm to him, her eyes on me. "Where did you get the—" she began, but at that moment a blur in short-shorts seemed to fly across the room and tackled her around the waist.

Mary.

Chapter 45

There was no sign of Katia, but I figured she was probably too weak to climb out, which meant she was too weak to fight. I had to trust that she was safe for the moment.

Declan began snapping at my limbs again, and I lost track of what Morgan and Mary were doing. I landed one good punch on his snout, then reverted to hammering my fists against him as he tried to get a grip on me. I knew what he was trying to do—get an arm or leg in his mouth so he could shake it, breaking bones—and my best bet was to keep hitting him with the silver cuffs.

Unfortunately, he was smart enough to switch to leading with his claws. For a while I was able to turn my wrists sideways and counter, so any time he tried to rake his paws down me, he got the silver cuffs first. This worked for maybe two minutes, but he was just too fast. Soon there were shallow scratches all over my arms and legs, and I fell down again. I was losing. I opened my mouth to yell for Mary—but then she came flying across the room, hitting the wall a few feet away from me with a very gross *crunch*. Declan advanced on me, his lips pulled back.

"Stop." Morgan's voice rang out sharply, and Declan made himself take a step back from me, though there was an unnaturally sullen expression on his wolf face. I wanted to take stock of my injuries, but there was no time. Morgan strode over to me with her hands on her hips. "Where is Keith?" she demanded. "Tell me the truth, or I'll let Declan bleed you out."

I climbed to my feet, ignoring the pain from my injuries. None of them were life-threatening. "He's dead," I told her. "His body is in the hallway."

"*I* wanted to kill him," Mary muttered under her breath.

"Hmph." Morgan's lips pressed together, and I could practically see her running new calculations in her head, reorganizing her plans to cover the loss. I used those precious seconds to scan the room, desperately looking for my revolver. Werewolf or not, Keith had been a coward. He wouldn't have wanted it to be far from him, not when I was in the other room with his ghosts.

"Well," Morgan said, "that's mildly annoying in the short term, but I suppose I can work with it." She looked at Declan. "You still want to move into Colorado?"

He didn't exactly nod, being a wolf and all, but he jerked his chin upward once in the affirmative. Morgan pointed at Mary like a haughty socialite sending back an entree. "Kill her first."

Declan's huge head swung away from me, toward Mary.

Where's the gun? It had to be in this room; he hadn't had enough time to shuffle sideways through the four o'clock exit. But there just weren't any decent hiding places where he could—My eyes traveled upward.

Declan's lips peeled back as he began stalking slowly toward Mary. He was obviously enjoying himself . . . but I was still just a little closer to her. "Mary," I said urgently, already starting to sprint. "Boost me!"

To her credit, Mary reacted fast, lacing her fingers in a stirrup like any kid who needs to help her friend over a fence or into a tree.

My timing wasn't perfect, but I had a superpowered foundation. As I jumped, Mary bent a little extra to scoop my foot into her hand, thrusting it upward so fast I went flying up to the shelf. *Damn* she was strong.

I heard Morgan yelling, and I scrambled to get all my limbs over the ledge as fast as I could, before she could zap me. In the process I lost the silver handcuffs, which went clinking down to the rock floor below.

No time to worry about them. The sandstone was dry up here, thank God, or I would have made a very comical sight slipping right back down onto my ass. Unfortunately, it was also a lot darker than the chamber below, and all I could really see at first was a fuzzy blackness.

I began crawling cautiously along the ledge, feeling with my hands. I had only about two feet of clearance, and this wasn't a man-made shelf, so there were hundreds of nooks and crannies, plus loose sand. Plenty of places to stash a gun.

"What was the point of *that*?" Morgan called up, sounding exasperated. Declan, who knew what was up here with me, must have crouched to jump up after me, because Morgan snapped, "Forget her. I'll get her in a minute. Kill the werewolf."

Then there were a lot of scuffling sounds, followed by a couple of lupine yelps. I forced myself not to look down. Morgan could throw a spell at me, and getting my night vision was more important at the moment.

After a few more seconds, I could make it out: the revolver was about twelve feet ahead of me on the ledge. I crawled toward it as fast as I dared—but Declan knew where the sidearm was too, and I was still six feet away when he sprang up onto the ledge like a fucking velociraptor.

I got one shoe under my stomach and pushed off as hard as I could, diving for the weapon between us.

My fingers touched metal and slipped, knocking the gun to one side. It seemed to teeter precariously on the edge; then my grasping fingers went around it and I pulled it toward me, narrowly missing the extended claws as they came at me from the other side.

I might have fumbled a different gun, but my grandfather had taught me to shoot on the revolver, and I had it turned and pointed at

Declan before he could do anything. I cocked it, aimed loosely at his center mass, and pulled the trigger.

Only Declan wasn't there. He had thrown himself sideways over the ledge.

I cursed, my ears ringing. Keith had fired the gun twice, which meant I had only three shots left.

I leaned my arm over, trying to aim, but he was so fucking fast on four legs, and he was already hiding underneath where I lay on the ledge. Morgan was in the center of the room trying to put another pair of silver handcuffs on Mary, but when she saw me with the revolver, she swore and straightened up, extending her fingers to catapult me.

Mary swept Morgan's legs out from under her with a vicious kick. "Shoot him!" she yelled.

Fuck it.

I dropped my head and shoulders over the ledge, like I was doing an upside-down crunch, leveled the weapon at where I thought Declan would be in two seconds, and fired.

The wolf screamed, falling back, but I couldn't tell where I'd hit him. My lower body started to slip off the ledge, so I flailed my arms, trying to get my balance back—but the back of my left hand struck the rock *hard* and I cried out and let go of the gun. With a massive effort, I got my right hand back on the ledge and flipped myself over onto my back, listening for the clatter of the old revolver hitting the cave floor. It didn't come.

"Mary," I said, more or less to the ceiling.

I could hear heavy breathing and the hum of the generator, but that was it. I peeked over the edge of the rock shelf—and saw a large, naked man, a pool of blood spreading away from his body. Mary was standing right beneath me, holding the gun. The barrel was pointed at Morgan Pellar.

Chapter 46

"Don't kill her," I blurted.

"Why the *fuck* not?" Her voice was ragged. She was close to the edge of her control, though I wasn't exactly sure if that meant she would shoot Morgan or turn into a wolf.

Because I'd promised Simon? Mary wasn't going to go for that, so I said, "Because she spent way too much time on the phone."

That made Mary pause to think, which was what I wanted. I slid my legs and lower half over the ledge first, hanging on, then dropped down, bending my legs to absorb the impact.

Morgan, I could see now, was completely still, but she had that calculating look on her face that I knew all too well. "Her bullet is faster than your spell," I snapped at her.

Morgan pressed her lips in a line, but she raised her hands slowly.

I turned to Mary. "Give me the gun, Mary."

"She killed Ryan. She has to answer for it."

"She will," I promised. "The right way."

Mary shot me a scornful look. "You mean like last time? How would you say that's working out?"

She had a point. "Mary . . . if you kill her now, she becomes a martyr, and the little witch uprising she planned might still happen. Besides, someone was funding her. We need to know who it is."

"What exactly are you proposing?" Mary demanded, without looking away from Morgan.

"We take her to Maven. She'll probably end up killing her anyway, but she'll be able to expose all of Morgan's lies first." And I could keep my promise to Simon.

I could see Mary thinking this over. "How do you know you'll get her to talk?"

It was a fair question. Maven couldn't press a witch, and I wasn't ready to resort to physical torture, but I thought we might be able to bribe Morgan, maybe with a visit with her kids. In the meantime, I could bluff. "One way or another," I said heavily, "we can make her talk."

Morgan visibly flinched for the first time, which made Mary cock her head with interest.

"No," Morgan said, her voice edged with panic. "You can't do this. You can't torture me."

"Don't be so dramatic," I told her.

"Just shoot me," Morgan begged.

Mary gave a little shrug. "If you insist."

She lowered the barrel and pulled the trigger. The silver slug hit Morgan in the soft tissue just above her hip, and she collapsed to her knees. Then she began to wail, and Mary darted forward and punched her in the side of the head. Morgan slumped to the ground, unconscious.

While I was still standing there with my mouth open, Mary held out her hand to give me the revolver, now hanging from her finger by the trigger guard.

"I'm starving," she said. "Wanna get breakfast?" She raised her voice. "Hey, Katia! Breakfast?"

Chapter 47

The sun was rising on an overcast haze as I drove the hell out of Wyoming.

The radio was playing a sickly-sweet Christmas song, so I reached over and clicked it off. I adjusted the rearview mirror to check on Tobias, who lay sprawled across the back seat, snoring gently.

When we had finally climbed out of the fucking tunnels, with me supporting Katia and Mary carrying a still-unconscious Morgan Pellar, Alex and Tobias had been on the stairs in human form—along with Lindsay and Nicolette, the two younger werewolves who'd sat out the earlier fight. The rest of Mary's pack had been on their way to rescue her.

Instead, Lindsay and Nicolette retrieved Barlow's body, carrying it to a more concealed tunnel exit, while Alex and Tobias helped the rest of us get out of there. Then Mary and Alex had personally escorted Morgan Pellar to a doctor Alex knew in Fort Collins, who would stitch up the bullet hole, no questions asked. I was a little wary about leaving Morgan in the hands of Alex and Mary, but in the end, I had to trust they wouldn't kill an injured, sedated woman.

Yeah, I may have given Morgan some of the morphine from the emergency kit before they took off.

Tobias was coming along to Boulder to retrieve the Ventimiglias' vehicle and hopefully collect Dunn's body, assuming Maven could pull strings to get it released. Mary and Alex would bring Morgan to Boulder that night, to hand-deliver her to Maven. I had already left messages for Maven and Quinn explaining the situation, and I'd called Lily and arranged for Hazel to drop the barrier preventing Morgan from coming into the state. The witches could set up a meeting with Maven and the werewolves later that night. It was about time all these people got in a fucking room and figured things out.

Which left me. As far as I was concerned, I was out of it. At the moment I had no standing at all in the Old World, and I was sort of grateful for that. When the dust settled, I planned to go to Maven and beg for my job back, but I was just as happy not to be around to complicate her negotiations with the witches. Most of them hated me, and I didn't want to distract Lily and Simon when they needed to focus on family.

Also? I wanted some fucking sleep.

Putting the mirror back where it belonged, I glanced sideways, to the passenger seat. Katia was sitting with her forehead pressed to the cold window, and for a long time I couldn't tell whether she was asleep. Then she turned her head to look at me, and I winced again at her bruised and swollen face.

"Stop looking at me that way," Katia said. Her words were still slightly distorted from the puffy lip. "I have had worse."

"*That* doesn't make me feel better."

Katia began to stretch her arms, but it must have hurt, because she stopped almost immediately. "Did you talk to Lily?"

"Yes. She's going to meet with Maven and the werewolves tonight, and Simon's going to be fine," I assured her. "He was just a little banged up."

"Is Lily okay?" she persisted.

Something in her tone . . . I glanced over again and took in the very casual, innocent way she was staring at the road in front of us.

"Oh. *Oh*," I said stupidly. "It's Lily."

I *felt* stupid.

"What is Lily?" Katia was still trying for innocence, but she didn't pull it off.

"You said you liked someone, romantically. It's Lily, isn't it?"

There had been signs—nothing huge, but now that I thought about it, Katia never asked after the Pellars—just Lily. When she'd asked me about Morgan, she'd called her Lily's sister. For crying out loud, Katia had *blushed* when Lily complimented her hair.

Katia craned her head around to check on Tobias. When she turned to face front again, she began to study her fingernails in silence.

Why hadn't I seen it? True, I hadn't known Katia was into women—but then, I hadn't known she was into men either. Katia was so self-contained, she often came off as cold. And maybe because she'd witnessed—and possibly been the victim of—so much sexual assault, I guess I hadn't . . .

I felt ashamed of myself. *Hadn't what, Lex?* Hadn't thought Katia could enjoy sex, or have feelings? I spent a few more seconds berating myself, then realized Katia was sneaking glances at me, and I had to take care so she didn't misinterpret my expression. "Why didn't you *say* anything?" I blurted.

She gave me a look. "She's your best friend, and you are the only family I have left," she said in a quiet voice. "I didn't think you would approve."

"Why not?" I asked, though I suspected I knew the answer.

"Because of the things I've done," she said simply. Unspoken were the words *because of what I am.*

I had no idea how to respond to that. "Katia . . ."

"Don't pretend you don't know what I mean," she said, her voice still subdued. "I pressed a vampire to kill innocent women. I stood by and watched as those vampires Oskar had imprisoned were tormented and raped, then I forced them to forget their pain, just so they could go through it again. I told myself I was helping them—but I never tried to save them."

"Do you think you could have?" I asked. "Could you have pressed Oskar?"

She shook her head. "I tried to press him once, but he was too strong for me. It . . . didn't go well." One hand lifted to rub her collarbone. Katia always wore crew-neck shirts, usually with long sleeves, but this one was ripped, and I could see the beginning of scar tissue. I forced my eyes back to the road. "But I could have done something else," she went on. "Found a witch to release them from their bonds, or pressed them to run as far as they could. Reported him to a cardinal vampire. Anything. But I was scared, and I did nothing."

My heart ached for her. She sounded . . . well, she sounded like me, really, when I'd first returned to Boulder after being blown up in the desert. Only Katia hadn't signed up for the army; she'd been kidnapped and victimized by a monster. He had literally killed her when she was fourteen, in order to activate her boundary magic. And yet she couldn't stop blaming herself for everything that had happened afterward. If I were a betting woman, I would put down every penny in my savings account that she had night terrors, just as I did.

"You've heard the stories about boundary witches," she continued, with the smallest tremble running through her voice. "There's death in our blood, that's what everyone says. But what if it's not just death? What if it's darkness?"

I had to admit, I'd had similar thoughts. Doing serious boundary magic, the kind where you played around with another being's soul, it felt *way* too good. Someone could get addicted to that kind of high, and if I hadn't had Simon and Lily and Quinn to keep me grounded, I probably would have gone . . . well, what Scarlett would call "full dark side."

"I raised the dead last night," I blurted.

Katia sat up straight. "*What?* When? Why?"

I shook my head. "It doesn't matter now. I did it, and I can't go back. And I'm still here, Kat. I'm still breathing."

She let out a soft grunt that suggested she was unconvinced.

I sighed. "Look. I'm the wrong person to judge good or bad. I'm definitely in no place to judge your actions twenty years ago. But one thing I'm pretty damn sure of is that you get to decide who you are and what you do *now*. And it never would have crossed my mind that you might not be good enough for Lily."

One corner of her mouth instantly tugged up, as though just thinking of Lily made it impossible not to smile. Then her frown returned. "Anyway. Nothing will come of it. I couldn't do that to her."

"Do what to her?"

She gestured helplessly at her chest, like there was an airborne toxin inside her. "Lily is like . . . sunshine in human form. I could never risk that out of selfishness."

"Well, that's just horseshit." That got a tiny smile out of her. "Lily is a grown-up. She has the right to make her own choices without you deciding what's good and bad for her."

Katia relaxed back into her seat and stared out the window again, her face betraying nothing. "I will think on it."

I drove straight to the hospital in Boulder, where I would check on John and Katia could go to the ER to get checked out. She thought this was unnecessary, but I badgered and insisted until she gave in. I was not going to be in another situation where I didn't find out about internal bleeding in time.

We pulled up to the ER entrance and I put the Jeep in park, watching the EMTs bustling in and out of the building. Katia and I both glanced into the back seat, but Tobias was still out.

"You should really come to the ER too," Katia said quietly. "I saw your arms and legs before you changed your clothes."

"They're just scratches," I said. It was true that the claw marks hurt, but they'd all stopped bleeding very quickly, and I didn't think they required stitches. I would have Lily take a look at them tomorrow, after I'd gotten some sleep and she'd finished meeting with Maven and her mother. "They look a lot worse than they are."

Katia let out a dubious grunt, but dropped the subject. Then she gave me a serious look and said, "Lex . . . thank you."

"For what?"

"For coming to get me."

I looked over in surprise. "Um, first of all, *you* saved *my* life just the night before, and secondly, it was my fault you were at Simon's place to begin with. If you hadn't been there, they would have taken me."

"And I would have happily paid that price, for Valerya's child," she said primly.

It hit me then, really for the first time: I was Katia's Charlie.

I had never really thought about it that way before, and I felt tears well in my eyes. "Katia . . ."

But I choked on whatever I might have said. She gave me a small smile and a nod, then turned and said very loudly, "Lex, look! Is that . . . a *mailman*?"

"That's not funny," Tobias said without opening his eyes. But I could tell he was fighting a smile.

Chapter 48

I told Tobias he could take the Jeep on to my house, but he insisted he was happy to keep napping while I went into the hospital to check on John. Apparently werewolves didn't mind the cold.

I walked Katia into the ER first, to make sure she actually signed in. The intake nurse dropped her eyes when she saw Katia's face, and I knew I'd made the right call to bring her in despite her protests.

When they came to get her for the exam, Katia gave my hand an awkward pat and told me to go see John. "Fine," I said, standing up, "but no lying to me about how bad your injuries are later."

Katia just raised her eyebrows in a way that said *I promise nothing*.

I knew BCH pretty well, after so many years of sustaining minor injuries while working for Maven, plus visiting various family members. I stopped at the intensive care unit first, but they told me John had been moved to a regular room, and he would likely be discharged that afternoon.

That thought cheered me as I made my way through the hospital to the correct wing. When I approached the room, I could hear talking and laughing, and I recognized Sashi's voice. I quickened my step, pushing the door open gently.

John was sitting up in bed, smiling. His color looked miles better than it had the night before, and although he was leaning his head back on pillows, he seemed to be lucid and alert. I felt my chest loosen.

"Lex!" he called as I walked in. "Welcome to the party. We've been shushed *twice*."

There was a guffaw from a strange man sitting on the glider chair in the corner. Sashi, who had been sitting on a folding chair pulled up to the bed, rolled her eyes and stood up. My friend was in her late thirties, with glossy, dark hair and a mild British accent. Her mother had emigrated from India to England, then from England to America, when Sashi was a little girl.

"Ignore him," she said, coming toward me with a smile. "They gave him more Vicodin than he strictly needs at this point, but he didn't want me to say anything."

"To protect her cover," John announced, still too loudly.

Sashi sighed and gave me a hug. I held on to her for an extra moment. "Thank you so much for coming," I said into her hair. "I can't tell you how . . . well. Thank you."

"Of course. You were right to call," she said as she pulled back. Her voice was light, but I understood her meaning and fought to keep my expression neutral. If Sashi hadn't gotten there in time . . .

Sashi held me at arm's length for a moment, inspecting my face. "What?" I asked, touching my cheek. "It's nothing, just a bruise."

"Not that," Sashi replied, shaking her head a little. "Oh, I almost forgot." She stepped back and held out her arm to the stranger. He was tall and handsome, in a cheerful, open way, like a great bartender or maybe a therapist. "I'd like you to meet my husband, Will."

"Husband?" I echoed as the man came over and held out his right hand to shake. His left arm, I realized, ended just below the elbow; he had pinned up the sleeve so it wouldn't flop around. "You got married and I wasn't invited?"

Sashi threw back her head and laughed. "It was a quickie Vegas thing," she assured me. "We only invited Grace, and she didn't want . . . Well. You know how kids are."

"Get this, Lex," John said, with great animation. He had lifted his head to see me better. "Will is Grace's *father*! That's why Sashi didn't want to marry me! She was still hung up on *this* dude!"

"John!" Sashi hissed at him, but he looked comically smug, like he'd just been found innocent of a crime.

I couldn't help it; I cracked up. It felt good to laugh, even if my voice had an edge of exhaustion. To my surprise, Will joined in the laughter. He gave off kind of a calming, easygoing vibe, not unlike John—at least, when he wasn't high on painkillers. I entertained myself for a moment with the thought that Sashi had a type.

"I'm glad you're doing so well," I told my brother-in-law.

John shrugged, smiling. "Eh. I was too good for her anyway."

"I meant physically," I told him.

"Yeah, I know you did."

Sashi rolled her eyes again, but now she was laughing too. Will smiled at her, and the look she gave him back was something else. Simple, pure love.

Now that I knew, I could see Grace in Will's posture, his movement. There were about a dozen questions I wanted to ask Sashi, but I was just too exhausted at the moment. For now, she looked happy, and John seemed comfortable and mostly healthy, and that was all I cared about.

"Lex," Sashi said, pushing her hair behind her ears, "I want to hear the whole story, if you're allowed to tell it, but could we take a walk first? There's something I need to ask you."

"Well . . ." I eyed John, then Will.

John flapped a hand at me. "Oh, we're cool. Will's cool."

The corners of Will's mouth twitched, but he looked at me and said very solemnly, "I'm cool."

"Okay then." I turned to Sashi and gestured to the door. "After you."

• • •

We ambled down the long hallway toward the cafeteria, where Sashi could get a cup of coffee. I had already had plenty—we'd stopped on the way back from Cheyenne—and suspected that more might actually make me start to vibrate.

"What did you want to ask me?" I asked after a group of gossiping nurses had passed us.

"First," she began, "did you do something to John?"

"Uh, yeah." I fingered the bandage on the base of my thumb. I'd had to apply a fresh one from the first aid kit. "I sort of . . . bled into his wound." It sounded *so* gross out loud.

Sashi stumbled and almost went down, but I caught her arm. "Sorry, sorry," she exclaimed. "I'm just . . . why on earth would you do that?"

I explained about the boundary magic in my blood, and how I was willing to try anything when I knew I was going to lose him.

Sashi nodded thoughtfully. "I see. I felt something strange in his bloodstream, but I couldn't seem to get at it, which usually only happens with others in the Old World. That explains it."

We turned into the cafeteria, and she looked sideways at me. "Just out of curiosity . . . now that John knows about the Old World, have you told him you can talk to Sam?"

I shook my head. "She asked me not to. She wants him to be able to move on, and she doesn't think he could if he knew." I shrugged. "It must be tempting for Sam to use our connection to interfere with John's parenting, but she knows it would be an abuse of our magic." I didn't say, "And that's not allowed." I may not have understood the strange powers that restricted Sam's communication, but I was pretty sure they wouldn't want me telling others about them.

"That sounds complicated for you," Sashi observed.

"Sashi . . . when is family *not* complicated?"

She sighed. "Quite. And I'm afraid that leads me right into my next question. I need a favor."

"Anything," I said immediately. Sashi had saved John's life, not to mention Simon's, and plenty of other people's. "Name it."

She held up a cautionary hand. "Hold on now, this is big. I want you to ask Maven if I can move to Boulder, at least temporarily."

We were almost to the coffee machines, but I stopped walking and turned to stare at her. "Seriously? I mean, I'd love to have you here, but you and John spent *all that time* doing long distance. *Now* you're ready to move here?"

Sashi pushed the hair behind her ears again. "It's not just for me, although this row between Grace and me has hurt, and I'd like to repair it."

Oh, right. I'd momentarily forgotten that Will was Grace's father. I blamed the comprehensive exhaustion. "Will."

She nodded. "He wants to get to know his daughter, and she has three more years here at CU." She turned to grab a cup and began filling it with light roast.

"How does Grace feel about that?" I asked.

"Right now, she's resistant. She doesn't understand why she hasn't heard from this man in nearly twenty years, why I never told him I was pregnant."

"You never *told* him?" I hadn't meant to say it, at least not in that tone, but it was too late to take it back.

Sashi winced. "I was only twenty when I got pregnant, and Will . . . Will was a different person. It's not really something I'm able to talk about, but he went away, for a very long time, and I didn't have the means to find him. Even when I did, I wasn't sure I could trust him. So I chose to do things myself."

"Okay," I said. I couldn't help but wonder what she meant by "went away." Will hadn't struck me as a former soldier, or an undercover cop. I wondered if Sashi was talking about prison. He hadn't seemed the type for that either, but the only other thing I could think of was witness protection, and that seemed sort of implausible.

At any rate, I could be as curious as I wanted, but I wasn't going to push her.

"Anyway, we'd like to spend the next few years in Boulder," Sashi went on. "We both want to show Gracie how important she is to us, and we can only do that by being here."

I nodded. "I'll talk to Maven, but you should know she's not very happy with me right now."

Sashi smiled, squeezing my arm. "I have complete faith that you'll do your best. That's all I'm asking."

I called Elise, but my parents had already stopped by and picked up Charlie, after giving her an update on John. "You made it sound way worse than it is," Elise accused. "Don't scare me like that."

"You're right," I said, smiling internally. "My bad."

Katia had to stick around the hospital for X-rays, and she assured me she knew how to use my Uber account to get to the cabin. I went back to the Jeep and drove home, where I opened the garage door for Tobias and bade him a bleary goodnight. "Do you want to hang out?" he said hopefully. "I've got some time to kill before Maven's up for the night."

"No offense, Tobias, but I've been up for a *very* intense twenty-four hours," I said, yawning. It was after eleven a.m. "Help yourself to food or whatever. Go hiking. Catch a movie. Imma go to bed."

I waved and trudged into the house. The dogs were ecstatic to see me—except for Stitch, who hid. I wasn't a detective, but I suspected this had something to do with the new stains on my living room carpet. I let everyone outside to do their business, cleaned up the mess, set out food and water, and even checked on Mushu. Katia had dropped him off in his old tank on her way north to rescue me, and luckily she'd brought along a few crickets. "Hey, grumpy old dragon," I said as I dropped them in the cage. "Remember me?"

Mushu ignored me. Just like old times.

When the dogs were back inside, I locked up, zombie-walked to my bedroom, and eyed the bed, facing what seemed like the hardest choice of my entire life: Collapse right then, or force myself to shower off the cave grime and dried blood first?

I fell onto the bed without actually making a decision.

Chapter 49

Someone was brushing hair from my face with cool, assured fingers. Quinn.

I smiled, though I wasn't ready to wake up yet. I rolled onto my back and stretched. I had gotten up twice, just long enough to stumble to the bathroom and pee. "Hey. Come to bed with me."

"Lex . . . honey . . ."

Even those two words were so solemn and formal. It was the tone you use to deliver bad news.

I opened my eyes and sat up. Quinn had turned on the bedside lamp, and was sitting next to me fully dressed. There were no dogs draped over me, so he must have put them in the back bedroom. I hadn't even heard them bark. "What happened? Where's Katia?"

"Asleep in the back bedroom."

"What time is it?"

"A little after midnight. We just finished at the Pellars'."

"Crap!" I flipped off the covers. Hadn't I set an alarm? I'd meant to . . . "Okay, I'll take the world's fastest shower, and then we have to go see Maven. I need to talk to her—"

"*Lex.*" It was his turn to interrupt. "She's here."

I froze, already halfway to the bedroom door, and looked back at him. "*Here* here?" I said. "At my house?"

"Well, outside, at the front door. You have to invite her in."

I looked helplessly at myself, my room. I smelled . . . I didn't even want to put words to what I smelled like. "Quinn . . ."

"It's fine," he said firmly. "She doesn't care."

I dug up clean clothes to wear, at least, and hurried to put them on. Well, I *tried* to hurry, but I was sore all over, and when Quinn saw my arms and legs, he almost had a cardiac event for real, vampire or not. He helped me get a sweater dress over my head and told me to skip the pants until I could clean out those cuts, for God's sake. I was too nervous about making the cardinal vampire wait to argue with him.

As I shuffled toward the front door, I could see through the glass that the snow was falling again. Big wet flakes dotted the neon-green hair of my former—and hopefully, future—boss. She smiled tentatively at me through the window, and I tried to move faster.

"Hi," I said, opening the door. "You changed your hair."

She touched it, as if she'd only just remembered. "Yes. It was time."

I opened the door wider. "Sorry—come in."

Maven stomped the snow off her boots and came in, looking around with interest. "You have such a nice home," she said.

It was such a normal remark that I fought down a chortle. "Yeah, well, it's not usually quite this messy. I . . . got in late." I gave her an apologetic look. "And I haven't showered. Sorry."

She waved it away. "I understand."

I led her into the living room and checked the armchair for dog hair before she sat down. Then I perched on the edge of the couch, while Quinn settled down on the next cushion.

I knew I should really let her speak first, but I was dying of curiosity, and hey, I didn't actually work for her at the moment. "So you guys were at the Pellar farm?" I said, looking back and forth between them.

"Yes." Maven smoothed her skirt, a thick denim number that wouldn't have been flattering on anyone. She had dropped the "corporate human" disguise and was back to her usual look. "We've been there since sunset. Things got . . . heated."

"Is everything okay?" What a stupid question.

"Not really."

"What happened with Morgan?"

Maven's face darkened, and Quinn looked away from me. "What?" I asked. "Mary didn't—"

"No, no, it wasn't her fault." Maven sighed. "As you know, the witches had a meeting, which ended up starting early this afternoon given all of the developments."

"Okay . . . ?"

"I don't know the details of their meeting, but the leaders of the witch clans left a message requesting that I come out to the farm to parley. I got the message at sunset, at the same time Mary arrived at the coffee shop with Morgan." A tiny smile. "Who was still rather sedated. At any rate, I asked Mary and her friend—Tobias?—to go ahead to the farm with Morgan so I could eat first."

There was a look on Maven's face that I hadn't seen before. Was it . . . guilt? "I suppose I thought if I made the concession of coming to them," Maven continued, "and we could get the truth out of Morgan . . ." She trailed off, her hands dropping to her lap.

I looked at Quinn, whose face was grim, but he waited for Maven to speak. "Twelve armed men arrived at the farmhouse just after Mary," she said in a detached, robotic tone that terrified me. "They wanted to recover Morgan, even had silver shot for the werewolves. I missed them by perhaps three minutes."

Unable to help myself, I blurted, "Simon and Lily—"

"Are fine," Quinn assured me. Then his eyes darted to Maven, as if to apologize for interrupting.

She just nodded. "They are."

"Mary? Tobias?"

"Injured, but alive," Maven said formally. "Thanks to your friend Simon. He had a spell that pulled the silver shot out of them like a magnet."

I relaxed a little. Yeah, that sounded like something Simon would come up with in his spare time, especially after Mary had saved his life.

But Maven's face was still grim, and I realized there was more. "The gunmen almost got away with Morgan," she continued, "but the Pellars, and a few of the other witches, fought back."

"Don't tell me Morgan escaped *again*," I said.

"No, she was too wounded to run fast enough. When the witches put up a bigger fight than was expected, the men began to retreat. They shot at Morgan, likely to silence her."

Maven, who had been a frickin' queen of some country that didn't even exist anymore and who had probably seen a hundred thousand people die, was actually too choked up to continue. She gave a little headshake and glanced at Quinn.

"Hazel pushed Morgan out of the way, Lex," he said quietly.

"Hazel is . . . dead?" Hazel Pellar was an institution. It seemed impossible, like saying the buffalo statue on Pearl Street had suddenly galloped off to greener pastures.

"Morgan, too," he replied. "Another gunman shot her as they made their escape."

"Oh, God." I clapped a hand over my mouth. It was my fault. I'd gotten Hazel to drop her wards to let Morgan back into Colorado; I'd sent Morgan with Mary—hell, I'd sent everyone to a meeting place without stopping to consider how vulnerable they would be.

Jumping up despite my sore muscles, I patted my back pants pockets for my phone—only I wasn't wearing pants, and I didn't have any pockets. "I need my phone, I gotta call . . ." I mumbled, looking around.

Maven cleared her throat. "You don't, at least not at this moment. There's nothing you can do right now, and your friends need to deal with their dead."

I stood there for a moment, swaying a little, but dropped back onto the couch. She was right. I would call Simon and Lily, of course, or probably just go out to the farmhouse, but a few minutes wouldn't make a difference. "I should have let Mary shoot Morgan in the fucking head," I blurted, looking at Quinn. "God, I'm such an idiot; I should have been at that *fucking* meeting—"

"And you probably would have been, if you hadn't quit my service," Maven finished. "It's possible that you could have helped, but given the odds, I suspect it's more likely that you would have been shot. Or lost control of your magic."

She sounded matter-of-fact, but I flinched. "Maven, I know I crossed a lot of lines the last couple of days," I began, but she held up a hand to stop me.

"Lex, I'm trying to apologize."

Well, *that* brought me up short. "What?"

"I put you in a position where the only way you could do what I wanted was to defy me. That's a pretty unforgivable thing for a leader to do."

"I know you didn't do it on purpose," I said.

She gave me a weak smile. "But I did."

I blinked, too surprised to be angry. "Excuse me?"

She was fiddling with her skirt, and I realized with a start that she seemed . . . *nervous*? Was that even possible? "You know that I am the last surviving member of the Concilium, the council that led the Old World many centuries ago," she said. "After that group fell, I kept to myself for a long time. I fell out of practice with trust. These last few months . . . I haven't been engaging you because I've been busy gathering allies again. Getting in touch with old contacts, trying to make new ones. I want things to change in the Old World, and I became so focused on my project that I paid no attention to the people I'm supposed to lead.

"When you called me with Ryan Dunn's problem, I was distracted, and I didn't think too much about it. Even when Dunn was killed, I thought . . ." She held out her hands, palms up. "I thought perhaps it would be a good test for you."

"A *test*?" I remembered the way she'd quizzed me on the phone after Morgan's town hall meeting. "People died for a fucking *test*?"

Maven sighed. "I'm so sorry, Lex. Part of my project would involve giving you more responsibilities. I thought dealing with a werewolf crisis more or less on your own would give you a chance to think and work independently, and I could observe how you handled it."

"So you hung me out to dry," I said flatly.

She didn't break eye contact. "I did. I don't need another sycophant, Lex. Every vampire in this state has already sworn an oath to me; they literally *have* to obey me." She shot Quinn a small apologetic smile, then turned back to me. "I hired you because you can go places that I can't, talk to people who would never talk to me. And during this . . . incident—I threw you into that without explanation, because I was too lazy to find another way for you to prove yourself."

"Perhaps," I said icily, "you could have let me actually apply for the job."

Maven just nodded. She looked contrite, but I was still tempted to tell her to get the fuck out of my house. She had left me dangling while good people were dying.

But wasn't that exactly what I'd done to my friends? Left them dangling in a dangerous situation? I had put Morgan Pellar in play and hadn't bothered to see it through.

Guilt, hurt, and anger raged in me for a moment. I saw Quinn's hand lift off his lap, reaching for me, but I could practically see him think better of touching me just then. Good call. I squeezed my eyes shut, trying to control my breathing.

Steady, babe, Sam's voice said. *You did the best you could. The best anyone could, under impossible circumstances.*

I wasn't where I was needed, Sammy, I thought back to her.

There was a soft jingle, and I opened my eyes to see Dopey trot into the room, coming over to sniff at Maven's ankles. She looked down at the little Yorkie with obvious surprise, then turned to Quinn. "She's . . . not scared of us?"

"She's very stupid," he said fondly. "Go ahead, you can pet her."

Tentatively, Maven reached down and scratched at Dopey's ears. There was wonder on her face. "I miss animals," she said softly.

I felt some of the anguish leach out of me, replaced by a bone-deep weariness. Maven was a person. A ridiculously powerful one, but still just a person. She'd made mistakes in this, yes, but so had I. "What happens now?" I asked.

"Now I make you a promise." Maven sat up straight and leaned forward, staring into my eyes. I felt the intense crush of her power, as I always did, and was struck silent.

Luckily, there was nothing I needed to say. "Allison Alexandra Luther," Maven said formally, "I swear to you, I will continue to consider Charlotte Wheaton under my protection until she reaches the age of eighteen. I offer this security to honor the service you have already given me, regardless of whether you ever work for me again. I give you my word and my oath."

For a moment, I thought I felt something in the air, just a quick little shiver, and I wondered if it was actual magic. Swearing oaths was about the only magic the vampires could perform, so I supposed it was possible.

"Thank you," I whispered. Quinn reached over and squeezed my hand.

There was a moment of awkward silence. I knew I should feel gratitude, and I did, but I also felt sort of panicky. If I didn't have a covenant with Maven to protect Charlie, what was I working for? Why was I getting up in the morning?

Maven gave me a faint smile. "Perhaps this would be a good time to explain my . . . project."

"Um, okay."

"You were in Los Angeles during what they call the Vampire Trials."

I blinked, but tried to roll with it. "Yes."

"So you saw how Dashiell shares power with the witches and the werewolves. I respect that; it's something I hadn't seen before. I've decided to try something like that here."

"You're going to share power?" Oops. I hadn't meant to sound quite so incredulous.

"Yes. With Lily, as the new clan leader now that Hazel is gone." She hesitated a beat, then added, "And with Mary."

"Uh . . . *my* Mary?" I said in disbelief.

Now her smile was wide. "I know. She's a bit coarse. But she has proved her value in both helping you apprehend Morgan, and in showing her mercy—at least more mercy than the witches expected from a werewolf." Was I crazy, or were Maven's eyes twinkling? "I also believe the witches appreciate having a female alpha, as it suits their matriarchal way of doing things."

I had to smile, because that part, at least, made perfect sense. "I think that's a great idea—but what does it have to do with the mysterious phone calls?"

"In a few months, when we've got this statewide alliance worked out, I want to pursue an even greater one."

My brow furrowed. "You . . . want to take more territory? I thought—"

"No, not that. I want to start a new Concilium: Dashiell, myself, a few others."

I was momentarily horrified. "You're not asking me to join!"

Quinn made a choking sound, and Maven let out a small, but very genuine, laugh. "No, no. I considered it, but—and I mean no offense—starting the group with a boundary witch onboard might not send the desired message."

I relaxed back in the couch. "Okay, good. What would be the objective of this group?"

"Self-regulation," she said frankly. "And a kind of higher court system. A parliament. It did not escape my attention that I myself had very few options when it came to punishing Morgan, save actually killing her."

"You want to start a penal system?"

"I want to start a conversation."

I thought that over for a minute. "Would this conversation include the topic of who the hell sent a bunch of gunmen to collect Morgan Pellar this afternoon? And who's been bankrolling her whole rebellion?"

Her face lit up a little, the way it did when she approved of something. "Indeed it would. I have an idea about that, but it bears further discussion."

"So if you don't want me in your parliament, what *do* you want from me?"

"Well," she said slowly, "I think it would benefit from having its own . . . well, for lack of a better term—its own knight."

"A knight?" I repeated.

"A paladin," she continued. "A marshal, a—" She turned to Quinn. "What was that word, from the television? One riot . . ."

Quinn's lips twitched. "A Texas Ranger."

"We may need to work on the title," I said, though I was dying to know what the hell TV show Maven had been watching.

"At the moment, this is all rather speculative, but if I can get the parliament up and running, you will still be my representative, but you will begin carrying out bigger assignments, like helping to recruit new members, or investigating crimes against the parliament."

I glanced at Quinn. "For that I would need my investigator."

"You'll have him," she promised. "When you need him. And a significant raise, of course."

"All right then, I accept," I said. "Under one condition."

Maven looked a little surprised, but not put off. "What is it?"

I thought of Sashi, and Katia. "How does one go about starting a new witch clan?"

Acknowledgments

As wonderful as it was to return to Lex's world with this book, I couldn't have done it without plenty of help. Thank you to Jill Pope and her team at Cheyenne Trolley Tours for taking the time to answer all my ridiculous questions—and help me look for evidence of tunnels that may or may not (but probably do?) exist. If you're interested in Wyoming history, Jill's book *Haunted Cheyenne* has some great stories of local ghost sightings.

Thank you also to the nice folks at the Wyoming State Archives, who taught me how to search historical blueprints and put up with the machinations of my five-year-old "research assistant" for much longer than anyone should have to. A big thanks to my team at 47North: Adrienne, Angela, Sharon, and more. You've made this book so much better than I could ever have done alone. My gratitude also goes out to Elizabeth Kraft and Amelia Barr for the superb photo that graces this cover. I'm so lucky to have you on this.

Speaking of my team, thank you to Brieta Ventimiglia, who was a huge help with local knowledge and even went cave-exploring with me for research. I'm sorry it ended up being a distressing experience for some members of the party.

A final, special thank-you to all those who have been asking me for the next Boundary Magic book. Whenever I get stuck or lost in the writing process, I think of your continued support, and it's the push I need to keep going. I hope you enjoy this adventure as much as Lex's previous outings.

About the Author

Photo © 2017 Elizabeth Kraft

Melissa F. Olson is the author of numerous Old World novels and stories, as well as the novella *Nightshades* and its two sequels. She lives in Madison, Wisconsin, with her husband, two kids, two dogs, and two jittery chinchillas. Read more about her work and life at www. MelissaFOlson.com.